A Time to Choose

EDWARD BLIGHT

PARK PLACE PUBLICATIONS
PACIFIC GROVE, CALIFORNIA

A Time to Choose
Edward Blight

All rights reserved under International and Pan-American Copyright
Conventions. Published in the United States by
Park Place Publications, Pacific Grove, California

Japanese translation by Shigeya Kihara
Japanese calligraphy by the Reverend Kisan Ueno
Book design by Patricia Hamilton

Library of Congress
Card Catalog Number:
2001087995

ISBN 1-877809-87-x

First Edition 2001

Printed in the United States of America

1 2 3 4 5 6 7 8 9 10

First U.S. Edition

When Japanese bombs destroyed Pearl Harbor on December 7, 1941, the world for Japanese Americans was changed forever. This fictional account by Edward Blight describes these changes primarily through two Japanese American families. The Hayakawas, fishermen from Los Angeles, are sent to the detention camp at Manzanar. Oldest son Ken, diverted from medical school, volunteers for service with the famous 442nd Regimental Combat Team, composed of Nisei from Hawaii and the US mainland. He joins the unit at Camp Shelby, Mississippi, for training and then ships out for Europe, where the regiment participates in some of the bloodiest fighting of the war in Italy and France.

Meanwhile, the Nakamura family, raised in Seattle, but having moved to Tokyo for their girls' college education, are caught by the war. For Aileen and her sister, they are aliens in a foreign land, a land at war with their homeland.

As the war progresses, Blight leads these two families and others through both the European and the Pacific theaters of war and the home fronts in the United States and Japan, until Ken and Aileen meet during the Occupation. Against a historically authentic background, Blight explores the issues of racial prejudice, assimilation, discrimination by their government, and loyalty to country faced by Japanese Americans during World War II and its aftermath.

Dedication

to Ben and Jean Suechika,
whose real-life story inspired this novel

Executive Order No. 9066

Whereas, The successful prosecution of the war requires every possible protection against espionage and against sabotage to national-defense material, national-defense premises and national-defense utilities...:

Now therefore, by virtue of the authority vested in me as President of the United States, and Commander in Chief of the Army and Navy, I hereby authorize and direct the Secretary of War, and the Military Commanders whom he may from time to time designate...to prescribe military areas...from which any or all persons may be excluded...

Franklin D. Roosevelt
THE WHITE HOUSE
February 19, 1942

Part I
A Time of War

CHAPTER 1

KEN HAYAKAWA STARTLED AT THE ALARM CLOCK AND
in one motion turned it off and swung his legs over the side of the
bed, not realizing that this would be the pivotal day of his life. He
looked at his roommate Dave, to be sure he had not been awakened but
knew it was a needless action since Dave Larson never awakened to any
alarm, his or anyone else's. In fact that was the only friction between
them in their year and a half as roommates. Dave could be bitingly
insulting when Ken, responding to pleas from the previous night, tried
to awaken him in time for class. The next night, apologies from Dave,
more pleas for an early wakeup, and the next morning the same scene.
The only time Dave had ever referred to Ken as a "Jap" was during one
of those half-awake early morning episodes. There'd be no problem today, however, since it was Sunday and Dave rarely got up in time for
church. He had accompanied Ken to his Japanese church on a few occasions, but it presumably had more to do with a cultural experience
than an opportunity to worship.

Ken moved to his desk and turned on his desk lamp, for it was 6:00
AM, and the Los Angeles December sun would not be up for nearly an
hour. He opened his Vertebrate Anatomy book and began tracing the
vascular system of the cat.

It was a full hour before he raised his head again and looked at his
roommate. As far as he could tell, Dave hadn't even changed positions.
He was both jealous and critical of his roommate's ability to sleep in
and to take life so lightly. Dave was a business major at UCLA, studied
no more than an hour a day, but all night before a test, and was elated
when he made C's. The previous semester, he had made two B's and
seriously discussed with Ken whether he was working too hard and

losing what he called his "common touch". He was planning to return to San Luis Obispo after graduation and eventually take over his father's Chevrolet dealership, and the common touch was more important than accounting, he assured Ken. Ken convinced him that an occasional B wouldn't dull his ability to talk a customer into turning in his old Ford for a new Chevrolet, and Dave seemed satisfied. Part of Ken, as he termed it, his "American side," wished he had Dave's attitude, while the other part, the "Japanese side," avoided the parties, the common touch development, and sports, except for the occasional Saturday afternoon football game (he had sat through a disappointing 7-7 tie with USC the previous afternoon), to press towards the goal. In his case the goal was medical school, and he knew it would require almost a straight A record for him to get there. The University of California, in Berkeley, the only school his family could afford, took only one Japanese student into its medical school per year. This Japanese half was fueled by *on*, the traditional sense of obligation to family and community. It was not that Ken came from a professional family or an elite community. His father was a fisherman, and the family of six lived in a five-room shack (it could hardly be called more than that) on Terminal Island, a predominantly Japanese fishing village next to Long Beach. Nor was it that Ken's parents insisted that he be a doctor - it was just an innate drive to be a man they would be proud of. Ken quickly set aside these musings, as he always did when he wrestled with his "American" and "Japanese" sides, covered his book and tried to name all the vessels a red blood cell would pass through from a cat's right ventricle to its paw.

The morning light was coming through the windows the next time Ken looked up from his studies. He checked Dave's still-sleeping form, shaved and put on his one suit - Dave had four - and quietly left the room. There weren't many in the UCLA cafeteria at 9 AM, mostly those on their way to church services. Ken got a large helping of bacon and eggs - that was one area where his American side had won out - his preference for American over Japanese food. For that he did not even feel guilty, although on weekends at home, he'd have to diplomatically turn down his mother's Sunday night dinner of rice, fish and pickled vegetables and leave early enough to get back for a meat and potatoes dinner at the cafeteria.

Finishing, he left the cafeteria and walked to the bus stop. As he waited for the bus, he thought again of his medical school application, sitting somewhere in the admissions office in Berkeley. He knew he'd be one of the top two Nisei applying from UCLA, but would there be better qualified students from Cal or elsewhere? He probably wouldn't know until late January. As always, he refrained from thoughts of the fairness or unfairness of the negative quota for Japanese students. The bus came, and soon he was entering the church. He noted in the bulletin that Pastor Kenda was preaching on "Jesus and the Money changers: When is Our Anger Righteous?" And he noted the date: Sunday, December 7, 1941. He settled into his pew and reached for a song book.

When the service ended, Ken was one of the first out of the church, but he then loitered on the sidewalk, greeting the worshipers as they came out. It was not that he was particularly gregarious, nor that he was a member of the evangelism committee charged with greeting visitors. He was hoping to wangle an invitation to lunch, and at that enterprise Ken was no amateur. He knew who ate American food and who ate Japanese; he knew who had eligible daughters they would love to hook up with a medical student; and he knew whose lunchtime talk would be interesting and whose would be mind-numbing. And it all had to be handled with courtesy and self-effacement. "Oh, I wouldn't want to impose on your family again. You've been so kind in the past...well, if you're sure you have enough?" This particular day, he accepted the invitation of Mrs. Kawamura. Dr. Kawamura, the only Japanese physician he knew, had written a letter of recommendation for him. Ken always came home from lunch at the Kawamuras bolstered in his medical school hopes. Mrs. Kawamura served mostly Japanese food, but the conversation and discussion of medicine always made it worthwhile. The doctor rarely made it to church because of hospital rounds but would always get home just as his wife was getting the lunch on the table.

On this day, the doctor was home in front of the radio when Ken and Mrs. Kawamura arrived, and he was more agitated than Ken had ever seen him. "The Japanese have bombed Pearl Harbor!" he said, standing as the two came in.

"You mean in Hawaii?" his wife asked.

"Yes, and apparently they sank several battleships."

"Have they invaded the islands?" asked Mrs. Kawamura.

"I don't know. The reports are pretty sketchy."

Ken sat down next to the doctor to listen to the news reports while Mrs. Kawamura started to prepare lunch. The reports were indeed sketchy. The two men were quiet except for an occasional question Dr. Kawamura would put to the radio: "Are they sure they were Japanese?"; "Where did they come from?"; "Have they invaded the islands?"; "Are the islands still in our hands?"

Soon lunch was ready. The doctor turned the radio up so they could hear it from the dining room, and the three sat down. Dr. Kawamura started to eat without saying grace, an omission Ken had never before seen him make. In fact, on the days he missed church, Ken noted he seemed to make up for it by an unusually long grace, almost like a second sermon.

"What does this mean, Father?" asked Mrs. Kawamura. She was a university graduate and knew very well what it meant, thought Ken, but he recognized the marital deference she always paid her husband.

"Well, it surely means total war. And Japan has an agreement with Germany, so I don't see how we can keep out of the European mess either. The Japanese have played right into Churchill's hands - he's been trying to get us into this war for a long time."

"What does it mean for us?" Mrs. Kawamura persisted.

"I'm too old to join the Army, but with all the young doctors going to war, I'll have to double my workload."

"But you're already working too hard, Father."

"But think of the younger doctors. They'll have to leave their families. I'll have it easy compared to them."

"With us at war with Japan, how do you think the patients will accept you?"

"Oh, I've never had much trouble with that. We were born in this country and both graduated from Cal. We're citizens, and with most of the doctors gone...I don't foresee a problem." He looked at Ken, seemingly noticing him for the first time since they had arrived. "Now, Ken here, they'll probably speed med school up, run it year round, and you'll be out in 2 1/2 or 3 years. I doubt the war will last that long."

By this time, Dr. Kawamura had reassumed his usual calmness and with his predictions Ken was reassured.

Before he left, Mrs. Kawamura insisted he call his parents. That was not easy to do. He had to call their neighbors, the Takahashis, and wait for them to go next door and bring them to the phone. For that reason, he never called except in an emergency, but it was not hard to convince himself that today's events qualified. On this day, it was difficult to get through because of the volume of calls, but eventually Ken was talking to his father. He restricted himself to three minutes and when he had hung up, Mrs. Kawamura asked him what his father had said.

"Not much," replied Ken. "He had heard the news, but he's pretty shocked by the whole thing. He said there have been a couple cars driving through the neighborhood, yelling 'Dirty Jap' and things like that. He's a little concerned for our safety, although he says my brothers and sister and I shouldn't have much to worry about because we're Nisei and speak without an accent. He's always been embarrassed about his accent, you know. Mostly, he just sounded shocked."

Ken firmly turned down Mrs. Kawamura's offer of a ride back to campus but soon wished he hadn't. Although he had never considered himself very sensitive, he had the undeniable feeling that all eyes on the bus were on him. He looked to the rear of the bus once, and in truth all eyes were on him, though they were quickly averted. Ken focused on the seat back in front of him. "Isn't it obvious that I'm American?" he said to himself. "If I were Japanese, my clothes would be different, and..." He stopped his thoughts in mid-sentence. "If I were Japanese...but I am Japanese...but I'm also American. I was born here...will I always be Japanese as long as I look Japanese? If your family comes over from England, when do you stop being English? Maybe if I stood up and sang 'The Star-Spangled Banner' or recited 'The Gettysburg Address'. I don't even know the Japanese national anthem."

His thoughts continued in a jumble. Eventually they came together in the conscious comparison of Dave and himself. "Maybe I should develop Dave's devil-may-care attitude. But could I? And would anyone be able to see beyond my face and recognize I must be American because I celebrated C's?" Some of his confusion began to slip away and his sense of humor to return. "I wonder what they'd do if I suddenly jumped up, made some jujitsu moves, yelled 'Banzai' and claimed this bus for the Emperor of Japan?" he thought. He looked up for the first time and realized he'd gone a stop too far. He pulled the cord and got off the bus when it stopped. He'd walk the three blocks back to his apartment, which was just off campus. There was a rule against assigning Japanese Americans to the dormitories, but the housing office cooperated in finding off-campus rooms. Dave had lived in the dorms his first two years but had forgotten to reapply for a room after his second year. When he returned in the fall, all the rooms were full, so he was assigned to room with Ken. If he had any reservations about that, he didn't have any options by that time, and soon he realized Ken would be a good influence on him. By the end of the year, they got along well enough together that he didn't consider moving back to the dorms.

As Ken walked back to his apartment, he couldn't put his finger on it, but there seemed to be more tension in the air than on the usual early Sunday afternoon. Was there more traffic, or was it just going faster? Again he noticed the glances of passersby, held just long enough to prevent their being described as casual. As he approached the apartment, he saw a car coming toward him, moving a little closer to the curb than necessary. He was sure he'd seen it pass the other way a block back. The window rolled down suddenly and a white face stuck out. "Dirty Jap son-of-a-bitch. Go back to Japan where you belong!" Spit came out of the face but missed him. Ken turned, started to memorize the license plate and then stopped.

"Who am I kidding? Are the police going to arrest a guy for spitting and cursing at a Japanese? They might give him a medal." He began to think of Dr. Kawamura's predictions of just an hour ago, "Maybe he was being a little optimistic." he thought.

He took the apartment steps two at a time, and when he entered he saw Dave, dressed and listening to the radio. "Did you hear what happened?" Ken asked unnecessarily.

"Yeah." Dave answered without turning his head. "They're saying five or six battleships were sunk. They have no idea how many people were killed."

"Did they invade the islands?" asked Ken,

"No. The Japs left and they don't know where..." He stopped his sentence, turned and looked at Ken for the first time. "I mean 'The Japanese left...'"

"That's O.K.," said Ken. "If they did all that, they're Japs. I'm Japanese." He wasn't convinced that that distinction had settled the problem for him.

Dave continued to look at Ken, more thoughtful than Ken had ever seen him. "How do you feel about this, Ken?"

"Well, probably the same way you do. I thought there were some Japanese diplomats in Washington that were going to come to some sort of agreement and prevent this kind of thing from happening. I hate the thought of what sounds like a major war. Dr. Kawamura thinks we'll have to go to war with Germany, too."

"I mean, do you have relatives in Japan? Will your parents take you back to Japan?"

Ken thought about those questions a few moments - not about the answers to them, but about what they said about the intimacy of their friendship. How could Dave think he'd ever go "back" to Japan? "My folks have brothers and sisters in Japan, and I have cousins there. I've never been there. I'm an American citizen because I was born here. My parents are permanent aliens."

"That's right. You were born in Long Beach, weren't you?" At least Dave remembered that aspect of who Ken was.

They listened to the radio awhile longer, without comment. Every new piece of information was worse than the last, and it was soon clear that it was a major disaster. What wasn't clear was where the Japanese fleet had gone. Were they returning to Japan, or were they coming towards the west coast?

Ken sighed and went to his desk. "Better get back to Anatomy," he said, but did not turn a page for the next hour, as he alternately listened to the news reports and tried to interpret what they would mean for his life.

Finally, Dave said, "Let's go get some dinner." He paused, and added, "Tell you what. You're studying. I'll bring you some back." They occasionally did that for each other, if Ken had a big test the next day, or Dave was taking a late afternoon nap, but this did not qualify for such an occasion.

"OK," said Ken simply, and added, "Thanks," as an afterthought after the door shut behind Dave.

Dave was back in less than an hour, and as he set Ken's dinner down on his desk, he was obviously struggling with something he wanted to - or didn't want to - say.

"Some of the guys are jackasses," he finally blurted out. "They thought I'd want to move out from rooming with you. I told them you were Japanese, but not a Jap... I mean, how do you put it...?" He hesitated.

"I've been trying to figure that out all afternoon," said Ken. "I'm proud of my Japanese roots, the family, the respect, the high standards, and all - but when I think of my future and my dreams, and stuff, they're all here. I think that makes me more American than Japanese."

"Yeah, that's what I told them, more or less," said Dave.

Not much more was said that evening and in fact Ken, and even Dave, were able to concentrate a bit more on their studies.

"You know," said Ken as they settled into their beds and the light went out, "if you want to change roommates, I'd understand. I..." He was interrupted by a book that came sailing across the room from Dave's bed.

"Shut up, you stupid Jap!" They laughed and fell asleep.

CHAPTER 2

THE NEXT TWO WEEKS WERE UNSETTLED FOR KEN. There was no open hostility towards him on the UCLA campus, but he sensed that all eyes were always on him. Was he overly paranoid? The war was the primary - in fact the only - topic of conversation, yet when he was around, people stretched to find other areas to discuss.

The only exception to this was Dave, who in his typical fashion, worked out problems verbally. "I don't think this will be a long war. I'll bet they dropped all their bombs on Pearl Harbor. If we can get a few battleships from the Atlantic and go shoot a few shells into Tokyo, I'll bet they give up right away. Is Tokyo on the ocean?"

"You must know something the government doesn't know, because they're in a panic the fleet will show up off the west coast any day now," thought Ken, but he didn't try to disturb Dave's progress towards personal peace. Instead, he said, "Yes, it's on the east coast of Japan," in answer to Dave's geography question.

"We'll still have the war with the Germans and Italians, of course, " Dave continued, "but surely they'll have the guys on the east coast fight that war."

Ken wondered if Dave had ever heard of the Selective Service Act. Ken hadn't heard that the draft was regional. Again though, no boat-rocking.

"And they're still going to need automobiles. We'll need a lot of people to stay home and keep things going, won't we? You don't think they'll stop making cars and use the factories to make tanks, do you, Ken?" Dave's face clouded.

"I'm sure we'll still need cars," Ken reassured his friend.

Relieved, Dave looked back at his textbook. That was one positive change. Dave had become much more studious since December 7. Most satisfying to Ken, though, was that Dave seemed to have no question where Ken's loyalty lay or about their friendship. He had settled that the first night.

Ken considered canceling the next meeting of the Japanese American Student Club but fortunately decided against it, for that meeting had the best attendance of any that year. The club had been organized with fairly vague purposes several years before. The by-laws said something about improving and maintaining understanding of the culture and economics of the United States and Japan, and they sponsored several talks per year by such men as the Japanese consul to Los Angeles and trade representatives. Ken had been elected president this year, more, he was sure, because of better attendance than because of any particular enthusiasm he'd ever shown. Usually several of the more internationally-minded Caucasian students attended the meetings, but there were none at this meeting. Whatever the agenda had been, it turned into an informal discussion of the events of the past week and what those events might imply for the future. Everyone assumed they'd stay in school until graduation, but what then? Getting appropriate jobs for Nisei college graduates was difficult in the best of circumstances, but what about now? Would they do better going east to look for jobs? The meeting ended without many answers.

The sermon at church the following Sunday engaged Ken more than usual. The text was the one in which Ruth tells her mother-in-law "...whither thou goest, I will go; and where thou lodgest, I will lodge; thy people shall be my people, and thy God my God." What interested Ken was the fact that Pastor Kenda was born in Japan. He had been converted in Japan and had been sent over to pastor this church. "If anyone should be torn over loyalties, it should be he," Ken thought.

Ken had had three more phone conversations with his parents during the two weeks after Pearl Harbor, which had been comforting and disturbing at the same time. His father had become more articulate than in their first conversation in denouncing the sneak attack and in pledging his loyalty to the United States. What was disturbing, however, was what was happening, officially and unofficially, at Terminal Island. It had always been a Japanese enclave, left undisturbed by the surrounding communities. Now there were FBI men going from house to house taking everybody's names - "a cross between a census and a prison cell check" his mother had said. Acts of vandalism by young whites, driving through and yelling obscenities and threats had increased. Some even had thrown bricks through windows. On the rare occasions when police had responded to calls, the caller was made to feel he was the instigator rather than the victim.

Nevertheless Ken was able to finish the semester with his usual straight-A record and climbed aboard the trolley to go home for the Christmas holiday with considerable relief. He noted that Dave had been more sincere than usual in his goodbyes.

If his last two weeks at UCLA had been somewhat uncomfortable, he was introduced promptly to the depth of the anti-Japanese feeling in Los Angeles on his return home. He was to take the trolley to Long Beach, then transfer to the bus for Terminal Island. While waiting for the bus, a car approached him, slowed, and a hail of eggs came towards him, one of them hitting him in the chest. The three angry Caucasians in the car yelled, "Go home to where you came from, you yellow Jap bastard!" In the years that followed, Ken thought of many a sharp retort, the most obvious being that he was going home to where he came from, but at that moment his only emotion was that of sheer terror. Though moderately proficient at judo in high school, his thought was that if the car had stopped, he would have run and never stopped. He remembered the impulsive spitting on December 7th. In contrast, today he was the victim of a premeditated act two weeks after Pearl Harbor. To his relief, the car didn't stop, but a shaken Ken Hayakawa entered his home on Terminal Island that evening.

Ken's mother took one look and understood. "Kenichi, take off those clothes and get into something more comfortable. I'll get them washed."

"What's been going on here?" asked Ken, as he complied.

"Well, we've had some problems, but I'll let your father talk about that. He should be home tonight." With that, the youngest Hayakawa entered the room, let out a war whoop, and ran over and tackled Ken.

"Hey, you're getting too big for that now," said Ken as the two of them rolled on the floor. "You must have grown two inches since Thanksgiving."

"Coach wants his linemen big," Peter answered. "He keeps calling me 'Sumo'."

"And it looks like you're obliging him," Ken laughed.

Dorothy, a year older than Ken, came home next. She had gone to business school after high school and then worked as a secretary in Long Beach the last four years, while she lived at home. Ken wondered if she'd ever gotten the egg treatment as she took the bus home but didn't ask.

Finally, Ken's father and brother Howard, sardine fishermen came home smelling like their business. Howie, the third child, had joined his father on the boat after high school.

After greetings all around, the fishermen bathed and changed clothes. Then the family gathered around the dinner table.

"Yeah. We have punks driving through here almost every night, yelling and throwing things. We've almost gotten used to it," said Shoji Hayakawa in English. Ken looked at his father, who had just violated his own house rule: the family would speak Japanese at home, since they all spoke English outside the home. The kids surreptitiously frequently violated that rule when their parents weren't listening. Somehow, "Hey, who's starting at quarterback for the Bruins this year?" didn't translate easily into Japanese. Ken didn't ask his father why he was now speaking in English.

Ken admired his father greatly. Brought up in a poor rural family in Okayama prefecture, he had taken to the sea as a teenager. In 1911, at the age of twenty, he left his ship in Los Angeles and never returned to Japan. He found his way to Terminal Island, then a company town owned by Van Camp's and French's canneries. The town men fished days at a time for sardines, mackerel and tuna. When they returned, the canneries' whistles would blow, summoning the women, day or night, to come process, can and pack the fish. They would work until the job was finished, and then they'd return to their families. After several years, Shoji had worked his way up to captain, and for the first time noted there were girls in the world. The first one to catch his eye was delicate, soft-spoken Toshiko Tanaka. Toshiko, a fisherman's daughter, born in Okayama also, was brought to this country as an infant. She was attracted to this muscular, tanned young captain who paid so much attention to her, and soon they were talking of marriage. In those days, arranged marriages were the modus operandi in Japan, so Shoji and Toshiko plotted to plant this idea in her parents' minds. Once Toshiko's parents determined the young people were Dokenjin (same prefecture people) and respecting Shoji, Mr. and Mrs. Tanaka played their parts willingly. The two were married on a sunny February day in 1917, three weeks after Toshiko's eighteenth birthday. Dorothy was born three years later, and her three brothers came every year or two thereafter. By the time Peter arrived, Toshiko stopped answering the cannery sirens and gave any extra time to seamstress work. Like so many poor people in those Depression days, Ken and his siblings didn't know they were poor. When he got into high school and college and visited his friends' homes outside Terminal Island, he learned that not everybody lived in barracks-style buildings, three brothers to a room, another family a quarter-inch of plywood away.

The only thing to mar what Ken considered a happy childhood was his father's drinking. Not that he drank very much, but what he did drink seemed to go straight to his brain. As a premed student, Ken thought it must have something to do with his father's lack of body fat. Shoji would become morose with alcohol. The children had learned early to stay away from him at those times. But Toshiko was not always able to distance herself from her husband. Ken had once seen evidence of physical harm to his mother. His father had not drunk alcohol for two months following that episode, and when he started again, he had behaved himself better.

As Ken watched his father, he didn't see that he had aged over the past ten years. His hair was still black, his arms well-muscled and his skin taut. Around the eyes, he could see some thickening of the wrinkles, the result of years spent scanning the sea's horizon in the Southern California sun.

"I'm not as worried about those punks," Shoji was saying, "as I am about the men they've taken away."

"The FBI took Mr. Furutani and Mr. Tatsuno and Mr. Endo. They're just gone," Toshiko explained.

"Why did they do that?" Ken asked.

"No reason. They're just prejudiced." answered Howie, a little too quickly.

"Howie!" Toshiko frowned disapproval, "They said they'd found short-wave radios in their homes and they might use them to signal the submarines."

"What submarines?" Ken asked, "Have they found subs off our coast?"

"No!" said Ken's father. "I tried to tell those FBI guys that we all use the radios to communicate with the canneries and our homes when we're out at sea. They got so pissed off at me, they almost arrested me too." Shoji had a strong accent when he spoke English, but he had no trouble with the vernacular.

"You be careful, Father. Don't give them any excuse to arrest you," said Toshiko, forgetting for once to complain about his use of the vernacular "in front of the kids".

"What are they doing with those men?" asked Dorothy.

"I hope they execute them as spies!" blurted Peter. The family smiled, remembering that it was Mr. Endo who had reported Peter and two other boys to their parents for smoking. Toshiko lectured Peter on revenge and forgiveness, while Dorothy's question went unanswered.

The next two weeks were both better and worse than the usual holidays. The nightly drive-bys continued and once the thugs threw a firebomb instead of the usual brick or garbage. One building, housing two families, burned to the ground. Widespread catastrophe was avoided by a hastily-organized bucket brigade. All but the embers were out before the Long Beach Fire Department arrived. Arrests of Terminal Island men continued. Charges were always vague, and the destination of the arrested men unknown. Those residents who ventured outside Terminal Island reported more and more signs in store windows, advising "American-owned", and "Help Wanted. Japs Need Not Apply".

However, Ken noted much more community spirit because of the harassment. The bucket brigade was only one example. When neighbors got together and cleaned up the garbage thrown the night before, they stayed to help weed gardens, trim hedges and fix loose porch steps. Community centers were busier at night, the music turned up louder. Still, two or three of the bigger teenage boys were always stationed at the door.

Ken noted that his family seemed happier to be together. They talked about the situation frequently, but someone always finished the discussion with an optimistic prediction. "Well, I'm sure the war will end soon and everything will return to normal." or "They'll realize pretty soon that we're more American than Japanese and let those men come back." Even Peter decided that they'd soon have to let Mr. Endo go, "...because they'll see he's not smart enough to be a spy!"

The only exception in the Hayakawa family was Howie, who became more and more angry with each insult. "What have we ever done to them except be good Americans? Maybe we need to raise more hell and let them know they can't push us around." Toshiko started to say something, but stopped. She sensed that Howie's problem was more deep-seated than the use of an occasional profanity.

Even the religious aspect of Christmas did not become a sore point this year. Dorothy and Ken had converted to Christianity and particularly liked the Japanese church on Terminal Island. Their father didn't understand why they did not follow Buddhism. Many long conversations over the past years had convinced nobody and rarely had ended on a pleasant note. This year though, Dorothy and Ken attended Christmas Eve and Christmas Day services without a word of protest from Shoji.

And so it was that Ken returned to school in January with a more confident feeling than when he had left. He wondered about that on the trolley back to the university. "I should feel even more frightened than when I came home two weeks ago," he thought. "We're fighting a war in two hemispheres. The Japanese are running rough-shod through Southeast Asia. The Nazis seem unbeatable in Europe. And the fate of the Japanese Americans is still completely unsettled. No one in the family has any real answers." But nevertheless, he felt he could handle his responsibility, whatever that would be. He pulled his Chemistry book out of his suitcase and settled back in his seat.

The reunion with Dave in the apartment was different than ever before. Usually, Dave filled his ears with stories of all-night, hard-drinking parties and his conquest of pretty girls in San Luis Obispo. Now it was a quiet Dave, listening to Ken's description of the holidays. His only response as Ken described the drive-bys was, "Yeah, we had a few incidents in San Luis with some of our Japanese too." When Ken had finished his tale, Dave asked "What are you folks going to do? I mean, what does your father say?"

"Well. I guess just business as usual. Dad'll take his boat out tomorrow and come back with a load of sardines. We need canned sardines for the war effort, just like we need more cars. Dorothy's back on her job in Long Beach. I should hear later this month if I get into med school. Pete has high school to finish, and Mom will keep the home fires burning - not literally, I hope." He smiled briefly at his little joke but then realized he hadn't included Howie in his litany. He decided he wouldn't, and Dave apparently didn't notice the omission.

The rest of January was relatively quiet on the UCLA campus. The only problem for Ken was when he ventured off campus. He limited that to church going. Each Sunday, he could see the problem playing out in store windows. "Jap, go home" was the most popular. The second most popular was "American owned", which seemed to be sufficient, until one saw the sign in the window of Ogawa's Fresh Produce Market: "I am an American". Ken wondered if anybody was listening. He and his Nisei friends on campus had an ongoing game–how to respond to the most common question yelled at them by whites: "Why don't you go back to where you came from?" Ken, with his usual quirk of mind, thought they should answer a question with a question: "Why aren't all babies born in this country born with a Caucasian face?" or "Why aren't all naturalized citizens given a white face instead of an American flag?"

Word came from home that the arrested Terminal Island men were being held at a place in North Dakota called Ft. Lincoln ("What an ironic name," thought Ken). They were suspected of espionage, though no charges had been filed. Ken continued to aim for Sunday after-church invitations from the Kawamuras and continued to be assured by the doctor that they as Japanese Americans had nothing to worry about.

What concerned Ken most as February came was that he'd received no word on his medical school application. His Caucasian colleagues had gotten their acceptances in late January, but Ken and the other Japanese boys had heard nothing.

He received an answer, of sorts, on February 19, 1942. That day President Roosevelt issued Executive Order 9066. Ken read about it the next day in the newspaper. All persons of Japanese ancestry, citizens or not, in California, Oregon, and Washington would be relocated to camps, not yet built, in some of the western states and Arkansas. Ken read and reread the article. How could this apply to him? Surely it couldn't include citizens! And what would happen to their property and businesses? The more he thought about it, the less he decided it could be true, and he finally set the newspaper down, satisfied it was all one big mistake. "I'm sure they'll reconsider it in the next few days and rescind the order," he reassured his friends in class that day. He was shaken, however, when on Sunday Dr. Kawamura departed from his usual optimistic position on such matters.

"That's going to wipe out everything we Japanese Americans have tried to establish over the last fifty years. It'll be devastating, just devastating!" said the doctor. Ken chose not to share his own thought that the order would be canceled.

Ken's father also thought that the order was serious. In their periodic phone conversations, each strictly limited to three minutes and always conducted in English now, Shoji kept him updated on the latest instructions from the authorities, regarding selling their homes and their businesses. He had put the boat up for sale but had no offers yet.

Ken watched the papers, looking for the editorial outcry against this order forcibly moving Americans from their homes to isolated camps on the basis of race alone. He found none. He did find a considerable amount of support for such a move. Even those columnists who were uneasy about the fairness or constitutionality of such an order resolved their doubts by deciding it would be for the protection of the Japanese Americans, if nothing else. "Let's do the expedient thing now, and we'll worry about the morality of it later," seemed to be the majority opinion of the more responsible commentators. Ken's earlier conviction of a reprieve began to waver.

Finally came the phone call that it was time to come home. Posters had appeared all over Terminal Island that all Japanese residents would be moved two days hence. From a certain point they would be bussed to an assembly area for later movement to their permanent camp, the location not specified. In the two suitcases allowed per person, they were advised to bring heavy clothing, not an easy task for Southern Californians.

Ken packed quickly and had a moving goodbye conversation with Dave. The usually verbose Dave had been remarkably quiet over the past month. He didn't think the order was fair, but he agreed that the Japanese would be safer away from the coast. What he couldn't resolve was that his father was buying back cars he'd sold to Japanese in San Luis Obispo for much less than their worth. Somehow the market principles that Dave had been studying did not apply here. You needed a "willing buyer" and a "willing seller". Here you had "duress sellers". As he shook Ken's hand and said good-bye, he searched for some encouragement he could give Ken, but he came up dry. His platitudes had deserted him. Finally all he could say was, "Hope to see you soon," and he shook Ken's hand a little longer than necessary.

Ken arrived home none too early. The house was in a mess as six people spread clothes and belongings over the small home, deciding what to take. He had not anticipated such a problem, since he had never thought his family possessed many material goods. But with the unloading of closets not emptied for years and the uncertainty of where they were going, the task was a difficult one. The family had only two old suitcases, one of which Toshiko's parents brought with them from Japan when she was an infant. It fell to Howie to arrange alternate means of carrying their goods. He found a good length of twine and several empty cardboard boxes, and it looked as if the Hayakawas would resemble the Okies and the Arkies of a decade before.

The family owned two things of potential value. Two absurdly low offers on Shoji's boat, he rejected. He eventually left it in the care of Mr. Brandt, the owner of the Terminal Island Boat Works and the man who initially sold Shoji the boat. Mr. Brandt agreed to sell the boat for the best price he could get and send Shoji the proceeds minus a 10% fee. Ken worried that the agreement was not on paper, but it was too late to change that. The other Hayakawa possession of value was Toshiko's kimono and obi, bought at the time of her wedding at great sacrifice to the Tanakas. Since then, Toshiko had kept it carefully wrapped and stored except on the very few occasions when she took them out to show Dorothy. The family debated long and finally decided it would be safer to leave the kimono and obi rather than to take them to the unknown destination. Further discussion, and Ken took them to the local church he and Dorothy attended. The Caucasian pastor readily agreed to keep them.

The next morning the Terminal Island Japanese Americans climbed aboard their buses. Layer upon layer of their heaviest clothes protected them from the unseasonable cold and ensured that their suitcases were liftable.

"Where are we going?" Ken asked Peter for the fiftieth time. His younger brother, having found a peephole in the cardboard that covered the bus windows, was keeping the passengers apprised of their progress through the streets of Los Angeles.

"We're coming to a racetrack!" shouted Peter. "We're going to spend the war at a racetrack! Think I'm too big to be a jockey?"

Ken looked through the peephole and announced "Santa Anita. This is where they'll keep us until they move us to the permanent camp."

For two weeks, they milled around the racetrack, their numbers swelling daily as buses full of Japanese Americans arrived from all over the Los Angeles basin. The Hayakawas were fortunate in that they stayed in tents raised in the infield of the track. The less fortunate were housed in the stables, still reeking of horse manure despite recent whitewashing. When the new inhabitants examined the walls, it was apparent they had not been washed before the whitewash had been applied! Warm meals were served them, and the bathrooms were overcrowded. But the impassivity of the guards struck Ken the most. They carried rifles and talked to the inmates, as the Japanese were beginning to consider themselves, only to give orders. One lieutenant Ken recognized from UCLA. They'd been in the same physics class a couple of years before, but when Ken spoke to him, his brusque response showed no hint of recognition.

After two weeks, orders started coming for groups to be moved to their permanent camps. The Hayakawas' name appeared on one of the first lists. They would go to Manzanar—"a place in the California desert, between the Sierra Nevadas and Death Valley," they were told. Nothing more. None of their friends had even driven through that area.

They boarded long-distance buses and headed east. In other circumstances, it might have been a pleasant drive. Ken had driven that road a couple times on winter trips to Big Bear and none-too-successful attempts to ski. He decided Japanese were made for sumo wrestling if they were big; baseball, if they were small. But not for skiing! He didn't seem to notice that few were successful regardless of their ethnicity, in those days of long skis, loose bindings and no chair lifts. A ski run was an uncontrolled wide-based slide down a snowy hill at ever-increasing speeds, until it ended in a crash at the bottom for almost everyone. But the fear of damaged bodies was nothing, Ken thought, compared to the fear on this trip. The fear of the unknown loomed large. However the sense that whatever occurred would be bad overshadowed that. He assumed there would be physical deprivations. What kind of facilities could they have built for thousands of people even if they had begun on the day of the exclusion order? Of more concern to Ken though was what would they do in camp? His people thrived on hard work and progress—moving towards goals. Now those goal seemed far away. He didn't worry about his mother, or Dorothy, or Peter. They always seemed to land on their feet, but what about Howie? He had become more angry and rebellious as the scenario had unfolded. Never a happy, cheerful type, he had seemed to find himself as a fisherman. The days on end of near solitude had allowed him to avoid expressing an unfelt sociability. And the success in landing fish dependent upon his talent to find them and his strength to bring them in, gave him a sense of accomplishment denied him in school. But probably the time spent with Shoji had done more for Howie than anything else. Ken had accompanied them on a few trips during summer vacations. He estimated that no more than a hundred words passed between the two of them on a three-day trip. But the way they worked the net together and loaded and unloaded the bin spoke of a oneness that he regretted he'd never be able to experience with his father. As the fishing prohibition was imposed, and the "sentence to prison", as he termed it, was announced, Howie changed. He started to spend time with the few in the community who were beginning to speak of violence and refusal to cooperate.

Ken worried about Shoji too. This man had struggled for everything he had gotten in life. Now he was losing his fighting spirit. He had subtly turned the family leadership over to Toshiko, and the last days at Terminal Island spent all his evenings in the bar drinking too much sake.

The bus wound its way up Route 66 through Cajon Pass and was soon traveling north through the High Desert. At sundown, they reached their destination. The sun was setting behind the Sierra Nevadas as they turned west off the highway and drove through a gate in a fence topped with barbed wire. Two unsmiling soldiers with rifles opened the gate. The camp was arranged in rows of wooden barracks separated by wide streets of blowing sand. This was Manzanar! A silent group of Japanese Americans left the buses that cold March evening in the desert to start a phase of their lives that none of them had chosen—a forced separation from society that none felt they deserved. The deep-seated chill that Ken felt in his bones that night, he knew was due to more than dropping temperatures.

CHAPTER 3

AILEEN NAKAMURA WAS LOST IN STUDY. SUDDENLY the book she held was struck from her hands and landed on the floor of the trolley. She looked up, startled to see an angry, elderly face looking down at her.

"Shame on you, young lady, reading enemy literature! You must throw away such trash and read only books that honor our Emperor and our brave soldiers and sailors!"

Aileen could only watch the man as he continued his tirade, drawing the attention of the whole car. Her sister, Myrna, hastily picked up the book, a book in English on the labor movement in America. She stuffed it quickly into her schoolbag. Myrna tugged at her sister's elbow, and they got off the trolley one stop sooner than they planned. The two girls started the long walk to their home in the Daitoh district of Tokyo.

"I wanted to get away from that old man," explained Myrna in English without a trace of an accent. "Why didn't you tell him *why* you were reading that book?"

"I was frightened, and besides, I couldn't think of anything to say," Aileen answered. They stopped talking until out of earshot of other pedestrians. "I should have told him I was studying about *my* country, the country that's going to win this *baka na senso*." She spit out this last phrase—a literal translation of which would simply be "stupid war". But if said with vehemence, it has the emotional impact of cursing, a habit neither girl exhibited in English. "And then I should have slugged him!"

Myrna chuckled at this picture of her little sister, only one year younger than she, measuring one inch over five feet and weighing 100 pounds only after a large meal. The chuckle evolved into a laugh, and the laugh into a guffaw. Tears came to her eyes as she described the imaginary scene.

"...the whole car would have fainted in unison when they saw you punch out that old grandpa..." was all Aileen could pick up through Myrna's laughter. Soon she was laughing too. There was no way passersby could understand what had amused these seemingly normal, pigtailed Japanese schoolgirls dressed in middy blouses over long, navy blue skirts.

The incident wasn't nearly so funny when later they described it to their parents. The part about Aileen "punching the old grandpa", they wisely left out. Also, when related in Japanese, it almost seemed she should feel guilty of disloyalty.

"You should pay attention to what he said," their mother admonished. "You've heard the orders about reading enemy propaganda..."

"Yes, Mom, but that's the course I'm taking at the university. If it's about the American labor movement, an American book is certainly more accurate. The professor recommended it even though he told me it was illegal and he could not officially do so."

"Well," said Aileen's mother, as she searched for a compromise, "maybe you should read it only at school or at home and keep it in your schoolbag at other times."

"And maybe next semester, you should take a course on the Japanese labor movement," added her father.

"But, Daddy, I'm not taking Japanese Culture and Politics. I'm taking American Culture and Politics. That was our agreement!" Aileen blurted out.

"I know! I know! But that was before the war," said her father.

"But this *baka na senso* is not my fault!" answered Aileen loudly. Her parents initially had tried halfheartedly to correct her when she used that phrase with such feeling. They no longer commented on it. Though they didn't verbalize their feelings, they agreed the war was a *baka na senso*. "My plan still is to return to America. Maybe I'll represent some Japanese firm there, but I'm an American citizen and I plan to go back. Before you say it, I know, I won't say this outside our family. When I'm out, I'm a well-behaved little Japanese girl. And I won't read 'alien propaganda' on the trolley anymore."

"You're Japanese too, Aiko," said her father, using her Japanese name. "You can choose either one."

"I know, Daddy, and I'm proud of being Japanese - I don't want to have to choose. I want to remain an American citizen who happens to be Japanese." Her tone became more demanding. "I know I'm registered as a Japanese national, but I'm also an American citizen by birth, and I'll never renounce that. In fact, I hope you'll have my name removed from the family registry one day." She referred to the tradition that all Japanese living abroad should register their foreign-born children in the family registry, thus conferring dual-citizenship.

"Me too, Daddy," added Myrna.

"And by the way, there is no Japanese labor movement," added Aileen, as they sat down to dinner—cold rice, broiled dried fish and pickled daikon. Aileen yearned for a good, juicy hamburger. She wondered if there were food shortages in Seattle as there were in Japan since the war in China had bogged down. Fish was plentiful enough, but rarely could they get beef or pork. Sugar was in short supply, and when they got rice, it was mixed with wheat.

"The Nomuras said that the *kempeitai*...," started Mrs. Nakamura, then asked "How do say that in English?"

"I think that would be 'military police'," answered Myrna.

"Yes, but they were in civilian clothes. Anyway, they came by the Nomuras and pressured them to renounce their American citizenship." The Nomuras were a family of Japanese Americans similar to the Nakamuras. Together, they were part of the 10,000 Americans of Japanese ancestry living in Japan for one reason or another when war broke out—some there for short visits; some for education. Of this group caught in Japan by the war, some were American citizens; others had dual citizenship; still others had been resident aliens in the United States for many years, shut out of the naturalization process because of race.

The status of most families, like the Nakamuras, was even more complicated. Jun Nakamura had gone to the United States as a 19-year old in 1899. He worked in the mines and in the fields but eventually began an import/export business in Seattle, dealing with Asian goods. Enjoying a bit of financial success, he returned to his Japanese village in 1916, sporting western clothes and western ways. That same year he married twenty-year old Mieko, clearly the prize of the village. Immigration papers for her were slow in coming, and it wasn't until 1920 that she joined him in Seattle. Myrna and Aileen were born in the next two years, and the Nakamuras settled down to become a middle-class American family.

Business was good, and for many years, Jun did not doubt his choice. Gradually however, he became more and more aware of prejudice directed against Asians on the west coast. It seemed that it was all right if they stayed "in their place"–Japan towns or Chinatowns–and did stereotypical jobs–launderers or gardeners. But when they stepped out to experience the "American dream", they encountered subtle, and not-so-subtle, barriers. The Nakamuras lived in a middle-class Caucasian neighborhood, but after fifteen years the parents still had not been accepted as part of the community. Their rejection was softened by the fact that the girls were accepted, and that alone kept them from moving to a Japanese community.

The girls excelled at whatever they put their minds to. Myrna was one of the top students in any class she attended–winning the math and science prizes on a yearly basis. Aileen, too, was a good student, but she excelled in "anything having to do with talking", as her father put it. A speech or an essay, running for a school office, or a pep rally–Aileen was first in line.

Jun and Mieko basked in the glories of their girls' achievements, but that did not make up for a growing sense for Jun of not belonging. He could get bleary-eyed when he described America as "a land of opportunity, where sons of subsistence workers from the old country, through sweat and sacrifice raised families in relative affluence and comfort". Except when it came to Japanese. He had done all that but was prevented from becoming a citizen and was denied the friendship of others because of his facial features. That wasn't true for immigrants from Europe, and that fact began to bother Jun more and more. His memories of Japan became progressively more nostalgic. He soon forgot that Japan was hardly a land of opportunity, much less of social acceptance, for those born of a humble background.

Myrna had received a scholarship from the University of Washington when she graduated, at the top of her class, in 1939, and she registered for a premedical course. But, during that year, Aileen's senior year in high school, Jun began to talk of going to Japan for the girls' education. His suggestion was initially met with disbelief, then by refusal, then by tears, and eventually by grudging acceptance. Myrna spent hours trying to reason with her father. She cited the necessity of getting the right premed courses. Aileen spent hours in tears, cajoling, pleading, and threatening. Jun's reasoning was that Japanese students were more serious about their studies and not distracted by pep rallies and extra-curricular clubs. Furthermore, they could "meet their Japanese roots." He said it in Japanese, and the girls, who thought better in English, never did understand at gut level what that meant.

Deals were made. Myrna received assurances from the University of Washington School of Medicine that premed courses from an approved Japanese university would qualify her for application, and Jun agreed she could return for medical school. Aileen and her father agreed that she could study U.S. politics and economics.

Jun had approached the trade officer at the Japanese consulate in Seattle and gotten his whole-hearted encouragement for his proposal to establish an import/export business in Tokyo. The trade officer, impressed with Jun's credentials and U.S. contacts, assured him the Japanese government would do everything possible to help him start his business. In the summer of 1940, after Aileen's graduation, the Nakamuras sailed for Tokyo.

The first year had been better for the girls than for their parents. They found that the Japanese university students were more liberal in thought and speech than they had believed. That was particularly true for Aileen, who in her course of study encountered an interesting amalgam of Japanese Americans like herself, and Japanese who were interested in America and other western countries. Animated discussions often lasted long after the class bells rang.

The girls found that their spoken Japanese, though fluent and proper, was laughably out of style. Their new-found friends were not always gentle as they taught them to speak idiomatic 1940-style Japanese. Also, to their glee, boys suddenly discovered them. The one area of American teenhood that had been denied them was dating and boyfriends. There had been few attractive Japanese boys in their classes, and Caucasian boys seemed to be happy to have them as friends, not girlfriends. That was all right for picnics but not for proms. But in Tokyo, they were discovered. Not that there was dating in the American sense, but in informal get-togethers, the Nakamura girls were clearly the queen bees.

Jun's experience that first year was not as positive. He had sold his business in Seattle with plans to establish a Japanese source of products to ship to U.S. businesses, creating a demand for Japanese goods. Trade regulations had gotten in his way. There were numerous documents to fill out for each contract, and each document had to be approved by the appropriate government office. It was not as easy as the Seattle trade officer had promised. He also sensed prejudice by the Japanese against doing business with him, "a foreigner with questionable motives". Within a year he was forced to leave that business. He now worked part-time for Domei, the Japanese news bureau, translating English language news reports into Japanese. The girls laughed privately over that, wondering how he would handle an article about a Frank Sinatra performance at the Hollywood Bowl. "'Frank' means 'sincere', but I don't know what a 'sinatra' is," Myrna mimicked her father, "and it must mean rice from Hollywood - eaten in a bowl." Apparently the rest of the articles dealt with other topics, for Jun continued in his job. It paid poorly however and never was more than part-time. Twenty-five dollars a month could not support a family of four, and Jun, to his great dismay, was invading their savings.

His disillusionment with life in Japan, though, was not enough to make him heed the State Department's warnings, which started coming in late 1940, that all American citizens should leave Japan. Despite the girls' pleas, and to a lesser extent Mieko's, Jun reasoned that the warnings were just part of the American government's negotiating strategy and that soon the two governments would patch up their differences. Aileen paid more attention to the details than the others in the family, and she voiced serious reservations about the ultimate success of the negotiations. Pearl Harbor crushed Jun's optimism and even caused him to look into passage on the first repatriation ship that left in March, 1942. It was then that the girls' lack of passports became a problem. When they came to Japan in 1940, they had been given certificates of identification and told they could apply for passports from the American embassy. But when Jun applied, the list of documents required, particularly after the war started, was overwhelming. The certificates of identification were not sufficient. As far as the first repatriation ship was concerned, it was a moot point anyway, as it was filled with diplomats, newsmen, and businessmen.

"Well, I hope the Nomuras didn't fall for that renouncing citizenship business. It'll only get them in trouble if they ever want to go home," said Aileen.

"I don't believe they did," answered Mieko. "How was school today, girls?" she asked as she took an unhurried sip of tea, indicating an end to discussion of serious or upsetting topics.

The next day while the girls were at school and before Jun left for Domei, two men from the *kempeitai* came by.

"We recommend your daughters renounce their American citizenship so they can be recognized as 100% Japanese nationals," they told Jun.

"I've always told them they can make their own decisions," Jun answered.

"But as their father, we think you'll see the advantages of declaring their loyalty to the Emperor. Life may get more difficult for the enemy living in Japan in the near future." said one of the men, carefully measuring his words for emphasis.

Color rose on the back of Jun's neck, but all he said was, "I'll talk to them about it."

"See what I mean about how our family structure is destroyed after they live in America for awhile?" said the older of the two men as they left the Nakamuras, "That man is going to let his daughters decide!"

That night, Aileen spoke for both of the daughters as she said, "Not on your life! When this *baka na senso* is over, I'm going back home and take up my life where it left off. I don't have any loyalty to the Emperor, Daddy. I've never even seen him or heard him. At least we could hear President Roosevelt on the radio and see him in newsreels. Look, I'm proud of being Japanese. I really am. I've even sort of enjoyed the last two years here, or at least parts of them. Daddy, if it'll make it easier on you, I won't insist on taking my name off the register, but I will never renounce my American citizenship."

"But...," Jun started, then shrugged and went back to his rice balls. Aileen noted that that sort of outburst from her a year ago would have committed them all to at least an hour of heated discussion, with her father getting the last word. Was Jun changing his mind on the perfection of the Japanese system? Or was he just giving up trying to tell anything to his stubborn, too-American daughters?

A month later as Aileen and Myrna were walking home from school, they suddenly heard the roar of an airplane flying much too low. They looked up and saw an olive drab bomber flying right over them.

"It's American!" Myrna yelled in English, then quickly switched to Japanese, "See the red, white and blue stars on the wings? Where did it come from?" They looked in the direction from which the plane had come, and saw three plumes of smoke rising in downtown Tokyo. They remembered hearing explosions a minute before but had ignored them, assuming some sort of construction noise. "We're bombing Tokyo," Myrna said softly, now in control of her enthusiasm.

That night, the Tokyo radio described "some accidental industrial explosions in the downtown district". Nothing was said of enemy airplanes. Surprisingly, Jun believed his daughters' report that they'd seen an American bomber flying over. The family decided to pay a social call on the Nomuras that night. As the wives socialized, kneeling on thin *zabutons* on the *tatami* floor in the front room, the husbands and the girls went to the back room to listen on the outlawed short wave radio for an English language explanation. Late at night came a truncated report of a B-25 raid on Tokyo that day. There was no report of where they'd come from–Jun and Mr. Nomura were sure they couldn't have flown all the way from Hawaii–or where they'd gone. The next day, the girls saw two partially damaged factories on their way to school. But repairs on them had already started. Reports over the short wave the next few days referred to the bombing as the Doolittle Raid.

Following the raid, the visits by the *kempeitai* increased in frequency, but the girls, emboldened by the raid - "Finally we're fighting back!" - continued to resist the ever-more-threatening requests to renounce their American citizenship.

CHAPTER 4

"LOOK, MAMA, WE DON'T EVEN NEED DUST PANS."
Dorothy exclaimed, as she swept sand through a knothole in the floor. An afternoon sandstorm had blown sand between the sheets of tar paper and the wall boards of their barracks, and soon the amount of sand in the Hayakawas' unit equaled that on the strip of land they called a beach at Terminal Island.

Each barracks had six sections, four intended for families; the two at the ends for a couple of bachelors. One light bulb hung from the ceiling, and one pot-bellied stove occupied the space below that glare. Each family area had six Army cots but no other furniture. No dividers between families were in place the first night. Latrines were in a separate building, far from the barracks. Inadequate numbers caused long lines, which discouraged many a would-be user. Plenty of them left the line, disappeared into the shadows, returning a few minutes later to head back to their barracks. Perhaps worst of all was the absence of partitions between the toilets. Though cardboard dividers were eventually erected, many a woman, conditioned by a lifetime of modesty, would sneak out late at night to visit the latrine.

Dinner, served in the community mess hall, was the highlight of the day, it was generally agreed, even though the menu was canned wieners and spinach, served on tin plates. "Just like they serve the soldiers," said some of the boys who were ROTC veterans. Before they settled down for the night, they were issued Army blankets and mattress covers, which they filled with hay. Most slept that cold first night in the multi-layers of clothes they'd worn all day.

"Well, I think we can make this into something like home," said Dorothy as the Hayakawa family turned out the light. There was no answer except Peter's deep breathing–not even detention camp with barbed wire, guards and hay-filled mattresses could keep Pete awake.

If it was a dispirited group of Japanese Americans that went to bed at Manzanar that night, they recovered quickly the next morning. The transformation of the camp began as soon as they finished breakfast. Some supplies and tools were available, and soon the larger openings in walls and floors were covered with strips of board and more tar paper. At Dorothy's request, the Hayakawas left one of the floor knotholes open, and soon their floor was almost sterile. When they eventually covered the knothole with a rug, the phrase "sweeping the dirt under the rug" had an entirely different meaning for the Hayakawas than for most families. The blankets hung the first day to separate families soon gave way to cardboard partitions and ultimately to plywood. In most family areas, the parents' "room" was partitioned off, while the rest of the area was open. The number of electrical outlets was increased, and when that began to overload the power supply, Captain MacDonald, the camp commander provided more generators.

MacDonald, an infantry officer, barely missed combat in World War I. The Armistice was signed while he was aboard ship on his way to France. He stayed in the reserves after he was mustered out, while he attained moderate success as a high school football coach in Connecticut. He requested active duty the day after Pearl Harbor. Finally he would get his chance to command troops in combat! What a disappointment when he was assigned to Manzanar. Shoji got to know him well. He, appointed block captain for a block of fourteen barracks, made a habit of visiting the commander daily with a list of needs.

"I don't have the manpower to do all these jobs you want done," MacDonald told Shoji authoritatively on their first meeting.

"We've got plenty of manpower. All we need are these tools and supplies right there on the list," replied an uncowed Shoji.

MacDonald studied the list, the bluster gone from his face. "Well, we'll see what we can do," he conceded.

From that first list, Shoji only came away with fourteen brooms to replace the makeshift brooms they had been using, but it was a start. The next visit, Shoji presented their need for shovels and bricks to replace the open sewers that drained the latrines with septic tanks. Because of that, Ken was convinced that their block had a lower prevalence of the "Manzanar trots" that soon swept the camp.

Captain MacDonald gradually began to take pride in his job, and he was not above playing his block captains off, one against the other. "Why don't you go check out Mr. Hayakawa's area?" he might say to one of his less-imaginative block captains. "They're growing a hedge around their area." It was clear to Ken that the old football coach loved the teamwork of the camp and probably bragged about Manzanar, as a coach would about his team.

The camp began to develop its own organization. Block captains picked eight men and women from the group who had been professional cooks and could prepare Japanese and American food. MacDonald was only too happy to agree to that. They selected two women as librarians. A Los Angeles high school which had to merge with another high school had donated its library. Ken appreciated the irony of this, because the school that closed did so because it had lost so many Japanese students. Applicants were selected for teachers, recreation directors, drama teachers, band leaders–and most important for the Hayakawas, a baseball coach! Men and women who filled these and other positions requiring special abilities and leadership were paid the exalted sum of $19 a month, compared to $16 for the rank and file worker.

Peter, though not a particularly gifted athlete, loved sports and played them all in their season. Baseball was in season for at least half the year in Manzanar, and the leaders asked Harry Toyoshima to coach. He had learned his baseball as a boy growing up in Hawaii, and then as a young man in Los Angeles, he coached neighborhood teams. At Manzanar during the season, three age groups kept him busy from the end of school till sundown weekdays and all day on weekends. Peter was the first-baseman on the high school-age team, a big target for the infielders though not very mobile around the base. He'd occasionally hit a long ball, and what he lacked in batting average, he made up for in enthusiasm. When Peter was at home, his conversation centered around two topics–what a great coach Harry was, and Peter's prowess as a slugger. The family did not particularly regret that Pete ate most of his meals in the messhall with the other boys on the team–at least other topics could be discussed over the dinner table.

Dorothy soon found her niche in the administrative office of the camp. The main change in her life, she commented, "Now I walk to work instead of taking the bus." Howie fit in right away with the maintenance group. Ken worked with him and admired the way in which his brother innately knew how to fix toilets, rewire a shorted lamp, or replace a broken step. Howie enjoyed Ken's admiration. The relationship between the brothers was better than ever before, particularly the times Ken was the premed student and Howie the fisherman. But after three weeks, Ken, noting his black-and-blue fingernails and his blisters, decided he'd served Howie's ego enough. He offered his services at the hospital.

He walked into the first-aid room and smiled as he recognized Dr. Kawamura, the man who, a few months before, had assured him it would all "blow over". "I heard your family was here," said the doctor. "I was going to look you up. We can use your help."

"That's what I'm here for," replied Ken. "I was hoping you could teach me to sew up lacerations, and put on casts..."

"All in due time," interrupted Dr. Kawamura. "What do you think's more important than sewing up cuts and setting broken bones? It's prevention of disease. We're lucky to have Dr. Togasaki here. She's a specialist in communicable disease, and she has us inspecting mess halls and giving typhoid vaccinations and teaching the mothers who give their babies powdered milk to boil the water first. The doctors take turns doing this. If we could teach you and some others to do this, it would free the doctors to see patients."

So Ken became a public health specialist. He was convinced of the importance of his job, and he did it with great diligence - too much so for the cooks, who quickly realized that no greasy utensil or stove top would miss the eye of this young former premed student. But he felt he was missing a great opportunity to be exposed to clinical medicine. He soon found he could get an early start on his public health rounds, then spend most of the afternoon with Dr. Kawamura. He was enthralled by the practice of medicine, but he was also overwhelmed by it. The doctor would explain everything he did in a rapid-fire way such that Ken thought himself lucky if he retained 10% of what he heard. The apprentice system of medical education, which had been replaced just after the turn of the century, was not an easy way to learn, Ken concluded. He did learn how to suture lacerations and looked on those times as his break periods. It didn't take nearly as much brain power to sew up a simple cut as it did to follow Dr. Kawamura's rapid discussions of the cause, diagnosis, and therapy of the varied illnesses they saw. Ken would take home any excess suture of the day and practice tying knots on his bed frame - first two-handed knots and then one-handed knots - a practice engaged in by medical students from time immemorial.

Patient care suffered from lack of medicine, and Captain MacDonald was not as able to get medicine as he was construction materials. Dr. Kawamura, at Ken's suggestion, used the tactics that Shoji had perfected of a daily visit with a list of needs. But he knew the captain was not lying when he said the priority for medicine was the battle front. Even outside the camp, shortages of medicines for civilians existed. One episode served to convince Dr. Kawamura that Captain MacDonald was doing his best. At one of their morning visits, the captain was obviously distracted.

"It's my daughter. She awakened this morning with a stomach ache. I took her to the doctor, and he said it was just an upset stomach and gave her some medicine. She threw it up, and now she's worse than before. She even has a fever now," he told Dr. Kawamura.

"How old is she?"

"Eighteen."

"Where's the pain?" Captain MacDonald pointed to his right lower abdomen. "Has she had this pain before?"

"No. She's always been very healthy, and she felt fine when she went to bed last night."

"Well, captain, I would take her back to the doctor, or to another one, and ask him to look at her again. Ask him if it could be appendicitis."

"You think so?" asked Captain MacDonald.

"I haven't examined her, but it fits."

"Thanks, Doc. I'll take her back when I get home tonight."

"No. Go home now and take her right away. Appendices can rupture, you know."

Captain MacDonald looked at Dr. Kawamura for a few seconds and then grabbed his hat and left.

The next morning, the commander was late getting to the camp but went straight to the hospital when he did. "You hit the nail on the head, Doc. They operated last night, and sure enough, it was appendicitis. They said they got it just in time."

Dr. Kawamura smiled. "We always say that." Although medicines remained in short supply after that, the doctor was sure that Captain MacDonald was doing his best to obtain the medicine available.

Despite the evidences of community spirit, however, nobody (except perhaps the children) felt that life at Manzanar was better than it had been at home. The one stove per family was not enough for warmth in the winter. And in the summer, the wind from Death Valley, a few miles to the east, brought oppressive heat.

The toilets frequently stopped up, causing not only inconvenience but intestinal disease, despite the typhoid vaccinations.

And yet, for the internees the spiritual privations were worse than the physical ones - the knowledge that despite having done nothing wrong, they were prisoners behind barbed wire and armed guards in their own country. Floodlights played back and forth along the sand streets at night, and anything they wanted to do required permission. Trips outside the camp required escorts. The family table was a distant memory, replaced by messhall eating. Toshiko had tried to keep the family together for at least one meal a day, but without success. Dorothy often joined her parents, but Ken usually came in late with the doctor. Sitting at one of the peripheral tables, they discussed cases of the day. Peter ate with "the team," but most distressing was Howie. He was completely unwilling to accept any platitudes, Japanese or American, for the actions of his government. He spent most of his time with a small but increasingly vocal group of young men of similar conviction. They ate together, and when not working, could be seen standing and talking together quietly but intently. Shoji and Toshiko tried reasoning with him whenever possible. Their main argument, *shikataganai*, "It cannot be helped", failed to satisfy their son. Such reasoning always resulted in an argument, and Ken was happier the more time Howie spent away from his parents. He tried to spend time with his brother to continue their improved relationship from their working together on the maintenance crew, but he avoided any discussion of the camp–and what else was there to talk about?

The challenge of making his block of barracks livable and the competition with the other blocks had initially caused Shoji's spirits to rise. After about six months, though, his goals had been reached, and his renewed vigor waned, giving way to boredom. The family leadership passed back to Toshiko. He also began drinking again, having found a source for smuggled whiskey. When Ken was not listening to his parents and Howie arguing, he could hear his parents doing so with each other, usually late at night. One night, the bickering took a more strident tone, and Ken heard a loud slap. He jumped out of his bed and rushed behind the blanket partition to his parents' area. Toshiko was pulling herself up from the floor. "It's O.K.," she quickly said, "I just fell off the bed. You know how clumsy I am." Tears welled in her eyes.

Shoji, who had been standing over his wife, turned away and stared at the wall. "Do you want to sleep in my bed?" asked Ken, immediately wishing he could have thought of something more appropriate to say.

"No. No. I'm fine. Thank you, anyway. You go back to bed, now." Ken heard no more noises that night.

By the autumn of 1942, the boredom that had overtaken Shoji had settled on the whole camp. It was relieved for awhile when the men taken from their homes on Terminal Island in the first few days after Pearl Harbor returned to their families.

"What did Mr. Furutani say about his time in North Dakota?" asked Ken of his father one evening.

"Well, they asked all kinds of questions day after day. They seemed to suspect him of delivering messages to submarines off the coast," replied Shoji.

"They had that one episode where they thought a sub shelled Santa Barbara, but they never proved it one way or another. Even if it did it was at least two months after they took those men away," said Ken.

"I can't imagine Mr. Furutani doing anything like that." added Toshiko. "He's always the one organizing 4th of July parades and that sort of thing."

"Why did it take nine months for them to figure out he hadn't done anything?" asked Dorothy.

"I don't know." answered Shoji. "None of them are saying much about what happened. It was a bad experience."

"Did they torture them?" asked Peter. "Even old Endo doesn't deserve that."

"I don't think they actually tortured them," answered Shoji quietly. Ken was glad that Howie was not with the family that night.

But Howie and his friends had talked with the returned men, and their anger was increased to even greater levels. Some in the group were openly pro-Japan and were talking about repatriation to that country. To his parents' satisfaction, Howie spurned that position. "How can I be repatriated to a country I've never been to or been a citizen of? I want my country to do what's right, and that's not to keep us behind barbed wire."

One night, Howie's particular peeve was the Japanese American Citizens League. "You know, they've sold us down the river. They come across as being our great protectors, and then they give in on everything the government wants them to do. They don't protect us worth a damn! As far as I'm concerned, they don't represent me."

"If you had your wishes," responded his father heatedly, "we'd be at constant war every day. At least we live in peace now."

"What do you mean 'live in peace'? I don't call this peace. We're like prisoners of war."

"Well obviously, Howard, this is not the way we'd choose to live, but give the JACL time. If they can convince the government that we're loyal citizens, we'll have our freedom back earlier than if we fight them every step of the way," said Shoji.

"But how much respect are they going to have for us if we just lie down like slaves and say, 'Thank you, master. Thank you, master,'" every time they tighten the screws a little more? And as for the JACL men, they'd better watch out. There are enough guys who don't like what they're doing that they'd better watch their backsides." With that, he left the room.

"What do you think he meant by that last statement?" asked Toshiko.

Her question went unanswered that night, but Shoji and Toshiko were alarmed three days later when they heard that a Mr. Tatsuno, the most vocal of the JACL supporters in camp, had been beaten badly enough that he'd had to be hospitalized.

"No. I didn't do it, but I wish I had," answered Howie to their question.

"Do you think he's telling the truth?" asked Toshiko of her husband after Howie had left.

"I'm not sure. I hope so. He's never lied to us before."

They were relieved two days later when they heard that three men had been arrested for the assault. But that night, an hour after supper, they heard noises outside their barracks, as if crowds of angry people were milling about. Ken and Peter, the only two of the children home at the time, went out to see what the commotion was. They came back shortly.

"There are hundreds of people out there all upset about the arrests. They're going to the camp office to demand their release," said Ken to his parents.

"Shoji, Dorothy's there! She went back after supper to finish off some work," said Toshiko, in panic.

"Kenichi, go get your sister, and don't get involved in the demonstration," Shoji ordered. And then, as Ken and Peter started to leave, he yelled "Peter! You stay home. I told Ken to go, not you!"

"But, Dad...," Peter looked at Shoji and said no more, retreating towards his bed.

Ken ran to the camp office. When he arrived, he saw six M.P.'s with rifles at the ready standing in front of the main office door. Across the street was the angry mob he'd seen minutes before passing his barracks. They were loudly demanding the release of the arrested men. An unarmed Captain MacDonald stood on the porch behind the M.P.'s, shouting to the mob. He was not being heard.

Ken remembered that the office had a back door, and he took a long detour around the adjacent barracks so he could approach it without being seen. He went up the steps and tried to open the door. It was locked.

"Dorothy! Dorothy! Come to the back door!" he yelled, hoping to be heard above the noise from the other side of the building. A few seconds later, a relieved Dorothy opened the door.

"Boy! Am I glad you're here. It's beginning to get ugly..." Before she could finish her thought, a shot rang out, and then another, and another. Then there was a volley of shots. The angry shouting turned into screams. Ken looked under the elevated building to the other side and could see that the mob was running away. His heart sank when he saw bodies lying in the street.

"Let's get out of here," he said and took his sister by the elbow. They walked and ran back to their barracks, taking the long way to avoid any confrontation. They entered their home to find their parents beside themselves with anxiety.

"You're safe!" said Toshiko. "What were those shots?"

"I don't exactly know," said Ken breathlessly "There were M.P.'s with rifles facing the mob, and Captain MacDonald was trying to quiet them down. I don't know who fired the first shot - probably the M.P.'s."

"Was anyone hurt?" asked Toshiko.

"Yes. That's the worst part. I saw bodies in the street. I better get to the hospital and see if I can help," answered Ken.

"Kenichi...," started his father.

"I've got to go, Dad. I'll be careful. Here, I'll wear this Red Cross arm band," said Ken as he fetched the arm band he'd worn for a recent mass casualty exercise at the hospital.

When he reached the hospital, confusion reigned regardless of the mass casualty training. He found Dr. Kawamura and asked how he could help. "This man has had a gunshot wound to his flank. It may have hit his kidney. He's stable, but we're getting a urinalysis. Help me start an I.V., and we'll transfer him to the hospital in Independence."

After the I.V. was started, Ken looked up to see one of the other doctors pulling a sheet over the face of one of the wounded men. "That makes two who've been killed. One was dead when they brought him in. Let's hope there are no more," said Dr. Kawamura. They looked at another man with a wound to his thigh. The doctor started to dress it and said, "You go check out that man over there. He has a wound in his upper arm. I'll be with you in a minute."

Ken went and checked the arm. When he could feel a pulse and elicit good arm motion, he said, "I think this is pretty superficial. I'll get the doctor to check it out and then get it bandaged."

"Yeah, it'll be O.K," said the owner of the arm.

Ken looked up, startled. "Howie!" After a few seconds, he added, "Well, it should be O.K. What were you doing?"

"Nothing. We were just protesting the arrest of those three men. There was no evidence that they had done it. They were just looking for scapegoats for beating up that JACL guy."

Ken started to ask why he thought the men were innocent, then decided he didn't want to know how much Howie knew. Dr. Kawamura came up at that time, confirmed that the wound only needed a bandage and said "Now they're saying all the wounded need to be transferred to Independence. I guess they'll need to investigate."

"O.K., Howie, I'll check on you every day. Just keep your mouth shut, and don't antagonize anybody," said Ken.

"All right," answered Howie quietly, rare for him in recent months.

Ken told his parents about Howie when he got home that night, emphasizing how minor the gunshot wound was. "I'll call the hospital in Independence and check on him every day. He'll be home in no time." He declined to say anything about the investigation. As he settled into his bed that night, he noticed the date: December 7, 1942.

Howie was home in four days with no charges against him. The investigation revealed that none of the internees had had guns and that there had been no provocation other than the angry protest. There were reports that some of the M.P.'s had been reprimanded. At Manzanar, life soon settled back into its normal, boring routine, except that is, for the families of the two men who were killed in the riot.

Part II
Wartime Choices

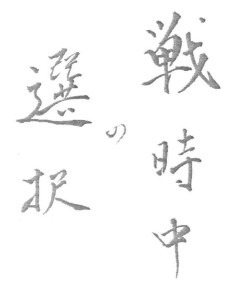

CHAPTER 5

Y OU SHOULD SEE THE NEW QUESTIONNAIRE WE
are all going to have to fill out." Dorothy fairly burst with
this information as she got home from work one day the
following February. "The two main questions are whether you would
serve in the military and whether you're loyal to the United States."

"Why do they need to ask us about our loyalty? We've never done
anything to make them doubt it," said Shoji.

"Do all Americans, or just us, have to answer it?" asked Ken in an
uncharacteristically cynical tone, when he got home from the hospital.

Dorothy was right about which would be the two most controver-
sial questions, questions #27 and #28. All conversation for the next two
weeks centered around those two questions. People split into the "Yes.
Yes's." and the "No. No's.", the first group far outnumbering the latter.
It took courage to speak for the "No. No's.", because no one knew the
consequences of answering the questionnaire in that way. There was a
widespread rumor that the "No. No's." would be sent to Japan. There
was confusion even amongst those whose loyalty to America was un-
complicated. Every man and woman over the age of seventeen had to
fill out the questionnaire, so the women and the older men wondered if
the government was getting ready to expand the draft to include their
respective categories. Some were afraid that to renounce any allegiance
to Japan, in the words of the question, would imply that they had previously had allegiance to Japan.

Shoji, Toshiko, Dorothy, and Ken were all "Yes. Yes's.", but not
without comment. Shoji was offended by the whole matter, and Ken
thought it all foolish. "Do they think there are a bunch of spies in the
camp who will answer "No. No.", and then they can arrest them?"

Howie did not say how he filled his out, but Dorothy, who was in charge of distributing and collecting the questionnaires, whispered to the family one night, "Howie said 'No. Yes.' Yes, he was loyal to America. No, he wouldn't serve."

"What will that mean?" asked Toshiko after that bit of news settled in for awhile.

"I think he'll be O.K," said Ken. "They're not drafting us, anyway. Wouldn't that be funny, for one of us here behind barbed wire to get a draft notice? Think they'd train us to be camp guards?" The family chuckled at such an absurd picture.

Dorothy was first out. The internees were allowed to leave camp if they had a sponsor and went somewhere other than the west coast. Dorothy had answered an advertisement for a young woman with secretarial training to work in New York City, and the job offer had come back by return mail.

"Did you tell them you're Nisei?" asked Peter.

"Yes. I told them I don't belong to that well-known Scottish clan of Hayakawas. I think they can figure that out, Petey, particularly with a Manzanar return address."

"Fumiko," said Shoji, using her Japanese name, as he did only when speaking of important things, "That's a long way to go, and you won't know anyone. Maybe you should wait a couple years."

"She's twenty-three. That's seven years older than you were when you left your family," said Toshiko to her husband, interrupting Dorothy's planned protest.

"But she's a..., a..."

"Girl?" asked Toshiko. "She's also got an education and five years' experience behind her. And as for being a girl, this is 1943. Who do you think is running the country while the men are at war?"

Dorothy left with several other young people, men and women, a week later. The night before, she and Ken walked the sandy streets of Manzanar and talked. He sensed her excitement at being on her own and seeing a part of the country not many California Japanese had ever thought they'd see. He noted the next morning however, that if anyone not knowing the situation had watched her goodbyes to her parents, they would have thought she was devastated at leaving them. "Smart girl," thought Ken. It allowed Shoji to be the protective father.

"You'll do fine, Fumiko," he said, "and if things don't work out, you've always got a bed here."

"We'll keep your knothole in the floor open for you, Dor," said Peter. Toshiko gave her a teary hug, and so did Ken, and the bus was off, heading eastward.

***

"I'm going! We've all got to go!" The speaker was Horace Yamashita, and he was speaking to a couple hundred young men scattered around the mess hall after supper. "if we're ever gonna prove we're true Americans, we have to be willing to be shot at and even die to show them that they had no reason to put us here."

"Bullshit!" came the reply from Howie Hayakawa. "Why do we have to prove anything? We're as much citizens as any of the white guys. And they didn't put any of them in jail."

Ken sat on one of the benches along the wall and listened as the discussion continued. He rarely attended these after-dinner bull sessions, but on this evening they'd had a recruiting visit from the Army. The new rule was that Niseis could volunteer for the Army, specifically an all-Japanese unit originating in Hawaii.

At first, listening to the debate, Ken was amused. Here was little Horace, a young man he'd known a bit at UCLA, taking the warrior's position and Ken's muscular brother, six inches taller and sixty pounds heavier than Horace, taking the pacifist role. "I think I'd rather go to war with Howie by my side than Horace," Ken chuckled to himself and leaned back against the wall.

Very few of the men were taking Howie's side.

"I want to get out of this damn prison any way I can," said Frank Oshima.

"We need to show them the *samurai* spirit," started one man whom Ken didn't recognize.

"Yeah," interrupted another, "I can see us getting off the bus at training camp swinging our *samurai* swords like a bunch of characters from a *kabuki* play. They'll send us to the loony bin." Everyone laughed at that, but most of the discussion, as the evening wore on, was serious. No longer leaning against the wall, Ken was beginning to feel uneasy, his earlier amusement gone.

"We can't let those guys from Hawaii show us up," said Ko Kawahara, "You heard those guys say that they wanted 1500 volunteers, and the first day 10,000 showed up. I mean, I thought those guys just sat on the beach and ate coconuts and strummed their ukuleles."

"Look. We shouldn't be trying to keep up with anybody else. This isn't like who can make the best float for a parade. This has to do with who we are and what we think of ourselves," said Howie. "Someone said something about the *samurai* spirit. What about *giri*, the idea we have to make our family and ancestors proud of us? Will they be proud of us if we sit like a bunch of sheep in this jail even though we've done nothing wrong, and then when they give us a chance to fight for the system that does that, say 'Thank you, sir, for your kindness. Sign me up.'?"

A longer than usual silence followed that speech, but soon the discussion was raging again. The overwhelming opinion was still against Howie's position.

Ken became more and more agitated and finally had to stand and speak. "I can see both sides. I can see my brother's point. They had no reason to put us in here. But, you know, they never had much respect for us before Pearl Harbor. We've been in this country for how long? Fifty years? And yet they mostly think of us as a funny, little, different people, who make good gardeners, and that's about it. You know Dr. Kawamura. He's the smartest man I know, and yet he was always looked upon as a second class doctor. You guys know what I'm talking about. And now with the war, you see how they portray Japanese - buck-toothed, near-sighted, sneaky. When this war is over, they'll apply that to us too. I think this may be a chance to change their perception of us. Yeah, Howie, I know it's not fair." He raised his hand to forestall his brother's objection. "But this might be our opportunity to change the last fifty years of our history in this country. I think we've got to go." As Ken sat down, Howie stood up. He left the mess hall, slamming the door behind him, and the discussion was terminated.

"I've got a couple letters for you to read," said Dr. Kawamura, as Ken entered the hospital the next morning. Ken had long since given up trying to beat the doctor to the hospital in the mornings. "Read the opened one first."

Ken sat down to read:

> UNIVERSITY *of* CALIFORNIA
> *School of Medicine*
> *Office of Admissions March 12, 1943*

Dear Tosh,

I'm sorry I took so long to answer, but your letter hit a guilty chord. Indeed, we did accept Mr. Kenichi Hayakawa in January 1942 for the class beginning that September. Because of Pearl Harbor and the events taking place in California, the committee thought it best to delay sending the letter of acceptance. I regret to admit I was part of the group making that decision. We felt justified when the order came out sending all west coast Japanese to detention camps. But I continued to feel bad about our decision. When I received your letter, I felt I had to do something about it. I honestly feel Mr. Hayakawa would have trouble in California if we accept him here. I think the anti-Japanese animosity would hamper his studies. In fact, I don't think we could even have him here legally. Therefore, I sent his file to a friend of mine, Mike Greenway, who's the admissions dean at Creighton in Nebraska. Mike wrote me by return mail that Mr. Hayakawa would be acceptable to him. He'll be sending him a letter, c/o you at Manzanar. I'm glad we could get him in somewhere.

I feel terrible about you being in the camp, Tosh. I know you said in your letter that it wasn't too bad since they let you practice medicine, but I'll bet it's hell. When this mess is over, let's get together, have a couple of drinks, and you tell me what it was really like.

Sincerely, Brod

Broderick L. Wilson, M.D., Dean of Admissions

Ken quickly opened the second letter, which was a standard acceptance letter from the dean of admissions, Creighton University School of Medicine. He set the letters down and stared at the wall. Normally, he would have been ecstatic, reading this letter for which he'd worked for four years.

"I think I told you that Brod Wilson and I were classmates at UC. The more I thought about your not hearing anything on your application, the more I thought I needed to contact him," said the doctor. He paused. "You have a tough decision to make, don't you? I heard about your speech last night."

Ken finally looked at Dr. Kawamura. "Yes sir. I sure do. Thank you very much for writing that letter, Dr. Kawamura." Together the two men rose, as if on cue and went to the treatment room where patients were already beginning to gather.

After supper, Ken shared his problem with his family. "But Ken, you can be a lot more service to people if you're a doctor than if you're a soldier," said his mother. "You've been dreaming about medical school since high school. This is your chance. You can get your degree and then join the Army. I'm sure they'll need you to take care of the wounded soldiers."

"Mom," said Peter, "the war'll be over by the time Ken finishes med school, and he'll have missed it. Anyway, you should have heard his speech last night. It sorta' ended the argument. He was more convincing than the recruiting sergeants. I'm going to volunteer!"

"Be quiet, Peter. You're not even seventeen yet, and I'm not going to sign my permission for you to go early. But Ken, suppose you go and get killed? What kind of doctor would you be then?" asked Toshiko with logic that Ken thought indisputable.

"Mom, Ken's too smart to get shot. He'll probably talk his way into some job away from the front line. He'll be O.K. He'll probably be a medic. Yeah, a medic. They don't get shot at as long as they wear that red cross on their sleeve. I saw a movie about that." said Peter.

Ken looked at his father, thankful that this was not one of his whiskey nights. "What do you think, Father?"

Shoji sat for a minute, puffing on his cigarette. Finally he spoke. "Kenichi, it's your own decision. We'd be very proud of you if you were a doctor, and nobody could criticize your decision. But how would you feel after this damn war is over?"

Ken sat still a few moments and began to smile. "You all are a big help. One says 'medical school'; another says 'Army'; and the third says 'It's your own decision.'"

Ken lay in his bed that night, unable to sleep. The arguments of the day rushed through his mind, one on top of the other. Every point had its counterpoint. He turned so often that he had to get up twice to pick his blanket up from the floor and re-tuck it under his mattress. By 3:00AM, he was desperate for sleep. "Maybe I should pray about this," he thought. When sleep didn't come for another fifteen minutes, he started: "Lord, I feel embarrassed coming to you in prayer after having prayed so little over the last year. I guess I felt sort of abandoned when we had to come to camp. And maybe I felt that since our lives were in someone else's hands here, you didn't have power in our lives. I know that's all wrong, but I think that's why I haven't prayed much. Anyway, I really need your direction now. Should I take the easy way out and go to med school, or should I volunteer for the Army?" He stopped and thought of the phrase he'd used for the medical school choice: "easy way out". How could medical school ever be easy? Yet that was how he was viewing it. He continued his prayer, lying there on his bed, rehashing the arguments he knew so well by now. Sleep overtook him before he even uttered a formal "Amen".

He was surprised at how refreshed he felt the next morning in view of his lack of sleep. He arrived at the hospital early with his mind made up. "Dr. Kawamura, I really appreciate what you've done for me, getting that acceptance at Creighton, but I'm afraid I'm going to have to turn it down. I..."

"I know," Dr. Kawamura interrupted. "It was a tough decision. But you'll be able to go to med school after the war. I don't see how it can last much longer. And think of how you'd be accepted by other doctors. Would you rather be known as a Japanese who went to school and got a head start on them while they were away fighting, or as one who served along with them?" Ken and Dr. Kawamura sat down to write letters to two medical school admission deans.

CHAPTER 6

"WHAT SORT OF LIES DID THEY HAVE YOU WRITING today?" Jun Nakamura asked of his younger daughter. "Oh, just the usual, about all the victories of the glorious Japanese Army and Navy for the emperor. Now, remember Daddy, I don't write them. I just translate them. That may be an important distinction after this *baka na senso* ends," Aileen defended herself.

"I know. Did they say anything about Admiral Yamamoto?" asked Jun.

"No. Why?"

"Apparently his plane was shot down near Guadalcanal. It came over the news reports."

"Well, they'd never announce that on our programs," responded Aileen.

Jun still worked for Domei, translating American and British news reports into Japanese. Aileen now worked for NHK, the Japan Broadcasting Corporation. The university had discontinued all the courses she had planned to take on the American political system, and she had been forced to leave school. She had briefly considered taking other courses, but the Nakamuras, along with all other families in Japan, were becoming more and more desperate. Jun's job was still only part-time and poorly paid, and his savings were now nearly exhausted. In truth, there was not much need for money, since there were price controls and the supply of food had dwindled. Still they did enjoy a better house than most, and the girls did not want to give up their room, furnished in western style with beds and study tables. Since Myrna was able to continue her premed studies, Aileen felt obliged to look for work.

Not many choices existed. She could work in a silk factory, making

18 cents a day - many farm girls had moved to town for that. Or she could work in a munitions factory. That would earn her $30 a month, but it would also require twelve hours a day, seven days a week. Worst, she would be making ammunition that would be fired at Americans.

Jun had come home one day saying that NHK was looking for bilingual employees to translate Japanese script into English for broadcasting to American troops in the Pacific. She struggled with that decision. She would be part of the process that broadcast propaganda to American fighting troops. And yet, what was actually broadcast seemed pretty innocuous - news from the Japanese perspective, and introducing American music records. Furthermore, it paid enough that the Nakamuras could stay in their house. She reasoned further that it might mollify the *kempeitai*, who continued to visit them monthly to encourage them to renounce their American citizenship. At least she was doing something somewhat official. It was a difficult time for Niseis in Japan. Even those whose loyalty lay primarily with Japan - a small minority in the experience of the Nakamura sisters - were looked on with suspicion and sometimes disgust. Aileen felt that this job took some of the heat off her.

Jun and Aileen sometimes joked about their jobs. He took English news reports and translated them into Japanese. Someone else used this information, with subtle twists in emphasis, for propaganda broadcasts to American troops, and Aileen translated it back to English.

"Why don't you just slip me the reports before you translate them, Daddy, and I'll get them on the air?" suggested Aileen. "We'll skip the middle man."

"We'd both be in jail then," Jun said laughing.

"I wonder if there would be more food in jail than we get now," chuckled Aileen.

Food shortages were now epidemic. American submarines controlled the waters around Japan so thoroughly that very little food arrived from the Philippines, Saipan, and southeast Asia. The Nakamuras knew this from the English broadcasts Jun translated - not from the Tokyo newspapers. Japan, with so little arable land, was unable to raise enough food to feed its citizens. Chemicals, used as fertilizer before the war, were going into explosives, and then when a natural disaster occurred, the effect of it was hugely magnified.

One would expect in such a situation that a black market would arise, and so it did in Japan by 1943. As the black market became more successful, the supply of food available in stores became progressively less and of poorer quality. The Nakamuras, always law-abiding, had had to deal with that as a family. At first they ignored it. But soon they began to notice each other getting skinnier. Myrna talked of beriberi and other diseases of food deficiency. Eventually they joined the half of Japanese families who bought from the black market. It did not solve their food problem but allowed them occasionally to go to bed not hungry. In Myrna's words, it kept them from going from "skinny" to "cachectic".

When the reports of the segregation of the west coast Japanese into detention camps first began to filter through, they were incredulous, doubting that the United States could have done that. Eventually they became convinced, as the Nomuras shared with them reports of their cousins, who had been evacuated to Heart Mountain in Wyoming. As the Japan food shortages became worse, both families concluded they'd rather be in the detention camps than in Tokyo. The report of unlimited food in the camps, though not the tastiest, was the telling point for these families, who felt lucky if they could have fish once a week.

One night, two men in black coats came to the door. They were not *kempeitai* men - the Nakamuras recognized them all by now because of the monthly visits on the citizenship issue - but identified themselves as officers of the *tokko keisatsu*. *Tokko keisatsu* was another police organization, whose main job seemed to be to suppress non-patriotic activities. "Are you Mr. Jun Nakamura?" they asked politely.

"Yes," answered Jun.

"Would you accompany us to the station for questioning?"

"Why? What have I done?"

"Just come with us. You may get your coat," was the answer, the tone less polite this time.

"What are you charging him with? You can't just take him off without a charge!" said Aileen, as she jumped between her father and the policemen. They glanced briefly at Aileen and then repeated their demand to Jun, this time more forcefully.

Aileen continued her protestations, evidently to deaf ears, but Jun got his coat and went with the policemen. "Don't worry. I've done nothing wrong. I'll be back shortly," he said, as he left.

When the women visited him in jail the next morning, Jun said "I was turned in for unpatriotic thoughts."

"Thoughts?" said Aileen. "Who turned...what thoughts?...Who turned you in and for what unpatriotic thoughts?" as she collected herself.

"They weren't specific. The only one I can think of is Mr. Murakami. I've probably given my opinions in the *tonarigumi* meetings once too often."

The *tonarigumi*–or neighborhood associations–had been organized by the government a year before the Nakamuras moved to Tokyo. Their purpose was both practical and spiritual. With government help, they were instructed in fire fighting and bomb defense. They were taught to keep buckets of sand near their homes, how to form a bucket brigade, and how to dig bomb shelters. Strips of homes had been actually demolished, and the families resettled elsewhere, to create fire breaks. The bomb shelters were hardly more than trenches dug in the back yard over which planks of wood were placed. Some of the more esthetic of the families grew flowers in the dirt piled on top of the planks. The *tonarigumi* also supported community morale. They sang songs and pledged loyalty to each other and to the emperor in defending against the hated enemy and the expected air raids. The Nakamuras had thought their group, which included ten houses on their block, quaint when they moved in and had enjoyed the friendship. But when the war came and as it progressed, they became tired of the anti-American invective.

As the food shortages became more intense, the *tonarigumi*, through the elected representatives, were the source of supply of gas masks and some food distribution. By summer 1943, they had also become conduits of information to the *tokko keisatsu* of men and women who expressed thoughts not in keeping with respect for the emperor and the courageous soldiers and sailors defending their country against the assault of the western democracies. Mr. Murakami was their *tonarigumi* captain, and they all agreed he must have reported Jun for some of the pessimistic opinions he had expressed in the meetings.

Jun was home in 29 days, the limit he could be kept without a charge. "No, there was no torture," he said "They just asked me hundreds of questions every day. They made me write my memoirs."

"Your memoirs?" asked Aileen.

"Yes. All about my early upbringing, our life in America, why we came back and what life has been like since then," answered Jun.

"What did you say?" asked Myrna.

"I could be honest about everything through our coming back, though I implied I had always planned to return to Japan after I'd made my fortune off the gullible Americans. But you should have seen the lies I started telling about how I felt about Japan after we got back," he chuckled. "Anyway, I told them what they wanted to hear, and they let me go."

Two things changed after Jun's detention. Any lingering illusions about Japan were gone, and any openness of Jun to express his honest opinions was squelched. If he spoke in the *tonarigumi* meetings, it was to extol the virtues of the *Yamato damashii*–the spirit of Japan. He never mentioned his detention to Mr. Murakami.

As spring became summer and then fall in 1943, the Nakamuras noticed that the morale in Japan grew worse. There was more public realization that the war was not going well. The government had eventually announced in May, six weeks after his death, that Admiral Yamamoto had been shot down and killed in the Solomons. Although there was a great outpouring of love and even reverence at his state funeral in Hibiya Park, the loss of such a national hero was sobering. The truth came out that the Americans were indeed moving up the Solomon Island chain in the southwest Pacific. When the Allies started attacking in New Guinea in October, even the most militant patriot had to admit that there were problems on the war-front. The final blow was the admission that four Japanese aircraft carriers had been sunk at Midway in June 1942 and that that battle was not the glorious victory that had been claimed for more than a year.

The Nakamuras relished the Allied victories, but they also mourned with their friends and neighbors when they received increasingly more frequent letters of condolence from the government (and, if they were lucky, ashes in a box, plain and unpainted) for a son or husband lost in battle. They did not rejoice as a sort of national depression - the Valley of Darkness it was called - set in.

One day, late in the fall, Aileen came home obviously greatly troubled. "Do we have any pepper in the house, Mama?" she asked.

"We do, but do you have any food to put it on?" answered Mieko.

Aileen took the pepper Mieko gave her and started shaking it into her throat. Her parents sat dumbfounded. She began to sneeze and snort. Tears came to her eyes. Soon she was grabbing for a handkerchief and eventually a glass of water.

"What in the world are you doing, Aiko?" Mieko asked.

"Well," Aileen began to answer hoarsely, "I'm going to have a voice test tomorrow, and I have to fail it." Her parents could hardly understand her, but she persisted speaking, her words interrupted by sneezes and nose blows. "They want me - **sneeze** - to try - **cough** - reading the news I trans - **snort** - late over the radio."

"What's wrong with that?" asked her mother.

"They broadcast that to American troops in the Pacific - **cough, cough** - along with music and other - **snort** - propaganda. **sneeze** I've even felt guilty about translating - **cough** - it. You've heard Dad and me talk. **snort** I don't think I could handle reading it. **sneeze** What they say isn't really disloyal, at least - **sneeze** - what I've heard, but I'd always be thinking I was reading stuff that the Japanese government wanted guys I went to school with to hear." Her snorting and sneezing had stopped, but she was still so hoarse as to be almost unintelligible. Jun watched this unusual incident without comment and finally with a slight smile.

The next morning Aileen was still hoarse, but she gave herself another pepper treatment before going to work. That evening, she reported with relief that she had failed the voice test.

"That was smart, Aileen, but how are you going to keep hoarse, pepper your throat every morning?" asked Myrna.

"No. I've figured out another way." answered Aileen. With that, she pulled a pack of cigarettes from her schoolbag and rather inexpertly lit one up. She took a couple of puffs, coughed but persisted. "This ought to do it." Her parents both started to speak. "Before you say anything," she quickly said, "I'll only smoke at home."

Mieko started to say something a couple more times but finally gave it up and went into the kitchen. Jun went back to his newspaper and muttered something that sounded like "damn war" in English.

CHAPTER 7

IT WAS SWEARING-IN DAY AT MANZANAR. NEARLY 250 young Americans of Japanese ancestry who had been "detained" behind fences, barbed wire and armed guards for a year of their youth had volunteered to join the Army two days after the bull session in the mess hall. They would be sworn in and moved out to their training camps in two groups, ten days apart. Ken's name had come up on the first list, which he thought was fortunate, because even now he was having second thoughts as he read and reread the acceptance letter from Nebraska.

The plan was that the recruits would be uniformed before they were sworn in so that the ceremony would look more formal, but whether that goal was reached or not was debatable. The supply truck had brought uniforms with an equal number of sizes: small, medium, large and extra-large. Ken estimated than in this group of 125 young Japanese males there was one extra-large, one large, thirty medium, and forty-five each small and extra-small. The only one who had the right fit was a fellow from West Los Angeles who had been an all-city interior lineman two years before. His extra-large fit just fine. Ken and a few of the other mediums didn't look too bad in their larges, but Horace Yamashita, the self-professed warrior from the mess hall debate looked like a child on a Halloween trick-or-treat wearing his father's clothes. Ken, whose last job in the infirmary had been to weigh and measure all the recruits, knew that Horace checked in at 4'10" and 98 pounds. He also knew that Horace's card said 5'3" and 115 pounds, the Army's minimum. Ken also was struck by the incongruity of the scene: these young men, ready to go off to fight and possibly die in a war, stood in the street as their mothers helped them dress. They tucked in belts, stuffed hats so they wouldn't come down over their sons' eyes, and in some cases hemmed pant legs so that their soldiers would not trip on them. The recruiting sergeant stood by benignly and watched the scene, apparently not questioning the Army's wisdom that decreed that a quarter of all soldiers came in each of four sizes.

Eventually the last mother gave her provisional pat of approval to her son's appearance, and the recruiter lined them up in four ranks. "Cover down! Dress to the right!" and similar instructions finally gave way to his taking each young man by the shoulders and placing him where he wanted him to stand. When they ultimately resembled some sort of military formation, Captain MacDonald strode to their front, did a left face so he faced them and began the short ceremony that would change their lives and, if Ken was right, the lives of all Japanese Americans forever.

"Raise your right hands and repeat after me: "I will swear to faithfully...". One hundred twenty five young Americans pledged their loyalty, even to the point of death, for their country. What went through these young minds at that time cannot be known since their faces were all straight and serious. More could be assumed by watching the faces of their families. Tears streaked many cheeks, both mothers' and fathers', and if pride can be read into facial expressions, it was there in abundance that raw April morning in the California desert. But perhaps most could be learned by watching the faces of the young, white Americans in the guard towers as they watched the ceremony, their rifles now leaning against the rails. These men on the dusty street were now their equals, their buddies. Some of the guards had come from the west coast where they knew of the anti-Japanese prejudice; others had come from elsewhere in the country where they had never known a Japanese. Whatever their background, they had been told that these people they guarded were the enemy, men and women who were disloyal to the United States and who would spy and sabotage if given the chance. Some had read the testimony of Earl Warren, California's Attorney General, accusing them of living in a "fool's paradise" if they didn't think the American Japanese had planned sabotage. Their own commander, General DeWitt, had said, "There isn't such a thing as a loyal Japanese". The gentler of the guards had treated the inmates passively, obeying the non-fraternization rule, while the more aggressive had treated the people like prisoners, poking them with rifles when moving them from one place to another and baiting and goading them. And now, Captain MacDonald was swearing them in as protectors and defenders of the country they presumably would have sabotaged yesterday!

"I want to say a few words," the captain said when the men finished the oath. "I admire you young men for volunteering. The last year and a half has been as difficult on you as on any Americans, and you've handled the pressure well." His voice faltered a bit. "I volunteered to go with you as your company commander, but the Army thinks I'm too old. I pledge," and his voice faltered again,"...that I'll make life at Manzanar as easy as I can for your families, so that when you come back..." He stopped and pressed his finger on his upper lip. Whether he could have continued cannot be known, as Peter let out his characteristic war whoop and ran to throw his arms around his brother. The crowd followed suit.

The recruiter, seeing that the new soldiers didn't know if they were still supposed to be at attention or not, yelled "Dismissed!", and soon the main street in Manzanar was witnessing what appeared to be a victory celebration. The first step of victory over the enemy had been accomplished, but the enemy in this case was neither the Third Reich nor the Empire of Japan nor the Italian Fascist State.

"I want you to write once a week, like Dorothy," Toshiko told Ken a couple of hours later, as the new soldiers loaded their suitcases on the buses. "I just wish Howie were here to say goodbye to you."

"That's O.K., Mom, Howie and I had a good talk last night. Everything is all right." Ken realized an unbiased observer to their conversation of the previous night might have had a different opinion. They each had stated their positions several times with vehemence, but each had reluctantly agreed at the end that he respected the other for acting on his principles. Ken's final advice to Howie was not to do anything illegal and get thrown into jail, and Howie's advice to Ken was not to come home dead.

Shoji shook Ken's hand as he stepped on the bus and said "I'm proud of you, son..." and, like Captain MacDonald, could not continue. And, as in that previous incident, the tension was relieved by Peter.

"I'll join you next year, or earlier if Mom and Dad let me sign up before I'm eighteen."

"Hush," said Toshiko to Peter. "One soldier per family is enough."

The bus was quiet for the first fifty miles as the young men dealt with their thoughts and emotions of the last few hours, but soon the chatter began to rise as the men began to wonder out loud what the future might hold. The bus took three hours to get to Mojave, where they would board a troop train for Camp Shelby, Mississippi. There they would join other Japanese Americans from Hawaii and the mainland in forming the 442nd Regimental Combat Team. They were not surprised when they were told to stay on the bus at the Mojave train station until the train arrived. When it did, they were loaded directly onto the cars and told to keep the window shades pulled whenever they were going through a town. Apparently the government felt that Americans were not ready yet for a picture of Japanese faces in American uniforms. The cars were comfortable however, and they were allowed to keep the shades up when not going through towns. For the first day of the journey that was most of the time. Ken began to notice the beauty of the desert, which he had never done at Manzanar. The colors changed as the day progressed, and even the scrub brush took on a beauty this city-boy had never imagined the desert might contain.

About sundown, they crossed the Colorado River and pulled to a stop on a sidetrack at an isolated area. Most of the men soon fell asleep, but they were awakened at midnight when a few more cars were added to the train and the journey eastward continued. In the morning as they proceeded across Arizona, some of the occupants of the added cars began to pass through their cars. They were Niseis in ill-fitting uniforms just like the Manzanar soldiers, and they said they came from the Arizona detention camps at Poston and at Gila River. They were soon sharing stories of their internment, and each tale seemed more ridiculous than the previous. As the gales of laughter ran down the car, Ken wondered how it was that people who shared experiences that were insulting and degrading could laugh at them. He roared as he listened to a fellow from Gila River describe his urinating through the fence with two spotlights on him, because the plumbing had backed up. Ken remembered he had done exactly the same thing at Manzanar one night, and he could feel again the embarrassment and anger he had felt then. It was the camaraderie of shared suffering. One experience unique to the internees from the Arizona camps was their delight with the troop train. Many of them had been taken to camp from their San Diego homes in cattle cars, in which the stench of the animals was soon mixed with the stench of vomit.

The train pressed on eastward and soon they were allowed to keep their shades up even when passing through towns. The changing scenery continued to be a pleasant diversion, but otherwise Ken and the others became bored. Stories had been told and retold and eventually became drained of their humor. Even for those who played poker, the small amount of money that any of them had was soon concentrated in the hands of a few.

The most exciting part of the journey for Ken, and he marveled at this as he later reflected on the trip, was when they stopped at Amarillo. For the first time, they were allowed off the train. As they milled around the station, Ken felt free for the first time in more than a year. True, he had to get back on the train in a few minutes and proceed to an Army camp, but by comparison he was free.

Other passengers in the station were surprised to see the Japanese soldiers, but showed no hostility.

"Where y'all goin'?"

"Where y'all come from?"

"Ever been in Texas before?"

"They gwan send you boys to Europe or the Pacific?"

"I have a son in the Army. Any y'all know a Billy Joe Davis?"

"Y'all sure speak good American!"

The young men answered these questions with delight, even the absurd ones. It was the first time in over a year most had carried on a civil conversation with a white American. But Ken had to suppress a smile when he heard one of the Texans whisper to another "Of course they're ours! We haven't taken any P.O.W.'s yet. They say the Japs at Guadalcanal just won't surrender."

Their last day of travel took them across the green countryside of eastern Oklahoma, Arkansas and Louisiana, and the train crossed the Mississippi River at Vicksburg. All conversation ceased as the young men, none of whom had ever been this far east, stared in awe at the huge river. "Remember that year when the Santa Ana River flooded?" asked one of the Los Angeles boys of no one in particular. "That was nothing compared to the Mississippi when it's normal."

Ken remembered something about Vicksburg being the site of a big Civil War battle and reflected on comparisons. The Japanese in America had certainly never experienced slavery, but in a real way they were now fighting for their freedom, at least for the freedom to break out of stereotypes and to have an equal chance to make of their lives what they wanted.

As they crossed the state of Mississippi, they began to realize they'd very soon have to start functioning as soldiers. Ken had become friendly with one of the young men from the camp at Poston. Doug Furuya had been a pre-law student at San Diego State prior to internment, but more importantly he had been in the ROTC. Three months prior to his expected commission in June 1942, he was sent to camp.

"I don't even know the ranks, the stars, the bars, or anything," Ken said.

"One stripe is a private first class. That's what we'll be when we finish basic training. Two stripes is a corporal, and three is a sergeant. The higher sergeants get those rockers under the stripes. But when you see a guy with three stripes and three rockers and a diamond in the middle, that's a first sergeant. He's the top sergeant in the company, and he's next to God." Ken decided his and the Army's theology differed, but Doug continued. "And then there are the officers. The most junior officer is a second lieutenant - he wears a single gold bar. The next is a first lieutenant - he wears a single silver bar. And then there are the captains - they wear..."

"That's all backwards," interrupted the eavesdropping Horace Yamashita. "Gold is worth more than silver, and second is higher than first. The second lieutenant with the gold bar should be higher than the first lieutenant with the silver bar."

"Well, why don't you make a suggestion to the Army that they change that. They've probably only had it that way for two hundred years, but I'm sure they'll see the common sense of your suggestion and change it," responded Doug.

"You think so? You mean like a suggestion box?" asked Horace seriously.

"Yeah, Yamashita, you drop it in a suggestion box when we get to Camp Shelby. They'll probably give you a weekend pass for it," said Doug.

Ken made a mental note to keep an eye on Horace lest he follow through and then pursued his questioning of Doug. Doug answered, "They'll probably take those who've had no military training and give them a month or two of basic - drill, how to fire the infantry weapons, squad maneuvers, **...how to wear the uniform**..." as he surveyed the uniforms in the car, the disarray of three days on a train having added to the fiasco of the first uniform fitting on the Manzanar street. "Then you'll join the others training in squads, platoons and companies. They're building the 442nd from scratch, you know."

"What are squads, platoons and companies?" asked Ken. And so, the School of the Soldier continued, as the train approached the southeast corner of Mississippi.

Three hundred weary young Nisei carried their suitcases off the train in Hattiesburg at the end of the third day, bedraggled and not a little frightened. As Ken wandered around the station while awaiting the promised trucks from Camp Shelby, Horace rushed up. "They have two drinking fountains here. One says 'white', and the other says 'colored', but the water from both is clear."

"That's not the color of the water, Horace. That refers to who can drink from them - white or colored - you know, Negroes," answered Ken.

"Well if it's the same water, what difference does it make?"

"I don't know." replied Ken, "I guess the whites just don't like to drink from the same fountains as Negroes."

Horace thought a bit. "Where does that place us? Are they going to set up a third fountain now that we're here?"

"Horace, you can drink from whichever fountain you want to," said Ken.

Horace thought a bit longer. "I guess I'll just wait until we get to camp."

The sun had set when they arrived at Camp Shelby, and after a full meal, the best they'd had since Manzanar, they were shown the barracks. "Just like home," said one of the new soldiers, but in this case, he meant it.

"Take any bed for the night. We'll sort you out in the morning," they were told.

"Morning" was defined by a baton beating on the metal bed frames of all the beds in Ken's barracks. The wielder of the baton was the most intimidating man Ken had ever seen. He was tall and muscular, and he added to the noise of the baton by yelling, "Rise and shine! It's a bright, beautiful Mississippi morning! The sun's gonna shine today and so are you yayhoos!" Ken wasn't sure the man's uniform was the same as the recruits. It was the same color, but **it fit him**, and it was pressed. He had three stripes and two rockers on each sleeve, and his name tag said "Strong". Was that really his name or did that only describe him? What impressed Ken the most was the campaign hat he wore. It was pulled down in front to the point that each eye looked at Ken separately around the cap's bill. "On the street, dressed, shaved and beds made in fifteen minutes," Sergeant Strong commanded.

Those functions normally required thirty to forty-five minutes for Ken, but on this occasion, he accomplished them in ten. "Fear does amazing things," he thought. Noting the darkness, Ken sneaked a look at his watch. "Five o'clock," he groaned. Medical school looked very attractive at this point.

A few minutes later in the mess hall, Ken was amazed as he had been the night before at the efficiency of Army food service. The mess sergeant, all 300 pounds of him, cooked eggs to order. And yet, the line moved very rapidly. By the time the soldier had gotten bacon, toast and coffee, the egg order he had yelled when he entered the line was ready, and always accurate. The men from the west coast and Hawaii puzzled for a while over the Cream of Wheat. It tasted different. Finally a man who had lived in the south identified it as grits and informed them they should add butter and salt and pepper, not cream and sugar. As Yamashita noted, when treated that way, grits tasted just like butter and salt and pepper.

An hour later, the sun was coming up over the eastern trees as they lined up on the company street.

"Abe!" yelled Sergeant Strong. It sounded like the nickname of the sixteenth president. No answer. "Abe. Anyone here named Abe?"

"Ah-bay?" asked a voice from the rear.

"Yeah. Take your suitcase and line up over there. Aki...mani?"

"Akiyama?" came the response.

"Yeah. You go over there too. Ari...sho...something?"

"Ariyoshi?"

"Yeah. You join them two. Baba?"

Ken cringed. John Baba was a sarcastic young man, and Ken was afraid of Baba's response to the sergeant's finally pronouncing a name correctly. When "Yes, sergeant," was the only response, Ken sighed in relief. Even Baba must be intimidated.

The names continued until twenty men, including Doug Furuya, were standing in the group apart. Sergeant Strong was visibly relieved when he came to Tendo and Uno. He gave a manly try to the rest of the names, until he came to the last one on his list. "Yana...go...ah, whatever the hell it is."

"Yanagihara?"

"Yeah. Get the hell over there with the rest." He composed himself and addressed the smaller group. "You men have had previous military training, right? ROTC or reserve units, or something, right?" Heads nodded. "O.K. You go with Sergeant Davis," and they marched off, suitcases in hand.

"Now, you men, any of you have any previous military training?" Three hands went up. "O.K. You go with Corporal Denby, and he'll see if he can confirm it." Those three men walked off.

"Now, the rest of you. Fill in the places the other men left. Dress right. Cover down." He watched the pitiful job these fresh recruits made to look like an orderly group, and he eventually called "Platoon! Tensh-hut! You men are now Training Platoon #14. You are all volunteers. If you ain't a volunteer, you're in the wrong place at this time. Since you're volunteers, I expect 110% effort at all times. If the other platoons are sitting down, you'll be standing up; if they're standing, you'll be walking; if they're walking, you'll be double-timing; if they're double-timing, you'll be triple-timing. If a quarter can bounce a foot off their beds, it'll bounce two feet off yours. If they assemble in the company area at 0500, you was already there at 0400, and you've moved on out to train. If 95% of them qualify as expert with the rifle, 100% of you qualify expert. Training you men is my only job in life. I ain't got no wife - the Army didn't issue me none. My home is in the barracks, so I'll be with you all the time. If you screw up, I'm on your ass. If you don't screw up, I'm still on your ass, but just not as hard. Eight weeks from now, when I present this platoon to the regiment, they're gonna say 'Damn, Strong, this is the best damn platoon we've ever seen.'

"Now, I've noticed you're all Japs, and I understand you were all in some kind of detention camps before you come here. I don't know what that all means, but if the United States Army says to me 'These are now American soldiers,' that's good enough for me. If you turn out to be good soldiers, I don't give a damn whether you're a Jap or an American. Any questions?

"Now, do any of you speak Japanese?" Nearly all hands went up, though a little warily. The sergeant pointed to the nearest man and said "Come up here and help me with the rest of the names on this roster."

When he had confirmed that his roster matched the ragtag group of men he faced, and vice-versa, he marched them, or rather walked them, to the two barracks that would be their home for the next eight weeks. They were two two-story wood structures that had seen better days.

"There's brooms and mops and buckets in them barracks. Clean them spotless, and I'll be back in an hour to inspect. I wanna be able to eat my lunch off the floors!" Sergeant Strong said after he assigned them each a bunk and a locker.

When he returned in exactly an hour, he started his inspection with comments expected of Army barracks inspectors since time immemorial.

"This is the filthiest damn area I ever seen."

"I wouldn't let my pet pig live in here."

"Were you men raised in a barn?"

"I can see I have my damn work cut out just teaching you to live like human beings."

As the inspection proceeded, his criticisms were less frequent and less pungent. Ken, assigned to the second barracks, thought he saw disappointment in the sergeant's face when he wiped his fingers on top of a locker, opened his mouth to say something and then realized his finger was dust-free.

"Well, that's not too bad for a first try. Now gather around and let me show you how to make a military bed." First, he demonstrated hospital corners, then showed them how to stretch the sheets and blanket taut enough that a quarter did, in fact, bounce two feet when slung down onto it.

"What's your name soldier?" he asked the man whose bed he had used for the demonstration.

"Taniguchi, sir."

"You say 'sergeant', not 'sir'. I ain't no officer," snapped Sergeant Strong.

"Taniguchi, sergeant," replied Alvin Taniguchi.

"O.K., Gooch. I want to see that bed made like that every time I inspect this barracks."

Sergeant Strong found Taniguchi's bed made precisely like that for the next two weeks. Ken could attest to that because he saw that Alvin slept on the floor for the next two weeks and never put anything on the bed. Eventually the blanket sagged slightly, and Taniguchi decided it was time to learn to make the bed himself - gaining a softer place to sleep in the process.

They spent the rest of the first day being uniformed and receiving their equipment, and Ken was gratified to see that the Army had smaller uniforms. Some alterations were required for Horace Yamashita and a few others, but when they returned to their barracks after supper, Ken thought they were beginning to look like soldiers. He placed his equipment and uniforms in his lockers precisely as Sergeant Strong had shown them, took his first shower in four days and settled into his bed. Any idea of reviewing his thoughts after his first full day of Army life was lost a minute after his head hit his pillow. Ken was asleep before 8PM for the first time in twenty years.

"Rise and shine, platoon 14!" shouted the voice from the barracks door eight hours later. "You done such a good job yesterday I got the mess sergeant to give us the special privilege of an 0430 breakfast, so we can be out training while those other wimp platoons are eating. Let's get going–on the street shaved and looking like a soldier in 15 minutes!"

CHAPTER **8**

"HATTORI, TSUNEISHI," KEN SAID AS THE MEN, gathered in a thicket of pines, awaited another run through the obstacle course. The first obstacle, the wall, was the most difficult for the shorter men. "You guys are the tallest. When we come to the wall, you go first but instead of going over, stand against it and cup your hands so the rest of us can step there and then get over the wall."

Minutes later, Sergeant Strong, stationed just beyond the wall, had a quizzical look on his face as one after another of the men, came hurtling over it. Instead of the prescribed way of getting one leg over the top, pulling oneself up and dropping on the other side, many appeared to vault over it. They'd land in a heap, pick themselves up, yell "Go For Broke!" and run off. Suspicious of what was happening, Sergeant Strong said to his companion, "Davis, go back and see what they're doing on the other side of the wall. Go through the woods, and don't let them see you. Report back to me." Sergeant Davis returned in ten minutes with his report.

"There are two guys helping them over with 'hand steps'. Shall I go and stop them?"

"No," said Sergeant Strong "Let 'em be. I wondered how long it would take them to figure out how to do that." A slight smile softened the sergeant's expression.

The first four weeks were physically demanding for the men of Training Platoon #14. Life in the detention camps had not required much exercise, so most had come to Camp Shelby in poor shape. Calisthenics, marching in full gear, and 12-hour training days soon corrected that. Once they had corporately mastered the wall, the next major challenge was the rope pull–pulling oneself up a steeply slanted cliff by a rope secured at the top. Most could make it without their gear, but when half a man's weight with a rifle, a pack, an entrenching tool and all the paraphernalia of war was added, it became almost impossible. No subterfuge was possible here,–just brute strength and a bit of technique. By the end of the fourth week, all the men could get up the hill in full battle gear.

Ken experienced a major emotional change at the four week point in their training, coinciding with the victory over the rope cliff. Until then, everything he had done was underlaid with fear. He eventually decided it was not fear of battle–that was far in the future. And it wasn't homesickness–he would rather be doing this than whiling away his time in the detention camp. To his surprise, he rarely thought of medical school, perhaps because "his class" at Creighton would not start until September. The source of his underlying fear, he finally realized, was the fear of failure. For Ken, these physical challenges were in a new milieu. Except for a little judo training, and cross-country running in high school to which he had been only mildly committed, all his life's challenges had been intellectual and scholastic. Those he could handle. But, to get down to basics, could he train to be a soldier strong enough and quick enough to kill another man whose goal was to kill him? So, every morning when Sergeant Strong came through the barracks batoning bed frames at 4AM, Ken had been awake for an hour, fearful of what the day would bring. Objectively he was doing well and, as in the experience at the obstacle course wall, showing some leadership. But he was still intimidated by Sergeant Strong, and to a lesser extent the assistant platoon sergeant, Sergeant Davis.

However, as he stood at the top of the hill, having pulled himself up in full battle gear, and looked back down the cliff, it suddenly came to him "I *can* do this! I can handle whatever they throw at me. The next months of training will be hard, but I can do it."

His contemplations were interrupted by Sergeant Strong's yelling "Move on, Hayakawa! You ain't no spectator. If you was in combat, you'd be dead by now. Move on out!" A week before, Ken would have been mortified to be yelled at in such a manner. This time he merely smiled to himself and moved on out.

That afternoon, a Friday, training was stopped early, and Sergeant Strong gathered his platoon. "You men have done a good... I mean a not-too-bad job these last four weeks, and we're gonna give you passes to go to Hattiesburg. Now, you gotta wear your Class A uniform to town, which you ain't worn since you've been here. So you come by to let Sergeant Davis or I inspect you before we give you your passes. Your shoes gotta be shined so we can see our faces in them. Now you also gotta remember you're representing the United States Army, so I don't want no trouble in town. I don't want you to drink no alcohol. If you drink, I don't want you to drink no more than one beer; if you drink more than one beer, I don't want you to get drunk; if you get drunk, I don't want you to get into no fights; if you get into a fight, I want the other guy, not you, on the floor at the end. You're Training Platoon #14! Got that?"

"And I have another order from regiment here. When you're in town, you're considered to be white guys." He looked up to questioning looks. "What that means is that you drink at white, not colored, fountains, and you use white, not colored, latrines, and you eat in white, not colored, restaurants. Got that?"

That night, Ken went to town with Horace and Kaz Ishii from Manzanar, and Mike Matsunaga from Gila River. On his own! Free to do as he pleased! Making his own decisions! For more than two hundred years, most Americans had accepted such freedoms as normal. Not so of these Japanese Americans. On pass in Hattiesburg, Mississippi, really free for the first time in more than a year, Ken was not the only one with a lump in his throat.

"You know, I don't feel right sitting here," said Horace. The four sat in a diner eating hamburgers and trying to decide how to spend their next five hours of freedom.

"Why?" asked Kaz. "I've been dreaming of this moment since the day we first set foot in Manzanar."

"You heard what Sergeant Strong said. We're to consider ourselves white, not colored. Why aren't the coloreds free to come in here?" asked Horace, not touching his hamburger.

"They're free to go to restaurants, just so long as it's one of theirs. As far as I know, their restaurants are as nice as the white ones," said Kaz, struggling with the "separate but equal" distinction eleven years before the Supreme Court would decide that distinction to be unconstitutional.

"Nah, I don't believe that," said Horace. "You saw some of their restaurants when we passed through the colored part of town, didn't you? They sure didn't look very nice to me."

"But that's up to them. They're free to make any kind of restaurant they want," said Mike.

"That's a bunch of crap, too," said Horace. "You know the situation down south really doesn't let them get good jobs and earn good money and all that. You can't really say they're free to do what they want."

"Well, they could move up north and get jobs in industry," said Kaz.

"Yeah, that'd be like telling us, 'We don't want you on the west coast. If you want freedom, pick up your roots and move east.' That's essentially what they told us, and we didn't want to do that."

"Look, guys," said Ken, "they've got a problem. I feel bad for them. Maybe one of these days when we've earned the respect of the whites, we can help them too. But in the meantime, our time of freedom is getting less and less. What do you guys wanna do?"

"I don't know. What do you wanna do?" said Kaz and Mike in unison. Horace sighed.

A couple hours later, they returned to the same diner for dessert, having seen the latest Hollywood musical comedy.

"I'll bet y'all boys come from California, not Hawaii," said the waitress as she served them their pie.

"How'd you know that?" asked Mike.

"Y'all's accents. Those guys from Hawaii talk with a funny accent. Y'all talk American real good, even though y'all sound like Yankees."

"Yankees?" asked Ken.

"Yeah, but I don't mean nothin' bad by that. We been seein' a lot of Yankees down heah since the wah stahted, and some of them are nice fellas. Really. Ah talked with a boy from Michigan just last week, and he was a real gentleman, just like a southerner."

"We can't make stereotypes, can we?" said Ken.

"Nah. Whatevuh that is," said the waitress, as she departed for the kitchen.

The four soldiers were quiet for a while. Then Horace spoke. "You know, when we act neutral with the coloreds, isn't that like when our white friends said, 'I feel bad about you having to go to the detention camps, but I can't do anything about it.'?"

"Yamashita! Shut up!" said Kaz "Here we are, our first night on the town, and you're trying to make us feel guilty."

"I'm sorry," said Horace, "but it just doesn't seem right."

On the bus back to camp, all the men, save Horace, were in a jovial mood. Everyone tried to outdo the last storyteller in describing the wildness of their escapades. Ken had observed most of the groups at one time or another during the evening and realized that all the stories after the first couple were more fantasy than truth. Sergeant Strong would have no fences to mend after this first night on the town.

The next four weeks of training they learned to fire their weapons. What a surprise to find that their drill rifles, with the addition of a firing pin, could be fired. "I thought it was just a 9 1/2 pound weight we had to carry to build up our muscles, and we'd be issued our shooting rifles once we got to combat," noted the ever-naïve Horace. Learning to fire automatic rifles, machine-guns and mortars presented a pleasant change from the drill and conditioning of the first month. Except for the weather. A cool and fairly dry late spring had been perfect for training. In late May and June, though, the weather turned hot. It rained almost daily, and it seemed they were always on the edge of some hurricane or tropical storm. Camp Shelby turned to mud. Training went on, and if the lesson of the day was firing the rifle from the prone position, only the rifle and the aiming eye could be seen above the mud.

"Good camouflage!" declared Sergeant Strong, standing next to them in boots, poncho and campaign hat.

One thing the mud taught them was to know their rifles intimately. Each night, their first job was to clean their rifles. They soon learned to strip, wash the mud off, dry, oil and reassemble them in less than ten minutes.

"Where'd the base plate go?" asked Kaz one rainy day when they were first learning to fire and move with the 60 mm mortar. "I put it down right there." The base plate was finally found–right where Kaz had put it–but submerged 3" under the mud. Thereafter, they learned to attach the tube to the base plate first and then place it on rocky ground if possible.

"Who do you think has to clean these things when we bring them in tonight?" asked Kaz.

"Take a guess," responded Ken.

"Yeah, that's what I thought."

The men in Training Platoon #14 turned out to be excellent marksmen, even in the rain and mud. All met the basic qualifications, and 47% qualified as experts–less than the 100% Sergeant Strong had predicted but still obviously pleasing to him. Their accuracy with the machine gun and mortar was better than any of the recent platoons.

Ken noticed that much of the sergeants' bluster was gone the last four weeks. They spent more time training and less time harassing. Even Horace was more successful at escaping the sergeants' attention. Early on, he had been the butt of many of their jokes, undoubtedly because of his size. But, when he maxed the PT test and qualified as expert on the rifle range, their jokes rang hollow. Mike Matsunaga, unimpressed with Horace's perfect PT score, commented, "How hard can it be to do pull ups and pushups when the body you're pulling and pushing only weighs a hundred pounds?"

One evening when Ken was passing Sergeant Strong's room, he heard the sergeant talking with Sergeant Dubinski, a trainer of a non-Nisei platoon on the other side of Camp Shelby. "Hell, Dubinski, these guys pick everything up the first time around. A lotta them are college graduates, and more'n half have had some college. It's not like in the old days when you had to just hammer everything through thick skulls. Why, the first day of live firing on the mortar range, every tube was on target within three shots. You can only pound hell out of them targets so long. I finally had to bring 'em back early. We was back in garrison by 1000 hours. I had to tell Cookie to give 'em a hot lunch instead of field rations on the range. Boy, was he pissed. I don't know whether to be proud or embarrassed. What good's a training sergeant if he can't blow his stack at least once a day?"

Ken smiled and moved on.

The afternoon before the parade signaling graduation from basic training, Sergeant Strong called Ken aside. "Hayakawa,"(the sergeant had by this time mastered most of the names) "I'm going to promote you to corporal tomorrow. You've shown real leadership during basic, so when you guys get back to the regiment, you'll be an assistant squad leader, you and a couple other of the men."

Ken was stunned. "But, sergeant, I'm sure there are many others that deserve it more than I do. Yamashita, for example, has worked awfully hard and done very well. I appreciate the honor, but I just don't feel I deserve it." Ken tried hard to sound noble, but he knew his real motivation–the avoidance of responsibility.

"Listen, Hayakawa, I didn't say I was giving this to you as an honor. This ain't a prize for doing best on the math test. Before long, we're gonna be in combat, and I want the best men in the leadership positions. You know what a leader has to be? He has to be disciplined enough to follow orders and smart enough to know what to do if the chain of command breaks down. And then he has to be tough enough to tell his men to do something that might get them killed. It's a helluva job, but they tell me I'm gonna be a first sergeant in the regiment when I get you guys trained, and I want my noncoms to be guys I can trust. These stripes ain't no bonus for doing a good job; it's because we need our best men in leadership positions when we start getting shot at."

All Ken could say was, "Yes, sergeant." But as he walked away, he felt he'd had the most important lesson of his military career so far. Combat—he'd not thought much about that aspect of military life. The challenge of the training had been to get into shape and master certain skills. That he'd done quite well. But now this sergeant with the grade school education and the poor grammar had made clear to this almost-college-graduate what the *real* goal was. Although Ken had not been intimidated by Sergeant Strong for several weeks, he now began to sense a growing respect for him.

The graduation parade the next day—complete with class A uniforms and the regimental band—included two other platoons. The trainees, never having marched to a band before, were surprised at how much easier it was to stay in step with the drum beat. Colonel Pence, the 442nd Regimental Commander, spoke. "I've heard from the training sergeants that you men have learned your jobs quite well, and I'm proud to have you in the regiment. We're training now as platoons but soon will train as companies and then as the complete regiment. We'll then be ready for a combat assignment." Where and when that combat would be, he didn't say.

He then awarded corporal stripes to Ken and seven other men, reiterating in a more sophisticated way Sergeant Strong's message to Ken the previous day.

Later that day outside regimental headquarters, Ken ran into his old friend from San Diego. "Lieutenant Furuya. I'm impressed," he said, admiring his friend's shiny gold bars. "I'd heard you'd gone to OCS. How was it?"

"Not too bad. I knew most of what they taught us, from ROTC, but I hadn't realized how out of shape I was. Everywhere we went, we ran. If you saw any group running at Fort Benning, you could count on its being an OCS class. And while we're congratulating each other on promotion, I see you're wearing two stripes."

"Your teaching on the train did it," replied Ken, laughing. "I never once called the sergeant lieutenant."

They walked towards the barracks area. "What's the protocol now that you're a lieutenant? Do I call you Doug or Lieutenant Furuya?" asked Ken.

"Officers and enlisted men are not supposed to fraternize. On the job or in public, we'll be 'lieutenant' and 'corporal'. In private, we won't worry about it, particularly since we're in different battalions. You're in second battalion, aren't you?"

"Yes. Company E."

"I'm in the first battalion, Company C. But while we're talking protocol, you should be walking on my left."

"Yes sir." Ken smiled and moved to Doug's left. "Explain something to me. I saw in the paper a couple of weeks ago that the Supreme Court had ruled against us in a couple of cases. What were those all about?"

"They both had to do with breaking curfew. Remember the curfew they imposed on all of us right after Pearl Harbor and before they sent us to camp? Well these cases were whether the government had the right to do that, and the Supreme Court said it did."

"What about whether sending us to camp was unconstitutional?" asked Ken.

"I understand there's a case about that going the appeal route now that will probably end up at the Supreme Court."

The two men walked on in silence.

"How's your family?" asked Doug.

Ken took a deep breath. "Well, they're not doing too well really."

CHAPTER 9

THE HEAT WAVES BILLOWED OFF THE SAND STREETS of Manzanar. Every barracks window was open, gulping for air, but it helped very little. The searing easterly wind from Death Valley brought no relief. The camp was still, all activities including baseball practice having been canceled due to the oppressive heat.

"This is gonna kill us," Peter Hayakawa said as he lay shirtless in his bunk repeatedly slamming a baseball into his first baseman's glove. Recently turned seventeen, his torso reflected the change from the chubbiness of youth to the muscles of young manhood. "We have to play the American Legion team from Bishop on Saturday, and they're the only team we'll play all year that has a chance against us. We need to practice."

"The Bishop team can't practice in this heat either," Toshiko encouraged her son.

"Well maybe it's not as hot in Bishop; maybe they're still practicing." The ball-to-glove beat continued.

But Peter's forced inactivity was not Toshiko's greatest concern that day. An order had come the previous day designating forty-two people to be transferred to the Tule Lake detention camp. Tule Lake, in the mountains of northern California, had started as a regular detention camp like the other nine. But because some of the barracks were more secure, the government had started to send the "troublemakers" there. That included any who complained too loudly or who openly desired repatriation. After the infamous questionnaire with its two particularly troublesome questions, #27 and #28, came out, they sent all the "No.No.'s" there. It had taken a little longer to interpret Howie's answer ("Yes, I'm loyal. No, I won't serve in the armed forces."), because Howie's name was on the current list.

Their conversation the night before had been unsatisfactory. "Howie," Toshiko pleaded, "see if you can change your answers. Mr. Tanigawa is trying to change his. He says he misunderstood the questions. Captain MacDonald says they're deciding in Washington if you can change your answers. Go try!"

"Mom, you don't understand. I don't want to change my answers. I answered the way I felt. I never had any loyalty to Japan, so it's easy to say "no" to that. But if they continue to treat us like they have, putting us behind barbed wire for nothing–'cept we're of Japanese descent–I'm not going to fight for that. I know I had to repeat American Government in high school, but as I understand the Constitution, they're not supposed to do that."

"But no Hayakawas have ever been in jail," Toshiko persisted.

"That's my point, Mom. We're in jail now! Listen, Tule Lake isn't as bad as you think. I've gotten letters from some of my friends who went there with the first group of "No.No.'s". They say it's not much different than here. There are a few more guards, and they have to account for you a little more often, but they say it's not much more hassle than here. And I'm sure it's a lot cooler."

Shoji had been no help. His work as block captain took an hour a day, and with nothing of interest the rest of the day, he had started drinking his whiskey before noon. He wasn't available for intelligent discussion after dinner any more, and Toshiko had given up trying to cajole him out of his habit. The center of the Hayakawa family now consisted of Toshiko and the ever-ebullient Peter. That was a far change from the family of two years before, with all the activity and interests of the children, and the anchor of mother and father.

Dorothy's letters were a source of great pleasure for Toshiko. True to her promise, she wrote once a week. If Toshiko could believe what her daughter wrote (and she had no reason to believe otherwise) life in New York City was pure enjoyment. Dorothy had quickly been promoted to secretary to the national marketing director of her firm, and her pay was more than twice what it had been in Long Beach. She had a busy social life. It sounded to Toshiko as if wartime New York City with its blackouts and rationing gave an urgency to living that kept the young people busy all the time. How different from Dorothy's prewar Terminal Island life. She frequently described her volunteer work in a

perpetual "Save Scrap Metal" drive, but she mostly focused on her social activities. It didn't take much reading between the lines for Toshiko
to realize that almost all these friends were Caucasian, particularly the
men, most of whom were servicemen on furlough from the war in the
Atlantic or North Africa. Fortunately, Shoji was satisfied to have Toshiko
summarize Dorothy's letters, and she avoided the parts about her social
life except in the most general terms. The idea of Dorothy marrying a
non-Japanese would have been anathema to Shoji.

The next day, buses arrived to take the forty-two men and women
to Tule Lake. There were a few people to see them off, but the scene was
hugely different from that four months before, when the young men
left for Camp Shelby. The carnival-like atmosphere and blatant emotions of the former day were replaced by somber goodbyes, and in some
cases last minute pleadings to change their answers to the two questions.

"Ask them there if you can change your answer, Howie," Toshiko
begged. "You just have to change one, not two, remember."

"Yeah, Mom, I'll look into it."

"And write once a week like Dorothy, not once a month like Ken."

"O.K. Mom."

"And please don't do anything to make them mad, Howie."

"Yeah, Mom, I'll watch it."

"And don't get in with your old friends. They're no good for you.
They got you into this in the first place. Please, dear."

"We'll see, Mom."

"And write every week like Dorothy, not..."

"Yeah, you already said that, Mom."

Shoji stood aside, staring at the ground. As Howie got on the bus,
he stepped forward, still avoiding eye contact, shook his hand quickly
and turned to walk away. Howie held onto his hand a little longer.
"One day I hope you'll understand why I'm doing this, Father," he said
quietly. Shoji looked his son in the eye for the first time, nodded briefly
and walked away.

"Look here," Howie admonished Peter as he clasped his hand, "take
care of Mom. You're the only one left."

"Yeah, O.K.," Peter said quietly.

The buses left, and the others walked quickly back to their barracks. Comparing the two goodbye scenes left little doubt where the
loyalties of the Japanese Americans interned at Manzanar lay.

CHAPTER **10**

"HAYAKAWA, THEY WANT TO SEE YOU IN THE orderly room."

Ken had barely arrived at E Company barracks and set down his gear. "What'd I do wrong now? I just got here," he said and headed to the orderly room. There, a staff sergeant from regimental headquarters was waiting for him.

"Are you Hayakawa?"

"Yes, sergeant," answered Ken.

"I wanted to talk to you about being a medic. They tell me you were a medical student."

"Premed."

"Well we need medics, and I'd like you to volunteer. We send you to eight weeks of Aid man school, and then we assign you to one of the battalions."

"Uh, sergeant, I, uh, appreciate your asking, but I think I'll stay where I am," said Ken.

"What? I'm not offering you a cushy job. The medics have to go to work when the firing's the heaviest. They have to expose themselves to enemy fire without a rifle. You'll have just as much chance to be a hero as a medic as you would as an infantry grunt," replied the sergeant.

"Yes, sergeant, I know. It's not the heroism involved It's, uh, it's, uh,..."

"What is it, Hayakawa? Look, we need our best men as medics. We need guys who are cool under fire and know how to take care of men who are wounded, to stabilize them enough to get them back to the doctor. Hell, they sometimes have to be the doctor themselves. We can't guarantee soldiers they're not going to get shot, but we can guarantee them we'll get them the best battlefield medical care available, and that's where we want you to fit in."

"I don't know. I just think I'd better stay where I am."

"Well, it's up to you. If you think it over and come to your senses, get in touch with me. Have the next man come in when you leave. Maybe he'll be a little more sensible."

"Why in the world did I say 'no'?" thought Ken as he walked back to the barracks. He stopped, turned, hesitated, and turned back again towards the barracks. "That would have been a great opportunity to get some experience. What am I trying to prove?"

Deep in thought, Ken started up the barracks steps when a khaki bowling ball with flailing arms and legs hurtled out the door and down the steps, knocking him over. He picked himself up and started to dust himself off when he was knocked down a second time, this time by a khaki missile exploding out the door. As he picked himself up the second time, he saw the bowling ball and missile rolling in the dust. Ken jumped between them and with difficulty separated them.

The missile, whom he was holding with his left hand said "You kotonks, eh, you tink you own da' damn country. Hey! I nevah want you poot yo' hands on my stoff. You know?" Ken recognized his Hawaiian Pidgin accent and noted his name tag: Shimabukuro.

The bowling ball, struggling in Ken's right hand, started to speak. "Hey man! Don't be so sensitive. I just wanted you to show me how to play the ukulele." For the first time, Ken realized the bowling ball was Horace Yamashita.

"Eh! How come you nevah ask me to teach you? I nevah like see you just peek it up and staht playing it. And more, I nevah see a damn kotonk can play one uke anyway," answered Shimabukuro.

"Well look," Ken began, "I'm sure Yamashita won't pick up your ukulele without permission again. But you're in the same Army now, supposedly training to fight the Germans. You shouldn't be fighting each other. Save it for Hitler."

Several men from the barracks had poured out expecting a good fight. Seeing the peacemaking, they grumbled and filed back into the barracks.

"Well, you know da' firs' lesson you guys need learn?" said Shimabukuro, no longer straining to continue the fight, "is dat we Buddha heads, you know, we're here too. Dey nevah tol' us when we sign up dat all da' sergeants are mainland guys." He shook free from Ken's hold and dusted himself off. As he went back into the barracks, he had a parting question. "Eh. And where you tink we get 'Go For Broke'? Dat nevah come from no kotonks, you know?"

"Hey, Ken, all I did was pick up his ukulele and start to ask him to teach me to play it. How was I to know he thought it was the crown jewels?" Horace pleaded.

"Well, in the future you'd better ask him first if you can pick it up."

"I'm not going to talk to the sonofabitch in the future," said Horace as he tried to brush the clotted blood and dirt off the front of his shirt. "And what's this kotonk and Buddha head anyway?"

"Kotonk is the name the guys from Hawaii have for us, supposedly the sound our heads make when they hit the ground after they knock us down," answered Ken. "And I guess in return, we call them Buddha heads. Doesn't sound too friendly, does it?"

As it turned out, Horace didn't have the luxury of ignoring Tyrus Shimabukuro in the future. The men from the recently graduated basic training platoons had been formed into complete squads to form the third squads of each platoon. Shimabukuro and three others from Hawaii were joined with Horace, Kaz Ishii and Mike Matsunaga to form the third squad of the third platoon of Company E. Ken was the assistant squad leader, and a Sergeant Honda was the squad leader.

"O.K., men," Sergeant Honda said as he addressed the squad for the first time. "We're already a little behind. While you guys were in basic, the rest of the regiment trained at squad level. Beginning this afternoon, we begin to train as platoons, and they're going to assume we know how to work as a squad. Now, I'm told you learned a little bit about squad maneuvers in basic, so we're going to spend the morning in a crash course on how a squad works in combat. Now, you see that clump of pines over there? There's a machine gun nest in it and we need to clear it out before the platoon can advance. We do it by fire and maneuver. Now, Yamashita and Shimabukuro, you're a team. You go over to the right flank there by that line of trees. Matsunaga and Murakami, you go over there just short of the brow of that hill..."

Third squad practiced fire and maneuver, advancing "as skirmishers", and all the other intricate movements utilized by American infantrymen since the Minutemen spread out, hid behind trees, and fired at the Redcoats advancing in a straight line. When they broke for their field ration lunch, Sergeant Honda called Ken aside and described his concept of what was required of an assistant squad leader. When he had finished, Ken said, "There might be a problem with Yamashita and Shimabukuro. Last night..."

"Yes, I heard. That's why I assigned them the way I did. Did you notice that each of the pairs consisted of one guy from Hawaii and one guy from the mainland? I'm afraid our first job is to overcome this 'us' and 'them' concept and think of ourselves as American soldiers fighting the enemy."

Ken noticed he didn't say "Japanese American soldiers".

Honda continued, "I guess it's natural that the Hawaiian guys would resent us. Most of the noncoms are from the mainland. In my case, I'm from Fresno. My reserve unit was called up in early '41 and sent to train at Fort Benning. When they gathered you guys up and sent you to the camps, they took us out of our units and sent us to non-combat jobs. They made me the assistant supply sergeant for barracks supply at Fort Benning. I'm glad I didn't have to go to camp—my folks are in Minidoka—but my job at Fort Benning was the most boring I'd ever had. When I heard about the forming of the 442nd, I jumped at the chance. Anyway that's why most of the noncoms are mainlanders. Some of the officers, though, are from Hawaii. Our platoon leader, Lieutenant Watson, is ROTC from the University of Hawaii. The Hawaiians seem proud of that even though he's what they call a 'haole'."

"A 'haole'?"

"Yeah. A white guy."

"What we would call a 'Hakujin'."

"Yes," answered Sergeant Honda.

"You think we'll ever get away from pigeon-holing people on the basis of race?"

"I hope so. That's sort of what we're fighting for, isn't it?"

"That's the reason I'm here. No more 'haole', 'Hakujin', 'Nihonjin'—just 'Americans'," said Ken. "But are the rest of the Americans fighting for the same thing?"

"Maybe not, but it's our job to convince them."

That afternoon, all such lofty thoughts of motivation gave way to the dust and sweat of platoon maneuvers. Ken wondered if the mud caused by the rains was worse than the mud caked on his face formed from sweat and dust. At least when it rained, it was cooler. By the time his squad had seized its first objective of the afternoon, his uniform was as wet as if it had been raining. By the end of the day, he wondered why he had thought basic training was so physically demanding.

"I thought life would be easier once we got to the regiment," said Horace as they stood in the shower and watched the Mississippi dirt wash off their bodies and disappear down the drain.

"Me, too," agreed Ken. He thought of his and Sergeant Honda's conversation earlier in the day. "Why can't it be easier to make a statement that changes a country's perception?"

"What?" asked Horace.

"Nothing. Let's get to the mess hall and then hit the sack early. It's going to be more of the same tomorrow."

<hr>

Platoon training continued into the fall. Ken marveled at how small his world had become. It centered on how well his squad supported the mission of the platoon, whether it was laying down a base of fire or advancing in line on an objective. In the field, his universe was ruled by Sergeant Honda and Lieutenant Watson. When they approved what he and the men did, life was happy, and when they chewed him out for failure, life was unhappy. Once in a while, Captain Eastman, the company commander, and Sergeant Strong, now Company E's first sergeant, accompanied Lieutenant Watson to observe their work, and Sergeant Strong never failed to give Ken a quiet word of encouragement. Ken was only vaguely aware that the invasion of Sicily had been completed and that the Fifth Army had landed in Italy at a place called Salerno. It didn't sound as if the battle were going well, but Ken would have to leave that to the generals. His job was to have his squad do its part in platoon training.

The boys from Hawaii and the mainland had worked together, but the co-operation was more forced than natural. Ken noticed that when they went to Hattiesburg on Saturday evenings, they segregated themselves by where they had come from. Horace hadn't picked up Ty Shimabukuro's ukulele again, either.

"Go, Shimabukuro! Go! Don't let that haole catch you!" Horace yelled as he and the others cheered Shimabukuro as he circled end and ran untouched for a touchdown. That gave the 442nd the lead over the 69th Division, the other unit training at Camp Shelby. With the extra point and another five minutes of hard defense, the final score was 14-

7 in favor of the 442nd. The players of the 69th, who outweighed the 442nd's players by fifty pounds per man looked shell shocked on the sidelines. The handshakes after the game were insincere, and the 442nd men heard more than one muttered "Damn Japs" as the lines passed each other.

Returning to the barracks after the game, Horace talked with Shig Murakami and Ben Watanabe, two of the Hawaiians in the squad, about Shimabukuro's athletic abilities. "He's really a good athlete. He won two gold medals in swimming at the AAU championships in August, and today he was almost the total offense!"

"Hey! No surprise dere, bruddah. Shima's one good at'lete. He was all-Territory halfback at McKinley High two years running, you know," said Murakami. "He poot records in da book, hey, dey nevah gone be broke!"

That night, Ken, Horace and Ishii took in a movie in Hattiesburg, then went for dessert in the cafe they'd discovered their first night in town. Later, as they strolled the streets, they noticed a group of soldiers in one of the parks. As they got closer, they saw that a confrontation was going on. Shimabukuro, Murakami and Watanabe were surrounded by half a dozen men from the 69th. The biggest man, half drunk was pushing Shimabukuro repeatedly in the chest and talking angrily about the football game. He pulled his fist back, but before he could hit Shimabukuro, a khaki bowling ball struck him in the back, knocking him over. His friends jumped on the three original men and the newly-arrived Yamashita, and soon elbows and fists were flying. Whether Ken and Ishii jumped into the fray to stop the fighting or help their outnumbered friends will forever be a moot point. Fortunately a joint patrol of MP's and Hattiesburg police arrived promptly to break up the melee.

An hour later, Ken tried to explain to Sergeant Strong, who had come to collect them from jail, what had happened.

"Never mind, Hayakawa. I talked to the sergeant major of the 69th. He said his men were pissed off over losing the football game and had too much to drink. He said they were out of line." Once outside the police station, Sergeant Strong added "Who ended up on the ground?"

"Mostly them, sarge." Ken started to smile but then realized how much his swollen lip hurt when he smiled.

"Awright! That'll teach them to think they can push us around!"

The "us" was not lost on Ken.

With the excitement of the football game and the extra-curricular activity in town, the combatants were still chattering after they returned to the barracks. The talk involved mostly the game and the fight. "So, Yama," Shimabukuro was saying, "for one kotonk, you not so bad. Eh, no can call you Yama. Planty Yamas heah an' Yama means mountain. You no beeg like mountain. Call you 'Yam', tiny but sweet, eh? O.K. Kotonk? Ah, no mo' kotonk, Yam."

Horace considered that for a few seconds and decided he'd take it as a compliment. "O.K. And there are too many Shimas. Maybe we should call you 'Bukuro', or 'Buckaroo'. Yeah, that's more like it. O.K., Buddha head?" Shimabukuro chuckled his approval.

"What does 'Go For Broke' really mean, anyway?" asked Horace after an interval.

"Well," started Shimabukuro, "it's uh, well uh, ...let me poot it dees way. When you surfing Pipeline, you know, and one da biggest wave you evah see come. And you say 'I bettah let dat one go' and den you say 'Hey, eef I evah gone take da beeg one, dees is it' and den you come go take it. Hey, dat's 'Go For Broke'."

"So, it's like throwing caution to the winds... or betting everything you've got on one play," said Horace.

"Yeah. I guess dat's how da haoles would say it," said Shimabukuro, and then after a few moments, "So! Yam! You wan' me teach you play ukulele or what!"

"Yeah. That'd be great," said Horace.

"I teach you good song, eh? 'Manuela Boy'." With that, he picked up the ukulele and started to strum and sing.

> *"Manuela Boy, my deah boy*
> *You no mo hila hila*
> *No mo fi sen, no mo house*
> *Go Aala Pahk heya moi."*

He turned to Horace and began to show him how to press the strings on the frets and how to pick and strum the strings.

CHAPTER 11

"THINK WE'LL GET HOME BY CHRISTMAS?" ASKED Horace as he packed his duffel bag.

Ken answered the question for the third time. "Well, it just depends on how many people are traveling and if we make the right connections, Horace." He noted that Horace had used the term "home" referring to the 500 square feet of a dusty, now freezing, barracks at Manzanar, where the Yamashita family had been interned for a year and a half.

Training had proceeded through the platoon, company and battalion levels, and for the first three weeks of December they had trucked to a national forest in northern Mississippi for their first regimental field exercise. The weather had been cold, particularly for the men from Hawaii. Hot showers and hot meals were a rarity, and the men from the third squad, third platoon, Company E seldom knew where they fit into the big picture. Nevertheless, Ken had been thrilled by the experience. New challenges surfaced every day, such as how to maneuver his squad from one side of a hill to the other without being spotted by an umpire. Again his world centered on the immediate objective. Only rarely did he focus on the long-term goal of meeting with and destroying an armed enemy. Once in a while, he thought of the freshman medical class at Creighton. In Gross Anatomy, the first semester's main course, they'd be nearly through dissecting their cadavers, but Ken felt only a slight twinge of regret at not being among them.

"So! You guys ready?" The speaker was Ty Shimabukuro. Two weeks of furlough was not enough time for the Hawaiians to go home, so most would spend the Christmas holidays with their buddies from the mainland. Mike Matsunaga was taking Shig Murakami back to the camp at Gila River, and Horace had invited Shimabukuro to Manzanar. With

Kaz Ishii, the group of four lifted their duffel bags to their shoulders and boarded the bus for the Hattiesburg train station.

The next three days were an adventure. Traveling with Army furlough documents, they had priority but no reservations, so their routing was creative, to say the least. They found the station masters to be helpful to anyone in uniform, and they kept moving west although not in a straight line. While their trip to Camp Shelby took the southern route, their trip back took a more northerly route. The plains, even when covered with snow, were an awe-inspiring sight, and the Rockies kept them speechless. For hours on end, they rode with noses pressed against the cold windows of the train.

"Now I know what they mean by 'Thy purple mountains' majesty'," said Horace, and the others murmured agreement.

They approached Manzanar as they had left nine months before, by bus, but this time from the north. December 24th was a freezing night as the four soldiers departed the bus, hoisted their duffel bags and walked westward towards the Manzanar gate. The full moon perched over the snowcapped Sierras in the distance, and a light and unusual snow dusted the ground.

"Eh! Dat's one pretty scene," said Shimabukuro, stopping to appreciate the beauty of the moment. "So dees ees snow. I mean, we get beautiful scenery in Hawaii, but nutting like dees, eh?" The other three, intent on seeing their families, stopped briefly and agreed with him and then moved on. Soon they reached the gate.

"Halt! Who goes there?" came a call from the dark.

"What da hell! Who dat?" said Shimabukuro.

"Our parents are in the camp. We're soldiers home on furlough," Ken said quickly.

"One of you advance to be recognized. The rest stay where you are," said the guard, still hidden in the shadows.

"What is dees?" persisted Shimabukuro, as Ken advanced with his furlough papers. "Dey no let you see your momma and your poppa? Eh, let's take da buggah out!", the beauty of the area now quickly forgotten. Horace and Kaz restrained him.

"The guy has a gun, Buckaroo. Look, this is what we've had to put up with. Don't challenge him. We'll get in."

Ken and the now visible guard went to the gate house. The guard, still with a wary eye on Ken, phoned the camp headquarters. The conversation took a few minutes, and Ken had to explain why one of them did not have parents in the camp. Eventually the guard put down the phone. "O.K. You can pass," he said, as if granting a generous concession. Horace and Kaz stayed between Tyrus and the guard as they passed, but Tyrus said nothing loud enough for the guard to hear. The pace quickened as they walked into Manzanar.

"Where do they get these guys?" asked Ishii. "Did you see that that guy had his insignia on the wrong collar?"

"Yeah. I noticed it, but I thought I wouldn't say anything," said Ken. "Maybe when we leave."

"I'd like to see him training with the 442nd. I bet he couldn't handle one day," said Horace.

"I'd just like to see heem in one dark alley," added Shimabukuro.

As they approached the barracks, light and noise came from one of the recreation centers. "Let's check in here first," said Ken. They saw that many of their colleagues had beaten them home, and the reunions were taking place in the centers.

"Kenichi!" came a familiar voice. Toshiko threw her arms around her eldest son and proclaimed, "Oh, Ken, I've been waiting so long to see you. I was hoping you'd get here tonight, but when all the other boys got here, I thought you'd missed the train. Let me look at you. You've lost weight. Oh, Kenichi, I need to fatten you up while you're home. So, how was the trip?"

"Fine, Mom, it's really great to be home. I...."

"And, Kenichi, why didn't you write more?"

"I did my best, Mom. We were pretty busy, you know. And my goodness, Pete, you just keep growing." He broke away from his mother's embrace and heartily shook his younger brother's hand. Peter was now at least four inches taller than he. "How's it going Pete?"

"O.K., Ken. I've been really anxious for you to get home." It had only been nine months since he had left, Ken noted, but in that time, Peter had matured from an irrepressible, chubby sixteen year old to a mature, muscular seventeen year old.

"Let me go get your father," said Toshiko as she left.

"How's Dad doing, Pete?" asked Ken as they found a couple of chairs.

"Not very good. It's like the life is out of him. He does his block captain work, but by ten in the morning, he starts drinking his whiskey, and by dinner time he's plastered. I asked Harry–remember Mr. Toyoshima, my coach?–he asked Dad to help him coach the teams, but Dad turned him down. It's pretty sad, Ken."

"Well, you take a proud guy like Dad who's had to work for everything he's ever gotten and put him behind barbed wire, give him all the necessities of life and tell him you only need him one hour a day, I guess you can expect something like this to happen. How does he get the booze anyway?"

"He has a deal with one of the swampers. When the truck goes to town to pick up supplies, he buys a bottle for Dad. It's really too bad because there's plenty he could do if he had the heart for it. The co-op is really going swell. They said it did almost a million dollars in sales this year, and after you left, they got a few more tractors and they're now farming 1500 acres. There'd be plenty for him to do. I guess that whiskey, once it gets you, it won't let go."

"And what do you hear from Howie?" Ken added after a short pause.

"Things are getting rough at Tule Lake. They've been moving more and more of what they call 'troublemakers' into the camp and more and more of the regular people out. We've had some Tule Lake people move down here. Anyway, Howie says the MP's are hassling them more than before, and the inmates are having stuff like protests and work stoppages and stuff."

"How involved has Howie been personally?"

"It's hard to say," answered Peter. "He sort of downplays what goes on. Most of what we've heard is from other people with relatives up there." He paused. "Ken, why does he have to go through all that ? Why couldn't he just answer 'Yes. Yes.' and stay with us here? He wouldn't have had to volunteer to go to the Army. He could've just stayed here, and maybe Dad wouldn't have been as bad as he's been." Tears welled up in Peter's eyes.

"Pete, I don't think you and I will ever fully understand. Howie sees things differently than we do. He's a proud guy like Dad and doesn't like to be shoved around. When the government takes him from his fishing and says move to the desert and stay inside the barbed wire and twiddle your thumbs, it just makes him furious. I don't like it either, but I deal with it in a little different way."

"How do you like the Army, anyway?" asked Peter after a few moments, finally brightening up.

"Well, it's O.K. I mean it's tough, but it's a challenge. I realize that most of my challenges have been to read a book and then answer questions on it. Now my job is to get five guys across a river and be ready to take some objective. I really sort of enjoy it."

"Do they let you fire the weapons? I mean of course they do, but which ones?"

"Well, we all have M1's. They make a big deal that our M1's are "a soldier's best friend". If we don't keep them spotless, we have to field-strip them on the site, clean them and then sleep with them that night."

Peter laughed. "Has any one ever shot himself accidentally in bed?"

"Pete, we take out the ammunition first. Anyway, we also have the BAR–Browning Automatic Rifle–two per squad. We know how to fire the machine gun and the mortars, but they're in a different squad and we don't fire them very often."

"How about the howitzers? From what I've read, they're really the ones that cause the damage - BOOM!" Ken could see some of the old enthusiasm creeping back into Peter.

"They're in the artillery unit that supports us. We don't fire those."

"When I go, I'm going into the artillery," said Peter.

"When you go?" asked Ken.

"Yeah. After I graduate in June, I'll be eighteen, and I'm volunteering. Mom can't say 'no'."

At that point, Toshiko and Shoji entered the recreation center. Shoji was a little unsteady on his feet, and his eyes were red. Ken, who had not embraced his father for fifteen years, did so now, and tears flowed from both men's eyes. It took several minutes for both of them to regain some emotional stability, and when they did, the conversation was halting and superficial.

"How are things going, Dad?"

"O.K., son, we're trying to keep the block looking good. How's the Army?"

"Not bad. I'm learning things I never knew before."

Pause.

"What do you hear from Dorothy, Dad?"

"Well, she seems to be doing good in New York. She certainly stays busy. You know, work, scrap metal drives, and a lot of parties."

"Well, that's Dorothy. Always busy."

Father and son had made their connection, if only for a couple of minutes. The four of them sat in the noisy recreation center talking about life at Manzanar and Ken's army life, for the next hour, carefully avoiding the topics that caused them the most concern: Shoji's addiction, Ken's future, and Howie. Toshiko filled everyone in on the latest from Dorothy, again emphasizing her work activities and down-playing her social life.

The recreation center, a converted barracks like all the other buildings at Manzanar, was full of similar family groups now. The young soldiers bore no resemblance to the young men who left nine months ago. Now, their uniforms, displaying the new red, white and blue shoulder patch of the 442nd Regimental Team, fit them. More importantly, the men exuded confidence. They had endured everything the Army had thrown at them for nine months, and they had mastered it, individually and as a group. This group of Japanese Americans, shunned and reviled by many Americans over the past two years, were convinced they were on the verge of doing something that would finally earn the respect and gratitude of those same Americans. They did not doubt they would excel at whatever their mission would be.

The family groups consisted of mother and father, not even trying to disguise their pride; younger brothers, fingering sharpshooter medals and asking for repeat descriptions of all the details of how those medals had been earned, even though only on the firing range; and usually a couple of teenage girls. A careful observer might have wondered why the girls were dressed this Friday night in Sunday dresses, their hair neatly done in a stylish pompadour in front. It would have been easy to recognize that their behavior toward the soldier was not that usually seen between a brother and sister, but only a camp insider would recognize that the girls had attached themselves to other family groups.

The largest family group that night was the Yamashitas. Not only did Horace have several young brothers, but this athletic-looking young man with the funny accent who came home with Horace was a magnet for any previously uncommitted young woman. Mrs. Yamashita, however, was not about to give up her position as "the mother". "So, Tyrus, you come from da Shimabukuros of Kapahulu?" she asked. Horace's mouth gaped. He knew his mother had grown up in Honolulu, but he had never heard her speak with the Pidgin English accent.

"Yes, een fact, we live on Kapahulu Avenue."

"Well, when I was dere, my best girlfriend was one Gladys

Shimabukuro."

"No!," said Tyrus, "Dat's my auntie!"

"Oh, Tyrus!" and with that, Mrs. Yamashita threw her arms around the young soldier and launched into their girlhood exploits, the pidgin patois becoming more intense with each memory of her Hawaiian youth. This amused Horace, but unamused were the young girls gathered around, more interested in hearing about Tyrus.

Again, as when the boys left to become soldiers, perhaps more could be learned from observing the guards in the watch towers. To be sure, they were now inside the rooms atop the towers with the heaters on, but as they looked through the gently falling snow, they could sense the love and warmth radiating from the open doors of the recreation centers. Those who had been there from the opening of the camp remembered the bedraggled people arriving by car and bus and how easy it was to think of them as non-people. If they were on duty at the swearing in, they remembered their confusion at the thought that these non-men were suddenly fellow soldiers. And now, enjoying the bosom of their families, they were members of a proud fighting team ready to go fight for the country that had encouraged the perception of them as non-people. None of the guards in the towers that night would have admitted to any envy, but perhaps there was some there.

At first, the furlough passed rapidly. Ken happily escorted both parents to the Christmas morning church service, although he knew they were going for him and not because of any desire to switch from Buddhism. Later at home, the family exchanged presents. Ken was embarrassed when he opened the package containing a new suit ordered from the Sears catalog. His father earned $19 a month for his job as block captain, and Ken knew that they had received no money from Mr. Brandt for selling their boat. In fact, they had heard nothing from Mr. Brandt, despite their many letters of inquiry. Ken, with his relatively princely corporal's pay, had bought watches for his father and brother and a new sewing machine for Toshiko. The sewing machine had served as his chair for much of the way from Mississippi. The snow stopped on Christmas day, and when the clouds cleared, the towering Sierras to the west seemed within walking distance. Ken suggested the family take a walk that way, then remembered that in less than a mile they would come to a barbed wire-topped fence and be under scrutiny. They decided to walk anyway and stood for a long time at the fence talking about the things that families talk about during precious times. Frequently the guards challenged internees who approached the fence, but on this occasion, whether due to Ken's uniform or its being Christmas Day, the Hayakawas went unchallenged. In the years to come, it was this episode that Ken remembered most vividly.

The first few days were similar to Christmas Day, but then the days began to drag. Shoji returned to his whiskey, and Ken found he spent more time with Horace, Kaz, and Ty–that is, when Ty wasn't surrounded by girls. Their talk turned to the trip back to camp and to speculation over when they would receive the order to prepare for overseas movement, POM in Army terminology.

They left Manzanar on January 3. Ken promised Toshiko he'd do better with letter writing and silently purposed to write Dorothy to plead that she not write home so often. Shoji came to see him off–fortunately it was in the morning and he hadn't started his whiskey yet–but their goodbye was rather formal. Ken realized their first few days would be the ones he'd have to remember. When Peter promised to join Ken later in the year, he wisely did so out of earshot of Toshiko.

Again the train took the northern route back to Camp Shelby. Sitting on their duffel bags, they soon crossed the deserts of Nevada and Utah. Most of the conversation centered around Ty's exploits with women.

"Eh, I nevah know you one stud wit' da wahines!" said Horace trying to mimic Ty's Pidgin.

"Eh. Fo'get eet, Yam. You too haolefied. You nevah learn talk da' kine. And don't ask me teach you. Eet's hawd enough teach you da' uke, you know." Tyrus thought for a few moments and added, "But, you know, Yam, you have got one nice muddah and faddah. T'anks for bringing me home, eh?"

They spent the first night on their duffel bags but found some seats the next day as they started through Kansas. Soon they were asleep in their new-found relative luxury.

Ken thought he couldn't have been asleep more than five minutes when he felt someone shaking him by the shoulder. He looked up to see the conductor. "You boys'll have to get up and give your seats to these soldiers," he said.

Ken straightened up, shook his brain clear and asked why. "Well, our fighting men have priority on the seating," answered the conductor.

Ken looked behind the conductor and saw four Caucasian soldiers. He recognized from their uniforms that they had not been in combat. They appeared to be just out of basic training. "We're soldiers too. We have as much right as they do to these seats," Ken told the conductor.

The conductor returned to the other soldiers, consulted and then returned. "They said that because you're Japs, you must be in some construction units or something and not real soldiers."

Shimabukuro had heard enough. "Eh. You guys nevah heah of da' 442, da' 'Go For Broke' guys? Let me show you a ting or two!" He tried to jump past Ken into the aisle, and it was all that Ken and Ishii could do to restrain him.

"Stop, Tyrus, we can handle this without an incident," said Ken, but he and Ishii were losing their grip on the angry Hawaiian.

"What's the trouble here, conductor? Can I help?" came a voice from the other end of the car. Shimabukuro stopped in mid-struggle, and all four men looked towards the familiar voice.

"Lieutenant Watson?!" they said in unison.

"These men are members of the 442nd Regimental Combat Team, which is an infantry unit in training," Lieutenant Watson calmly told the conductor. "If those other men were combat veterans, I'm sure these men would be the first to offer them seats. But that doesn't seem to be the case." The other soldiers retreated to the next car, and the conductor, sighing in relief, went his way.

"Where'd you come from, Lieutenant?" asked Ken.

"Well, I live in Honolulu, as you know, but my aunt and uncle have a farm in Kansas, so I spent my leave with them. I just got on at the last stop. I didn't see you guys until Shimabukuro here started going for that haole soldier."

"Thanks for coming to our rescue, sir," said Horace.

"We can't let them take advantage of us, can we? Furthermore, I think I came to their rescue more than yours. See you in Hattiesburg," said Lieutenant Watson, as he retreated to his seat at the other end of the car.

The rest of the trip was uneventful. All too soon the men were back to training as a regiment, along with the artillery and engineer units that with the infantry would make up the regimental combat team. Ken, at his level, still could rarely see the big picture, but at least he was becoming aware that there would be an artillery officer attached to Company E to call in fire from the big guns. He met some of the engineers who could help them with bridging streams, removing roadblocks, and clearing mine fields. He had never doubted that the men of the 442nd would have the heart to fight ferociously, but now he was gratified that they would have the support needed to do the job.

Near the end of January, they were informed that they would return to the national forest in the northern part of the state and maneuver against the 69th Division. Both units would be given objectives, and umpires would be taken from both units to determine when those objectives had been met or blocked by the opposing force. The soldiers suspected this would be their last preparation for battle, and orders for overseas movement would be given shortly after the two-week exercise.

Again, as in the regimental maneuvers in December, Ken's squad was called upon to make a series of moves to outflank the usually unseen enemy. Once in a while they were told they had secured an objective by amassing an excess of firepower on that objective, and they would walk up and occupy a hill, watching the troopers of the 69th disappear into the distant forest.

"They say infantry is all 'fire and maneuver'," said Horace one day. "We've mastered the 'maneuver' part and it's time for the 'fire' part."

"That's a little frightening, isn't it, Horace?" responded Ken.

"What do you mean?"

"I know what he means," answered Kaz. "He means that when we fire, the other guy fires back. If we kill more of him than he kills of us, we take the objective, not because some umpire back at the fire direction center says we win. We may win, but some of us get killed."

Horace looked at Kaz and then at Ken and said, "Yeah, I know that." But the statement lacked the aggressiveness of his first statement.

The day before the maneuvers ended, Ken was told to take Horace, Matsunaga, and Murakami for a prisoner of war (POW) detail. Company E had captured an entire platoon of 69th men, and the four men were designated as the POW enclosure guards.

They arrived at the area where the embarrassed men from the 69th were milling about. They strung white engineers' tape around a group of trees, and after the "prisoners" were collected inside the tape, the umpire, a major from the 69th, reviewed the rules for POWs for Ken and the platoon leader from the 69th.

"As long as the white tape outlines an area and there is one guard for every ten prisoners, you have to stay for twelve hours. There are forty of you, lieutenant, and four guards, so you have to stay until 0200 hours. After that, there's not much need to go since the exercise ends at 0700 tomorrow. Got it?"

"Yessir," said the lieutenant without enthusiasm.

The afternoon passed slowly. Ken assigned two of them to stand guard at any given time, unloaded rifles slung on their shoulders. There were no fences, barbed wire or guard towers, but the irony of the scene was not lost on the four Nisei.

As evening approached, Ken noticed increased activity in the enclosure. More men stood and moved about, whispering. He remembered the POW rules for the maneuvers and decided there was nothing to worry about.

But then, as dusk came, the lieutenant stepped over the tape and said, "Come on, men, we're going back to where we belong."

"Halt!" said Ken, bringing his rifle to the ready, "You can't go. It hasn't been twelve hours yet."

"The hell with you. Watch us," said the lieutenant. "No Japs are going to keep us prisoner!"

"But, lieutenant, you, you..." Ken spluttered.

The men from the 69th now were following the lieutenant over the tape and into the forest. Ken dropped his rifle and ran at the lieutenant, tackling him around the hips. They rolled in the dirt, and soon Matsunaga and Murakami had joined in the melee. With the overwhelming numbers against them, it took less than a minute for the guards to be subdued.

"Now, corporal, you can stay here, or if you want we'll take you as our prisoners, but we're going!" said the lieutenant, leaning over Ken, who was being restrained by four soldiers of the 69th.

"Lieutenant," Ken tried to argue but had trouble talking because his lip was bleeding.

Suddenly there was honking, and all activity stopped as a jeep screeched to a halt. The umpire major from the 69th who had given them their instructions just four hours before, jumped out and came running to the scene.

"What's going on here, Lieutenant Baxter?" he barked. The lieutenant was silent.

"Can you tell me what's going on, corporal?" he asked Ken, now released and standing at attention.

"Sir, these men were, uh, doing what all American soldiers are supposed to do if captured. They, uh, were trying to escape." Ken tried to lick the blood from his lip but winced.

"Is that right, lieutenant? Speak to me!"

"Uh, sir, we were out of line. According to the rules, we were supposed to be prisoners until 0200. We, uh, I, sir, were violating those rules."

The major surveyed the scene and finally said, "O.K. You men get back into the enclosure, and I don't want to see any more of this. Lieutenant Baxter, I want to see you when this exercise is over."

"Yessir," answered Lieutenant Baxter.

Ken noticed for the first time that Sergeant Strong, with the white arm band of an umpire, had arrived with the major. The sergeant sidled over to Ken and said softly, "Good going, Hayakawa. I guess the guys from the 69th know what 'Go For Broke' means now, huh?"

"Corporal, you're going to need some stitches in that lip. You come back with us," said the major.

"Sergeant Strong," asked Ken on the way to the aid station, "how'd you know to arrive at just that time? They'd only started to leave about two minutes before you arrived."

"We were in the area and heard a call for help on the radio."

"On the radio? Who could have called?"

"Yamashita," answered Sergeant Strong.

"Yamashita?" asked Ken. "He had the presence of mind to call for help while I was deciding to take on ten to one odds in a wrestling match? Who's the hothead, and who's the cool-headed one now?" Sergeant Strong smiled, then chuckled and started to roar with laughter. Ken couldn't help but join him, which brought tears to his eyes because of the pain in his lip.

The major looked back from his front seat and wondered at this unusual display from the grizzled white first sergeant and the clean-cut young Japanese American corporal.

Ken was back at the POW enclosure a few hours later, with his lip now sutured and bandaged. At 2AM, the prisoners all stood up and started to leave. The lieutenant said, "Corporal, our twelve hours are up. We can leave and return to our lines."

"Yessir. You can, but you heard the major. The maneuvers will be over in five hours. You may as well stay until it's light," said Ken.

"I know," answered Lieutenant Baxter, "We've not lived up to the reputation of the 69th Division in the last twelve hours. The least we can do is get back to our lines by the end of the problem. The 442nd isn't the only unit in the U.S. Army with pride. Come on, men."

Ken and the others watched as forty men stumbled into the darkness of the forest.

Part III
Into the Battle

CHAPTER 12

"WELL, I THINK I HAVE AN ANSWER," SAID JUN, as he arrived home one cold day in early 1944.

"What was the question?" asked Aileen.

"There's not enough food for you girls. There's not enough fuel to keep our house warm. They won't let me work more than half-time. If Aileen didn't work, we'd starve."

"We're doing O.K., Daddy," said Myrna. "It's not your fault, and this war will be over one of these days. At least we don't hear as much propaganda about our glorious victories anymore."

"Yeah," added Aileen. "We'll survive, Daddy."

"Well, they were advertising for a position in Saipan today. Almost all the men who were responsible for supplying the civilian population of the island and then for shipping the produce back to Japan have gone to war. I talked to them today, and my background in import-export is just what they're looking for. The pay is four times what I'm making now, and they supply a room. I can send almost all of the pay back here."

"Why can't we all go together?" asked Aileen.

"Myrna should continue her medical studies, and you have your job with NHK."

The evening was spent discussing Jun's idea - in fact it was a fait accompli, as Jun had applied and been accepted - and they finally decided that Aileen would go with Jun, and Mieko and Myrna would stay home. Aileen happily volunteered to leave her job, as her guilt feelings had never really disappeared. She would keep house for her father, although he assured her they'd be lucky to have a two-room apartment and there wouldn't be much for her to do. Myrna would have been willing to drop out of medical school but seemed relieved when the family decided she should continue her studies.

Jun and Aileen were at the railing of the *Yawata Maru* as it tied up at the dock at Tanapag, the main harbor for Saipan, two weeks later. The cold weather of Tokyo had long since given way to the tropical climate of the Mariana Islands, situated just a little north of the equator. They watched as the ship was unloaded by Saipanese stevedores, their light brown skin glistening in the 80 degree heat. They were met on the dock by Mr. Kubota, the Director of the civil government of Saipan.

"Welcome to Saipan," said Mr. Kubota, both men bowing from their waists. "We are honored that you have accepted our offer. I have reviewed your resume, and you appear to be just the man who can help us at this time. But come, let us discuss this further over a meal. Mr. Villagomez will arrange to have your luggage delivered to your quarters." He nodded to a Saipanese, taller than the rest, probably in his fifties with graying hair, dressed in white trousers and an open-necked shirt. He was directing three men in the unloading of Jun and Aileen's baggage.

Mr. Kubota took the Nakamuras to a teahouse on a hill a mile from the harbor, with a panoramic view of the east coast of the island. As they ate a lunch of classical Japanese food, supplemented with mangos, pineapple and coconut meat, Aileen felt guilty. She thought of her mother and sister with their twice-weekly fish ration. They had fresh fruit only on the rare occasion they could find some in the countryside and barter for it. Mr. Kubota told them about Saipan.

"As you know, our goal from the 20s was to develop Saipan as a source of food for the empire. By the beginning of the war in the Pacific, we had a huge food industry here, mostly sugar cane. There were about 30,000 Japanese living here, including families, to support the industry, although, of course, all the physical work was done by the natives. In the last few years, it has been built up as a defense base." His voice lowered. "There are more than 30,000 soldiers and sailors here now. That's classified." Evidently he didn't consider Aileen a threat to be in possession of secret information.

"The military has their own supply system and has resisted my attempts to merge the civilian system with theirs. That's where you come in. There are still about 15,000 Japanese civilians on the island, and we need to fight for the use of the unloading and delivery systems. We also are in charge of sending the produce back to Japan, but there's not much of that. By the time the military confiscates what they need, there's not much to ship back. And much of what goes back is sunk." His voice lowered again. "That's also classified."

"You'll be helped greatly by Mr. Villagomez, the man taking your luggage to your home. He's a big man locally."

"What about supplies for the Saipanese? Who's responsible for that?" asked Jun.

"The natives?" Mr. Kubota looked surprised. "No. They take care of themselves. Their needs are pretty simple."

"What about medical supplies?" Jun persisted.

"Oh, I suppose they have their own remedies–folk medicine, you know."

Aileen left the men to talk further about the intricacies of Jun's new job. From the verandah of the tea room, she looked out across the white beaches to the Philippine Sea, peaceful and shimmering blue under the cloudless sky. She looked to the south to the town of Garapan, Saipan's capital, and it too seemed peaceful and quiet although it was a weekday. The last news reports she and Jun had worked with before leaving their jobs had described the battles with the American Navy and Marines at unknown places like Tarawa and Kwajalein. She had located those on a map and noted that the route of advance pointed towards Saipan. They were now 1500 miles closer to that route than when in Tokyo, but the difference in anxiety level was palpable. The Valley of Darkness had been replaced by the Beach of Carefreeness. How would Tennyson have described it - "a land in which it seemed always afternoon"? She thought of Mieko and Myrna, and her guilt returned.

When the men finished their conversation, the Nakamuras were driven to their living quarters, not a two-room apartment as Jun had predicted, but a three-bedroom house with a living room and verandah. The view equaled that from the tearoom. The young maid, who met them at the door, showed them the house. The rooms were sparsely furnished, but the tatami mats, ceiling fans and open windows promised comfortable living. Jun felt obliged to go to the office and start work immediately, so Aileen decided to walk into town. Starting down the main street of Garapan, she stopped short. She could be in Tokyo.

The architecture was only slightly different, making few concessions to the climate. Most of the people were Japanese, and many of the women wore kimonos, despite the temperature. All the signs were in Japanese, and the few Saipanese she saw spoke Japanese fluently. She remembered some references to Saipan as Little Tokyo, Japan's main effort at colonization in the Pacific, and some of the recent history lesson by Mr. Kubota began to fall into place. Few manufactured goods were for sale in the stores, but the open-air market was a cornucopia of fresh fruit. She bought a mango, which the farmer peeled for her, and she continued through the market. Hundreds of small reef fish hung in various states of drying. Some things she didn't recognize, particularly a great number of something that looked like soft cucumbers. She was told they were animals called "ocean cucumbers", harvested from the shallow water off the beaches. For the Japanese tongue, they were a delicacy. Aileen, whose food fantasies still ran towards hamburgers, decided to pass on them, preferring to buy a small piece of *sushi* to eat after her mango was gone.

Continuing through the streets of Garapan, she turned inland and came to an open-air hospital, as modern as any she'd seen in Tokyo. All the rooms, including the operating room, opened onto an inside atrium. She continued up the hill and came to an area which was the busiest of any she'd seen in Saipan. A little square steam engine chugged up to an unloading dock, pulling ten flat-bed cars piled high with sugar cane. Men appeared from everywhere and transferred the sugar cane to trucks, which headed towards the harbor. Perhaps the *Yawata Maru's* homebound cargo would be sugar cane.

Late in the afternoon Aileen returned home. Her father not yet home, she spoke with the maid. Her name was Masayo Tenorio, and she had worked at that house since she graduated from the sixth grade ten years earlier. The Saipanese, she said, were only allowed to go through the sixth grade. When they left school at age twelve, boys went to work in the fields and girls worked as domestics or as shopgirls. The Japanese selected a few of the girls to become teachers, and that group finished twelve years of schooling. This house had always been the home of the Director of Civilian Supplies for the island. When Masayo started work there, the director had been a Mr. Nishi, a young man with a family. Early in 1942, they had returned to Japan so he could volunteer for the Navy. She was sad to report that he had been killed when his ship was sunk far to the south off some island whose name she'd never heard before. Mr. Nishi was succeeded by Mr. Hirakawa, an elderly widower from Osaka, but his health eventually failed and he had returned home three months before. Enjoying the opportunity to talk with someone her own age for the first time in a couple of weeks, Aileen poured out her life story. When she came to the part about America, Masayo's eyes widened. She put down the duster she'd been idly using until then. "Tell me about America. I've always been fascinated by that country, but of course we can't even mention it here or we're showing disloyalty to the Emperor."

"I know what you mean," said Aileen and described the incident of the elderly gentleman striking the English book from her hands on the trolley.

When Jun returned at almost sundown, he saw the two young women, the one with light brown skin and a loose-fitting cotton dress typical of the tropics, and the other whose dress and facial appearance indicated she was Japanese, sitting and earnestly talking of a far-off land, the land supposedly of the enemy.

"Oh! Mr. Nakamura!" said the startled Masayo. "Please forgive me. I have not prepared your dinner." She rose hastily, hurried to the kitchen, and started to unwrap the reef fish she'd bought earlier that day.

Jun and Aileen sat on the verandah and watched the last traces of sun disappear below the sea horizon as they shared their activities of the afternoon. Aileen could see that her father was thrilled by his new job. He relished the opportunity to pour himself into his work again after the years of part-time work with Domei.

An hour later as they were finishing dinner, Aileen blurted out what had bothered her since they'd arrived on Saipan. "Daddy, I feel guilty living this well while Momma and Myrna are still in Tokyo."

Jun took a long drag on his cigarette and then another. "We'll bring them here during Myrna's summer break, and maybe she can even stay out for an extra semester. I'm sure she wouldn't want to come now since she's gotten a good start on the spring semester, and I know Momma wouldn't leave her by herself." Aileen knew the discussion was over. She also knew that was the best answer she could have expected from her father.

The next evening when Jun came home Aileen was surprised to hear him announce, "I've booked them on the *Yashima Maru*. It's due here on June 13."

The days passed slowly for Aileen. Masayo continued to grill her for every bit of information she could remember about America, but because of Masayo, she did not have to cook or clean. The highlight of her day was the nightly discussion of the challenges of her father's day. It was good to see him happy again now that he was the only wage-earner, to see his pleasure when he sent the first check to Mieko and Myrna.

Aileen spent most of her days walking around Saipan. Usually, she walked to Garapan and Tanapag with its harbor. One day, she walked all the way to the southwestern point of the island–five miles. She sat and ate lunch in the shadow of one of the pillboxes, its 8" gun pointed out to sea. There she talked with soldiers lazily enjoying the tropical sun. Had they been hearing of the relentless western progress of the American Navy and the probability that those guns would soon be in action? If so, they betrayed no sign as they talked with this pretty Japanese girl with the slightly unusual accent.

"What's that island over there called?" asked Aileen, pointing to the south.   "That's Tinian Island," answered one of the soldiers.

"What goes on there?"

"Nothing. I've been there. It's a very sleepy little island. Nothing of note will ever happen on Tinian."

When she got home, Aileen enthusiastically described her long walk to Masayo. After a pause, she nodded towards a mountain a mile to the southeast of their house. "Have you ever walked to the top of that mountain?"

"Yes, Miss Nakamura. That's Mount Tapotchau. I go there frequently. You can see all over the island from there. It's not too hard to get to. You go down that valley, cross the stream, climb that ridge and then it's a fairly easy walk to the peak."

"Could you take me up there sometime?" asked Aileen.

Masayo looked surprised. "Well, yes, Miss Nakamura. Whenever you want to."

Two days later, after Jun left for the office, the two young women packed a lunch and headed up to Mount Tapotchau. It was, as Masayo had said, a fairly easy walk, particularly after all the walking Aileen had done since arriving in Saipan. Many gun emplacements studded the road to the peak. Each emplacement, the girls noted, was near a camouflaged cave, enlarged to house the soldiers who manned the guns. Off-duty soldiers sunned themselves on the warm Saipan morning and re-acted with surprise and perhaps a little pleasure as they watched the two young women pass by.

From the peak on this cloudless day, they could see the entire length of Saipan, from the mostly flat southern half to the hilly northern half; the airfield to the south where fighters took off every few minutes; and the sparsely inhabited eastern half of the island. Wherever the ground was slightly flat, crops grew. In the nearer fields they could see the Saipanese farmers quietly tending their fields by hand. With machetes, they cut their crops, then they loaded them onto water buffalo-drawn carts.

Masayo broke the silence. "Tell me more about America, Miss Nakamura."

"Well, the first thing is that you call me Aiko. Everyone in America is very informal compared to Japanese, and if you're the same age, you call each other by their first names." She continued to describe everything she could remember, enjoying the opportunity to reminisce about days that seemed so long ago and a world away.

"Why are Japan and America at war?" asked Masayo abruptly. Aileen looked at the questioning dark eyes for a long time before turning her gaze to the horizon again.

"Well," she started, "I'm not too sure. I think the Japanese wanted to control Southeast Asia with their raw materials and were afraid the Americans would prevent them, so they sank the American Navy in Hawaii."

"When did they do that?" asked Masayo.

"On December 8th, 1941. I'll never forget that date. It changed my life."

"I never heard that," said Masayo.

"You never heard of Pearl Harbor?"

"No. Where's that?"

"That's the harbor in Hawaii where the American Navy was when the Japanese fleet sank them. How did you hear that the war started?"

"It was early 1942," Masayo answered, "when they announced that the Japanese fleets had been attacked by the Americans from the east and the British and Dutch from the west. The brave Japanese sailors won heroic battles and banished the westerners from this part of the world so that we would no longer be under their domination. But it seems to me that we're still under the domination of the Japanese. I mean, they treat us well, but we're not equals. Only a few of us can go beyond the sixth grade, and they send a few to Japan for higher education. That's why I'm so interested in America. Pastor Villagomez tells us of the opportunities there, even for immigrants." Aileen thought of her father's bittersweet experience in America, the success he attained through hard work but the lack of social acceptance, but she was more interested in something else Masayo had said.

"Pastor Villagomez?" Aileen asked.

"Yes. You know the man your father works with, the one who brought your baggage up the day you arrived."

"I remember him. He's a pastor? I thought he was in charge of the men loading and unloading the ships."

"Yes. He does both jobs."

"Don't you mean 'priest'? I thought most Saipanese were Catholics."

"No, there are some of each. The Spanish initially owned us, but then the Germans bought us in 1899 and had us until they gave us to the Japanese in 1919. During the German time, a lot of missionaries were here, and a lot of the people became Protestant. Not many have become Buddhist during the Japanese time. The Japanese don't get very involved with our religion, so we're both Catholic and Protestant. Aiko?"

"Yes."

"Can you teach me to speak English?"

"I could, but it would be a little dangerous, don't you think?"

"Maybe we could come up here two or three times a week, and you could teach me. We could find an isolated place here where no one would hear us."

Aileen chuckled. "We could probably work that out."

Later that afternoon as the girls started down the mountain, Aileen pointed to a small island two miles off Tanapag Harbor. "What is that island, Masayo?"

"Oh, Miss Nakamura, I mean Aiko, that's Managaha Island. It's the prettiest little island anywhere around here. Before the war, we used to go out there on Sunday afternoons for picnics. There's a beach all around the island, and you can climb coconut trees to get the cool coconut milk, and you can dive in the shallow water off the beaches and find pretty shells. That was my favorite place to go."

"Why don't you go there any more?"

"The Japanese confiscated most of the boats. They have some big anti-aircraft guns out there, and they try to discourage visits. But they let Pastor Villagomez keep his boat because of his position, and so we still go out with him occasionally. He used to take Mr. Hirakawa out there almost every Sunday before he got too sick to go. He said a trip to Managaha was better for his health than all the pills the doctors could give him."

The two young women followed through on their plans to hike to Mount Tapotchau three days a week for English lessons, and Aileen found Masayo a good student, a natural-born linguist. Some days, they walked down the eastern slope of the mountain, exploring that side of the island but being careful to revert to Japanese when they approached anybody. Aileen's hardest job was to convince Masayo to let her help clean the house on days they were gone a long time. The argument that finally won the day was: "It's more American and democratic to work together." They agreed that Jun didn't need to know.

One night when Jun came home, he said "Mr. Villagomez has offered to take us on a trip this Sunday to Managaha Island. Do you know where that is?"

"Yes. Daddy," answered Aileen and told him what Masayo had told her of the island. "Can Masayo go with us?" Jun looked a little quizzically at Aileen.

"I'll check with Mr. Villagomez," he said.

Jun and the two young women met Mr. Villagomez at the Tanapag docks at one o'clock Sunday afternoon and stepped down into his boat. It was a 32-footer with an inboard motor and a small cabin that slept two people. As they approached Managaha Island, it seemed perfectly symmetrical to Aileen–a flat island, with a tuft of coconut trees in the middle and a beach all around it. The sand was warm between their toes as they jumped onto the beach.

"Masayo, you show Mr. Nakamura and his daughter the island while I light the fire to cook the fish," said Mr. Villagomez. He was a tall man with chest and shoulders that showed he worked with the men he supervised, loading and unloading the ships. His full head of hair was graying around the temples, and his weathered face was more that of a compassionate pastor than of a hard-boiled stevedore boss, Aileen thought.

As they walked through the sand and the cool, shallow water, Aileen remembered the report Jun had brought home a few weeks before. The American Navy, he said, had struck at a place called Truk Lagoon, only 600 miles away. If Saipan were next on their agenda, it was hard to correlate with the general sense of peace that pervaded this island.

Suddenly the command "Halt!" was yelled from a grove of trees. "Who goes there?"

Aileen was so startled, she couldn't speak. Her father gathered his wits and answered, "Nakamura. We're here for a picnic."

"You are entering a restricted zone and may go no further," came the officious reply. Aileen could now see that the speaker was a young soldier standing with rifle pointed at them from just inside the line of coconut trees. Beyond him, she noted a huge gun, at least twenty feet long. It resembled guns she'd seen on a battleship in Tokyo Bay where her father had taken her on Navy Day before the war.

"We will turn around and return," said Jun, now self-controlled. It wasn't until they'd gone a hundred yards that Aileen became confident they would not be shot in the back. As they retraced their steps, they talked about how startled they'd been by the challenge. They passed Mr. Villagomez and walked around the island the other way. This time they noticed the sentry and the long gun in time to turn around and return to their picnic spot.

"Before the war, of course there were no guns here and this was the perfect spot for a picnic," Mr. Villagomez said after he heard their tale. "You could walk around the island in less than an hour, taking a dip in the water when you got hot, getting a coconut when you got thirsty. Let's pray the war is over soon and Managaha can go back to being what it was."

After lunch of fried fish, rice and fresh fruit, Aileen and Masayo swam in the cool water of the lagoon. "I understand you're a minister?" said Aileen, as she dried off and sat down in the warm sand.

"Yes," answered Mr. Villagomez. "The Germans didn't have time to do much in these islands during their time except start missions. My parents joined the local Liebenzell Mission when I was a young boy, and I was raised in the church. I learned to play the organ and helped the pastor with services. They were planning to send me back to seminary in Germany when the Great War came. After the islands were mandated to Japan, the missionaries were sent home. I was about the only one who could take over. I still wanted to go to seminary, but soon I had a family and never was able to go."

"That's not the whole story," said Masayo. "The people in the church always said there was nothing he needed to learn, and we'd never let him go."

"Now, Masayo, don't try to embarrass your pastor," said Mr. Villagomez, and both laughed in a happy, relaxed way that Aileen thought would not be taught as the standard for pastor-parishioner relations in most Lutheran seminaries in Germany.

"This has been one of the most pleasant days of my life," said Aileen as they motored back to Tanapag.

"We're proud to be able to show you 'our Saipan'," said Mr. Villagomez. "We come out most Sunday afternoons, and as many as can fit on the boat are welcome to come. Usually my daughters come, but they had a teachers' conference today."

"Are they both teachers?" asked Aileen.

"Yes. We were very fortunate that both Sumi and Asako were chosen to continue their education. Sumi—she's the older—teaches in Chalan Kanoa, and Asako teaches in Susupe. Both of them really seem to enjoy children. Maybe one of these days they'll get married and give us grandchildren close enough to enjoy."

"Masayo tells me you also have sons in Germany and Japan," said Aileen over the roar of the motor.

"Yes. Martin is our elder son. He had the call of the Lord on him, and we sent him to seminary in Germany. Juergen was selected by the Japanese to study medicine in Tokyo. He was supposed to come home to be a doctor, but they drafted him into the army and sent him to China. After three years there, we thought he'd be coming back, but now they've sent him to Burma. His wife and our grandson live in Tokyo, and she keeps us up to date on how he's doing. I think Burma's very tough on doctors, with malaria and all the other tropical diseases."

Aileen started to ask about Martin, but Mr. Villagomez quickly shifted the conversation to a discussion of the tides in that part of the Pacific, and her question was forgotten.

"Thank you very much for the afternoon," said Jun as they climbed onto the dock. "I should very much like to go again if you have room on your boat. It gives me an opportunity to think." Mr. Villagomez assured him there would be room.

"And then when Momma and Myrna get here on June 13, they'd love this trip," added Aileen.

Jun and Aileen took many more trips to Managaha with the Villagomezes that spring. Frequently, the girls and Mrs. Villagomez went along, as did Masayo. The more Aileen observed the Villagomezes together, the more excitedly she anticipated the arrival of Mieko and Myrna. One day she asked the sisters about their brother Martin, indicating she had the idea that Mr. Villagomez did not want to talk about him.

"That's right," answered Sumi. "Martin finished seminary in Germany and then after a two-year internship was to return here. He would have taken over for Daddy. But by the time Martin finished, it wasn't safe to return. They gave him a church near Berlin, but he started to protest the way the Nazis were imprisoning Jews and others. We've not heard from him for more than a year. Daddy fears the worst."

"Does he think they've put him in prison?" asked Aileen.

"Or worse. We've heard secret reports through the church that they've built a bunch of camps where they send what they call their 'undesirables'. And then they're never heard from again."

The next Sunday, Aileen asked Masayo to take her to church. She had attended church sporadically in Seattle, but it had never meant much to her. Jun and Mieko had never prohibited her from going, though they obviously were not pleased about it. So she had gone only infrequently when a friend invited her. In Saipan, she was the only pure Japanese in the congregation, but she discovered that she felt comfortable. The people sang hymns with gusto, and Aileen even recognized some of the tunes from her Seattle days. The love of the congregation for the pastor and his love for them was obvious. Aileen found herself listening to every word of his sermon, although she could understand none of it.

"Tell me what he said in the sermon," Aileen said to Masayo after church. From then on, Aileen attended church, began to participate in the worship but got the sermon translation on the walk home.

One Sunday afternoon in early June, as Aileen and Masayo were floating on their backs in the gentle waters off Managaha, Aileen saw a bird soaring high in the sky. *Why was it soaring in such a straight line and not changing direction as birds do?* she wondered. Then she saw a shiny glint off the "bird". As she started to call Masayo's attention to it, she heard commotion on the island, at both ends of the beach.

"That's where the long guns are," she told Masayo. Other guns, smaller, were rolled out on rails and elevated to an almost vertical position. When Aileen looked back at the airplane, she saw it turn and disappear into the distance.On the way home that afternoon, Mr. Villagomez said, "Mr. Nakamura and Aiko, I want you to sit back here with me. Let me show you how to run this boat." No other explanation.

CHAPTER 13

"L IEUTENANT FURUYA!" KEN CALLED AS THEY LEFT chapel on a Sunday in late February.

"Ken, what's going on?" responded Doug Furuya as he turned and joined Ken for the walk back to the barracks area.

"What's going on with you is more to the point. I heard you got orders for Italy."

"Yeah. They've ordered about twenty officers and two hundred men for replacements for the 100th Battalion," Doug answered, referring to the battalion of Nisei from Hawaii that volunteered early and the success of which had led to the formation of the 442nd. "They're decimating the 1st Battalion. There was a similar group that went just before our maneuver with the 69th. I don't know why they always take them from the 1st. Maybe they have their reasons, but it sure creates holes in our battalion."

"We keep hearing rumors that we should expect POM orders any day. How can they expect to fill and train those holes in the 1st before we go?" asked Ken.

"That's my point. They can't. We were pretty much combat-ready before the first group went. Now, after our group goes, all our companies are way under strength," answered Doug. On their walk back to the regimental area, the two friends complained, as soldiers have done from the time armies were first raised, that the senior officers did not know what they were doing.

Before they parted, Ken said, "I'm probably too naïve, but I think we're ready for combat. In fact, I wonder if we're not getting over-trained. That's probably a stupid thing to say when the test of it is going into combat and getting shot at and maybe killed."

"I think you're right. There is such a thing as being over-trained.

Just so long as we're not over-confident and take the enemy lightly," responded Doug.

"I guess you're going to find out before long, huh? When are you leaving?"

"We get all our immunizations and pick up our personnel records tomorrow and then have to be packed and ready to move Tuesday."

"Will we see you when we get over there? Are the 442nd and 100th going to be together?"

"Beats me," answered Doug. "I just go where they tell me."

"Well, don't kill 'em all and end the war before we get there. Save some for us!" The two friends parted and headed towards their barracks. Ken thought about his false bravado and then thought of the freshman medical class at Creighton.

"What has this world come to?" he thought. "I could be learning how to keep people from dying, and here I am talking lightheartedly about killing them? And the irony is that I chose this way and would choose it again if I had to. Life doesn't make much sense."

The next morning Sergeant Honda came through the barracks rattling bunks at 4AM, two hours before their usual reveille. "Rise and shine, men. We're having a parade today for General Marshall in full battle gear. Breakfast at 0430, and form up on the street at 0600. Let's get to it, men."

"General Marshall?" said a sleepy Horace, rubbing his eyes. "Inspecting us? Ken, how come you didn't tell us about this?"

"First I ever heard about it," said Ken, picking up his shaving gear and heading to the bathroom.

"Hey. Tell da' guy someting for me.' said Shimabukuro, pulling the covers over his head. "Tell da guy..." We'll never know the message Tyrus Shimabukuro had for General George Marshall because Murakami yanked the covers off the sleepy Hawaiian at that point, causing Tyrus to issue a profane message for Shigeo Murakami.

At 6AM, the men were formed up in platoon formation. Lieutenant Watson and the squad leaders checked each man for his pack, (either full of clothes or blocked in such a way as to make it look full of clothes,) entrenching tool, canteen full of water, and the myriad equipment that soldiers carry to war. Rifles, unloaded, were slung on their shoulders. When the platoon staff was satisfied they were ready, the men marched to the company area, where a similar inspection by the company staff took place at 7AM. By 8AM, they were in the battalion area for inspection by the battalion staff, and finally by 9AM, the entire regiment was formed. After inspection by the regimental officers, they were given the command "Rest", meaning they had to stand in place but could talk and be relaxed.

"Hey Sarge, what time da guy coming?" asked Shimabukuro.

"1000 hours." answered Sergeant Honda.

"1000 hours!" exclaimed Shimabukuro. "Den why da hell we need get up at 4 o'clock? Hey, if dey tell me 'Shimabukuro, da guy's coming at 10 o'clock. We want you be ready for him den.' Hey, I get up at 9, poot on all my junk, and I be standing here, one happy Hawaiian. Da way eet ees now, hey, I'm half pissed off already. I hope he no ask me question, or I have to tell him a ting or two."

"Well, you guys know the Army way. The colonel says 0900, the lieutenant colonel says 0800, the major says 0700, the captain says 0600, the lieutenant says 0500. That's what you call 'Hurry up and wait'," responded Sergeant Honda.

Ten o'clock came and went with no General Marshall. The problem now was not only boredom. It was an unseasonably hot early March day in Mississippi. As the sun got higher in the sky, the men could see the humidity rising from the field. Soon, some of the men, dressed in their winter uniforms and full battle gear, began to pass out. Medics with stretchers came into the ranks to pick up the fallen soldiers and transport them to the hospital for resuscitation. When they were finally called to attention at 11AM, there was many a hole in their ranks. If General Marshall noted that as he walked down the line with Colonel Pence, he didn't mention it. What he did mention, however, as they stood "At Ease", was their particular situation. He described the difficulty of the decision to evacuate them from the west coast and put them in detention camps. He seemed to understand the unfairness of it but also described what they thought at the time was the military necessity and did not apologize. He told them of the exemplary record of the 100th Battalion and of his great expectations that they would follow in the footsteps of the men of the 100th. He told them the American people would be watching them. As they trooped back to their barracks, Ken remembered back to the discussion he and Sergeant Honda had had several months before and decided that General Marshall was at least one Hakujin who understood what they were fighting for.

Ten days later, their Preparation for Overseas Movement orders arrived. The order specified that the 1st Battalion would stay at Camp Shelby. Holes in the other two battalions were filled with men from the 1st, and the remnant would stay to train replacements. The rumor was that when they got to Italy, the 100th Battalion would replace the 1st battalion to maintain a three-battalion regiment.

Ken remembered back to some war movie he had seen in which the preparation for going to war meant simply putting on your pack, grabbing your rifle and going up the gangplank to the ship. The reality was that they had to take with them all their equipment, jeeps, trucks, big guns, communication centers, aid stations, and all these things had to be packed so they'd arrive in good condition. Ken's squad spent most of its time helping pack the 105mm howitzers and loading them onto the train. It was more than a month before the men actually climbed onto the troop train to head east, and it was late April when they arrived at Camp Patrick Henry in Virginia. It took a week to load their equipment onto the Liberty ships, and on the first of May, the men of the 442nd Regimental Team, mostly comprised of Americans of Japanese Ancestry, moved to Hampton Roads to board the ships that would take them to war.

The Liberty ships did not have much speed, and with the zigzag pattern they had to take as defense against submarines, they proceeded across the mid-Atlantic slowly. Ken, remembering his occasional summer trips on the fishing boat out of Terminal Island with his father and Howie, feared seasickness. But the sea was calm most days, and the trip was a pleasant one.

"Think of this as 'The Grand Tour'," said Horace.

"What da kine 'Grand Tour'?" asked Tyrus.

"Well, you know, before the war in Europe started, rich people would sail to Europe for the summer, travel around and visit all the countries."

"Tink we evah goin' do dat?" asked Tyrus in a rare thoughtful mood.

"Yeah, I think we will," chimed in Kaz Ishii. "I think when this war is over, we'll have a chance to live free without prejudice, do what we want for a living, raise our families, travel to Europe if we want to..."

"What you wanna do, Ishii? I mean for a living?" asked Tyrus.

"Well, my folks raised strawberries in the San Joaquin Valley, but I don't know if we'll get the farm back. I know strawberries. I think I'll be a fruit broker."

"What da hell is a fruit broker?" asked Shimabukuro.

"He's the middle man. He buys fruits from the farmer in large quantities and sells it to large market chains. We always busted our butts growing the berries, worried about not enough rain, or too much rain, or pests, and then we'd work all day and night harvesting them. The broker would have come by earlier, signed a contract for us to send them to such and such a place, and his job was over. But who do you think drove the nice car and wore the nice clothes? Up till now, no Japanese has been allowed to be a broker. My hope is that after this war, we'll be free to do what we want."

"You guys from da mainland have it bad, I gotta admeet. In Hawaii, we got more Japanese dan haoles. Planty Japanese go into professions, you know, teaching, doctuh, and stuff. But you know what? Da haoles run Hawaii, very few Japanese in da government. Da haoles have all da power. So, Yam, what you gonna do aftuh da wah?"

"Well, I was in accounting at UCLA before the war, but I don't know, maybe there are more important things to do," answered Horace.

"Like what?"

"I don't know. We'll see."

"And, Hayakawa," Tyrus continued his survey, "I know you goin' fo' doctuh."

"Yeah. Probably. What about you, Ty, what are you going to do after the war."

"He's gonna have a surfboard shop on Waikiki Beach and teach all the women tourists to surf. I can just see him standing on the board with his arms around their waists," said Horace.

"Dere you go again wit' da kine—wat ya call it?—one stereotype." He feigned hitting Yamashita over the head with his ukulele, which he had been lazily strumming during their discussion. "No, but it about da ocean, you know. Da coral and shells under ocean around Hawaii beautiful, particularly around outer islands, Maui and Big Island. You can make all kine beautiful jewelry wit' it."

Most of the time aboard ship, however, was spent in a much less contemplative pursuit. A poker game went on almost around the clock. Shimabukuro and the other Hawaiians seemed to be masters of the game. Horace and Ken participated occasionally but were soon out of the game. Ken never understood poker and quickly lost the small limit he set himself, and Horace had never learned to keep a poker face. On one such occasion, the two losers were leaning on the rail watching the destroyer escorts dart around the convoy.

"You know there are Negroes in the Navy?" asked Horace suddenly.

"Are there?" replied Ken without much interest.

"Yeah, but they're all stewards."

"So?"

"They don't let them run the ship or fire the guns or anything like that."

"How do you know?"

"I was talking to one. He works in the Captain's Mess. I mean they're letting us form our own combat regiment so we can prove ourselves and one day have a little more freedom to do what we want. But with them, they're not being allowed to prove themselves capable of anything more than serving mess."

"But what do you think we can do about it, Horace? Like you say, we have to prove ourselves first and then, if you want, you can help them." There was a pause, and then Ken added "How would you go about doing it?"

"I don't know. Remember the other day when Ty was asking us about what we wanted to do after the war, and I said I wasn't sure I still wanted to be an accountant? Well, that's what I was thinking about. I don't know whether I could help them more as a lawyer, or a social worker, or a teacher...." Horace's voice drifted off, and the two men continued watching the destroyers.

By the beginning of the fourth week at sea, Ken had long since lost his quota at the poker table and had retired from that pursuit. He had studied the destroyer escort enough that he could identify each ship at a glance. He had explored every nook and cranny aboard the Liberty ship, and he had read every book he could borrow from his friends. The squads had met daily for "brain sessions" to go over and over every minute detail of command and co-ordination required for a squad to operate in combat, and he had accompanied Sergeant Honda to the meetings for the same purpose at platoon level. All these activities left him little time to contemplate what awaited him at the other end of the trip, and this is what he wanted.

One morning they could see land off the port bow for the first time in three weeks. As they approached, land also appeared to starboard. Word passed around that they were passing through the Strait of Gibraltar. "Just think," said Horace, "For twenty-one years, I never get further outside L.A. than Santa Barbara, and now in two years, I travel across the whole country, and now at the same time can see Europe and Africa. Why is everyone so quiet? This isn't enemy territory, is it?"

"It shouldn't be." answered Ken. That's Spain to the left–they're neutral–and that's Morocco to the right, and that's now in Allied hands. I guess the only danger is what we've been facing all across the Atlantic–U-boats." As Ken spoke, there was a tremendous explosion to their rear. One of the tankers was engulfed in flames. The Liberty ships plodded onwards, but most of the destroyers started scurrying around, some to the aid of the tanker, now dead in the water with men jumping overboard, and others to a spot to the right rear of the convoy, evidently where the submarine that fired the torpedo had been located. The destroyers dropped depth charges and after fifteen minutes the apparent frenzy stopped. Later that morning, the ship's captain reported that there was a confirmed sinking of the U-boat. It was a sober group of soldiers who passed the sentry-like Rock of Gibraltar and entered the Mediterranean Sea later that day.

They continued their zigzag course and after two more days dropped anchor in the harbor at Palermo, Sicily. Ashore for the first time in nearly a month, they swayed as they walked down the still rubble-strewn streets. Palermo had been captured ten months before, and the Italians surrendered two months later, so there was a combination of civil and military occupation government. The Allies were interested in it primarily as a place to build up supplies for the campaign in Italy and for an R&R area. The men of the 442nd were inhibited in their relaxing until they ran into some men from the 100th Battalion, there recuperating from wounds suffered at Anzio. Soon the beer and the conversation flowed freely. The men from the 100th described the long, bloody, unsuccessful assault on Monte Cassino, and then the prolonged stalemate on the Anzio plain before the recent breakout.

"How does it feel to see a man you've shot at get hit and die?" asked Horace of a PFC from the 100th.

"Fahst time tough, man," answered the young man. " But when I see my buddy get heet, I teenk 'Hell wit dem and dees damn wah. Eef eet's dem or me, you can bat eet no be me'." He guzzled his beer, asked for another one and added, "Den I feel good." But he didn't smile. "Anyway, wheah you buggahs from?" And so the conversations went, with the men from the 442nd probing, and the men from the 100th preferring to talk about home or the humorous or ridiculous anecdotes that occur in war.

The men watched as tanks were loaded onto their ship from the Palermo docks. "Eh! Where dose tanks going?" yelled Shimabukuro to one of the soldiers loading the tanks.

"Italy," was the disinterested reply.

"Yeah, I know. But what unit?" persisted Tyrus.

"Hey, buddy," answered the loader, stopping for a moment and throwing his cigarette butt into the water. "How would I know? Do I look like General Clark?" He lit another cigarette and went back to his work.

"Tink dey goin' suppoht us?" asked Tyrus, this time of his friends.

"You think we look like General Clark?" asked Horace.

"Eh! I nevah see dees General Clahk, you know, but I bet he look moah like dat buggah dan you guys." The men laughed, but Ken knew that they perceived they were being dealt with as 'buddies' and not as Japs, for the first time.

The ship left Palermo that night and entered the harbor at Naples two days later. They arrived off Naples during the night but had to steam around in circles until it was light. When the men saw the devastation of the harbor, it was clear why a pilot came aboard to steer them in to the dock. The men saw a sunken ship every half mile, and with the circuitous course the ship took, they realized there must be other ships just under the surface. It was nearly noon when the ship tied up at the dock and the men were hurried off the ship. Most of the Naples docks were still damaged beyond use, and the loading and unloading went on around the clock without time to stand at the rail and admire the beauty of Italy. In fact, there was nothing beautiful to see. If Palermo had been somewhat war-damaged, Naples was utterly destroyed. As the men formed up quickly carrying their full battle gear and marched to some waiting trucks half a mile away, they saw that no buildings had escaped the devastation. The trucks carried them through city streets that had been cleared out by bulldozing rubble into side streets. To Ken, it looked like a tunnel. As he looked over the walls of rubble from his elevated vantage point in the truck, he could see life going on. There were lines of people everywhere. People standing in line hoping to get food, water and heating materials, he found out later. Very few roofs were still intact, and most of the people lived in lean-to hovels created out of the rubble.

When the trucks left Naples, they headed south. After nearly an hour on the shell-holed road they arrived at Pompeii, which was to be their staging area. The afternoon was spent in setting up their tents, locating the field mess and getting used to the fact that after all this time they were finally in Italy.

Horace was trying to be the tour guide. "See that mountain?" he said pointing to the north, "That's Mt. Vesuvius. It erupted and covered the town of Pompeii. It's just been recently that they've excavated and found all kinds of interesting things."

"Hey. How you know dat?" asked Shimabukuro.

"From history, Buckaroo. They talked about it in my history courses."

"Hey, wen dat happen?" Tyrus persisted.

"Oh, uh, maybe a couple hundred years ago?" guessed Horace.

"Naw, loook, I come from Hawaii. Volcanoes all time blow up on Big Island. Eef dat volcano blow up couple hundred yeahs befoah, wheah all kind da kine lava? Dees all plain dirt and beeg trees and stuff. I bat eet tousands yeahs befoah."

"I think Buckaroo's right," added Kaz Ishii. "I think it erupted in Roman times. That's why the excavation is so interesting. It shows us what things were like in those times."

Horace sputtered a bit at having his authority as tour director undercut but did not pursue the argument. Later that day a Red Cross lady came by and tacked a notice on a telephone pole announcing a tour of the ruins of Pompeii the next afternoon.

"Now we can find out for sure when Vesuvius erupted," said Ishii as he and Ken read the notice.

"Yeah," agreed Ken. "Kaz, when was the last time you were interested in a notice on a telephone pole?"

"I was thinking the same thing. The notices that we had 48 hours to get ready to go to camp."

"We went to Santa Anita, which was a staging area for detention camp. Now we're in a staging area for we really don't know what." The two men studied the poster for a few more minutes, lost in their own thoughts and then walked back to their tents.

The next afternoon as the men were getting ready for their tour of Pompeii, Horace asked Tyrus why he wasn't getting ready.

"Eh, you guys go tell me about da ol' town. Eh, for me, I get one ride to Naples and goin' catch up wit' someting more modern," Tyrus answered.

"You mean you've no sooner got to Italy than you're going to find some prostitute and pick up the local diseases?" asked Horace.

"Hey, Yam, I nevah like heah you comment on what I do, eh? You do wat you like, and I do wat I like, eh? Dey have da kine purple stuff to treat you wit fo' prevent da clap, you know."

When the men came back from their tour of Old Pompeii, Tyrus was gone. The next morning, a somewhat hung-over Shimabukuro went to the medics and came back shortly with the tell-tale purple stain on his pants from the potassium permanganate treatment that was standard, though not very effective.

"So how was the tour of the dens of iniquity of Naples last night, Buckaroo?" asked Horace.

"Shut up," was the only reply.

"We had a great tour of Old Pompeii. You were right. The eruption was in..."

"I say 'Shut up!' Eef you no shut up, I goin' poosh your nose back to da back of your head."

Horace shut up.

For the next several days, the men from the 442nd cleaned their weapons, packed and repacked their packs and impatiently followed the news of the Allies entering Rome. The next day, they permanently broke camp and loaded onto trucks to return to the Naples docks. As they waited to load onto LST's, the Navy dock workers told them that the invasion of northern Europe had begun at a place called Normandy in France.

"I knew it," moaned Horace. "The war's going to be over before we get into it!"

CHAPTER 14

THERE WAS NOT MUCH TIME TO EITHER CELEBRATE the northern invasion nor to worry about missing the war. As soon as the LST's left the Naples harbor and entered the Tyrrhenian Sea, they turned north towards their destination at Anzio, and then they met the rough seas they had avoided on the trip over from America. Soon the soldiers were draped over the rails vomiting. At one point Ken realized he'd have to hold tight to the railings lest he fall overboard when the ship pitched. Eventually though, he decided he didn't care if he fell over. Perhaps the sea itself would cause him to be less seasick. It was an overnight trip to Anzio, and in the war zone no lights were allowed on the deck at night. After sundown, a trip to the rail was extra-hazardous because of the vomit on the deck. Many a soldier finished his trip to the rail sliding on his back. The 442nd Regimental Combat Team was therefore probably the unit most relieved to arrive on the Anzio plain during the entire war.

As they walked ashore, their nausea finally cured, they knew they had arrived in the war zone. The devastation in Naples was extensive, but it was mostly Italian and civilian. The devastation here showed destroyed tanks and jeeps and half-tracks, emblazoned with the white star of the American Army. The Anzio plain may well have been an attractive farming area, but now, after four months of intensive fighting, it was shorn of all vegetation. Occasional fields of stalks were recognizable as former corn fields or vineyards, but the landscape was black-brown instead of the lush green of an early June. It also afforded no trees to hide under when the sudden sound of approaching low-flying planes was heard. Men hit the ground and tried to burrow in as they heard the ack-ack of the air defense followed by nearby explosions. They looked to see less than two hundred feet up three dive bombers with black

Maltese crosses roar overhead.

"Eh. Now I've seen eet all," said Ben Watanabe. "I was in Aiea on December 7, and I see all da red suns on da planes. Now dees. Eh, when am I goin' be able deesh eet out?" The last question was an angry cry.

"Hang in there, Ben, I don't think it's going to be very long now," yelled Ken. "Stay down men, there may be more!" There were no more, but when the men got to the trucks, one was burning, the target of one of the Luftwaffe bombs. As they passed it, two men with a stretcher opened the driver's door, and loaded a charred corpse onto it. No one complained as the men were forced to squeeze into the remaining trucks.

"You know, that guy was killed waiting to drive us," said Horace to no one in particular. No one answered.

Slowly the trucks moved inland and then north. Finally, the men began to note that the burned-out vehicles by the roadside were mostly German, and Watanabe became a little encouraged that he'd soon be on the "deeshing it out" side. The convoy moved slowly, sometimes waiting at crossroads for hours for unknown reasons. The men needed no encouragement to unload from the trucks during those times and seek what shelter they could. They heard occasional air battles in the distance but experienced no more close calls. Averaging twenty miles a day, on the third day they crossed the Tiber River as it flowed from Rome to the sea.

"Look at that road sign!" called Mike Matsunaga. "But what's that under it?" The sign, bullet-marked and hanging precariously from its post, pointed to the right. It read "ROMA 10 KM". Under the sign was a new addition: "The one-puka-puka was here, June 4".

"Hey!" yelled Shimabukuro,"da one-puka-puka was here da night before dey take Rome. Eh, da one-puka-puka guys coulda been da ones take Rome."

"One-puka-puka?" asked Horace.

"Yeah. Puka means hole, so "one-hole-hole", you know, 100. You haole Japanese, you nevah goin' learn."

The convoy continued north through Civitavecchia and that afternoon joined the 100th in bivouac. After tents were set up, the men met with their friends from the 100th, in some cases the men who had trained with them at Camp Shelby and been early replacements for the 100th, and in a few cases for the Hawaiians, men they'd known from home. The reunions were initially joyous, but soon gave way to soberness.

"Eh, and you remembah Takano?"

"From McKinley? Da guy in da band?"

"Yeah. He *mahke* een Monte Cassino."

"Nah! Really?"

"And Soogs Sugiyama. He *mahke* een Anzio, I teenk befo' he even fire one shot."

"What's this *mahke*?" asked Horace of Tyrus.

"You know. Die. Sugiyama, hey, he one good football playah. Hey, I nevah make all dose yahds witout Soogs blocking for me. Soogs wen' get killed? Hey, I no can believe eet." And so the litany of soldiers killed and wounded from the 100th Battalion went on.

Ken sought out Doug Furuya but hardly recognized him. A twenty pound weight loss had made him gaunt.

"No, I haven't been wounded," answered Doug to Ken's question. "But almost every other officer in my company has been. If anyone ever thought this would be an easy and glorious way to win the nation's respect, they're wrong. I'm very thankful I haven't been hit, but it's almost as hard watching your men go down every day, sometimes men whose names you haven't even had a chance to learn yet. And then you look back over the territory you've won, sometimes just a couple hundred yards, and it doesn't seem worth it. And, you know, I'm only talking about the breakout from Anzio after I joined the battalion. I can't even imagine what it was like at Salerno and Monte Cassino and the mountains in the winter. The guys who went through those battles just say it was rough and go on to other topics. That's where the 100th got the nickname 'Purple Heart Battalion'. At first I thought it was an insult, you know, 'Don't you guys have the sense to come in out of the bullets?', but in the weird thinking of war, it's a complimentary term. Anyway, how have you guys been doing since I saw you last?"

Ken described the loading and movement to Virginia of the regiment and the slow trip over to Europe. He described the sinking of the tanker and the U-Boat, the day in Palermo and then the devastation of Naples.

"Yeah, Naples really got it coming and going," interjected Doug. "We bombed it coming in, and the Germans bombed it going out. And then they left a lot of booby-traps in town. We may have had more injuries after we got into town than we did going in. Did you see all those wrecks in the harbor? They sank a bunch of boats intentionally and then destroyed the docks to try to slow us up. Fortunately, they didn't do that with Rome. They declared it an open city or something like that, so it escaped a lot of damage. Not that they let us enjoy it."

Ken's eyebrows raised at that last sentence."What do you mean?"

"Well, we got within ten kilometers of Rome the night before the official capture. We could have been in the center of the city in two hours, but they stopped us. It seemed the whole Fifth Army rolled past us that night, and the next day we just continued on north through the outskirts of the city. A lot of us were really upset, and, of course, some thought it was prejudice again."

"Was it?" asked Ken.

"Oh, probably not. It turned out they'd sent the battalion staff back to arrange the meeting-up with you guys, and that's why we stopped. The brass has been very complimentary of the 100th. General Clark has said we're his best unit."

"Well, we saw a very unofficial sign saying the 100th had been there," said Ken.

"Oh, yeah," Doug chuckled. "I saw that. You mean the 'one-puka-puka' sign. I probably should have taken that sign down, but it expressed the feelings of so many of the guys, I just left it there."

"So are the two units together now?" asked Ken.

"Yes. That was the reason for the meeting of the battalion and regimental officers. We are now your first battalion, and the regiment is part of the 34th Division. But we maintain our designation as the 100th Battalion, and that's a big deal in the Army. It means they feel that the combat record of the 100th is good enough that they want to keep the name. Not bad for a bunch of Japs in nine months, huh?" Ken smiled his agreement but remembering back to the listing of the killed and wounded he'd heard that morning wondered if it was worth it.

The next ten days were spent in establishing co-ordination between the battalions and in the attempted transfer of war wisdom from the men of the 100th to the newly arrived battalions. The 100th/442nd, as they were now generally referred to, left the staging area on June 21 and five days later relieved the 517th Parachute Infantry Regiment on the front lines.

"Ken, I want you to take your men, cross that road up there and then advance along the side of the road under the trees," Sergeant Honda said as the two men peeked over a small ridge at what appeared to be a peaceful Italian countryside. "We'll cover you from here, and if you make it to the trees without opposition, we'll go down to that stream bed, then we'll both converge on that group of buildings at the crossroads. Intelligence says Germans were in the buildings yesterday, but maybe they cleared out overnight."

"Let's hope so."

"Now, when you're going up along the road, you be ready to lay down some covering fire for us, because we'll be exposed for about 100 yards."

"O.K. Sarge."

The half of the squad that was with Ken made it to the road without drawing fire, but as they started advancing and watching the other half with Sergeant Honda starting out across the field, a sudden onset of fire erupted from the crossroads aimed at the other group.

"Get down, men! Lay some fire on the crossroads. See where the fire's coming from?" yelled Ken. No sooner had his men done that than they started drawing fire on themselves. The fire was heavy, and the trees, which had seemed so thick a few seconds ago, provided very little protection. The bullets kicked up dirt and leaves around them.

"Keep it up, men. Let Honda and his men get down into that stream bed!" But it was hard to get their heads up enough to fire off a few rounds without drawing all the fire from the crossroads onto themselves. There was a scream to Ken's right.

"I'm hit! Medic!" cried the panicked voice.

"Whose voice was it?" thought Ken. "Matsunaga or Murakami? The medics aren't close enough to help him before we can silence that crossroads. He kept firing. When will Honda get there? It must have been half an hour since we've been pinned down here! They must have a platoon at that crossroads."

After what was closer to five minutes than a half-hour, Ken heard increased firing at the crossroads and then three hand grenades. The firing stopped.

"Come on up. We got them," called Kaz Ishii from the crossroads. Ken went over to the wounded man. It was Mike Matsunaga. In the lull, Mike was sitting up and inspecting his right forearm. His sleeve, now torn off, was soaked with blood, but he seemed to be able to move his forearm and hand well.

"I guess it's not as bad as I thought it was," said Mike quietly. Ken wrapped the wound and sent Mike back for care and then joined the squad at the crossroads. They were looking at two dead Germans, who had been manning a machine gun from the upper floor of one of the buildings.

"You mean it was just one machine gun? I thought it must have been a platoon," said Ken. "What are you guys doing all standing around in a group here? Why doesn't Sergeant Honda have you in defensive positions? Where is Sergeant Honda?"

"He was hit back there. I think he's dead. It was the first burst from the machine gun," said Kaz.

"What? Where is he?"

"Back in the field there, just after we left the crest of the hill."

"O.K. Spread around the buildings and stay out of sight," ordered Ken. He retraced the advance of the other half of the squad and found Sergeant Honda lying without signs of life fifteen yards from where he had started his war. "He didn't even have a chance to fire his weapon," muttered Ken. After a few more seconds, he picked up the sergeant's walkie-talkie, and returned to the crossroads.

"Raging Lion 3, this is Raging Lion Sugar, over," he yelled into the radio. After two more calls, the call came back.

"Raging Lion Sugar, this is Raging Lion 3, over."

"Raging Lion 3, this is Raging Lion Sugar," Ken said. "Tell Lieutenant Watson that Sergeant Honda is dead. Over."

After a few seconds, Lieutenant Watson's voice came over the radio. "Raging Lion Sugar, this is Raging Lion 3. Who am I talking to, and what is your situation? Over."

"Raging Lion 3, this is Raging Lion Sugar. Hayakawa, sir. We're at the crossroads. One man was wounded, in addition to Sergeant Honda. Over."

"Raging Lion Sugar, this is Raging Lion 3. Defend the crossroads and await further orders. Out."

Ken set his defenses around the four buildings at the crossroads and settled back to think squad leaders' thoughts. Despite the year of being assistant squad leader, it was a whole new challenge to make the decisions a squad leader has to make. What should we do if they counter-attack down this road, or down this other road? Suppose they come over that field? What if they start shelling us? He looked at the mountains that rose from the coastal plain. It reminded Ken of pictures he'd seen of ancient Roman amphitheaters. His squad was on the stage, but instead of the people throwing bunches of flowers from the stands, they might soon be lobbing shells. What was the medical school class at Creighton doing about now?

Several hours passed, and though they could hear considerable gunfire off to their left, the men of Third squad, Third platoon, Company E were uninvolved. In the quiet heat of late June, Ken was almost dozing off, when Lieutenant Watson came up from the rear. "The battalion's running into a lot of opposition. The objective is a town named Belvedere up there over that first ridge. We're on the right flank. Our new orders are to jump off at 1700." He showed Ken a map and described the route of advance and the first objective. There'll be an artillery barrage from H minus 15 minutes until H-hour. When the barrage lifts, you move your squad out. We should have about two more hours of light." He paused a few seconds. "That's too bad about Sergeant Honda. I'm going to have to write a letter to his folks. They're confined in camp in Idaho - Minidoka. It doesn't seem right, does it?"

Ken didn't answer that question but asked one of his own. "Who are you sending up to take Sergeant Honda's place, Lieutenant?"

"You're it, Hayakawa. Any doubts?"

"No, sir," Ken lied.

The squad moved out when the artillery barrage lifted and started moving up the hill. When they were twenty minutes out of the crossroads, German artillery started dropping all around them. They retreated to cover behind some boulders. When they tried to move out again, they drew more fire, this time machine gun fire.

"Ishii, you take your men and go up that draw while we lay down some cover, and see if you can find that machine gun," said Ken. "When the four men left the cover of the rocks, they drew an overwhelming amount of fire and quickly turned back.

"There's more than one machine gun there, Ken," said Kaz. "Maybe we should go back down the hill a ways and then cross over and see if we can get above them."

"O.K. Give that a try and see how you do." Kaz and his men left while the rest fired in the direction the machine gun fire had come from. But every time they raised their heads to fire, a torrent of bullets came their way, chipping the rocks and driving them back to cover.

Eventually they could see Ishii and his men moving up the ridge to their right, but the Germans evidently discovered them at the same time and again a hail of bullets pinned them down. When they disappeared below the horizon, they were split into two groups, with the Germans returning their fire ten to one every time they looked out from behind their cover.

"...We're pinned down, Lieutenant," Ken called over the walkie-talkie.

"...O.K. When it's dark enough, move back to your crossroads and set up defensive positions. The whole battalion's bogged down..." came the reply.

It was nearly midnight by the time Ken got the message to the other half of the squad and they were able to move back to their crossroads and take up defensive positions.

"Talk to me, Horace. You haven't said a thing all day," said Ken as he checked the men at their posts.

"What's there to say? This is a ... this is a...mess," said Horace, choking back tears. "I didn't know war was going to be like this."

"What the heck did you think it was going to be like? Some umpire saying 'You guys did a better flanking maneuver than the other guy, so you get to occupy that town?'"

"No. I don't know. But here we are after one day of combat and one guy's dead and another wounded, and we're about three hundred yards from where we were this morning. Are we going to lose two men for every three hundred yards? To hell with it! And this evening, the Germans must have shot ten thousand bullets at us, and we're in the same place we were. It's a miracle no one got hit in that little trip up the hill. And did you see those Germans rotting up there?' he indicated the two machine gunners killed earlier in the day. "That one kid can't be more than fifteen years old!"

"Horace, I believe I remember you standing up in the mess hall at camp and telling us how this was the way to prove our loyalty." The tears were flowing freely, but now silently from Horace's eyes.

"Yeah, I remember that," Horace said after a little while. "I didn't know it was going to be so hard to do."

The next day, the squad tried a different approach but again were thrown back to their crossroads with a huge deluge of shells coming from the hills. When a third day's attempt was thrown back, Lieutenant

Watson told them to stay at the crossroads. By that day, the dead Germans were beginning to smell, and at Ken's request, some men from Graves Registration came up to identify and bury them. The men of the 442nd somberly watched the men go about their unpleasant task.

"You know, I teenk I should be one happy Hawaiian to see dose SOB's who keel Sergeant Honda get buried, but you know...." Shimabukuro's voice trailed off, and none of the others asked him to finish his thought.

That night, there was the sound of a terrible battle up in the area of what had been their objective, the town of Belvedere. In the morning, they moved out, without opposition and took up defensive positions beyond Belvedere.

"When 2nd and 3rd Battalions couldn't take the town head on," Lieutenant Watson explained, "the 100th came around behind, sealed the town off and wiped out or captured the whole garrison occupying it."

"Maybe we ask da one-puka-puka teach us how to deesh it out," commented Watanabe.

"Don't worry," Lieutenant Watson assured him, "this is a big country, and we've just started. We'll have plenty of opportunity to dish it out before we're through."

"But at what cost," said Yamashita, loud enough for only Ken to hear.

The next ten days proved the lieutenant right. There were a series of battles, with first one battalion and then another leapfrogging to be in the "hammer" position against the anvil of the other two battalions. Towns with names like Sassetta and Castagneto and Bibbona fell to men with names like Kazumura and Takahashi and Masuda. The squad finally began to see some success in their maneuvers. Even Horace's depression began to lift slightly. Though he had been effective in doing his job, Ken had begun to worry that the terrible toll of dead and wounded would soon overcome Horace. There had been no time for preventive psychology, however, and Ken had done nothing more than try to cheer him up on the few occasions when there was time to rest. So when he began to show some of the old Yamashita spunk as they crossed the Cecina River, Ken was relieved. Their next objective had the unromantic name of Hill 140, and Company E's mission was a frontal assault. Soon they ran into more machine gun fire than they'd seen since the debacle at Belvedere.

"Kaz!" said Ken, "Take Horace and Ben, and see if you can get the high ground over there and lay us down some fire on those machine gun nests." Ken and the rest tried to keep the attention of the machine guns but in the process seemed to be receiving much more fire than they were giving.

"So what? You tink dose guys stop fo' beah?" said Tyrus, as he ducked back behind a rock. "Eet must be half houh seence dose guys take off."

"It's been ten minutes, Buckaroo," said Matsunaga, now back with the squad, a bandage covering his right forearm. "Keep firing, man."

Finally the machine gun fire dropped down considerably, and the men started up the hill, firing their weapons from the hip. Suddenly there appeared a figure on the ridge top to their right, running towards the machine guns, firing and yelling something unintelligible. He fell once but got up and continued forward, this time staggering but still yelling. Ken could now hear "Go For Broke" and "deesh eet out" among some obscenities, and he recognized Ben Watanabe. Watanabe threw three hand grenades, stumbled one more time, got up and fell again, this time staying down. The machine guns were silent. Ken and the rest of the squad met Ishii and Yamashita at the scene of the disaster. Seven Germans lay dead around three machine guns.

"How's Watanabe?" asked Ken.

"Dead," answered Kaz. "He must have taken ten bullets."

"Why'd you have him rush the guns?" asked Ken.

"I didn't tell him to do that. We were distracting some of their fire, but they were well covered. We weren't going to be able to move them any better than you guys were. Ben just suddenly jumped up, said something about dishing it out, and started running."

"Yeah, we saw the rest," said Ken. Shimabukuro and Murakami had brought Watanabe's body back and laid it respectfully in a place where it could be retrieved. The others took defensive positions while the rest of the platoon moved up on their left.

"Horace! What's the problem with your right hand?" asked Ken, suddenly noticing a blood-soaked bandage around it.

"Nothing."

"Whaddya mean nothing? That bandage is soaked."

"It's just a flesh wound," answered Horace.

"Let me see it. Flesh wounds don't bleed like that. Against Horace's objection, Ken began to unwrap the bandage. As he got it undone, the blood began to spurt forth, and the little finger was hanging by a small piece of skin. He hastily rewrapped it and applied a tourniquet.

"Tyrus. Come here and take Horace back to the aid station. They're going to have to amputate this finger the rest of the way."

"No. Ken. It's going to be O.K," argued Horace, but by that time Shimabukuro had him firmly in tow.

"Look, hero, I no need lose two good friends een one day. You shut up and come wit me, or I peek you up an' carry you on my shoulder," Tyrus lectured him as they walked down the hill. When he returned an hour later, he said Horace had passed out as they arrived at the aid station. The battalion surgeon had revived him with blood and sent him back to the field hospital "for a formal amputation."

When Hill 140 was finally secured, the 100th/442nd continued their drive to the north with the ultimate goal of securing the port of Leghorn. Every little town and every hill that afforded some cover for their artillery became a defensive stronghold for the German Army, and each one required meticulous clearing out by men of the regiment. Individual heroics became commonplace, and the toll of wounded and dead rose alarmingly.

Four days after he had been evacuated, Horace returned to the squad. When Ken saw him and his wound, he was suspicious.

"Didn't they give you 'return to duty' papers?"

"Naw. They just said 'go'."

"Horace, there are still stitches where they amputated your little finger."

"Yeah, they said you could take them out. I told them my squad leader was almost a doctor."

"Horace, I know they don't do that. They would assign you to an R&R center and then probably to some non-combat job if not back to the States."

"Well, they said just to go back and join my unit."

"I'm going to look into this Horace. I don't believe they told you that, and if they did, it was wrong." Ken started for platoon headquarters.

"Wait, Ken. You're right. They didn't send me back, but before you say anything, listen to me. You understand what we Japanese are doing over here, right? We're trying to prove ourselves. Well put yourself in my position. I've always been the shortest guy in the group. I was always the last guy chosen for baseball and football. Whenever anybody wanted to prove his manhood, he'd always start a fight with me because I'm so short. You've heard the 'short jokes' even here in the platoon. I've heard them all. That's why I was so vehement about our volunteering. Now I get a minor wound after ten days of combat and I'm out for the rest of the war. I've got a whole lifetime to go of being short. Don't turn me in."

Ken sat down and thought for a whole minute. "Horace, I thought I understood you. Now I don't know. You're crazy, you know that? We'll see what happens."

Four days later, Lieutenant Watson called Ken to his headquarters. "I got a report that Yamashita went AWOL from the field surgical hospital. You know anything about that?"

Ken took a deep breath and told the lieutenant the story Horace had told him four days previously. "He seems to be getting his strength back. We've kept him off the front line. I got a pair of surgical scissors from the medic and plan to remove his stitches in about a week. The wound is clean."

It was Lieutenant Watson's turn to sit and think for a while. "Well, we can't keep him here in AWOL status, but Sergeant Strong knows someone at division that can take care of that. In fact, he was telling me he did the same thing for a guy in first platoon just the other day. You guys are crazy, you know that?"

"Yessir. I know that," answered Ken.

CHAPTER 15

A ILEEN WAS BESIDE HERSELF WITH ANTICIPATION. "Miss Aiko, you've hardly touched your dinner," said Masayo. The "Miss" was added when Jun was around.

"I can hardly wait for Momma and Myrna to get in," said Aileen. "First thing in the morning I'm going up to Mt. Tapotchau and watch for their ship. As soon as it passes through the reef, I'll come down to your office. Won't it be fun to see them again, Daddy?"

"It certainly will, Aiko. Will you be able to get down from the mountain in time, once the ship crosses the reef?"

"Oh, yes, I'll come running. I bet I can make it in fifteen minutes. Well, maybe an hour, but it'll take them at least that long to clear the harbor red tape." She immediately realized she'd hit a sore point with her father.

"I don't mean red tape, Daddy. I mean the customs and medical clearance that all ships have to go through." Too late.

"Well, I certainly hope you don't mean red tape, young lady, because I've worked hard over the last six months to smooth the process for entering and leaving Saipan. I've instituted..." and so the lecture began. At least, Aileen thought, it would relieve some of the acuteness of her anticipation to listen to her father's lecture on harbor-clearing procedures in Saipan.

Her plan was to arise at daybreak, dress quickly and climb to the peak of the mountain. She awakened, however, about 3AM and when she couldn't get back to sleep, dressed and headed up the mountain while it was still dark. When she arrived at the first gun emplacement, she was surprised by the frenetic activity in the dark. She startled at the challenge: "Who goes there?" She mumbled who she was and where she was going. "You may not go further. You must go back!" She was so frightened that she did not ask why but turned around and started down the mountain. As soon as she was beyond the vision of the soldiers, she sat on a rock to gain her composure. After a few minutes, she noted the dawn was beginning to break and for the first time looked to the west. She could not believe her eyes. There in the growing sunlight, just beyond the reef the sea was gray. Gray with ships. It appeared to Aileen that the ships were lined up deck-to-deck. It looked as if one could walk from ship to ship from opposite Garapan down to the corner of the island where she had picnicked and talked with the artillery pillbox soldiers a few months ago. So today was the day of the invasion. She looked to the north where the ship bringing her mother and sister would come from but knew there would be no way it would arrive today. What would happen to it? Would it be sunk? Suddenly there was a terrible noise that hurt her ears even though it started five miles away. Seemingly every ship in the fleet opened its fire at the same moment. Ten seconds later the southern beaches began to explode as the first volley hit. From her vantage point, Aileen could see the coconut trees snap in two and huge geysers of sand and water spray into the air. Straight south from where she sat was Aslito Airfield. Dive bombers were hitting the airfield wave after wave. Although from that distance she could not distinguish one plane from another, it did not appear that many planes were taking off from the airfield.

For two and a half years, Aileen had dreamed of this moment, when the Americans would fight back, end the war and allow her to "go home". Her dreams always culminated in the American Navy invading for the sole purpose of whisking her up and taking her back to Seattle. She had not bothered herself with the practicalities of how that would work, and now that it was here, all she felt was fear. Thoughts raced through her mind. Was her father safe? Should they stay in their house and wait to get overrun and rescued? Or would their house get shelled? If she was "rescued", would they believe who she said she was? She looked and dressed like a Japanese. How could she convince them she was true-blue American? And what about her mother and Myrna? Were they alive?

In this confusion of thought, she continued down the hill. She could no longer see the shelling, but the volume of the noise was intensifying. When she got home, she found Masayo collecting a few of her things, but Jun was not there.

"Where's Daddy?" she asked.

"He left for his office. He said his place of service was there. He said that if you got home before I left, you should go with me to my family's house in the interior."

"No, Masayo. I need to go be with him."

"But Aileen, they're bombing down at the harbor. It's too dangerous. Come with me."

"Look, Masayo, my mother and sister are probably dead, and I just can't leave my father now. I remember where your family lives. I'll try to convince Daddy that he can't stop the invasion and we should both go to your home."

"But your father gave me strict orders to take you with me. I…"

"Masayo, I'll handle my father. You go now, and we'll join you as soon as possible." Aileen started out the door but then turned and embraced Masayo, who was now weeping. With a tone of courage she wasn't sure she felt, she added in English "Be brave. This is the beginning of the end, Masayo."

As Aileen started down the hill towards Tanapag, she saw six dive bombers aiming for the docks. Antiaircraft fire was heavy in the dock area, and one of the planes was hit as it pulled out of its dive. The explosions from the bombs shook even the ground Aileen was walking on, and when the smoke cleared she saw the damaged plane splash into the sea just off the coast of Managaha Island. As she stopped to watch that, she saw the big guns from the island firing south towards the American fleet. Remembering how close the ships were to each other, she figured that every round must be hitting a target. She hurried on, taking cover every time a wave of dive bombers aimed at the docks, or fighters came flying low strafing the antiaircraft batteries. Soon she was so close and the action was so fierce, she had to take shelter behind a wall.

When there was a lull in the bombing, she ran towards her father's building, just next to the main dock. The building was burning at the opposite end from her father's office. She ran up the steps and burst into his office. Jun Nakamura was sitting quietly at his desk looking out over the harbor. All the windows in the office were shattered, the dock itself was burning, and all the ships in the harbor were either afire or sunk with only their masts above water. Through the roar of the fires, Aileen could hear men screaming. Just then the explosions and the antiaircraft fire began again.

"Daddy! We've got to get out of here!" Jun turned quickly, a glazed look in his eyes.

"Aiko, you were supposed to go with Masayo to her home!"

"Not without you, Daddy. Let's go!"

"I can't go. This is my post!"

"Daddy! The harbor's destroyed. There'll be no civilian ships in or out today. It's a war zone, now. We're civilians. We've got to get out."

"Your mother and Myrna should be arriving today. We must wait for them."

"Daddy! Snap out of it. They're not coming. I don't know where they are, but if we don't get out now we'll never see them again." Jun looked again at his daughter, this time with a clearer look.

"Yes, of course. Do you know where Masayo's family lives?"

"Yes, Daddy, let's go now. The bombs have stopped, but they'll be back. Do you have your truck?"

"Yes, it's just outside."

They ran down the steps, turned the corner of the building and encountered Jun's truck, now a burned-out shell, the tires still smoldering.

"We'll have to walk, Daddy. It's a long way, but let's get going. Maybe we can catch a ride. They started north on the paved road that ran around the island, but immediately had to dive into the ditch as they saw a fighter plane coming towards them strafing the road. Aileen rolled over on her back just in time to see the red, white and blue star on the wings, and the wing guns spurting death aimed at her.

"I think we better go cross-country, Daddy." They headed straight inland and in minutes were walking through a rice field with the sounds of war receding behind them. They came to another paved road, but seeing it full of trucks loaded with soldiers and remembering the strafing planes decided to continue cross-country. After passing through a grove of coconut trees, they came to a field of sugar cane and walked along a dirt road for at least a mile. Now the sounds of war were far behind them. After the cane field ended, they started up a gentle slope and were soon looking out over the ocean to the east. Many American warships plowed back and forth, lobbing an occasional salvo of shells, but clearly the main invasion would come from the west. Below them was a wide dirt road full of troop-laden trucks all heading south to the battle, so far undetected by the American planes. They stopped there and rested.

"Where is Masayo's home?" asked Jun.

"When we went there, we went along that road about another mile north and then inland a bit . Her father has a small farm nestled up against this ridge. I don't know if it's safe going along the road or if we should continue up this ridge and hope we can find their place."

"I think we'd better go down to the road," said Jun. "The underbrush on this ridge is getting thicker and thicker."

"Daddy?"

"Yes, Aiko."

"What do you think happened to Mom's and Myrna's ship?"

"I don't know. We got confirmation that their ship left on time three days ago, and then we never heard anything more about it. Usually when a ship has to turn back to Japan, we hear about it. We've heard nothing more of the *Yashima Maru* since."

"There's no chance they could have been sunk, is there?"

Jun hesitated. "Well, there was a naval battle up there, but I've heard no details of it."

"Daddy! Why didn't you tell me?" Aileen burst into tears.

"I didn't want you to worry, Aiko, and we don't know if they were involved."

"They must have been, or else we would have heard, or they would have arrived this morning."

"Not necessarily," said her father "We just don't know, and aren't you glad they didn't arrive this morning?" Aileen continued to sob.

Finally, Jun said, "We should get going. Let's go down to the road. The truck traffic has been continuous since we've been sitting here. They must be moving all the troops from the north down to the battle. It's going to be a terrible battle."

With great difficulty, they forced their way down the hillside, trying to skirt the thick underbrush. At times they had to plow their way through. When they arrived at the road, their arms and legs were bleeding, and the dress that Aileen had worn specially for the arrival of her mother and sister was shredded. They followed the road north, moving into the ditch about every two minutes whenever a truck rumbled by, kicking up dust. After they'd been on the road for fifteen minutes, they heard an approaching roar behind them and turned to see a plane not a hundred feet off the ground firing at the truck currently approaching them. This time they dived into the ditch just in time to avoid the burst of flames as the bullets found the truck's gas tank. Peeking over the brink of the ditch, they could see soldiers diving for cover on the other side of the road, some of them aflame and screaming. A second airplane followed the first, its guns seeking the soldiers still on the road. When Jun and Aileen finally pulled themselves out of the ditch, they surveyed the scene of chaos in front of them. The truck was blazing and blocking the road for further travel. Several wounded men lay on the road while medics attended them. Charred bodies laid still, their screaming silenced. An officer was trying to assemble his remaining troops in order to continue their movement to the south on foot.

"We'd better get back up into the hills," said Jun. "With those trucks blocked up, they're going to be sitting ducks for more attacks."

"But, Daddy...," protested Aileen looking at her bleeding legs and shredded skirt. "How can we get through that underbrush?" But recognizing the wisdom of her father's decision, and since Jun was already striking up the side of the hill, she followed.

It took them more than an hour to get back up to the ridge, again with tearing of clothes and skin. Before they had gone far, they heard firing and explosions behind them. The Naval Air close support had evidently found the blocked road. Fortunately they could not see it and they hastened all the more up the hillside. When they reached the ridge and sat down to rest, they could see several pillars of smoke rising from where they estimated the convoy had stopped.

"I hope all the soldiers were able to get out of the trucks, Daddy," said Aileen.

"I do too," said Jun after a pause.

"Why do people have to fight wars?" asked Aileen. Jun did not answer his daughter's question. "I mean, I love the United States. I want to have my future there. But I love Japan too. I'm glad we came to Japan so I could appreciate what my heritage is. The Japanese have a gentleness about them and a respect for others and nature... and parents, at a level that we don't have in the United States. But now my two countries are at war with each other. The American boys flying those planes could have been my classmates in Seattle, but the soldiers killed on the road could have been my cousins."

"I can't explain it, Aiko," Jun finally said. "There have been wars since the beginning of time. It has something to do with people wanting power and the desire to dominate others. Once they get a little of the upper hand, they want to go all the way and subjugate the other group just because they're different. I don't know why that is. People have been trying to explain it for ages. That's why we call it the 'damned war'. My plan for you and Myrna was that you'd get a good education in Japan and then make your own decision where you wanted to live. But instead we're wandering around in the bushes on an island in the South Seas dodging bullets!" Aileen stared at her father. She had never heard his long-term plans for his daughters. "We'd better get going," he finally said, "We need to get to Masayo's house before sundown."

They proceeded north up the ridge. They found that if they stayed right on the ridge, they could avoid much of the thicker bushes and get an occasional glimpse of the coast road. Eventually, Aileen estimated they must be opposite Masayo's home, and they headed down towards the coast again. Before they got to the road, she recognized the path to the small valley where the Tenorios' farm was.

"Oh! Aileen, I mean, Miss Aiko. I'm so glad you got here!" called Masayo as she ran to the bedraggled pair walking up the path to their house. She stopped briefly, bowed to Jun and then continued to blurt out, "We've been seeing the planes and hearing the bombs and seeing the smoke, and I was just sure you wouldn't be able to get through. Here let me get you a cup of tea. Let me introduce you to my family." She calmed down long enough for introductions to her parents. Bows all around.

"Mr. Nakamura, you are welcome to our humble home. I regret the circumstances of your visit," said Mr. Tenorio, a large man, nearly completely bald and with laugh lines in his face that belied his currently somber expression. Mrs. Tenorio also was a large woman but moved gracefully as she led Jun to the one overstuffed chair in their home and served him a cup of tea. As they drank, Jun and Aileen described their overland trip and the bombs in Tanapag and along the road. As they listened to the tales of death and destruction, the Saipanese couple silently shook their heads. Eventually, Mrs. Tenorio disappeared and soon returned with a large basin of hot water and a cloth.

"Mr. Nakamura, please come into the bedroom and wash all your wounds. I will get you some of my husband's clean clothes while I wash yours."

"Aileen," whispered Masayo, "Come. Let me show you where you can wash." She led her out the back of the house and up the valley between rice fields. Soon they were following a small stream coming out of a steep escarpment. "Here." said Masayo when they came to a small pool. "Here's where I wash when I want to be cool and refreshed." The usually modest Aileen quickly stripped off her dress and jumped into the pool in her underclothes. The coolness of the water and the shock of the water on all her scratches made her gasp audibly, but soon she was able to relax reclining on a rock and letting the cold water bubble over her. She lost track of time and might even have fallen asleep when Masayo offered her a towel and told her it was time to go home. She also produced one of her own dresses to replace Aileen's torn garment.

It was dark when they returned to the house. Aileen had to stifle a chuckle when she saw her father in Mr. Tenorio's clothes. The waist of the pants had been gathered and rewrapped half way again around his waist and then secured with a rope. The shoulders of the shirt hit him somewhere around the elbows. But he was his usual respectable self as he sat, sipped tea and discussed the program for civilian supply for the island of Saipan, a topic now made obsolescent by the events of the day.

Sleep was fitful that night for Aileen. Masayo had insisted she sleep in her bed while Masayo curled up on the floor. The sound of battle was distant to the south, but the roar of trucks on the coast road half a mile away was nearly constant, punctuated occasionally by strafing from low-flying fighter planes and the shelling from the ships off the coast. At one point, she went out to the porch and was surprised to see her father sitting there.

"What shall we do, Daddy?"

"I've been thinking about that, Aiko. The island has no evacuation plans, and even if they did, the Navy has the island surrounded. The only thing the government did to warn the civilians was to tell them that the Americans love to rape and torture. We know that's a lie, but I'm afraid most Japanese are going to believe them, and there will be wide-spread suicide even among the civilians. I guess there's enough American in me that I don't plan to commit suicide, but I'd hate to be captured and spend the rest of the war separated from your mother."

"Daddy, we don't even know if Mom and Myrna are alive."

"You're right, Aileen. We don't."

"What will happen if we stay here?" asked Aileen. "Wouldn't it get the Tenorios in trouble if they were found to be sheltering Japanese when they're finally overrun?"

"Probably so. I don't know."

The next morning, Jun started to announce that they would leave to continue the trip north, but Mr. Tenorio interrupted him forcefully.

"No! Mr. Nakamura, you cannot travel. It's too dangerous. I've been hearing reports all morning. The American planes are strafing all the roads, and the countryside north of here is even rougher than what you came over yesterday. You must stay here. We have plenty of food. No one knows what's going to happen, but I insist you stay here where it's safer." As an after-thought, he added a bow. Jun argued some more halfheartedly, but when Jose Tenorio mentioned the harm he'd be exposing his daughter to, Jun caved in.

"Well, you are very kind, Mr. Tenorio. We will have to assess the situation daily." The two men bowed to each other.

CHAPTER 16

THE ROAD NORTH FROM HILL 140 DID NOT GET easier for the 100th/442nd. The Germans continued to defend every defensible terrain feature until they were nearly surrounded or the American artillery became overwhelming. They would then evacuate only to set up strong defenses at the next hill. To the men of the third squad, it was a series of flanking maneuvers and frontal attacks. The difference from their first experience with the futile attack on Belvedere was that now they knew they would be successful, even though the battle would be fierce. But it was not without casualties. One of the men in the squad was killed in the battle for the village of Castellina. And Kaz Ishii took a bullet in his helmet as they tried to gain control of the high ground of Monte Pisano. When Ken saw his friend lying still, his face covered with blood, his heart skipped a beat. But when he found a strong pulse and removed his helmet, he saw that the blood was coming from a deep scalp wound and that Kaz' skull was evidently intact. A compressive bandage stopped the hemorrhage, and Kaz had begun to regain consciousness as he was carried to the rear.

After ten days of continuous fighting, there was a lull of sorts. The port of Leghorn, vital to the continuance of the battle up Italy's west coast, had been taken, and the 100th was detached to secure it. General Clark, in an almost embarrassing statement, had "personally selected" the battalion for that job because of his faith in it. The other two battalions were to secure the highway from Leghorn to Florence. For a few days, the men had a little rest and time to heal wounds not severe enough to warrant evacuation. Rifles and BAR's were given a thorough cleaning, and they were served three warm meals a day for the first time since they entered combat.

"Do you realize we've only been on the line for three weeks?" Horace asked Ken as they ate hot franks and beans. "It seems we've been here forever. We were in training for more than a year, but I think everything I've learned about war I've learned in the last three weeks." Ken had noticed a year's worth of change in Horace's emotions in the last three weeks. The anger and tears of the first day when Sergeant Honda was killed had been followed by a morose despondency. He was gradually pulling out of that when he was wounded. After his return, Ken noted a certain carelessness, almost an invitation to get himself killed. He decided to talk to him about it, but after Kaz's injury, Horace stepped temporarily into the position of assistant squad leader. With that responsibility, he began to show a balance of courage and caution as he led the other half of the squad when it was split up.

"You're right, Horace. When I think of my past life, I think of Monte Pisano and Hill 140 and the Cecina River and Belvedere. It's hard to get my mind back to Camp Shelby or Manzanar. And UCLA and Terminal Island might have been in a previous lifetime."

"How do you think the folks are doing back at Manzanar?" asked Horace.

"I don't know. I haven't gotten a letter for two weeks. I was hoping they might bring up the mail in this lull. But I don't know how much to believe of what my mother says. She always says Dad and Howie are doing OK, but then she goes on at great length about Dorothy and Pete. I think that means Dad and Howie aren't doing too well."

"Did she let Pete volunteer?"

"Yes. Of course, now they're drafting Nisei so she didn't have much choice, but Pete volunteered the day he graduated. He's at Shelby now."

"You mean he might be one of our replacements one of these days?" surmised Horace.

"Let's hope the war's over by then."

The next day, Ken and Horace were called to Lieutenant Watson's tent. "Ken, I want you to lead a long-range patrol into Pisa. Our next job is to get across the Arno River. We've heard the Germans have blown all the bridges across it, but we've also had contact from Italian partisans in Pisa. We need to find out if there are still any bridges intact, and if not what's the best way across the Arno. I'm detaching four men from second squad, including a BAR, to you. That'll give you twelve men all together. Here, let me show you on the map. Pisa is about seven miles as

the crow flies. We think the enemy concentration is fairly weak between here and there, but you know our intelligence isn't always the
most reliable. Sergeant Kubota will talk to you about radio frequencies,
extra chow and so forth. I want you to leave as soon as it turns dark
tonight."

"How will we know who to get in touch with when we get to Pisa,
Lieutenant?" asked Ken.

"Well, that part's a little iffy. We think the leader of the partisans is
a fellow named Luigi. The message from them is to go to the Piazza
Venezia, and he'll find you...we think."

They were barely out of earshot on their way back to the squad
when Horace started, "'A little iffy'? He'll find us? What do we do,
stand in the middle of this Piazza Venezia and wait for Luigi to find us?
And Ken, how many people in Italy do you think are named Luigi?
Whatever it is we're trying to prove, they don't make it any easier, do
they?"

The opinions of the rest of the squad were not much different from
Horace's.

"So, Ken!" said Shimabukuro, "Let me get dees straight. We take
off at night and go seven miles troo da woods - no light - carry extra
junk, look for one town we nevah see befoah, but hey, dat's O.K., because intelligence say 'we tink dere's no enemy dere'. Now dese buggahs
are da same guys who say all da Krauts left dakine Monte Pisano, and
hey we get our asses shot off. And den wen we get een Pisa we go up to
da plaza and say 'Hey, Luigi, come get us'. So, Yam! Dees ees wat you
mean by da Gran' Tour?"

Each complaint was more colorful than the last, but Ken noted
they were also very carefully packing extra rations and ammunition,
taking care to remove or tie down anything that would rattle.

As they silently one by one ran across the highway they had guarded
the last two days, no moonlight shone to betray their movements. Horace
led the patrol, and Ken brought up the rear. Soon the canopy of the
forest covered them. Barely able to see the man in front of them, they
picked their way carefully. Every ten or fifteen minutes someone would
stumble over a root and fall. Everyone would hit the ground, expecting
a hail of fire from an unseen enemy. Thankfully, none came. Even when
Tyrus fell, there was no string of invectives, as Ken would have expected.
Rather, he scrambled to retrieve his rifle and get into a firing position.

After three hours, they came to a clearing on some high ground. Before them, they could see in the distance a broad river. Ken left his place at the rear of the patrol to join Horace. Together they surveyed the picture.

"That must be Pisa," said Ken, pointing to their left front. "I hope this Piazza Venezia is in the part of town on the south side of the river. I'd hate to be trying to find a way across the river at sunup." Ken and Horace picked a route to the town and after a fifteen minute rest, the men resumed their advance. Soon, they were in the dark of the forest again.

Suddenly Horace hit the ground, followed in turn by the other eleven men. The word was whispered back down the line, "German outpost. Move back." They did, and Horace came to tell Ken he'd heard and seen a small group of Germans manning a defensive position.

"I'm sure they didn't see us, but I think we should backtrack a ways and make a wide detour," whispered Horace. Ken agreed, and Horace led them far to the west. By the first rays of dawn, they reached the outskirts of town without further excitement.

"What do we do now?" Horace asked Ken as twelve pairs of eyes peered over the edge of a ditch at a farmer loading some newly-picked vegetables onto a dilapidated truck.

"We have to trust him," said Ken. "Let's go." He stood up from the ditch and started to move towards the farmer, followed by the others. When the farmer saw the men approaching, he let out a yelp, dropped his vegetables and raised his hands in the air.

"*Non tiri! Non tiri!*" Then "*Americani! Americani! Amico! Amico!*" He dropped his arms and started to run to the men but stopped suddenly. "*Giapponesi?*" The befuddled farmer stood for a few seconds, his hands half-raised, and then a look of understanding came across his face. "Ah. Goa for Broka Boice. *Aspettari! Aspettari!*" With that, he turned and ran down the road.

"Shall I shoot eem?" asked Tyrus, raising his rifle.

"No!" yelled Ken. "I think he's a friend. Let's move into the barn and wait for him to come back. Each of you take a window."

As the minutes passed, Ken began to wonder about the wisdom of his decision. Finally the farmer reappeared, dragging a somewhat reluctant companion. The companion was a thin young man trying to adjust his glasses, tuck in his shirt and not trip on his untied shoelaces all at the same time. Ken motioned from the barn door, and the two men entered.

"You're American soldiers, Marco says," said the young man in New York - accented English, blinking in the semi-darkness of the barn.

"That's right. Who are you?"

"I'm Paulo diPietro. I'm from New York," answered the young man.

"What are you doing here?" asked Ken.

"I was born in America, but my parents sent me to Italy for my education. I got caught by the war. And what are you doing here?"

Ken hesitated for a moment but quickly decided things couldn't have worked out any better. "We're here to make contact with the partisans. Have you ever heard of Luigi?"

"Yes, of course we've heard of him. But no one knows exactly who he is or where he is. Lately the partisans have been more and more active, sabotaging the Germans and all. It's hard when you go into Pisa not to get caught in a gun battle."

"We're supposed to meet him at Piazza Venezia. Know where that is?"

"Of course. It's not too far from here." Marco, on hearing the words 'Luigi' and 'Piazza Venezia', started talking rapidly with Paulo. Finally Paulo turned to Ken. "Marco knows more about it than I do. He says that the Piazza Venezia is the center of the partisans' activity. He seems to think if you went there, they'd find you."

"Sounds to me like we'd be sitting ducks," said Ken.

Paulo and Marco talked some more, and Paulo said, "He doesn't think so. He says the Germans stay out of that part of town except for one patrol a day around lunchtime." Paulo hesitated a few seconds and then added, "You want me to take you there?"

Shimabukuro spoke up for the first time "Eh. Eef you one American citizen, how come you don't know much about da underground? Hey. Eef it's me, hey I'm een da meedle of all dakine sabotage from da staht."

Paulo looked slowly at the Hawaiian and said in a tone reminiscent of his New York upbringing "Think about it, buster. If you're the Germans trying to root out the underground, wouldn't you go first to the American citizen in the area and torture him for information? I talked to the men from the partisans early on, and we agreed I'd do better to remain a student of the Italian Renaissance and await my time. I've been questioned a few times but was able to convince them I knew nothing, which is true. But I think now is my time."

"O.K.," said Ken. "Take us to the Piazza Venezia."

"O.K., but first tell me why you're Japanese. I mean, are you from Hawaii? We've heard of a unit called the 'Go For Broke Boys'. Is that you?"

"Yes. We're Japanese Americans mostly from California and Hawaii. Our motto is 'Go For Broke', which is Hawaiian slang." He remembered Tyrus' definition of the motto and decided not to get into a discussion of monster waves on the north shore of Oahu.

And so the young American of Italian parentage led the twelve young Americans of Japanese parentage into the town of Pisa early that morning in late July, 1944.

As they got closer into town, the men spread out and tried to stay in the shadows of the buildings, but with the town waking, Ken knew that the approach of twelve American soldiers in full battle gear could not have gone unrecognized. After about a mile, they came around a corner to a widened area where several ancient paths had converged. A fountain, from which water had not sprayed for some time, stood in the middle of the area. The pock marks on the fountain looked recent. Evidently, the Germans did not leave that area of town completely alone.

"This is the Piazza Venezia," announced Paulo. "Marco said to wait here, and someone would find us."

"Shouldn't we wait inside somewhere?" asked Ken. The traffic on the square was increasing.

"Yeah, let's go into this cafe. I know the people here," said Paulo. After a few knocks on the door, a sleepy gentleman opened the door and greeted Paulo. He then looked with surprise at the patrol.

Quickly, he motioned them in. *"Avanti. Avanti,"* he invited and closed the door after them. He and Paulo spoke in whispers.

"We're lucky, you guys. He's associated with the partisans. See? I come here every day for a coffee and I didn't know that. Anyway, he says he's sure our arrival has been seen and that Luigi or one of his lieutenants will be here shortly."

Ken appointed two men to watch the square through the front windows and two more to watch the back alley. He then settled down to contemplate how easily this could be an ambush.

"Two guys approaching!" said Mike Matsunaga from the front window. A quiet tap on the front door signaled the cafe owner to open the door quickly. The first man who entered was a slight, balding man with glasses. He was followed by a husky young man in an undershirt.

"*Professore?*" said Paulo.

"*Si, Paulo,*" said the man, and the two conversed briefly.

"This is my professor. I did not know he was Luigi, the leader of the underground."

"Welcome," said the man in highly accented English. "We have awaited you." He and Paulo spoke again briefly.

"The professor asked me to translate. He says he's happy I'm here, because his English is not very good."

Ken, Horace, Paulo and the professor sat at a table, and Paulo translated while the professor described the bridges over the Arno river. Except for the Ponte Vecchio in Florence, all were destroyed. He then described parts of the river where crossing would be easiest. He opened up a cloth napkin from the table. After courteously asking permission of the cafe owner to draw on the napkin, he drew out the areas of the minefields the Germans had planted guarding the approaches to possible river crossings. When the professor finished drawing, Ken asked about German troop deployments. He had barely started to add those to the napkin, when a sudden alarm from the front window alerted the men of danger.

"Here come the Germans. There are..." Matsunaga's further description was muffled by explosions from the square. The sound of machine gun fire was deafening. Through Paulo, the professor directed Ken and his men to follow the man who had accompanied him to the cafe out the back door. He grabbed Paulo by the wrist and led him up the stairs, and the cafe owner quickly put the chairs and tables back in order. He remembered to replace the map napkin with a clean one from behind the bar. Within ten seconds, no one would have known that anyone had been in the cafe since the night before.

Ken and the patrol followed the professor's burly associate down the alley and away from the sounds of the gunfire in the square. The man moved rapidly for his size, and the men from the 442nd, in their battle gear, had a hard time keeping up with him. They had approached the piazza from the south, now they were leaving to the west.

They were led down narrow alleys, crossing streets only after careful observation. After about a mile, they came to the edge of the city, crossed a shallow creek and climbed up into the surrounding forest. They saw smoke rising from a place that must have been the Piazza Venezia, and Ken wondered how many men had lost their lives because of their meeting with Luigi. Their guide finally stopped and in a combination of English, Italian and hand gestures indicated they should go a little deeper into the forest and then wait for nightfall before returning to their lines. After a quick "Arrivederci," he disappeared down the hill.

The patrol kept moving until they found a thicket which gave them shelter and for the first time in twelve hours they took off their gear and relaxed. After a brief meal, Ken sent Horace and Shimabukuro out to decide how they would get back to their lines after dark. They did their job well, and the patrol reached the front lines without further trouble about 3 AM.

"What's the password?" Horace asked Ken as they lay hidden in the trees on the enemy side of the highway.

"I don't think Sergeant Kubota gave me one," answered Ken.

"Well, what are we gonna do? I don't want to walk across the road and get shot," said Horace. "If you don't know the password, they shoot first and ask why you didn't know the password later, when you're dead."

"You guys don't know da password?" said Tyrus, who had been listening to their interchange. "You need one Hawaiian bail you out again?" With that, he stood up, removed his gear and his shirt. He then took off his undershirt, started to swing it above his head and walk up to the highway, yelling as loud as he could, "I surrendah! I surrendah! I surrendah!" When he was half-way across the road, a faltering voice came from the other side.

"Green." Pause. "Green." When Tyrus kept yelling that he was surrendering, the voice said "What's the password?"

"How I know da password, you dumb ass? I'm one German geevin' up. How I know da steenkin password?"

"Shimabukuro? Is that you?" came the voice.

"Yeah. Who you?"

"Nakashima. Wat da hell you doin' out dere, Shima?"

"Eh! Eet's one long story. Let me an' my buddies come een an' we can seet down talk story."

"Come." said Nakashima, and the rest of the patrol hustled across the highway.

Thirty minutes later, Ken and Horace walked into regimental headquarters to describe their findings to the regimental S2. As Ken took the napkin from his pocket, the major's eyebrows raised. He took the napkin from Ken. "Pure linen. I've got to give it to the Italians. They do everything in style, don't they?" The three men lowered their heads to decipher drawings about river crossings and minefields from an Italian linen napkin.

CHAPTER 17

THE AGREEMENT BETWEEN JUN NAKAMURA AND Jose Tenorio to assess daily the level of danger on Saipan turned into a confusing task. The air battle appeared to have finished, since all the planes flying overhead were American. Not so on the ground. After two days of round-the-clock bombing, the Americans had landed on the southern beaches, only to find tremendous resistance. The roar of distant battle could be heard almost continuously and was moving slowly closer. On one occasion, it appeared that the Tenorio home was a target, but the bomber's aim was errant, and the bombs missed the house badly. Smoke had obscured the sky ever since the invasion. Jose, who took daily information-gathering trips, reported that the Americans had secured the southern half of the island and were advancing northward. Noting the number of field ambulances going north on the coast road and the slowness of the American advance up the 13 mile long island, the two men judged it to be a very bloody war.

On one occasion, after they'd been at the Tenorios' a week, Jun insisted they pursue their trip to the north of the island. They struggled back up to the ridge of the island where the hiking was less impeded, but after two American fighters buzzed them, Jun had second thoughts.

"One of those boys is going to get itchy fingers. I think we'd better go back."

"A very wise decision, Mr. Nakamura," said Jose Tenorio once they returned. "I hear that American planes are patrolling all the roads and strafing anything that moves. You're much safer here."

"But I worry about what it will mean for your family if we're here when the Americans overrun this area."

"Who can say what's going to happen when the civilized countries go to war," said Mr. Tenorio. "They say that if the American soldiers capture you, they torture the men and rape the women. You've lived in America. Is that true, Mr. Nakamura?"

"No, Mr. Tenorio. Americans may not accept foreigners as equals—at least if they're Orientals. But I don't think they would ever rape and torture. So I don't think that would ever be true"

"Oh, Daddy, you know that would *never* be true," said Aileen as she entered the room. She had just returned from a refreshing soak in the cool stream she and Masayo had gone to the first night at the Tenorios'. "I went to school with those boys, and I can't see them torturing anybody."

"Well, the official word is that soldiers and civilians should commit suicide rather than be captured by the Americans."

These discussions went on daily. Jun continued to talk about leaving; Jose continued to assure him that he and Aileen would be safe in his house. Aileen, whose opinion swayed back and forth from day to day, found she could forget their plight only by soaking in the stream, probably the only peaceful place on the island, with Masayo. There, the English lessons continued.

One morning near the end of the third week, Aileen asked her father if he knew what day it was.

"Tuesday," Jun answered.

"I mean the date."

"Yes. It's July... uh, July the fourth. Oh, I see what you mean."

"Think this'll be our day of independence?" asked Aileen.

"I wish I knew what was going to happen, Aiko."

At the stream that morning, the English lesson centered on the meaning of Independence Day. Aileen was having trouble explaining the concept of all men being created equal.

"I thought I heard your father say the Americans didn't accept Orientals as equals?" asked Masayo innocently.

"Well, that's true. I, uh, guess, uh, that 'created equal' might mean that theoretically everyone's equal. Or, I mean, they have equal opportunity. Like, we could go to school with everyone." Aileen thought of the earlier years of the century and the attempts to segregate Japanese children into their own schools, and the segregation of Negro students in the south. She decided not to pursue that line of explanation.

"Well," she continued, " they're always telling stories of the poor immigrants from Europe who came over late in the last century and early in this century and how they set up fruit stands and eventually owned a grocery store. There are thousands of stories like that."

"But they were all white people," Masayo persisted. "Maybe they mean 'all white people are created equal'?"

"No, they mean everybody. I know they mean everybody is created equal. I guess it just takes time. Maybe it's up to us to earn our right to be treated equally."

"How long have Orientals been in America, Aileen?"

"The first Japanese started coming over in 1885, and the Chinese before then."

"That's been a long time."

Aileen was uncomfortable with this conversation. "Well, all I know is that the United States is a great country. There's been prejudice, and there will be prejudice, against people of a different color, but one of these days that prejudice will disappear, whether because we had to earn our rights or the white people just came to the conclusion that America is best as a country of many races. And I want to be there when that happens. Anyway, Masayo, let's talk about the past tense, when you want your verb to refer to something that's already happened...."

As the girls returned to the house, they saw a distant figure pedaling rapidly up the road. Soon Masayo said excitedly, "Oh! It's Pastor Villagomez!" She ran to greet him.

Pastor Villagomez jumped off his bike and hugged Masayo. "Good morning, Miss Nakamura," he said. "I need to talk to you and your father."

"The battle for Saipan is almost over," said the pastor once they were seated in the Tenorios' living room. "I'm afraid the Americans will soon control the whole island. I think they will overrun this house by tomorrow. I don't know how they would treat you. I know Aiko is an American citizen and that you have American connections, but they may also know you were an official in the government. Do you remember Bird Island? We went there a couple of times and picnicked on the beach."

"Yes, I remember it very well," said Aileen. "It's very isolated, and the birds are so noisy."

"That's it," said Villagomez. "My boat is there. I had taken it there a few days before the invasion and had to leave it there. I think God had his hand in that, because all boats on the west side are now sunk. I want you to use it to escape the island tonight. The tide will be low, and you can walk over from the mainland. Both of you know how to run the boat. I'll leave you a map and instructions on how to get to Pagan. That's an island about 200 miles north of here. I have a friend there, a young man named Yuichi Camacho. He's the part-time pastor there, and he'll take you in. If there's any way to get you back to Japan, he'll know the way. Submarines and small freighters occasionally dock there."

"Mr. Villagomez," said Jun, "you are very kind, but you are putting yourself in great danger for my daughter and me. I cannot let you do that."

"Never mind, Mr. Nakamura. You have treated my men and me very fairly over the last several months. That has not always been the case with the Japanese and the Saipanese. I want you to be able to get back with your wife and other daughter before this damnable war ends. Oh! I forgot the most important news. The last message we got before the radio closed down was that the *Yashima Maru* had made it back to Tokyo."

"What?" yelled Jun as he jumped up. "They're safe?"

"No details were given except that the ship arrived in Tokyo on June 28. The message just came in yesterday."

"Oh, Aiko, they're safe!" Jun grabbed Aileen and hugged her in a way he had not done in years.

"Yes, Mr. Villagomez," Jun finally said, calming down and taking his seat again, "you are very kind. We will accept your gracious offer if it means our family gets back together again. Go over the details with me one more time, please."

Carlos Villagomez discussed his plan again with Jun and Aileen, occasionally speaking with Mr. Tenorio in the Saipanese language to co-ordinate the plan.

Finally, the tall, distinguished-looking Micronesian stood up, bowed slightly to Jun and Aileen and pedaled away.

"I must hook up the ox cart," said Mr. Tenorio. We should get going quickly. It may be a long trip, even though it's only about three miles to Bird Island. My wife will pack some food. And Masayo, you pack a change of clothes for them." Before Jun could protest, all three had scurried out of the room to fulfill their assignments.

"Aiko, it looks as if my children will have American

names...Joe?...Mary?...," Masayo said to Aileen as the girls packed for the trip. Aileen looked quizzical. "You know," Masayo continued, "we name our children depending on who owns us at that time. Pastor Villagomez and my parents were born in the Spanish time, so they have Spanish first names. Children born in the German time, like the Villagomez boys, Martin and Juergen, have German names. Children like me, born in the Japanese time have Japanese names." Aileen thought about one country "owning" another but only briefly because Mr. Tenorio was ready to load.

"Goodbye, Masayo, stay safe. Maybe we'll meet next in America."

"Thank you for all your teaching," said Masayo softly, still not certain she wanted everyone to know she had been learning English. "I hope you have a safe trip."

"I'm going to cover you with this tarpaulin and lay some sugar cane over you." said Mr. Tenorio, directing them to lie on the floor of the ox cart. "Pastor Villagomez said it would be safer this way, so soldiers won't stop us and ask where we're taking two Japanese people. They may insist you go with them so you can die for the emperor." He stopped quickly and looked at Jun as though afraid his disdain for dying for the emperor might have shown through his usually respectful speech. Jun was climbing onto the cart, apparently not having noticed Mr. Tenorio's verbal slip.

The ride was distinctly uncomfortable. Saipanese ox carts, unchanged for hundreds of years, did not include shock absorbers. Jun and Aileen, squeezed between the floor of the cart and several hundred pounds of cane, felt every bump on the road. The trip became a little smoother when they turned north onto the coast road, but it was still a bruising ordeal.

"Quiet now," said Mr. Tenorio. "There's a lot of traffic, and we may get stopped. I'm sorry it's so bumpy."

After fifteen minutes, Aileen was almost ready to crawl out from under the tarpaulin and take her chances, when they heard a loud "Halt!"

"Move onto that side road and make way for the convoy!" came the command. The cart moved a short way and then there was blissful rest as the convoy passed.

"What are you doing on this road?" came the harsh voice of the military policeman. "This road is restricted to military traffic."

"Huh. I do not speak Japanese," Mr. Tenorio, whose Japanese was in fact very good, stumbled through the sentence.

"I said this road is restricted to military travel!" said the M.P., raising his voice with the universal assumption that people will understand a foreign language if one speaks loudly enough.

"I do not speak Japanese," Mr. Tenorio repeated.

"And what are you doing carrying sugar cane on a day like this? There's a war going on. Where are you taking it?"

Aileen tensed. They had discussed the fact that it was ludicrous to be transporting sugar cane in the midst of a war.

"Stay here! Here comes another convoy," said the M.P.

The convoy passed. "O.K.," the M.P. said abruptly, "Get out of here, but get off the road whenever you see military vehicles coming."

"Thank you, sir," said Mr. Tenorio haltingly as they drove on.

It took another hour and three more stops before they turned onto a side road and away from the noise of the main road.

"I'll be behind the trees in a few minutes, and I'll let you out then. The island will be just a short walk down the hill then," said Mr. Tenorio.

Soon they stopped. After the sugar cane had been unloaded, Jun and Aileen climbed out of the cart and gratefully walked around, gulping the fresh ocean air.

"I'll leave the sugar cane here and wait an hour or two before I go back." said Mr. Tenorio, "so our friend, the M.P., will not be too suspicious. There are a couple hours until sundown. Pastor Villagomez will be here in about an hour and lead you over to the island. Jun and Aileen looked down the cliff at Bird Island. It rose steeply two or three hundred feet from the small bay and was connected to the beach by a natural causeway under water at high tide but now almost exposed. Palm trees grew out of every crevice in the island's sheer cliffs. A path led to the top of the island, and Aileen remembered the difficulties she and Masayo had when they climbed it on one of their picnic outings. On the far side of the island was a beach just wide enough to build a cooking fire and then to lie down and enjoy the afternoon sun. That was where the boat was. The birds, which gave the island its name circled by the thousands, their calls drowning out all but the loudest conversation.

"Pagan has about a hundred people," Mr. Tenorio said over the bird screeches. "It has a volcano and a large enough flat area that can grow a lot of food, mostly sugar cane of course but also vegetables.

There's a natural harbor, and the Japanese built a good dock when they realized how much the island could produce."

After an hour, Carlos Villagomez arrived. Jun tried to thank Mr. Tenorio in his usual formal way but found the words eluded him. Finally he bowed and squeezed the hand of the Saipanese.

"My father wants to thank you and your wife very much for your kindness," said Aileen, "and I do too. And please thank Masayo also and tell her we'll meet next in the United States." Both men looked a little surprised but turned to their respective journeys.

Villagomez was already halfway down the hill, and father and daughter hurried after him.

"Here's the map. Take a heading of 350° to this first island in the chain—that's only about fifty miles away—and then just go from island to island until you get to Pagan. Can't miss it. I've put extra fuel and food in the boat. Also some extra water. You should be getting there before sundown tomorrow. You'd better get going now."

If there had been any idea of a special goodbye, it was lost in the final instructions on navigating and running the boat. Mr. Villagomez had shown the two Nakamuras the nuts and bolts of running it, but that had been within the reef of Saipan. The idea of navigating towards a target over the horizon and at night seemed a challenge of a different magnitude. Aileen knew that had it not been for the news of Mieko and Myrna, she and her father would have backed out at that point. When he had finished his instructions, Mr. Villagomez waved a quick goodbye and started for the causeway to the mainland, and Jun and Aileen were soon motoring around the point and turning north.

Within minutes, a destroyer came into view. A searchlight illuminated their small boat, and both awaited the shot that could obliterate them. After two minutes, the searchlight switched off and the destroyer sliced away, evidently deciding they were not worth even one shell. The moonlight and the few lights visible on shore allowed them to start in the right direction. But after a couple hours and two more visits from other destroyers, with Saipan gone from view, their confidence waned. Jun sat in the stern handling the tiller, while Aileen, compass in hand, sat on the bow and directed him.

The sea, though calm when they started, began to roll. Aileen found it harder and harder to keep the boat pointed in the right direction.

They estimated they should have passed the first island by one or two in the morning but neither saw it.

"I'm sure when the sun comes up, we'll see the islands, and then we can just go from one to the other until we get to Pagan," said Jun, his voice not as confident as his words.

When the sun did rise, there was no island in sight. As far as Aileen could tell, they were still going 350°, and they had gone far enough, but were they to the east or west of the islands? The sea swells were getting worse. The 32-foot boat seemed smaller and smaller as it traveled up one side of a swell, its propeller breached, and then down the other side. Neither Jun nor Aileen wanted to frighten the other, but their occasional words of encouragement rang hollow. Finally at noon Aileen left her bow post and went to get some food for the two of them. She found that Pastor Villagomez had stocked the boat well. They would run out of fuel before they ran out of food and water. However, that was the concern. Jun had refueled twice and had enough for two more refuelings. If they didn't find an island soon, they'd be drifting free in the Pacific Ocean.

"Look, Daddy! Pastor Villagomez packed two flags for us, one Japanese and one American." Aileen showed the two flags to her father. "Why do you think he did that?"

Jun thought for a minute. "I suppose he figured we might get picked up but he didn't know by whom."

The day progressed, and now the sky clouded over. Soon, they could see rain clouds approaching from the west. Aileen found two raincoats, but when the tropical downpour hit, they did little to protect them. Worse than the drenching, though, was the lack of visibility. If there were an island in the vicinity, they would not be able to see it. The rain continued until nighttime, and they were still heading north, unable to see anything but the sea.

"We've been going twenty-four hours now. Maybe we've overshot Pagan also." wondered Jun.

"I don't think so, Daddy. By dawn, I'll bet it'll be just on the horizon."

"I hope so, and I hope our fuel will last until then."

When Jun refilled the gas tank just before dawn, he said "There's enough fuel for one more refill, about eight more hours."

When dawn came, the storm had disappeared and the sea had become calmer, but still there was no land in sight.

When Jun made the last fuel change about noon, he said "I'm going to turn off the motor and let us drift. That way, if we see some land, we'll have enough fuel left to be able to go towards it. You stay on the front looking that way, and I'll stay back here looking out the back."

"Aiko," said Jun after an hour of unrewarding searching of the horizon. "I'm sorry I got you into this. How stupid of me. If we'd stayed on Saipan, we would be in American hands by now, and you'd be safe. Instead, we're drifting…"

"Daddy! Don't say that. Both of us had the goal of getting back with Mom and Myrna. It wasn't just your decision. As much as I want to get back to America, I'm not going without the rest of you. The three of you are more important to me than where I live. And furthermore, Daddy, don't give up hope. We *will* get rescued. We've still got plenty of food. What we need now is rest. Daddy, you go and get some rest. I'll keep a lookout, and then we'll switch in a few hours."

Jun started to protest but realized the wisdom of his daughter's suggestion. He was asleep as soon as his head hit the bunk.

It was late afternoon when Aileen awakened Jun to take the watch. It seemed she'd only been asleep a few minutes when she heard him yell, "Here we are! Here we are! Aiko! Wake up. It's a submarine! Here we are! Here we are!" Aileen was wide awake and hurried up out of the cabin. Two hundred yards off the port bow, she saw a submarine surfacing.

"Is it Japanese or American, Daddy?"

"I don't know. Go down and get ready to get a flag. As soon as I know which it is, I'll call you and you bring up the right flag." Aileen went quickly down to the cupboard where the flags were.

A head peeked up over the conning tower and looked at the drifting boat through binoculars. Two seamen descended the tower and went forward to man the bow machine gun.

"I still can't tell." whispered Jun to Aileen. "I can't call to them. I don't know what language to call in."

"Raise your hands to surrender, Daddy. I don't want them to shoot you first."

"Who are you?" came the call over a bullhorn finally. The language was Japanese.

"Friends!" yelled Jun in Japanese and then whispered to Aileen "Bring the Japanese flag, Aiko."

Aiko came out of the cabin, unfurling the Rising Sun flag as she did.

"Stay where you are. We will come to you," came the command. The officer spoke through the pipe to his boat, which slowly approached the Nakamuras. "Come aboard quickly. It is not safe to stay surfaced very long," he said once the boats were together. The seamen helped Jun and Aileen onto the sub and hurried them into the conning tower and down the ladder. "I'm sorry," the captain said, "We do not have time to bring your possessions on board, nor do we have room for them." The conning tower closed, and the submarine dived. Aileen thought of the American flag aboard their boat and was thankful that no one went aboard to help her move. It would be hard enough explaining what they were doing drifting in the small boat, much less explain the presence of an American flag.

"What were you doing drifting in that small boat, Mr. Nakamura?" asked Commander Ito after introductions.

"We are from Saipan, Commander. We were planning to evacuate Tanapag and go to the north of the island, where General Saito was going to mount a counterattack and push the Americans back into the sea. Our boat's propeller was damaged on the reef and we were blown out to sea. We have been drifting for two or three days."

"Counterattack, Mr. Nakamura?" asked Commander Ito skeptically. "There will not be a counterattack. Probably the island has been lost even now. The Americans have control of the sea and the air. There's no way we can supply Saipan or even evacuate it anymore. You're probably the only two people to escape, although I understand you were not trying to escape." He added the last phrase with a knowing nod. "By the way, do you know how far you 'drifted'?"

"No, commander," answered Jun with a straight face.

"We're three hundred miles northeast of Saipan."

"Are we near any islands?" asked Aileen.

"The nearest island is about two hundred miles away. That would be Pagan, in the Northern Marianas archipelago."

Life aboard the submarine was not pleasant for Aileen. Commander Ito insisted they stay in his room, and they had a little more privacy than the rest of the boat. But the submarine was stuffy and hot and smelled of sweaty bodies. They got a little relief when the sub surfaced every night to recharge batteries and exchange a little of the air. The food, after Saipan, was nutritious but not tasty. Aileen wished she'd brought some of the fruit from Mr. Villagomez's boat. Nevertheless, they were safe and apparently headed for Japan. Commander Ito said he could not tell them their destination but implied they'd see their family soon. The commander had been in submarines for the entire war and though obviously competent seemed to have lost his confidence in the ultimate victory for the emperor.

Still, Jun and Aileen were awakened once to a frenzy of activity in the command area. From the captain's room, they could ascertain that the sub had come upon an American fleet. There seemed to be choice of targets, and finally Commander Ito settled on a battleship. A hush fell when the torpedoes were dispatched. After about a minute, the captain announced quietly, "Two explosions on the starboard side, midships and stern."

A cheer went up from the crew, then rapid activity as the sub dived and moved to evade the destroyers sent to find it. Suddenly everything went quiet. One of the seamen whispered, "There're one or two of them overhead now." and that was followed shortly by four explosions, none of them close enough to do anything but rock the sub slightly. Quiet again, and about an hour later, the sub moved slowly away, risking periscope depth on one occasion to look for the battleship.

"It's still afloat," Commander Ito reported, "but moving very slowly, and the fires are not out yet." They dived and moved away.

"That's about all we can do anymore. Hit and run. We don't have enough subs to concentrate and do a lot of damage," the captain confided to Jun and Aileen at breakfast that morning.

Two weeks later, the submarine docked in Yokohama harbor, and Jun and Aileen, after sincere thanks to Commander Ito and his crew, went ashore. Jun shocked Aileen by announcing they would take a taxi all the way home. She noticed that in his negotiations with the taxi driver, he didn't mention that he was trusting that Mieko had the money at home, since the two of them were penniless. Soon they were riding in the taxi. Its charcoal-burning engine perched on the trunk, belched black fumes as it completed the final twenty-five miles of Jun and Aileen's long, perilous journey home.

時 選
の
期 択

CHAPTER **18**

"HOW FAR HAVE WE GONE SINCE WE ENTERED THE line?" asked Horace of Ken. With the rest of the regiment, they were in trucks headed back to a rest area near Rome. They had barely gotten back from their patrol into Pisa when the order came reassigning them. At the recreation area, they would do some training and stand some honor guards, but they also looked forward to plenty of R&R.

"It's been about forty miles. I was noting it on Lieutenant Watson's map the other day," answered Ken, as the 2 1/2 ton truck rumbled south over the route they had fought north over the last month. "It seems longer than that, doesn't it?"

"I don't know how fah eet's been, but I know we should get some real Ah&Ah," said Shig Murakami. "Eh, we gone poot Rome upside down. Dat true, Shima?"

"Yeah, Shig," said Tyrus with surprising lack of enthusiasm.

"Ken, you say you heard Kaz is going to join us at the R&R camp?" asked Mike Matsunaga.

"That's what Doc said. He said it turned out to be just a scalp wound."

"Eh, tank God for dat, eh?" said Murakami.

"Yeah, tank God for dat, no keeding," said Tyrus with more enthusiasm.

❧

Late in the day, they pulled into the R&R area and moved into large tents with wooden floors, a luxury Shimabukuro and Murakami decided must be the equal of the Royal Hawaiian Hotel on Waikiki. After a warm shower and a huge dinner, the squad decided they were ready for Rome. It was only with great difficulty that Ken was able to convince them they'd be able to celebrate better with a good night's sleep on cots.

The next day, as predicted, Kaz Ishii joined them. He and Matsunaga and Yamashita compared wounds, while the rest gave various clinical opinions about the effect of the wound on Kaz' brain–or lack of one.

On the way to Rome, the group decided to take a tour first and then find a glass of beer or two. "You gonna join us for the tour, Tyrus, or find a girl?" asked Horace.

"Eh, Yam, how many times I gotta tell you, mind yo' own business bout dat. Eh?"

In Rome, they were herded into large groups by Red Cross personnel for the various tours. Their group started at the Colosseum and the ruins of the Roman Forum, where Horace wondered out loud if two thousand years hence people would be viewing the ruins in Naples they'd seen two months before. As they toured the Pantheon and the Trevi Fountain, a sense of awe began to envelop them.

"I remember seeing pictures of these places in school, but I never thought I'd see them," said Kaz Ishii in a hushed tone.

The tour continued through magnificent piazzas and buildings left mostly undamaged by the decision of the Germans to declare Rome an open city. The suffering of war, however, was reflected in the people if not the architecture. As in Naples, the people were gaunt and in some cases emaciated. The black market served only the clever few. The vast majority spent most of their waking hours looking for food.

The trucks crossed a river, passed the citadel-like Castel Sant'Angelo and approached St. Peter's Square. They stopped outside the square and allowed the soldiers to cross the square and enter the cathedral. Wordlessly, they entered St. Peter's and were led to the altar. The tour guide described the history and art of the building and the altar. Ken tried to pay attention to the facts but could not help noticing Tyrus. Oblivious to the guide's lecture, he was looking up at the ceiling of the cathedral, and then Ken noted tears coming down his cheeks. Ken looked away in embarrassment. The guide led them into the Sistine Chapel and after a short course on Michelangelo, led them back to where they had left the trucks. She told them they were on their own for the rest of the day and where to meet the trucks for the ride back to camp.

They stood for a time thinking about the sights they had just seen, but soon these lofty thoughts were replaced by the more visceral desires of soldiers who'd been in combat for a month. They talked of exploring the pleasures of a city that had been issuing its siren call to men and women across the world for three millennia. The discussion was open-ended since none of them knew clearly what he wanted to do or where to do it.

"Where's Shimabukuro?" Horace suddenly asked. Nobody knew. They all agreed they'd last seen him at the altar in the cathedral.

"Eh, we'd better go find da guy," said Shig.

"Maybe he's taken off on his own to find some prostitute," suggested Horace.

"No, I don't think so," said Ken, remembering his actions at the altar. "Let's go find him." They crossed the huge square again, looking to see if he were among the columns that lined the sides of the square. As they started into the cathedral, they met Tyrus coming out.

"Eh, bruddah, we tought you were lost," said Murakami.

"No, I was O.K," came the reply.

"Well, what were you doing?" asked Horace.

"I, well, I start tink of all da bad tings I wen do in my life wen I stand at dat altah. An', ya know, I have one bad life. Shig can tell you, yeah, Mura? An' I teenk of Ben and Sergeant Honda, and man, I start to cry, no lie. And den I remember wat da Catholics call 'confession', and man heah I am in da centah of all Catholichood, so I wen' go confess."

"You did *what*?" asked Murakami.

"Yeah. You know dose booths along da side of da church, I mean da kine catedral? Dose for confession. Hey, I find one wit' minister in eet, so I confess. Man, I covah everyting from little boy on. Eet take me one long time, you know."

"But the priest didn't speak English, did he?" asked Ishii.

"Eh, I don' know. I no geev heem much time fo' talk. But he say someting wen I finally feenish, you know. I teenk he fahgeev me. Anyway I feel much bettah now."

If the men thought that confession for Tyrus would rid him of all his guilt so he could get his mind back onto the worldly pleasures of Rome, they were mistaken. Two conversations ran simultaneously as the men sat at a sidewalk cafe: Tyrus' and everyone else's. Whatever the others were talking about, Tyrus would interrupt with a discussion of the grandeur of the cathedral or the altar, or a description of how good it felt to be forgiven. He sipped his beer slowly compared to the usual way he drained it. The men's 'night on the town' eventually consisted of going from one sidewalk cafe to another, drinking a beer and retelling the stories of the last month. When the stories began to include Sergeant Honda and Ben Watanabe, the stories switched back to Camp Shelby. Even Ken was a little unsteady on his feet as they climbed onto the trucks to return to the R&R center.

"So, Kaz. You teenk confession no work eef not een your own language?" said Tyrus, as the trucks started back.

"No. I don't know. I guess it's God who does the forgiving, and He can understand every language, even pidgin," said Kaz. He belched, pulled his cap over his eyes and settled back against the side of the truck, indicating that his theological advice, filtered as it was through the alcohol, was over for the night.

"Maybe I need confess to some buggah who speak Eenglish," continued Tyrus, ignoring the crack about pidgin.

"Look, Tyrus, we'll talk to Chaplain Hirano about it tomorrow. Now be quiet and let us get some sleep. It's a long way back to camp. I'm glad you confessed and feel better, but we've heard enough of it for one evening," said Ken, uncharacteristically.

"O.K.," said Tyrus, uncharacteristically.

<hr />

When Shimabukuro awakened him the next morning, Ken's head ached and his stomach was sour. The latter was helped by a trip to the latrine where he vomited, but he realized for the first time what a hangover felt like. Tyrus wasn't much help.

"Yeah, I had dem plenty times. Da best way to get ovah one is take one long sweem een da ocean. But hey, you said we could go see da Chaplain."

"Did I say I'd take you?"

"Yeah, you said dat. And moah, you know da guy bettah dan me."

"Well, O.K. Let me see if I can find an aspirin."

Half an hour later, they were in the chapel tent talking with Chaplain Hirano. The chaplain let Shimabukuro go through his whole story, the guilt, the magnificence of St. Peter's, his overwhelming compulsion to confess his sins, and the sense of peace he'd had since his confession. He was a little uneasy with Tyrus's request to confess again, in English.

He repeated Ishii's opinion of the previous night that God was the for-giver whoever the listener was. But when he saw the seriousness of the request, he said, "We Baptists believe in confession, but not necessarily formal ones. However, in chaplain's school, they gave us some instruction on dealing with soldiers of other faiths, so come on into my office. I can find the order for confession, and we'll give it a shot." Chaplain Hirano was from Hawaii, and though he spoke more "proper English", Ken could still hear the lilt in his voice that signaled his origins. He had also noted that sometimes in his sermons, particularly when he wanted to drive home a point that would "hit you where you lived", he would revert to pidgin. He wondered whether the chaplain's part in the con-fessional would sound more like it came from Rome or Waikiki. He never found out, but both men seemed satisfied when they came out of the office nearly half an hour later.

"Tanks, eh, chaplain," said Tyrus.

"I'm glad you came by, Tyrus. I think you had a real encounter yesterday. While we're in garrison, some of the men have been coming by for Bible study at 0800. Come on by. You know, I like that confes-sional. Maybe Baptists need it more. Ken, you don't look well. Have you been to sick call?"

"No, sir. I think it's a hangover. We celebrated a little too much last night."

"I didn't know you were a drinker," said Chaplain Hirano.

"I'm not. That's my trouble."

"I see," said the chaplain in a tone that neither condoned nor con-demned. "You're welcome to come to the Bible studies with Tyrus, you know."

The first week in the R&R center was, as the name implied, spent in rest and recuperation. Ken was amazed at how long he could sleep night after night and still take an afternoon nap. Letters from home were read and reread, and he even wrote a few himself, wondering what would escape the censor's scissors. The news from home was not par-ticularly good. Although Toshiko tried to keep her letters upbeat, it was clear that the same problems persisted. Shoji was still under the influ-ence of his whiskey much of the time, Peter was training at Camp Shelby and not writing home any more often than Ken had, and she didn't hear from Howie very often. Ken's letters from Dorothy were encouraging. She was still staying busy with her work and the scrap metal drive as well as what sounded like a non-stop social life.

They played baseball in camp, and trips to Rome continued, though none as alcoholic as the first trip. Ken and Tyrus attended the Bible study faithfully but were unsuccessful in getting the others to come. They looked on Tyrus's newfound commitment as a healthy correction but not one that would last very long. Ken wasn't sure he agreed.

Near the end of the first week, an awards parade was scheduled. General Clark would present the awards. The regiment was under strength since the promised replacements had not yet been assigned. Then when the men to receive awards were taken out, there was almost no one left in the ranks. In the first place, the entire 100th Battalion would receive the Presidential Unit Citation for its actions at Belvedere. From Ken's squad, Yamashita, Ishii, and Matsunaga would receive Purple Hearts, and he would belatedly receive his sergeant's stripes. Watanabe would posthumously be awarded a Distinguished Service Cross, and he and Sergeant Honda would be named for Purple Hearts posthumously. It was a huge group of awardees who marched forward on command to receive their awards, and it took an hour and a half to hand them all out. Despite that, General Clark wanted to address the men. If there was anyone who looked like a general, it was General Mark W. Clark. Tall and slender, he had the bearing of a soldier and the aquiline nose that communicated command. He had a voice to match.

"Gentlemen, there's no one on the parade ground today more proud of your magnificent achievements than I. When I was in the War Department at the beginning of this war, I was asked by General Marshall to evaluate any military threat that the Japanese on the west coast might constitute. After traveling there and consulting with a great number of people, I concluded that they constituted no threat at all. Unfortunately, the politics of the moment decreed that the Japanese should be moved away from the coast and housed in detention camps, and my report and advice was ignored. Last year when the War Department was deciding where the 100th battalion was to be sent, I told them, 'I know these men. I know they can be great fighters, and I want anybody who can fight. Send them to me!' They did, and you have fought magnificently. Everything you have been asked to do, you have done splendidly. When we have a tough job to do, I tell my staff, 'Send the Niseis. They can do it.'

"The war, of course, is far from over. The Germans are giving every indication that they are forming another defensive line, and so there will be much more blood spilled before we can achieve the victory, secure freedom and go home. And then I'm aware that more battles face you because of your heritage. I pledge my support for that war. I will tell everyone I can of your splendid fighting spirit, fighting for the country you love."

After the first week, the regiment started to get assignments. The first—to receive and orient the replacements. Next—a rather curious assignment—to act as honor guard for the king of England, visiting the Italian front. It would require a four hour truck ride each way, and Murakami was not convinced that should be their job.

"Eh. I nevah want go spend one whole day fo' stand one houh for da kine king."

"Look, Shig," said Tyrus, "pretend we gone be honah guard for King Kamehameha or Queen Liliuokalani. Eh, you nevah go complain about dat."

Though none of them would mention it, they felt that that was one way General Clark was showing his pride in them, and there was no murmuring any more serious than Shig's.

The next week, training started again. When fistfights started the third week, it was clear they had had all the R&R they could tolerate. In mid-August, they went back to the front.

"This is where we were when we left," said Horace. "I thought at least they would have crossed the river while we were gone. The whole point of us exposing our butts going into Pisa was to get information on where they should cross."

"Maybe they thought our feelings would be hurt if we didn't have the honor of being the first across," suggested Kaz.

"Can't they do anything without us?" asked Horace.

"They went into southern France without us," said Ishii, referring to the recent invasion by the Seventh Army. "I noticed you didn't worry about what we were going to miss like you did when they invaded Normandy without us."

"You're right. I guess there's enough war to go around for everybody. Italy should be enough for us."

They had looked at the Arno River for two days. Orders were to cross it just down river from Florence, but the Germans' defenses had proven impenetrable. It had been mostly a battle of artillery. The Germans had pounded every engineers' attempt to build a pontoon bridge across the river, and the American artillery tried, without success, to silence the German artillery. The men from E Company, sheltered in woods away from the exploding shells, watched the vain attempts to span the river.

"What we need is a bridgehead on the other side. If we can get our infantry harassing their artillery, we can divert their fire and get a bridge across." The speaker, Captain Eastman, had come up from company headquarters to Ken's observation point. Sergeant Strong and Lieutenant Turner, the forward artillery observer accompanied the captain. "If we could put a bunch of men ashore at that little beach over there, it's sheltered. If we could get enough across to break out and create confusion, maybe we could do it."

"We got the boats, Captain, but no outboard motors," said Sergeant Strong. "With the strong current, we couldn't count on all the boats getting to that little beach. They'd be spread all over the far shore. If only we could get a rope across to the beach, we could pull the boats across."

"How do we get the rope across?" asked the captain.

"Strong swimmer?" asked Sergeant Strong.

"He'd have to be an awfully strong swimmer."

"Eh, Captain, now you talkin," said Tyrus Shimabukuro, who had been listening to the conversation.

"Can you swim across with a rope, Shimabukuro? That's an awfully strong current," said the company commander.

"No problem, Captain. You nevah surf da Pipeline?"

"No, Shimabukuro, I never surfed the Pipeline."

They discussed the tactics. Lieutenant Turner, a tall, blond officer from rural Illinois, said he would lay a barrage on the bluffs along that section beginning at 2315 hours. Fifteen minutes later, Shimabukuro and another strong swimmer from H Company would start swimming across the Arno with small ropes around their waists. If they could get one or both ropes to the sheltered beach, they would loop the ropes around trees and pull large ropes across and secure them to trees twenty yards apart. The men from the Second Battalion would then get into the boats and pull themselves across by the ropes. Lieutenant Turner would move his artillery back further from the bluff when the men started across.

The barrage started promptly at 2315 hours. Frank Oguri, the swimmer from H Company, and Tyrus stood near the shore, stripped to swimming shorts, ropes tied securely and discussed previous swimming competitions, four years earlier and half a world away.

"So, Shima," said Oguri, barely five feet tall but all muscles, "I have one moah chance to beat you."

"Eh, Frank, I no keah dees time who beats who. Jus' meet me on da uddah side. Eef we get two ropes ovah, mo' bettah, eh?"

"Eh, Go For Broke, uh?"

At the signal, both men dashed for the river, dived in and started swimming with strong strokes. They had started upstream so the current would land them on or near the beach.

The men from the third squad watched with anxiety to see if they would be spotted. When they were thirty yards from the opposite shore, the bluff awakened with machine gun fire, spraying the two swimmers.

"There, by that big tree!" yelled Ken. "Get some fire on that!"

The Niseis' fire was accurate, and the German firing stopped momentarily, allowing Tyrus and Oguri to scramble ashore.

"Keep them pinned down, so they don't decide to find their way down to the beach!" yelled Ken.

The swimmers tied one rope to a tree and then together pulled on the other one. When they had the big rope across, they tied it to a tree and then repeated the process with the second rope. Before they got the second one secured, men were already pulling themselves across by the first rope. While half the men would pull, the other half would try to cover the bluff with rifle fire.

With only the brute strength of the two swimmers available to pull the ropes across, they sagged considerably downstream, so the pull across the river was easy until mid-stream but much harder for the second half of the journey. Some boats lost their hold on the ropes and bobbed downstream, so it was difficult for awhile to judge success. Eventually though, several squads landed on the beach. As they started up the draw, they ran into a German squad coming down. The fire fight that ensued in the dark allowed more and more men to land on the beach and start climbing to the bluffs above. By 0100, Company E was on the bluff, establishing a perimeter, and the rest of Second Battalion was pouring across, now using four ropes that had been winched tightly.

By first light, the men of the third squad were in the outskirts of Florence. Third Battalion, downstream from Second Battalion had exploited the success of the river crossing and now were crossing themselves. Long-distance German artillery still harassed the building of the bridges, but without forward observers, it was inaccurate.

"I hope we get to spend some time in Florence," said Kaz, as the men feasted on a cold C ration breakfast. "I remember hearing that it was the center of the Renaissance. We had a seventh grade teacher who loved all that history. According to her, that was all the history that mattered."

Some of the men looked up with slight interest, but most kept working on their C rations, exhausted from the night's battle.

"Good work, Ty," said Ken. "If it weren't for you and Oguri, we'd still be on the other side of the river." A chorus of agreement showed that the men obviously were more moved by the immediacy of Shimabukuro's heroism than the contemplation of the Renaissance, regardless of its meaning for all of history.

Ishii's wish was not realized. The three battalions of the 442nd moved directly north towards the mountains above Florence. The Germans' defense was weak, but word passed around that they were building another strong defensive line in those mountains. They apparently hoped to hold up the Allies until the snows came and made movement difficult again. But the Niseis did not have a chance to see if they could break the line before winter as they were withdrawn again, barely a week after crossing the Arno.

"So it's Captain Fukuda now, eh?" asked Ken of his friend when they returned to their original staging area near Florence.

"Yes. They've moved me to the S2 section of the regimental staff."

"So you can tell me why they moved us out of the line so soon after we'd just gotten back. Not that I'm complaining. Those mountains look intimidating, particularly when they get covered with snow. The rumor is they'll be shipping us to France," said Ken.

"Well for once the rumors are right. I guess at the very high levels, they've decided the push should be into France and Germany. They'll be satisfied to let Italy tie down a bunch of German divisions. You know, the people at regiment were very impressed with the way your group crossed the Arno."

"Yeah, Shimabukuro and Oguri were very courageous. When I saw those machine gun bullets landing around them there in the river, I thought they'd be hit for sure. I hope somebody seriously considers them for big-time medals. I know Captain Eastman recommended them."

"Yeah, it's in the works. I'm sure they'll get something."

"You know, Doug," Ken said after a pause, "what makes me mad? They're drafting Niseis out of the camps. I mean it was one thing for us to volunteer, but the guys who don't volunteer for the sake of conscience shouldn't be forced to. When they put us in the camps, they told us in essence that we did not have full American citizenship, because our loyalty was in question. How is it fair that they can then force us to serve if we don't want to?"

"Are you talking about your brother?"

"Yeah. Howie got his draft notice and refused to go. They tried him, found him guilty and sent him to federal prison in Washington state. My Mom is devastated, and I'm mad as hell."

"Obviously I have no answer. The only thing we can hope for is that after the war when the hysteria dies down and people have a chance to look at things a little more rationally, we can reverse some of these things."

"How can we reverse Howie's being sent to prison?" asked Ken.

"There's a way to legally reverse his sentence, as if it had never occurred. Of course, he still will have spent some time in prison."

"You know, Doug, I'm beginning to lose hope. One of the guys from our battalion lost his leg at Cecina. He was awarded the DSC and went home to his place in the Stockton area to try to see what had happened to his family's farm. He was in uniform with his medals and on crutches and all, and they still ran him out of town. Wouldn't even tell him who was farming his place. What do we have to do to prove ourselves?"

Doug again had no answer.

CHAPTER 19

I THOUGHT THEY HAD FOUGHT UP THROUGH THIS area. It hardly looks like there's been a war at all," said Horace The men were on a truck traveling up the highway along the Rhone River in France. Some evidences of war were noticeable, but compared to Italy, where every tree, vine and rock gave testimony to the bloody, bitter fighting, southern France was nearly unmarked. The Seventh Army had covered 350 miles in less than two months. What Horace didn't know was that Allied intelligence had reports that the Germans were setting their winter defenses in the Vosges Mountains to prevent entry into southwestern Germany.

"I think I prefer this type of campaign to Italy," Horace continued.

"Eh, Yam, I nevah like hear dakine talk. I mean I no superstitious, but evah time you talk dakine, we go get ouh butts keecked," said Murakami.

"What do you hear about what we'll be doing, Ken," asked Kaz.

"Nothing except that we'll be attached to the 36th Division," answered Ken.

"Well I hope they're as good to work with as the 34th," said Mike Matsunaga, referring to their time in Italy. "They were a bunch of good guys."

"Yeah, but they no can play pokah worth a damn, eh Shima?" said Murakami.

"Nah," said Tyrus, looking up from his Bible. "Dose haole faces no can hold one bluff evah." He looked back to his Bible, and Shig didn't mention that Tyrus had not joined in the poker games since his encounter in St. Peter's Cathedral.

"Will we be going through Paris?" asked Horace. "I'd sure love to see that city. They say the Germans left Paris, like Rome, without much damage."

"I don't know Horace. I think the 36th is quite a bit east of Paris, so I doubt we'll go through it."

"Well, they'll probably put us in reserve, and we can take a few days' leave there."

"Dere ya go again, Yam. Now fo suah, dey gone poot us een da front lines," said Murakami.

The trucks rolled on, and the men intermittently dozed and watched the French countryside, well on its way to autumn. Late that day, they stopped for a break near Lyon, and Tyrus pulled Ken aside.

"Ya know, Ken, I make one decision," he said softly. "Wen I go back to Hawaii, I gone study for priest."

"Y'you are?" Ken stammered. "Well that's great, Ty. I'm a little surprised, but I think you'd make a good one."

"One ting fo suah, nutting evah gone surprise me at confession. I wen' do all kine evil teeng you can teenk of."

"I'm not sure about that, Ty. But are you sure you want to be Catholic? You know those priests can't get married."

"Yeah, I know, but, hey, dat not important like being een da true church."

"But I think a lot of Protestants would disagree that that's the true church. You've heard of the Reformation. That's when a bunch of people said the Roman church had strayed from the truth and they needed to make a lot of corrections," Ken said.

"Eh, I nevah know dat, but wat I know ees wat I feel at da altar in St. Peter's dat day. Dat must be true."

"Well, Ty, more power to you. We need priests and ministers who've experienced life at its hardest."

"And, Ken, one ting moah. Don't tell da guys, eh? Dey nevah understand, eh?"

"I won't say a word, Ty."

After two days, the trucks left the highway and turned to the northeast along small country roads. Signs of war became more prominent. Burned out tanks and trucks sat in roadside ditches, and in the towns, many buildings were in rubble. It was clear that Paris was not on their itinerary. The trucks stopped a little beyond the town of Epinal, and the 100th/442nd Regimental Combat Team went into bivouac, awaiting orders. The first order was for Ken and Kaz to see Captain Eastman at company headquarters.

"Lieutenant Watson is going to battalion as the S-3 officer," said the captain. "and you, Lieutenant Hayakawa, are going to be my Third Platoon leader." With that, Sergeant Strong pinned a gold bar and the crossed rifles insignia of the infantry on the under side of Ken's collars.

"Keep 'em out of the sunlight, sir, so they won't be such a damn target," said Sergeant Strong, as he stepped back and saluted Ken.

"Does this mean I owe you a buck?" asked Ken of the first sergeant.

"Yessir, first enlisted man to salute a new officer." Sergeant Strong stepped a little closer to accept the greenback and said quietly, "I'm proud of you, Lieutenant Hayakawa. I knowed I'd see this day from the day you done earned your corporal stripes out of basic."

"Thanks to you, sergeant," said Ken, remembering the sergeant's short sermon on leadership the day he'd tried to turn down the stripes.

"And Ishii, I want you to take over the squad. We're all out of stripes, so, Ken, we're going to have to use yours."

When the transfer was completed, Ken and Kaz headed back to the platoon area.

"They're not doing us any favors, you know, Kaz. Rank doesn't seem to protect people from getting shot."

"I know. I hate to be fatalistic, but I think when your number's up, your number's up. When Sergeant Honda was killed before he even got one shot off, I decided there's no fairness in war. We try to kill the German before he kills us, and if we're alive when the war's over, we consider ourselves lucky and go home and try to justify our having made it through."

Two days later, the men hefted their packs and marched into the Vosges Mountains. If Horace thought they'd be in reserve for the 36th Division, helping them out here and there, it was soon clear he was wrong. They were in the forefront of the division with the initial goal of securing the town of Bruyeres. The mountains in France were much more thickly wooded than those in Italy, and every tree might be hiding a machine gun. The first goal always had to be the securing of the high ground since any advance up the valleys was subject to heavy fire from the surrounding hills. As the battle for Bruyeres began, the cold and the fog settled in. The pleasant temperatures and blue skies of France to that point had disappeared. Cold and fog then gave way to rain. The men of the Third Platoon, Company E were fighting up a steep hillside, vision restricted to less than a hundred yards by the fog and slipping in the mud. They had to defend against machine gun fire seemingly from behind every tree. If the Germans had not defended to the last man as they retreated up the Rhone Valley, it was different in the mountains. Blocked trails, interlocking fields of fire and booby traps in any buildings that looked like they might provide some cover made the advance of the Japanese Americans very slow and dangerous.

However, determination had become as much a part of the 100th/442nd as their motto. With the combat skills learned in Italy, the 100th and the 2nd Battalions slowly cleared the hills, while the 3rd entered the town. Fighting house to house, they soon found that the most dangerous job was clearing out the basements. From most basements, French civilians flooded out with embraces, tears and bottles of champagne for their liberators. In other basements, where German soldiers had taken refuge, the men would be met with a hail of fire when they opened the door. A couple of hand grenades did not always silence the opposition, and more than one soldier lost his life in basement-cleansing.

By the time Ken's platoon got into Bruyeres, the town had been cleared of Germans, and the celebration of the townspeople rivaled those of the Italian towns they had liberated. The war continued, however. Instead of a night spent in a warm building with a sip of champagne before falling asleep, the men shivered in newly-dug foxholes a mile out of town. They ate field rations and tried to keep their feet out of the water accumulated in the bottoms of the foxholes. The water was becoming a problem. Once boots and socks got wet, it was hard to find a way to get them dry again, and the flesh of their feet got soft and blistered easily. Because of the cold, it was hard to feel the damage to their feet, and they were shocked when they took off their boots and saw the ugly, bloody messes they'd been walking on. Nearly as many men were evacuated for trench foot as for wounds. Now in addition to all the other requirements of a platoon leader, Ken had to continually remind his squad leaders to watch their men's feet.

The day after the liberation of Bruyeres, Ken's platoon was ordered over a hill and down into the hamlet of La Broquaine. Ken stood on the hillside with his binoculars watching his two lead squads enter the town, hardly more than a crossroads. Suddenly a German tank rolled out from behind a building and fired a high explosive round down the street at the advancing soldiers. They dived for cover, but when the smoke lifted,

Ken could see three men—unidentifiable except they were from the third squad—lying in the street. With quivering voice, he tried to call artillery onto the lone tank, but before he could make contact, he saw two bazooka teams approaching the tank from alleys on either side of the main road. One fired at the tank, but the shell missed. The tank backed into its previous hiding place. That however allowed the other team to place a shell in the motor at the rear of the tank. Flames immediately engulfed the tank. The hatch opened, but the man who started out was shot immediately and fell back into the tank. No one else came out and the tank stood, a burning mess. Ken scurried down the hill and into the town. One of the men lying in the street was Kaz Ishii. A medic was bending over him but shook his head as Ken approached.

"Kaz! Kaz! Can you hear me?" yelled Ken.

Kaz groaned, opened his eyes and said in a voice Ken could barely hear, "I told you it wasn't fair." With that he closed his eyes, and his breathing stopped.

"Is he dead?" asked Horace who had just come up, his bazooka slung over his shoulder.

"Yeah," answered Ken, standing up. "Kaz died in a town that's not even on the map. It's not fair."

"Of course it's not fair," said Horace.

"O.K. Horace," said Ken after a short pause, "You're squad leader. Keep moving up the road. Our objective is Hill 617. You can't see it in this fog, but here it is on the map. Get Kaz's map." Kaz's two friends moved back into the war, leaving his body for the men from Graves' Registration.

⸎

"One of the battalions of the 36th has gotten cut off," Captain Eastman said. "They're over on this hill here, surrounded by Germans. The other battalions have been trying for two days to get through to them but no luck. With this weather, there've been no air drops, and the battalion is running out of ammunition and water. Division's putting us into the effort now." To his platoon leaders, he pointed on the map where the 100th and 3rd Battalions would be and then what the 2nd's orders were. "The Germans are really strong between here and there. Basically, it's going to be strength against strength."

The company commander was right. No sooner had they started out than they ran into heavy opposition. It seemed every tree in the thick forest had to be fought for. The fog restricted vision to less than a hundred yards and made artillery support too dangerous to call in. Casualties mounted as the three "Go For Broke" battalions moved to the hill where the surrounded battalion was. Fortunately there was no snow, but temperatures hovered around freezing at night and only slightly higher during the day. Day became night and night became day, and it was hard to tell if they were progressing. Ken had access at times to the big picture and encouraged his men that they were slowly getting to their objective, but he did not share with them that casualties were terribly high in all the battalions. On the third day, the weather cleared enough to allow planes to drop supplies to the battalion–now called "The Lost Battalion". The diversion allowed Ken's platoon to make a flanking maneuver that secured for them more ground than they'd covered in the last day and a half. They could finally see the hill where the battalion was, but the territory between was very defensible. The fighting ground on.

On the morning of the fourth day, the fog returned, but the men now had a clear picture of their objective. They determined to reach the battalion that day. Ken's platoon, on the left flank, had secured some high ground but were being held up by two machine guns on the other side of a clearing.

"I'll take two men over to the right and lay down some fire, Buckaroo, and you take the rest of the squad through the trees to the left," Horace said. Horace and the other two men found cover under some trees and started firing on the machine guns. As planned, that allowed Tyrus and the rest of the squad to approach the guns from the other side and silence them. No sooner had that been accomplished, however, when heavy artillery started coming down on Horace and the other two men. The first volley destroyed their tree cover, and as the men started to run for safety, the second volley hit. All three were knocked to the ground, but one of the men jumped up and ran to the safety of the newly silenced machine gun nest. The other man lay still, but Horace tried to get up, fell down again and lay moaning on the ground.

From the protection of the machine gun nest, Shimabukuro watched his friend. "Come, Yam! Come! Get up, Horace!" he yelled. Horace continued to roll on the ground and moan, his right pant leg getting bloodier by the second. Shimabukuro jumped up and ran the hundred yards to Horace, jerked him up over his shoulder and started the run back to safety. The third volley landed as he started up over the dirt embankment surrounding the machine gun nest. Khaki missile and khaki bowling ball hurtled over the dirt and both rolled to a stop and lay still.

"How are they?" asked Mike Matsunaga.

"Yamashita's lost a lot of blood from his leg, but I've got a tourniquet on it, and his wrist pulse is strong," said the medic. "But Shimabukuro's dead."

Later that day, Ken tried unsuccessfully to be gracious as he received the thanks of the men of the Lost Battalion as they filed back through the corridor the 100th/442nd had opened for them. He tried to smile but couldn't. He nodded and mumbled something in response to their words, but all he could think of was the terrible cost. In addition to Tyrus and Horace, he knew there were hundreds of casualties in the Second Battalion alone. Was it worth it? When could they stop proving themselves?

The war continued. The 36th Division's objective was the town of Saint Dié, from which the division would sweep into southern Germany. The 100th/442nd continued to lead the advance, although replacements had not yet arrived. Companies were at platoon strength; battalions were at company strength. Ken's platoon, which called for fifty-one men had eighteen who could carry rifles. He reorganized them into two squads. Even then they were undermanned. But by this time they were seasoned soldiers, and much of the coordination happened with very little direction from above. The tactic of fire and maneuver was so ingrained that it required not much more than pointing to the routes the two elements would take. But the snow began to fall, and the toll of non-battle casualties began to rise. With Ishii, Yamashita and Shimabukuro gone and Murakami evacuated because of frostbite, for Ken, the camaraderie that to some extent had balanced the horror of war had disappeared. Of the original men from third squad, only Mike Matsunaga remained, and he had been promoted to platoon sergeant in the first platoon, so Ken didn't see him very often. His war continued to be one snowy hill after another. The Germans employed more delaying tactics than in-depth defense, but that included a lot of long-distance artillery delivered more or less at random. When a shell exploded thirty yards from Ken one morning and he awakened in an ambulance with only his right hand injured, he had to admit to himself he had no regrets.

"Don't amputate," Ken said in the field hospital. "I'm going to medical school when this is over, and I'm going to need it."

The doctor examining his hand raised his eyebrows a bit. "Medical school, lieutenant? Where?"

"I wanted to go to California, but I was accepted at Creighton."

"If you were accepted, why didn't you go?" asked the doctor.

"That's a good question. I'm not sure my answer would make sense anymore...if it ever did."

"Well, we'll do our best to save it, lieutenant, but I'm not sure about the function of it. Psychiatry, maybe? Radiology?"

When Ken awakened from anesthesia, the first face he saw was that of Doug Furuya.

"What are you doing here?" Ken asked through the ether-induced haze.

"The colonel sent me down to check on our men in the hospital. Turns out about half of the men here are our men."

"Have you seen Yamashita?" asked Ken, shaking his head to try to clear it.

"No. But he's apparently going to be O.K. They had to amputate his leg above the knee–A.K. they called it–and they evacuated him out yesterday," Doug answered.

"I wonder how the Negroes in the south are going to accept a short Jap with a peg leg trying to help them after the war," Ken mused, his brain much clearer now, as he breathed the ether out of his system.

"Aren't you curious about your hand?" For the first time, Ken looked at his right hand, covered with a huge white bandage.

"Yeah, what's the story?"

"I talked to the doctor. He said he saved most of it, but you wouldn't have much function. With a lot of luck and physical therapy, you'll be able to write with it. He asked if you were right-handed?"

"Yeah. Right-handed." Ken could turn the arm but had no feeling in it.

"The doctor called it a 'million-dollar wound'."

"What did he mean by that?"

"He meant the wound was bad enough to get you shipped home, and the disability would be enough to keep you out of further combat. But you're alive, and the disability is something you can learn to live with." Ken dropped his bandaged arm and sighed.

"You know, Doug, I'm to the point I don't care anymore. All the guys I came over with are either dead or wounded. Our objectives are just one hill after another, and they all look the same. Meanwhile, Howie's in prison, Dad's still hooked on whiskey, Peter'll probably be over here in a few months and lead a 'banzai charge' into some machine gun nest so he can die gloriously...and what about that 'Lost Battalion' fiasco? Did they ever figure out how many casualties we took?"

"The best estimate is 800 dead or wounded, to rescue a little over 200."

"Does that make sense, Doug?"

"Only if you have to prove you're more loyal and ready to die for your country than the next guy."

"Well, I think we've done it!"

"I think we did it long ago. Let's just hope they're listening," said Doug. "One other thing the doctor said - he said you'd know what he meant."

"What's that?"

"With therapy, you'll be able to 'put X-rays up'." For the first time, Ken chuckled, but his chuckle held no humor.

Part IV
The Conclusion of War

保勝
の
訨利

CHAPTER 20

KEN WRAPPED HIMSELF TIGHTLY AGAINST THE freezing wind off the North Atlantic. He leaned on the railing of the USNS Encouragement, the hospital ship carrying 2000 wounded men home. Staring into the predawn darkness, his thoughts went to his parents in Manzanar; to Dorothy, whom he anticipated seeing in the next couple of days with great pleasure; to Howie, in federal prison near Tacoma; and to Pete, just now joining the 442nd. He thought of the last two weeks he'd spent in the hospital. Compliments concerning the reputation of the 100/442nd from wounded soldiers there and from the evacuation chain team were numerous. But he experienced no joy in hearing those compliments, because he could not divorce the heroic deeds from the carnage. When he had studied the roster of the wounded soldiers aboard ship, looking for Horace or others, he was saddened by the number of Japanese names he saw on that roster. It was one thing for the soldiers with whom they had fought and died in the mountains of Italy and France to recognize their valor, but would that translate to whole-hearted acceptance by Americans at home? Stories he had heard so far did not seem to support that notion. The one positive note as he searched the ship's roster was that he found Horace's name and then was able to locate his friend.

"Well, at least it's clear. We'll be able to see Old Lady Liberty." Ken looked to his right and saw a soldier on crutches leaning against the rail.

"Will we? We'll be able to see the Statue from here?"

"Yes sir. It'll be just off our left bow as we get into the harbor. And just beyond it, we'll be able to see Ellis Island."

"Ellis Island?" asked Ken.

"Oh, yes sir. That's where thousands, probably millions of immigrants from Europe entered the U.S. My parents came through there around the turn of the century. They were just kids."

"Where did they come from?"

"Poland. Some of their aunts and uncles had come before them and settled in Chicago. They actually met on the ship. Ma says they fell in love then. Pa's not so sure. Anyway, they met again in Chicago about a year later and when they got old enough, they got married. When Hitler invaded Poland, Pa tried to join up. They wouldn't let him because he was too old, but me and my brothers got into it." The two soldiers continued to stare into the lightening dawn. "Did your people have an Ellis Island on the west coast?" Ken's companion asked.

"Not exactly. There was an island in San Francisco Bay - Angel Island - where they checked some immigrants from Asia for diseases, but not everyone. For the most part they came over on work contracts with the intention of earning a lot of money and eventually returning to Japan–*dekasegi,* they call it. In fact, there is a law against foreign-born Orientals becoming citizens."

"No kidding?"

"No kidding. Children born in the U.S., like me, are citizens, but my parents can't be, even though they've lived here for twenty-five years."

"That ain't fair, lieutenant. And are they in a camp?"

"Yes, they're in a camp in the California desert."

"Hell, Lieutenant, that ain't fair!" The two men continued staring at the horizon. After ten minutes, the soldier spoke up suddenly. "There, lieutenant! See the shoreline over there? That's Jersey. It won't be long before we're seeing the Statue."

Ken watched the New Jersey shore come into view and then the Long Island shore off the starboard bow and then suddenly he spoke out. "Horace! He's gotta see this!" He dashed to the aft stairway and ran down three decks. Further back he came to Horace's area.

"Horace! You gotta see this. We're coming into New York Harbor and the Statue of Liberty. Come on up!" Horace sat up in bed and looked questioningly at Ken. Ken grabbed his uniform and began to put it on him.

"Wait, Ken. I can do that. You're getting it on backwards."

"Well, hurry up. I don't want to miss it." Horace finished dressing, picked up his crutches and started for the stairway.

"Now, hold the crutches," Horace said. "I do better if I hold onto the railing and hop up one stair at a time." Progress was slow and laborious. After half a flight, Ken could be patient no longer.

"Horace, climb on my back. We're going to miss it."

"I'll be too heavy for you, Ken," Horace said as he climbed piggyback onto Ken's back.

"Horace. You forget I saw how much you weighed when you joined up, and you sure didn't gain any weight on C rations. Now hold on tight!" He decided not to mention that Horace was also missing his right leg from the knee down.

This unlikely-looking pair, a lieutenant with a bandaged hand, piggybacking a sergeant with an empty pant leg, climbed three flights of stairs, then jockeyed for a place at the rail, now lined with soldiers, most with as many bandages as the unlikely pair.

"There!" yelled somebody. "There she is!" The Statue of Liberty began to appear in the distance off the port bow. Cheering started and within a few seconds the noise exceeded any Ken had ever heard at UCLA-USC games. Cheers, now mixed with tears, continued until the hospital ship passed the Statue. If anyone had believed the stereotype of the inscrutable Oriental, he would have been shocked to see the tear-filled Japanese faces along the rail, yelling with hoarse voices.

As the cheering died down, Ken heard a voice call, "Lieutenant! Where's the Japanese lieutenant?" He looked up to see his friend from earlier in the morning coming down the railing.

"Here, Corporal," he said, his voice hardly a whisper.

"There, Lieutenant." The corporal pointed to a long, low series of buildings on an island just beyond the statue. "That's Ellis Island. That's where my parents came through." He looked at the island intently, occasionally wiping tears from his cheeks. "I'm sorry your people didn't have an Ellis Island, sir. Maybe it would have been different."

⁕⸺⸺⁕

The boat docked, and confusion ensued. The goal was to ship the 2000 wounded soldiers to rehabilitation hospitals spread throughout the northeast. No hospital could receive more than about a hundred men at a time. So the attempt was to group all men headed for a certain hospital and then move them out. During the trip the men were told which hospitals they'd be going to, but these war-hardened men felt they were entitled to make their own decisions. Some trades had been approved, but many merely joined the group going to the destination of their choice, thus confusing both rosters. Ken and Horace had been assigned to the group going to Halloran Hospital on Staten Island. Since there were no destinations near California, they dutifully joined their group. It took most of the rest of the day to load onto the ferry to Staten Island, be trucked to the hospital and assigned their beds.

"Ken! Where are you?" Dorothy's voice on the other end of the telephone line became teary.

"I'm here in Staten Island, a place called Halloran Hospital."
"How are you? You said something was wrong with your hand?"

"Well, it's not too bad. They say I've lost some function but with rehab I'll be good as new."

"I don't believe you, Ken. They wouldn't have sent you back if it was that minor. Anyway, when can I see you? Is Horace with you? You said in your letter that you thought he was still alive and might be on the same ship as you?"

"Yes, he's alive, but he lost a leg. He'll have to be fitted with a prosthesis."

"You mean a peg leg? Speak English now, Doctor." Brother and sister shared their first laugh in a year and a half.

"They say we can have passes to the city beginning next week. Tell me how to get to your place, and you can show me New York City," Ken said.

"That can wait, dummy, I'm coming out there. The ferries don't run at night, but I'll be on the first one in the morning. If they're starting your rehab, they can just wait until your sister has a chance to welcome you home!"

⊶

Later that evening, Ken sat on his bed, writing a letter to Shoji and Toshiko, and tried to describe his injury in such a way that his parents would not be concerned. He was aware that his writing with his left hand would probably tell them more than the words he chose.

From behind the curtain came a loud voice. "You're not putting any Jap there! You don't expect me to bunk next to any Jap! They're all spies! 'The only good Jap is a dead Jap!'" Ken took a deep breath, put down his writing materials and started to stand up. With that the curtain was flung aside revealing a tall blond man resting on crutches, who threw his head back and started to laugh.

"Dave? Dave Larson?" said Ken. "But if you're Dave Larson, you must have lost thirty pounds."

"Yeah, you old sonofagun. I figured there could only be one Lieutenant Ken Hayakawa." The two old roommates shook hands vigorously and sat down on Ken's bed. "What brings you here? You obviously don't have the sense to stay out of the line of fire when people are shooting at you. The last I'd heard, you'd been shipped to that camp in the Owens Valley. What's happened since then?"

Starting with Manzanar, Ken filled his friend in on his life over the intervening years, leaving out the part about his acceptance to medical school.

"Now what's been going on with you. I thought you'd be selling cars in San Luis Obispo."

"Well, I graduated, barely, and went home. I had flat feet and was classified 4-F. For a while, it was O.K., but then my father began to get on my nerves. He had bought back a lot of cars he'd sold to Japanese, for less than 10% of what they were worth, and he thought he was doing them a favor. He thought the order to send all of you to those camps was great. Whenever I tried to tell him that no one had ever proven any of the Japanese Americans were spies, he'd go nuts, call me a 'Jap-lover' and everything. I finally had to get out of there. Actually, when I heard about the formation of the 100th Battalion and then the 442nd, I figured if you guys, with all you'd had to go through, could do it, I couldn't let flat feet be an excuse. I'd never even heard of flat feet before my draft physical. Ironically, I used some of Dad's connections at the draft board to get reclassified. I went through basic and then OCS and then foolishly volunteered for parachute training."

"You? A paratrooper?" said Ken.

"Yeah, crazy, isn't it? War makes you do strange things. Anyway, they assigned me to the 82nd Airborne Division. I joined them after they jumped at Salerno. I survived Normandy, but after the jump in Holland, where we didn't have many casualties comparatively, I got a bullet in my left knee. It wasn't much, they say, but enough to have a fused knee the rest of my life. But, Ken, I'm lucky. Both of us are lucky. So many good men getting killed. I know you've seen it at least as much as I have. This war business is horrible. There's gotta be a better way to settle our differences." The two men talked well into the night, until a medic had to remind them them it was time for lights out and for Dave to return to his ward.

"I'll be back tomorrow after therapy, and we can talk some more," said Dave as he rose to leave.

"My sister will be visiting tomorrow. Did you ever meet her? She's been working in New York for a couple of years."

"Yeah, I must have. I remember one time your whole family came up for some award you received—you know, Jap of the Year, or something like that. I must have met her then. What's her name?"

"Dorothy."

"Yeah, Dorothy. Anyway, I'll see you tomorrow, Ken. Work on that hand. You'll need it when you're a doctor."

True to her word, Dorothy caught the first ferry to Staten Island and arrived shortly after breakfast. Ken was struggling to make his bed with one hand when she entered the ward. She let out a yell and ran to him, embracing him so hard, they both fell on the bed laughing.

"Kenichi! You've lost so much weight!" said Dorothy.

"Kenichi? You sound like Mom."

"Well, before you see Mom, we're going to have to fatten you up."

"You look great, Dor," Ken said holding his sister at arm's length. She was dressed in a navy blue suit with nylons and high heels. Her long dark hair was piled up in a large bun billowing out over her forehead. "You didn't have to get dressed up just for me."

"This is about what I usually wear."

"This is what secretaries in New York City wear?" asked Ken.

"Well, I'm the assistant marketing director for the company. We meet with potential customers several times a day, and they like us to look presentable."

"You look more than presentable, Dor. Tell me about your business and everything else you're doing here in New York."

"First, you tell me about your hand," Dorothy said, lifting his bandaged arm.

The two talked all morning, jumping from one topic to the next. Dorothy had found life in the city stimulating and energizing. Her work took at least ten hours a day, and in addition, she now headed up the scrap iron drive for Upper Manhattan. And yet, she seemed to find time for a busy social life.

"Do people accept you, as a Nisei?" asked Ken. "I can't imagine this happening in Los Angeles."

"Yes. It's sort of funny. At first, they pretend they don't notice. Then as I get to know them a little better, they find a way to bring up the topic of race. But it's more a question of never having known any Japanese before, than any preset prejudice. But there are always the stereotypes. Many are surprised that I don't wear glasses, you know, since 'all Japanese are near-sighted'. I've run into a couple of unpleasant situations, but they've always been with people who have lost someone in the Pacific. I've mentioned you many times to let them know I'm vulnerable to that also."

"But now, Dor, the question of the hour. Is there any special guy?"

"No. Not really. As busy as my social life is, it seems like it's all false, like a drama, and soon the curtain will come down and we'll all go home. I've gone out with many guys on leave from the war who thought they were in love with me, even a couple who wanted a quickie marriage before they went back. But when all this is over and the lights go on again, I don't want any regrets. When life is real, then we'll make real decisions." Ken looked again at his sister and wondered if this was the same girl he'd known in Terminal Island.

Dorothy went with Ken to therapy. Their conversations ranged from Manzanar to McNeil Island Penitentiary to Peter. Neither knew exactly where he was at that time. Ken described his experiences in Italy and France. He carefully avoided the despair he had eventually begun to feel about whether it was all worth it, or the almost relief he felt when he was wounded and could stop struggling. At one point, Dorothy spied Horace across the room. Remembering him from Manzanar, she went to talk to him.

"Horace seems almost cheerful, despite losing his leg," she said when she returned.

"Did he tell you what his plans are?" Ken asked.

"Yes. He said he was going to go law school and then go try to help the Negroes down south. Is he serious?"

"Yeah. He was very disturbed by the way we saw them treated when we were in Mississippi. You know, separate bathrooms and drinking fountains."

"He also told me you carried him piggy-back up three flights of stairs so he could see the Statue of Liberty."

"When I saw it in the distance, I said Horace has gotta see this."

"Ken, you're not as bad a guy as I used to tell everyone you were,"

Dorothy said with a laugh.

The two went back to Ken's bunk before lunch. As they sat down, Dave Larson came up. "You're Dorothy?" he said, as he studied her from hair bun to high heels. "I don't think I would have recognized you."

"It's been a long time. Ken said you were here, and we remembered we'd met when Ken received the scholarship from the Japanese American Club of Los Angeles." She stood and shook Dave's hand.

"Yeah, that was it," Dave said and continued to shake her hand. "Ken says you've been in New York a couple of years now?"

"Yes. I came out in the spring of '43 and have been here since."

"How do you like New York City?" Dave continued to look her in the eyes and shake her hand.

"I like it. It's a very energetic city. I have a good job, and I, uh...we could stop shaking hands and sit down and I could still tell you about New York City."

"Oh, yeah, sure," Dave said. They continued to talk non-stop. Ken noted it didn't matter whether he was there or not. After awhile, he informed them that the lunch announcement had been given several minutes before.

"Well, let's go to the P.X. to eat. Visitors can't eat in the mess hall. He led Dorothy to the door, allowing Ken to trail after them. The two-way conversation continued, although every once in awhile Dorothy made a lame attempt to involve her brother in it.

"Would you show us New York City?" Dave asked later that afternoon.

"I'd love to," she answered. "When will you be free to come in?"

"This Saturday. We can catch the first ferry in and meet you wherever you want about 8:30."

"Hey, Dave," Ken said. "Let's have breakfast first and catch a later ferry. We can still be in by 10." Dave looked a little pained but agreed, and the three of them settled on where they would meet that Saturday.

"I thought you liked to sleep in on Saturday mornings," Ken said after the two men had bid Dorothy good-bye.

"Yeah, I do, but, uh, there's a lot to see in the city. Your sister has sure changed, Ken. You should have warned me."

The day after Dorothy's visit, Ken went to visit Horace. They had spent some time together on the ship, but after Dorothy's comments, he realized he had been so tied up with his own thoughts,he had not been listening to Horace.

"Dorothy said you were pretty cheerful when she talked to you yesterday."

"When I first awakened in the field hospital and found that my leg had been amputated and that Tyrus had been killed, I felt terrible. I was mad at the war, mad at my country, mad at myself for volunteering, mad at everything. I didn't care whether I lived or not. If I'd felt any stronger, I probably would have killed myself. After a couple of days, though, something dawned on me. Tyrus lost his life saving mine, isn't that right? I wouldn't be alive if it weren't for Tyrus Shimabukuro." He paused. "Did you know he was planning on becoming a priest?" Without waiting for an answer, he continued. "He told me that the night before he was killed. He was going to go back to Hawaii, become a priest and deal with young boys in trouble. Instead, he gave his life for me. And here I was, feeling sorry for myself. Now I'm not religious like you, Ken, but if God was ever trying to send me a message, that was it. And then I thought back to the Negroes–haven't been able to get them off my mind since we left Camp Shelby. I don't know how to help them, or even if they'd be interested in my help, but I want to try. I think the law may be the way to do it, so those are my plans. As soon as I get my prosthesis and get discharged, I'll be looking for a law school willing to take a one-legged Jap who's so short he'll need to sit on two pillows so he can see over the desk." Ken was silent for several minutes.

"Whatever happened to the meek accounting major I knew at UCLA three years ago?" he finally said.

Saturday morning dawned cloudless. Despite the freezing spray off the waves, Ken and Dave stood at the railing of the Staten Island Ferry and took in the Manhattan skyline for the first time. Fully-dressed, Dave had awakened Ken that morning and insisted they eat breakfast in the snack bar, because "it opens half an hour before the mess hall." They had arrived at the ferry dock forty-five minutes early.

"I was just amazed at how much your sister has changed," Dave said for the third time that morning. "I mean, it must be something about New York, or I don't know what."

"What do you want to do in New York?" asked Ken trying to change the subject.

"Whatever your sister wants. She's the one who lives here. Wasn't that our agreement, that she'd show us the city?"

"Sure, but we can make suggestions. What have you always wanted to see in New York?"

"Oh, I don't know, the Empire State Building?" Dave said without conviction, his mind obviously on something other than sightseeing.

Dorothy met them at the pier, dressed in a long blue overcoat and a matching hat, designed more for style than for keeping her head warm. A hug from Ken and another long handshake from Dave, and they were off to see the city.

"Is it too cold for you guys to walk? This is a city you need to see on foot," said Dorothy.

"No problem," said Dave. "It's not too cold." He offered his arm to Dorothy and started walking.

"Oh, Dave," said Dorothy, "I forgot your leg. Maybe we should take a taxi."

"No. No problem. Let's go. It's good therapy." Ken hurried along to catch up with the other two.

"I thought we'd go by the Stock Exchange first," said Dorothy, " and then go to the Fulton Fish Market. It's the busiest place in New York on Saturday mornings with all kinds of fresh fish, people bargaining and yelling at each other in all kinds of languages. It's wild."

The Fulton Market was "wild", as Dorothy had described it. Though it was only 9:30 in the morning, they sat down for a shrimp cocktail at a table overlooking the East River and the Brooklyn Bridge.

"You know," said Ken, " I guess I never knew a street named Wall Street really existed. I always thought that was just a term used to refer to the financial establishment."

"What's it like living in New York City, Dorothy," asked Dave, ignoring Ken's revelation. "Tell me all about it."

Dorothy described her life there, with an emphasis, Ken noted, on the work, the energy of the city, the Scrap Metal Drive, and not the social life. She was obviously warming to Dave's attention, Ken noted with some concern.

"You've certainly made the best of a bad deal," Dave said after she finished. "I mean uprooting you from your home, sending you to that camp at Manzanar, and then only allowing you to get out if you came east."

"It's been a blessing in disguise, Dave. We west coast Japanese had almost no concept of what the rest of the country was like. If I'd stayed home, I would probably have continued working and living in the Los Angeles area and never known what the east coast was like. I shouldn't really refer to the war and the Japanese evacuation as a 'blessing', but there are some good aspects of it."

"Well, like I say, you've certainly made the most of it."

"Let's go, boys," said Dorothy, rising. "City Hall's next on our tour, and then the Empire State Building, but that's a long walk. How's your knee holding up?"

"Fine, no problem," said Dave.

"I'm holding up fine, too, thanks." said Ken. Dorothy looked at him and then blushed and smiled.

Three hours later, the trio sat eating lunch in a restaurant across from Rockefeller Center and watched the huge Christmas tree being raised. Dave rested his leg on a chair, a bag of ice on his badly swollen knee. He had limped noticeably the last several blocks of their walk. Even Ken was solicitous over Dave's leg now, but Dave would hear none of it. "Give it a little rest and elevation, and we can keep going." They finally agreed that after lunch, they'd walk the few blocks to Central Park and take a carriage ride.

"Hey, lootenant, are youse with that 442nd American Jap group?" asked the carriage driver, as they climbed into the carriage. Dave maneuvered himself and Dorothy into the seat facing forward.

"Yes, the 442nd Regimental Combat Team," said Ken, a little warily.

"Well, let me shake your hand. I read how youse guys saved the, whaddya call it, 'Lost Battalion', those Texas boys. I mean, that was sump'n special. And I mean it's criminal what those guys are doin', puttin' all youse American Japs in those, whaddya call it, detention camps. I gotta tell youse, I thought it was O.K. at the time, but now, hey, it ain't fair." By this time he had climbed into his seat and was driving the carriage up into the park. His commentary continued. "I got a boy in the Navy, you know. He was on the *Yorktown* at Midway Island. They got sunk, but he got out all right, and now he's on the new

Yorktown. He's a gunner, ya know. They're out there somewhere near the Philippines now, I think." The carriage driver's patter continued, requiring only an occasional grunt of agreement from Ken. That was fine with Dave and Dorothy, who were lost in their own conversation.

A cab ride took them back to the ferry dock, and as they waited for the ferry, Dave said, " Are you free tomorrow to continue the tour, Dorothy?"

"Dave!" Ken said. "Your knee is as big as a beach ball. You won't be able to walk tomorrow, even if they let you come back."

"Sure. If I elevate my knee tonight, it'll be fine by tomorrow. And they don't need to know. They don't check us on weekends."

"Look, Dave," Ken started, but his sister interrupted him.

"Why don't I come out and visit you two. I could go to early church service and catch the first ferry out after that."

"Would you do that?" asked Dave.

""Sure. I'd be happy to."

"What a nice sisterly thing to do," said Ken. When Dave looked the other way, Dorothy slugged her brother in the chest.

"Smart alec!" she whispered.

The 1944 Christmas season in New York was the most cheerful one in four years. In Europe, the Allies were on the verge of entering Germany, and in the Pacific, they were relentlessly retaking the Philippines and looking north towards Japan. The North Atlantic crossing was still a dangerous one, but not nearly as much so as in the past three years. Victory, though it would require many more lives, finally seemed inevitable. For Dorothy Hayakawa and Dave Larson, it was a particularly cheerful season. It was clear to Ken that his sister and his old roommate were falling in love. But what would usually be a happy situation sent warnings through Ken.

"Dor, you know how Mom and Dad, particularly Dad, are going to react."

"I know, Ken, but it's just something they're going to have to deal with. I'm not sure what will happen. Maybe this is just one of those wartime romances they keep warning about, that will fizzle as soon as the war's over. But right now I feel about Dave like I've never felt about anybody before. It sort of snuck up on me. From what you told me about him before, I thought of him as a happy-go-lucky guy with an eye for the girls and barely smart enough to make it through college. But he's different. He's a man with serious thoughts and serious plans. And as for the racial part, he's going to have more trouble than I will, I mean if anything comes of this. His parents aren't going to be any happier than mine, and how will it affect him in business to be known as the guy with 'the Jap wife'?"

"Well, if you're 'the Jap wife'," Ken said after a few moments, "it'll be to his benefit."

His warnings to Dave were no more convincing than those to Dorothy. "Look, Ken, you remember I always had a lot of girlfriends, but I hardly remember their names. They were just like challenges. Dorothy is the first woman I've ever met that I want to share my deepest thoughts and ambitions with, who I want to be a part of whatever I get into, whose opinion I care about. I can't imagine the future, whatever it holds—work, family and growing old— without her. If that's love, man, I got it! I know this racial thing will be a problem. I don't care now what my father thinks, but I know one day it would be nice to have doting grandparents for our children. I know when Mom meets Dorothy, it won't take more than ten minutes for her to be converted. I imagine your parents aren't going to be too happy, either, huh? Guess I'll just have to do my best to convince them I'm worthy of their daughter...if she'll have me."

It didn't sound like a wartime romance to Ken.

<hr/>

"Lieutenant, there's a Captain Furuya to see you," said an orderly one morning in early January.

"Doug! You show up at the oddest places," Ken greeted his friend.

"I've been reassigned, Ken. My job now is to recruit students and instructors for MISLS, you know the Military Intelligence Service Language School in Minnesota."

"So you think there's a hidden colony of such people in Staten Island?"

"Yeah. I have a list of about twenty men here in Halloran Hospital, including you, that we think speak and write Japanese."

"I speak it all right. We spoke it in our family, but I'm a little rusty on the writing. I haven't done much of that since the Japanese language schools in the afternoon that my parents made me go to," Ken answered.

"Because of your experience in combat and since you can speak the language and write a little, you're the kind of guy we're looking for. You'll have to take the course first, and then if you do well, we ask you to stay on as faculty. In your case, actually, we'd plan to keep you on regardless and expect you to become an expert in the Japanese military. I'm sure their military terminology will be foreign to you at first, but I have every confidence you can pick it up rapidly. I took the liberty of talking with your doctor. He said you've got about as much function back in your hand as you're going to, and he's going to start discharge proceedings."

"What? Discharge proceedings. I hadn't even thought of that, Doug. I've been so busy as a chaperone, I haven't had time to think of my future."

"Chaperone?" asked Doug.

"It's a long story. I'll tell you later. But I guess your pitch is that if I volunteer for MISLS, I can stay on active duty."

"That's about it. Whaddya say?"

"What can I say? Captain Furuya, I'd like to volunteer for MISLS."

"I'll see what I can do about it, lieutenant." He pulled some books out of his briefcase. "In the meantime, this will help you brush up on the writing and the military lingo. Your orders have been cut to leave here on Thursday."

時期の選択

CHAPTER 21

"EH, BU. YOU GON' GO PEE AX?"

"No, no go."

"Why no go?"

"No need go."

"I go."

"Yeah, you go stay go. I come bumbye."

Ken slowed a bit and smiled as he listened to this Pidgin English conversation on the steps of the headquarters building at Fort Snelling. Two years ago, he would have had grave doubts, in fact did, that men whose English was no better than that could function in a world that required thinking and decision-making in multiple syllables. His experience at Camp Shelby and subsequently had turned that opinion around one hundred eighty degrees. The men from Hawaii had turned out to be an intelligent, clever, and innovative group. He had also noted that even those who were college educated used their colorful patois in informal conversation, switching to "gude Eenglish" when the occasion demanded. He had no doubt that the two men deciding whether they should go to the P.X. were good language students. He continued up the steps to the headquarters to sign in.

Fort Snelling, Minnesota in January was colder than the Vosges Mountains, but there were no slush-filled foxholes, and when one got cold, one could go inside a heated building and have a cup of coffee. Warm showers were available whenever desired, not just once every two weeks when one's unit was taken out of the front lines for a few hours. The Military Intelligence Service Language School was a bustling concern in early 1945. Begun as a shoestring organization on the Presidio of San Francisco before the war, it had moved to Camp Savage, Minnesota and in the summer of 1944 to Fort Snelling in Minneapolis. The purpose of the School was to prepare Japanese linguists for service in the Pacific. Nearly all the students were Niseis with at least a basic understanding of the language. For those who spoke and wrote well, the training lasted six months and emphasized document translation, military terminology and monitoring radio transmissions. For those whose Japanese was rusty, the course lasted nine months and included speaking and *Kanji* writing. Many Kibeis (Niseis who had studied in Japan) stayed on the faculty after graduation because of their superior language ability. Graduates were sent to join front line units and headquarters in the Pacific and China-Burma-India theaters. Their activities included prisoner interrogation as well as the skills they had learned at MISLS. More recently, they had been involved with talking soldiers and civilians out of the caves on the limestone and volcanic islands of the South Pacific. When Ken arrived, thousands had been trained and sent out, and hundreds were there in various stages of preparation.

When he handed his orders to the administrative clerk, the clerk said, "Oh, Lieutenant Hayakawa, Major Aiso wanted to see you as soon as you checked in." Ken looked up from his signing in with interest. John Aiso, the Director of Academic Training, was already gaining almost legendary status amongst Niseis. A graduate of Harvard law school, he had been rescued from the motor pool a month before Pearl Harbor. He had been invaluable in organizing language training from the school's beginning .

"At ease, Lieutenant Hayakawa," said the scholarly-looking major, returning Ken's salute. "Have a seat. Let me get straight to the point. Captain Furuya told me of your background. Our plan is to use you primarily to teach map-reading. You'll have to take the language course obviously. Your tests indicate you should take the six-month version, but while you're doing that and afterwards, we want you to get very familiar with Japanese tactics, order of battle and so forth. With your experience, you should be able to integrate all of that into an effective plan to teach these young men to read Japanese maps. You may have to start with American map-reading since the only military exposure for most of them was two months of basic at Fort McClellan. We have a library I'm sure you'll find more than adequate for that purpose. Any questions?"

"Yes sir, I'd like to know when I start. I'd like to take a couple weeks' leave to visit my brother and my parents. I have plenty of leave..."

"Your class starts on the twentieth, Lieutenant," said Major Aiso. He looked at the wall calendar. "That'll give you six days. That ought to be plenty of time. Tell the librarian that I gave you permission to check the material out and take it off post. You can study it on the trip. That'll be all." He returned to his papers, looking up only briefly to return Ken's salute. He was lost in study as Ken did an about-face and left his office.

The next day Ken checked into the BOQ and repacked his duffel bag for a short trip, then caught the train going west to Tacoma, home of McNeil Island federal prison. As he sat at the train window watching the snowy northern plains, he remembered the trip to Manzanar for Christmas just over a year ago. He thought of Shimabukuro and Ishii, and he thought of Horace getting used to his prosthetic leg. He looked at his own right hand, the fingers strung up with rubber bands so he could continuously exercise the small amount of muscle remaining that would give him discriminate finger function. He was relearning to write with that hand, although it was a toss-up which hand he did better with. His thoughts went to medical school.

"Where would they be now?" he thought. "Half way through their sophomore year...still in the basic sciences...starting their clinical work this summer." He looked at his hand again and wondered if he'd ever be able to tie a surgical knot.

The snowy plains gave way to the Cascade Mountains, and then the apple orchards of eastern Washington, in hibernation now, awaiting the awakening of spring and another opportunity to display their sweet glory. After a change of trains in Seattle, Ken arrived in Tacoma late on a drizzly afternoon. As he climbed into a taxi and directed the driver to the docks, he noted the driver's frown. The driver dropped him off and accepted his money without comment, but Ken remembered that the order expelling all persons of Japanese ancestry from the west coast was still in effect. At the office for the McNeil Island ferry, he identified himself as the brother of an inmate and was told that the last visitors' ferry for the day had departed. He saw that the first ferry the next day would leave at 10AM and took a taxi back into town.

"We don't have any rooms," said the paunchy desk clerk in the first hotel he entered.

"You don't?" asked Ken. "I'm surprised you'd be full at this time of year."

"Naw. We're full." Ken left and went to another hotel further down the block. He waited while the clerk assigned the man ahead of him in line a room and then stepped up.

"A room for one for one night, please."

"O.K," said the clerk without looking up as he made a note in the registration book. He looked up as he turned the book around to Ken and then suddenly pulled it back and shut it. "We're all full," he said quickly. "No more rooms."

"You just gave one to the man in front of me," Ken said.

"That was the last one. We're all full." Ken felt the blood rising in his face as he glared at the clerk. He was small, and Ken was sure he could grab him at the collar with his good hand and pull him up over the desk. But he was elderly, and he was looking more frightened by the second. Quickly he added, "Down a block and around the corner, you'll find the Puget Sound Hotel. They take Japs, uh, Japanese." Ken stared at him a few more seconds and then left.

"Yeah, we got plenty of rooms, Lieutenant," said the clerk at the Puget Sound. "They been giving you a hassle at the other hotels?" The clerk was a young Caucasian with a hook for a left hand.

"Yes. They said they were full," answered Ken, as he registered.

"They ain't full. They don't understand what you guys are doing in Italy. I was at Monte Cassino–that's where I lost this," he said, indicating his hook, "when the 100th came in to save our asses. I try to tell these guys, but they don't see no distinction between Japs from Japan and our own Japs. What happened to your hand, Lieutenant?"

Ken described how he'd been wounded and brought him up to date on the actions of the 100th/442nd. The clerk told him at which restaurants he'd be welcome, and Ken went up to his room.

⋆⊸⊶⊷⊱⋆

The gray prison looked dreary as Ken watched it appear out of the drizzle from the ferry railing. "How else would I expect it to appear?" he thought. "What am I going to say to Howie? I'm sure he doesn't need any more reminders that he's the first Hayakawa in memory to go to prison. Should I just talk about how much fun we had with Dorothy in New York and how soft and safe my present job is, and ignore where we happen to be? Do I want to let him get going again on how unfairly the government is treating us? Maybe coming here to see him wasn't such a good idea. Maybe wearing my uniform will just rub it in." He reached up and unpinned his ribbons and Combat Infantryman's Badge and stuffed them into his pocket.

When Howie was escorted into the visitors' room half an hour later, Ken stood up, started to shake his hand, and then embraced him. "It's good to see you, Howie," replaced all the articulate phrases he'd come up with over the last thirty minutes.

"Good to see you too, Ken. I'm glad to see you followed my advice, even if I didn't follow yours."

Ken looked at his brother quizzically as they sat down. "Followed your advice?"

"Yeah. Remember at Manzanar the night before you left. I told you not to come home dead, and you told me to stay out of prison. Sorry I couldn't keep my part of the bargain. I was doing O.K. and staying out of the riots and work-stoppages and all at Tule Lake, but then when they said they were going to draft us, I had to refuse."

"How many refused?" asked Ken.

"I'm not sure. Thirty or so from our camp, and some from the other camps. I hear there were quite a few from Heart Mountain. Some are here at McNeil, others at Leavenworth, and I guess they're planning to deport some to Japan when the war's over. I'm glad they sent me here."

"Glad?" asked Ken.

"Sure. I broke their law, even if in my mind it was for a good purpose. When I've served my time, I'm a free man and can get back to life." Ken searched his brother's face and though he could not say he saw a smile, he saw the look of a contented man.

"How is prison life?"

"Not too bad. Everything's regimented of course, and some of the guards like to hassle you, but if you keep your mouth shut, they move on to someone else. We spend most of our time with others in for draft refusal, so they're not a lot of violent men. Many of them are Jehovah's Witnesses, who don't believe in war. Anyway, I'm handling it. Tell me about what you've been doing, Ken. How's your wound coming?"

Now it was Ken's turn to soft-pedal the situation. "Aw, it's not much. Just enough to get me out of combat. I'm getting strength back daily. I can write with it now."

"Yeah. I saw the results in your letter. Come to think of it, though, it wasn't much worse than your regular chicken-scratching. If there's anybody who deserves to be a doctor on the basis of bad handwriting, it's you." Howie laughed a real laugh, and Ken joined him, more because it was the first time he'd seen mirth from his brother in four years than because of his handwriting.

"You said you'd seen a lot of Dor in New York, at least that's what I think the letter said." Howie laughed again, still enjoying his joke.

"She's doing great. She's assistant marketing director for her company now, looks real professional when she goes to work, you know, suit, nylons, hat, the whole picture. She seems to love it, and she knows everywhere to go in New York City. She showed us a great time."

"Us?" asked Howie. Ken had intended not to tell Howie about Dave but realized his slip.

"Yeah. Remember Dave Larson, my roommate from UCLA?"

"Yes. I remember meeting him the time we all went up to watch you get some sort of honor or fellowship."

"Well he was there in the hospital with me. He'd gotten his knee all shot up in Holland. Anyway, the three of us must have covered every square foot of Manhattan together." If Howie suspected anything about the relationship between Dorothy and Dave, he didn't show it. But why should he? Ken thought. Howie would still picture his sister as a shy secretary in Long Beach, dressed in a summer dress, and Dave as a self-centered college student looking for the prom queen. Their conversation went on and on until the guard came to call Howie for lunch.

"Can I talk to my brother after lunch?" asked Ken. The guard looked at the patch on Ken's right sleeve and his deformed hand, continuously working the rubber band.

"Were you with that Jap unit that rescued the Lost Battalion in France? The 400-something?"

"Yes. The 442nd."

"That where you got your hand shot?"

"No. That was a little later."

"You can visit your brother as long as you want to, Lieutenant. I read about you guys in the paper. Not much, of course, this being the west coast. But one of the other guards has a son that was rescued in the battalion, and he told us all about it." He directed Ken to the snack bar for visitors and took Howie back to lunch.

That afternoon, the two brothers continued talking, far and away the best talk they'd ever had, Ken thought. They were interrupted by the guard who had called Howie to lunch. He brought with him the guard whose son had been in the battalion rescued by the 100th/442nd. He was effusive in his thanks and during the conversation, Ken was obliged to bring his ribbons and Combat Infantryman's Badge out of his pocket and describe what they were and how he had earned them.

After the guards left, Howie asked his brother, "Why were they in your pocket? Did you think I couldn't handle them?"

"No, no," Ken said quickly, "well, uh, ...I wasn't sure. I've gotta tell you, Howie, you're handling this prison sentence better than I thought you would."

"It's a funny thing, Ken, it was almost as if when I got here, the slate was wiped clean. We didn't deserve to be in the camps. Your way of showing them that was to go be a war hero, and I'm honestly proud of you and your medals. My way of showing them was to refuse and make them put me in prison. One of these days I really think they'll realize how wrong they've acted towards us. I was sentenced to three years, but I'm sure I'll be out as soon as the war's over. I guess it sounds crazy, but I feel I've done my part."

"I'm not really sure I understand your choice, Howie, but if you think it's best for you, I'll just have to trust you."

"I've been going to - now don't fall off you chair - to chapel lately."

"No kidding? That is a surprise," said Ken. "Did you make peace with yourself and then start going to chapel, or did you start going to chapel and then make peace with yourself?"

"I don't know," Howie said after thinking a moment. "Does it matter?"

"I guess not."

⸺⸺

"It's hard to believe but I think Howie is more content than he's been for years," Ken told his parents two days later. The three of them sat in their barracks room at Manzanar, a cold wind from the Sierras blustering outside. Their living quarters seemed luxurious compared to where they'd lived nearly three years earlier. How well Ken remembered the bleakness of those same rooms they had entered that cold March day of arrival. With the kids gone, Toshiko had created a living area separate from the sleeping area. And she had accumulated enough furniture and draperies to give a feeling of home. The drafts had long since been plugged, and now a pot-bellied stove kept their quarters warm.

Words of protest–almost the first time he'd spoken that afternoon–came from Shoji. "No way he can be happy in prison. That's no place for a Hayakawa. No Hayakawa has ever been in prison..."

"Tell me about Dorothy again, Kenichi," Toshiko said quickly. Ken described their time in New York City again, careful not to emphasize the time Dave spent with them. He wasn't sure his mother would overlook that as easily as Howie had. When he finished, he reread the last two letters from Peter.

"What I don't understand," said Toshiko, "is why he's not in your group. I thought he'd be in the 442nd like you, but he's in the 542nd–or something like that."

"522nd, Mom. 522nd Field Artillery Battalion. They're attached to the 442nd. They're all-Nisei too." Toshiko still looked confused.

"I don't know why they couldn't have given them the same number if they're all together."

"Well, Mom, it means they're detachable, capable of their own command and control."

"Now you've really made it confusing. Anyway, Peter seems to be happy with the 500th- whatever it is. When he left, he said he wanted to be an artillery fellow. But Kenichi, it doesn't sound like they're fighting much. All he talks about is spending his free time on the Riviera, with beaches and girls. I guess I should be glad he's not in combat like you were."

"They're in southern France over by the Italian border, mostly guarding against the Germans invading from Italy. They're still seeing some combat, Mom, but not too much." Ken knew that although what they were calling the Champagne Campaign was not the equivalent of driving up the west coast of Italy, or driving for southern Germany, there was still considerable fighting going on with opportunities for casualties, but he decided Toshiko would be better off thinking of it as light skirmishing. If Peter was harmed, he could deal with that later.

"How's it going Dad?" Ken tried to get Shoji into the conversation. "You're still the block captain?"

"Yes. Still block captain, but there's not much to do, you know. Everybody's gone. All the young people gone to war or to jobs outside like Dorothy. Old people dying. Some of the men have gone to work on farms in Idaho and other places. I tried to see if they needed any fishermen, but they weren't interested. Not much to do."

"I noticed when I came in that your block looks real good, Dad. You're doing a good job."

"Yeah. Pretty easy." That was the extent of the conversation Ken could get from Shoji. He decided that if his father invited him to join him when he went for his whiskey, he would accept even though he didn't like whiskey. But no invitation was extended. Evidently that place for Shoji was a solitary place.

"Not much has changed, huh?" Ken asked Toshiko after Shoji left.

"No." Ken noted resignation in her voice. "It's the lack of feeling that he has any control over his life, that's gotten to him. When I first met your father, he was the strongest man I knew, both physically and mentally. He didn't have any education, but he knew he could handle whatever life threw at him. There was a lot of prejudice in those days, but Shoji learned how to beat the system. He could get what he wanted without a lot of confrontation because he knew what he had inside *him* was better than what they had inside *them*. They weren't able to beat him until they put him in here and said, 'We'll give you three meals a day and put a roof over your head, and you don't have to work for it.' That's what broke him, what took away his pride. We haven't even made love for two years."

"Mother!"

"I'm serious. Having sex for a man means being confident of himself, and I always felt honored to be the one to share that with Shoji Hayakawa. It's all different now." Ken never thought he'd learn about sex from either of his parents, particularly not from his mother.

"Mom, I uh...isn't there more to, uh, making, uh, love, than the man showing his self-confidence?"

"Maybe it's different for different people, but that's the way it was for your father and me."

"I, uh, well uh, how are the Yamashitas doing? Has Horace visited them yet?" Ken knew he hadn't, but it was the first question that came to mind in his effort to change the subject.

⚬⚬⚬

Back at Fort Snelling, Ken found himself quickly into the hectic mainstream of the school. The course in Japanese was more difficult than he had expected, but he forced himself also to spend time researching his new area of Japanese map-reading. As he did so, he was exposed to everything related to getting an army into the field, transportation, supply, armaments and medical care, as well as how the infantry, armor and artillery did battle. It was no surprise to him that the Japanese soldier required much less support than the American soldier. As tough as it was being a front-line infantryman in the U.S. Army, the life of a Japanese soldier was much more spartan.

After four weeks, when he had become fairly familiar with his topic, Major Aiso told him it was time to add his course to the curriculum. Not that his responsibilities as a student decreased, it was just an added job. Though he doubted it at first, he soon found that he could teach his course as well as take the language course. In fact, his teaching gave him considerable pleasure. The students were serious about the subject, continuously pumping him to identify every little mark on the stolen Japanese tactical maps he used. And although he had prepared himself to interpret maps thoroughly, in the evenings he found himself in the library looking for information that might give the future interrogators a slight edge. Unit identification was extremely important. POW's would never identify their unit or wear their unit's patch, but if they mentioned their hometown in the interrogation, that might give a hint, since certain units represented certain areas. Ken soon knew where all the units originated. He also knew the Japanese chain of command . Some nights he dreamed he was in the Japanese army and familiar with all their inner workings. At times in his lectures, he would catch himself and question whether he was sharing information gathered from intelligence study or from his dream the night before. In his dream the Japanese soldiers were not fanatics with a death wish. Rather they were men like himself. Men who would rather be doing something else. Men caught in the maelstrom, doing the bidding of their country even if it meant death. He was glad he would not have to face those soldiers on the battlefield, for he knew that his war was over except for his teaching about them, the enemy he felt he was getting to know.

CHAPTER 22

M YRNA," SAID AILEEN, AS SHE SAT DOWN BESIDE
her sister, "I'm sorry to interrupt you, but have you seen
Mom's kimono lately?"

"Isn't it in the back closet?"

"No. I've looked all over for it,and it's nowhere to be seen."

"What do you want it for? You planning on getting married?" chuckled Myrna.

"I'm serious, Myrna. I think Mom bartered it. Notice we've been
having more turnips and sweet potatoes and cabbage recently? Well, I
checked out the old pantry in back, the one we never use. It's full of
those vegetables. Remember two weeks ago when Mom was gone all
day? She said there were long lines at the market, but I think she went
to the country and traded her kimono for all this food. But she wants to
add the food in a little at a time so we won't notice."

That night when confronted, Mieko admitted to having done what
Aileen suspected. She started to cry. "Everyone else has made such sac-
rifices. Aiko, you left school and got a job where you had to pepper
your throat. Then you and father went to Saipan and nearly got drowned.
And Myrna studies her medicine with bombs dropping every night. All
the money father sent home from Saipan is gone, and the taxes to support this foolish war are going up every month. I hated to see that kimono go, but it was time for me to make a sacrifice, as little as it was."

"Oh, Momma. I wish you'd let me know. I could have gone back to
my job at NHK. Maybe they would have given me a job in a different
area." When Jun and Aileen had returned home the previous July, they
felt as though the money from Saipan would last indefinitely. Jun had
returned part-time to Domei, with its inadequate salary, but he and
Mieko assured Aileen that she did not need to return to work. She had
joined a volunteer group that stood on downtown street corners and

collected *Senninbari* stitches from passersby. One thousand stitches of red thread on a white cloth were collected, then sent to a serviceman at the front. There it could be worn as a sash around the waist–supposedly providing the wearer protection from bullets. Although Aileen doubted the theory about protection, she felt no guilt at collecting stitches, since she thought of the servicemen as patriots rather than as aggressors. She avoided a similar activity, that of collecting written messages on a flag, which would then be sent to the front encouraging the men into valiant battle. Perhaps it was a fine distinction, she thought, but she carefully restricted her activities to solicitation of *Senninbari* stitches. Now when the *kempeitai* came by, less often lately, she could describe her volunteer work "for our courageous soldiers and sailors".

The fall and winter had not been too bad for the Nakamuras. Although raids by the B-29s (*bee-nijuuku* they were called) became more frequent, they were ineffective. Bombing from high altitudes, they rarely hit their targets, and they were looked upon as a nuisance, though sometimes a deadly one, more than a factor in the war. As spring approached, a somewhat more ominous program started through the *tonarigumi*. They issued pointed sticks and held classes on how to protect their homes if the invasion of *Nihon* occurred. "I know how to use this." Aileen said when they got home. "When I see American soldiers coming up the street, I'll tie a pair of my white panties to this stick and wave it out the window."

"Don't think they'll get the wrong idea, do you?" smirked Myrna.

"*Baka na senso,*" said Jun and Mieko, in unison.

Friday, March 9, 1945 had been a particularly pleasant day. It was the first warm day of the year after a cold winter, and though the wisteria and cherry trees were not yet in bloom, Aileen sensed spring in the air. Evidently others had sensed the same and had ventured out to shop, because she had gotten a huge number of threads sewn into her cloths. She had gone to bed after a dinner of turnips, rice and fish. A little after midnight, she awakened to a roar of planes overhead. The sounds came from the east and left to the west. When she heard no bombs, she went to look, because she had never heard planes that low before. They were distinctly *bee-nijuuku,* and they gained altitude and turned south as they crossed over their house. When she turned to the east, she saw a growing light, as though it were dawn. Joined by the family now, she watched with rising horror as the light increased. She could now see flames even though the fire was three miles away. The planes continued to fly overhead and head south. Soon sirens sounded as fire trucks from their district of Daito rushed to the scene of the fires, which clearly covered many square miles by now. Aileen went back to bed, but sleep did not come easily. The winds had been high, and she knew that the fires were spreading faster than they could be contained. In the morning, through the huge black cloud, she could still see flames, further south now. Judging by the fire trucks racing back and forth, the fire was still far from extinguished. Thinking they could possibly help, Jun and Myrna and Aileen walked towards the fire. When they came to the Sumida River, they were sickened by what they saw. Charred bodies were floating in the river, some of them still alive, but only barely. On the other side of the river, it appeared that nothing was left standing except a few brick skeletons. The fire continued to burn far to the south.

"Not much you can do here," said a weary fireman. "We'll just have to let it burn itself out. Those damned Americans have changed their tactics. Now they're coming in low and using incendiary bombs. They're trying to burn Tokyo to the ground. Well, damn them! It won't work. We'll show them that we Japanese will never surrender. They do not understand the *Yamato damashii*! They may have the bombs, but *we're Japanese*!" He yelled these last words and shook his fist to the south at planes long gone.

If the fireman at the Sumida River did not need their help, they soon found some who did. For the next week they worked nearly around the clock helping with disaster relief. At first they were assigned to look for survivors in the burned-out area, which officials estimated covered sixteen square miles. Aileen's first survivor, a two-year old girl burned from head to foot, died as she carried her to the ambulance. She went behind a crumbled wall, and there her tears mixed with her vomit. When she recovered, she told the organizers that she would join the group arranging housing for those who had fled the fire. That job was almost equally heart-wrenching, but at least the small amount of food she ate that week stayed down.

"Mom and Daddy, Myrna and I think we should take some of our turnips and sweet potatoes to the people in the shelters," Aileen said one night at dinner several days after the fire-bombing. "We know Mom traded her wedding dress for them, and we know there's only a few more weeks' supply for our family. But you've seen the people in the shelters. There's almost no food. We're trying to get them evacuated to the country, but there's so little transportation they'll starve before they get there!"

Jun and Mieko, as exhausted as the girls were, continued to stare at the walls and then nodded their assent.

"It hardly made a difference," Myrna said that night. "By the time we unloaded our vegetables, they had already been distributed. It was a drop in the ocean."

"When is Japan going to surrender, Daddy?" asked Aileen. "Surely everybody knows the war cannot be won. I thought when they got rid of General Tojo last summer more rational people would take over, but that's been eight months. Now the Americans have Whats-its-name, that island that just makes it closer to bomb."

"Iwo Jima," said her father.

"Yeah. If they do many more bombings like last week, Japan's gotta surrender. We're all starving!"

"I'm afraid they won't," said Jun. "You heard that fireman at the river the morning after the bombing."

The next day, Aileen decided her father was right. As she returned to her *Senninbari* stitch-gathering downtown, she was inundated with women of all ages, eager to stitch a knot. Her friend, collecting messages on a flag on the opposite street corner, said that the messages that day were more aggressive than usual, more of an emphasis on a warlike spirit than of the comfort of the beautiful homeland they were fighting for. Aileen gathered her thousandth stitch shortly after dark.

"I don't know whether to be happy or depressed," she told her family that night. "I'm proud of the people and their spirit, but maybe if everyone would tell the government they're ready to give up, they'd surrender, and we could get this *baka na senso* over with."

<hr />

The next day, the line to sew a stitch was as long as it had been the day before. Aileen had to convert the long line to three shorter lines to keep from blocking traffic.

"Aileen?" said a voice in English. Startled, Aileen looked up to see a young man in uniform. He looked familiar, but Aileen could not place him. He was slender and only slightly taller than Aileen. His face was a soft face and needed a razor only rarely. From her time in Saipan, Aileen recognized his uniform as that of an Army pilot.

"Yes?" she answered in Japanese.

"Do you remember me?" asked the young man, switching back to Japanese.

"You look familiar."

"From the university. Hideki Iimura. I was in English Literature. You and your sister came from America, and all our discussions became more interesting." He spoke haltingly. Aileen remembered him now, as a shy young man who had obviously had a crush on her. He was one of the smarter students and spoke English better than most, but his shyness had kept him in the back ranks of the Nakamura girls' admirers.

"Yes, Hideki, I remember you. I'm surprised to see you in the Army. You're a pilot?"

"Yes. I would like to talk to you. When are you finished?"

"Well, I, uh,...probably around sundown."

"Can I come back and talk to you then?"

"All right, Hideki, I'll see you then."

Hideki was back an hour before sundown but stood unobtrusively to the side until the second sash of the day had been completed. Aileen carefully folded it and placed it with the needle and thread case into a knit bag. She and Hideki started walking.

"So, tell me what you've been doing since we last saw each other," Aileen said, remembering Hideki's shyness.

"When they closed the university to students in the humanities, I didn't want to join the service. I thought it was a foolish war. I had wanted to go to America to study. Anyway, I switched to Electrical Engineering so I could stay in school. But I was hopeless." He chuckled at himself, the first time Aileen had seen him smile. "I stuck it out for a year, but I was so lost that even the Army looked better. Finally I left the university and joined the Army. I thought what little engineering I had learned might make it easier for me to learn to fly, and I'd rather do that than learn to live in foxholes in the jungle. I can't picture myself killing somebody, but if I did, I'd rather do it from the air so I couldn't see them. But pilots' training was tough too. In order to impart to you the fighting spirit, they put you in a ring to fight people, and you don't get out until you beat somebody. I'm not very...fierce, I guess. I had a hard time. Finally they found someone less fierce than I, and I fought my way out."

Restaurants did not abound in Tokyo in those days, but Hideki and Aileen found a place that served ersatz tea. The table was lit only by a candle, not for atmosphere, but to conserve electricity and to conform to blackout regulations.

"Was it hard to learn to fly?" asked Aileen.

"Yes, very hard. I'm sure I would have washed out, but they need pilots, so I eventually soloed and got my wings."

"What kind of planes do you fly?"

"Zekes. They're small fighter planes." Hideki had been having trouble maintaining eye contact with Aileen, whom he obviously still worshipped. Now he looked her intently in the eyes. "We have just been redesignated a Special Attack Corps squadron." He continued to look at Aileen, almost questioningly. She felt she should recognize that designation.

"That's nice," she said. Hideki looked relieved.

"Tell me about you now," he said. Aileen initially planned to just outline the last three years but soon was responding to Hideki's requests for more detailed information. After two more cups of weak tea, she realized she'd shared with him her guilt over her translating job and the pepper incident. She also told him about Saipan and Masayo and their desperate escape, even including her despair when the submarine had torpedoed the American battleship. Something about this young man opened up Aileen's vulnerability.

Suddenly, Aileen looked at her watch. "Oh, I must get home!"

"May I pick you up when you're finished tomorrow?" asked Hideki. She agreed and told him she'd be at the same corner collecting stitches.

"Where were you, Aiko? We were worried," said Mieko, when Aileen arrived home two hours late.

After explaining her lateness, Aileen asked, "Daddy, what's the Special Attack Corps?"

"Is this young man, Hideki, in the Special Attack Corps?" Jun asked, suddenly more interested. "Those are the suicide squads - the *kamikaze*."

"You mean those crazy men who crash their planes into ships?" asked Aileen.

"Yes. They arm the plane with a heavy bomb and give it just enough fuel to go one way and send them to their death. They think that's an even more glorious way to die for the Emperor," Jun answered. "*Baka na senso*!" He turned back to his newspaper.

"That's hard to believe, Daddy. Hideki does not seem to be that kind of boy."

<hr/>

The next afternoon after Aileen had put away her paraphernalia and as she and Hideki walked towards the tearoom, she said "Hideki, my father said Special Attack Corps is just another name for *kamikaze*!"

"That's right," said Hideki softly.

"I thought they were all volunteers. You didn't volunteer, did you?" She stopped and looked Hideki in the face.

"We were standing in formation when we were told our squadron had been redesignated and that anyone who refused to give his life for the Emperor should take a step forward. When none of us did, they said we were all volunteers."

"But you can go to them now and resign, can't you?"

"Probably I could, but..."

"Hideki. Your future is in the university teaching English Literature, not in some empty gesture in a war that's already lost. When this war is over, Japan will need scholars and professors. They don't need one more plane crashing against a ship for no good reason!" The two stood in the middle of a busy sidewalk, people passing rapidly to either side of them.

"You don't understand, Aileen." Hideki spoke Japanese but insisted on calling her by her English name. "The world's changed since 1941. If there were any way to get out of this, I would. You're right. My goal has always been the university, but the choice has been taken from me. How could I live in the post-war time if I had refused to do my duty as a Japanese?" The two resumed their walk to the tearoom, and Aileen resumed her argument. Hideki's mood was one of resignation, not of boasting or manliness. It was simply something he had to do.

By the end of the second cup of tea, Aileen had made her last argument, in fact they were now pleas, but to no avail. Conversation turned to other topics. They reminisced about their university days before the war, the last time of happiness for either of them.

"Tomorrow's Sunday," Hideki said as they stood to leave. "You're not collecting stitches then, are you?"

"No. I take Sundays off."

"Can we meet somewhere then?" If Aileen had wanted a day at home with her family, a look at Hideki's face gave her no option.

"Yes. In fact, let me bring a picnic, at least some rice balls and sweet potatoes and some real tea. You won't miss this kind of tea, will you?" She pointed to their empty cups.

"No." Hideki's intent look had relaxed with her acceptance. "I will not miss any kind of tea as long as you're with me."

⊷⊶

The next day, Aileen met Hideki in the park just after noon. "You're lucky I showed up," she told him.

"Were you thinking of not coming?" Hideki looked worried.

"No. I didn't mean that. But today is the first of April. In America, we call it... April Fools' Day." She said the latter in English. "Can you translate that?"

"Uh...fool is *baka*..." Hideki put it in Japanese but still looked confused.

"There's a tradition that you pull a practical joke on April Fools' Day and then yell out 'April Fools' Day!'"

Hideki still looked confused. "I'm glad you came. If you had not, it would not have been a joke."

"Don't worry, Hideki." She squeezed his arm as they walked towards the fountain at the center of the park. "I would not have stood you up." They spread their blanket and lunch under a freshly-blooming cherry tree. After the fire-bombing just three weeks earlier, many had predicted that the smoke would prevent the blossoms that year.

"Today is also a special day for Christians," Aileen said as she gave Hideki a rice ball and poured him a cup of real tea from the portable tea pot. "It's Easter."

"Is that the day they said Jesus died?"

"Actually, no. He died on Friday - Good Friday they call it - but came alive again on Easter Sunday."

"How could he do that? Was he really dead?"

"They say he was. And then when he came alive, they called it a miracle."

"Maybe the story is symbolic," said Hideki. "Much of American and English literature is symbolic."

"Well, Christians say it really happened. In fact they base their whole religion on whether it really happened."

"You keep saying 'they'. Are you not a Christian after living there all those years?"

"No. I don't think I'm a Christian. I guess before you become a Christian, you have to deal with the truth or falsehood of Easter, and I've never done that."

"Don't they make you become a Christian if you live in the United States?"

"No. You can pretty much believe what you want, or nothing. A lot of people don't seem to believe anything very seriously."

"I'm sorry the picnic is so sparse," Aileen said after a several minute lull in the conversation. She thought back to the picnics on Managaha Island and the fresh fruit and fried reef fish and decided not to describe those to Hideki.

"The picnic's fine, Aileen, much better than we get at the base. And when I lie back and see the blue sky through the cherry blossoms, and...and you sitting beside me, I..." His sentence trailed off. Aileen was glad lest she be expected to reply. She changed the subject.

"What course did you like best at university?" she asked.

As the lazy afternoon progressed, Aileen and Hideki began to sense a buzz in the conversations of passersby. The level of intensity was growing from that of earlier afternoon when couples strolled and enjoyed the sky and the blossoms. Finally Aileen asked a couple what the excitement was all about .

"The radio is announcing that the Americans are invading Okinawa," came the reply.

"Okinawa?" said Aileen as she and Hideki sat back down. "Isn't that only a couple hundred miles from Japan?"

"Three hundred twenty-seven," said Hideki. Aileen looked up, surprised at the precision of his answer.

"That must be one of your targets," Aileen said, referring to Hideki's assignment for the first time that afternoon. He nodded.

The light-hearted specialness of the afternoon vanished. Aileen ventured into several conversational areas, but it was obvious that Hideki's thoughts were elsewhere.

"I don't know if I'll be able to meet you tomorrow afternoon," he said as they parted. "The Okinawa invasion will put all our plans into action. But I will see you before I go. I will!" He held her hand briefly as he bowed solemnly and turned quickly to leave.

When Hideki did not meet her on Monday or Tuesday afternoon, Aileen began to worry. She pumped Jun repeatedly for reports on *kami-*

kaze attacks on Okinawa. Many were reported, but Aileen was unable to tell from the propaganda-covered news whether Hideki's unit was involved.

It was with great relief therefore that she saw him, dressed in his flight suit, approach her late Wednesday afternoon. She left her sash and ran to him, taking his hands. "Oh, Hideki, I'm glad you haven't gone!"

"I don't have long," he said. "In fact I'm not supposed to be off base now, but I need to ask you to come to the base tomorrow evening. We are having the *sake* ceremony, and then we leave later that night. Can you come?"

"Of course I can, Hideki." Hideki sighed and continued to study Aileen's face and hold her hands, ignoring the disapproving looks of passersby at the vulgar public display of affection.

"Can you, uh, can we..." Hideki stammered, "can we talk some more? Would you come with me to a *ryo*...er...*ryokan* and we can talk more?"

"To an inn, Hideki?" Aileen thought of their usual visits to teahouses and knew that they were private enough. But she said, "Yes, Hideki. I'll go. Let me get my sash."

Together they turned off the main avenue and walked down a narrow alley until they came to a modest looking building with *Kanji* characters indicating it was the *Tatsumi Ryokan*. As they slid the entrance door open, they were met by a loud *"Irasshai mase!"* from a middle-aged woman.

"I would like a quiet private room for a ... a short period of time. We want to talk," Hideki said nervously. The woman appraised the two of them slowly. "I don't have much money," Hideki continued.

"That should be no problem," said the proprietress with a knowing grin. "For those in service to our country, there will be no charge." She led them along a dark hallway to the back room, and with a barely audible *"dozo"* slid open the door. "I'm sure you'll find this room satisfactory."

The small room was unfurnished by western standards. There was one window, which opened onto an alley, and along the other wall was a *futon* for sleeping. As soon as the door slid shut, Hideki took Aileen by the shoulders and said, "Aileen, I...I love you. I...." Gently, he sat her down on the *futon* and knelt in front of her. Slowly he took off his flight jacket and then his shirt. He began to unbutton the front of Aileen's dress. She looked up at him, and tears rolled down her cheeks. He pulled the dress off her shoulders. She did not resist. He started to pull the straps of her slip off her shoulders and then stopped.

"I cannot," he said and sat down beside her, putting his head in her lap, sobbing. She pulled his head up into her chest and held it tightly as her tears dripped down, mixing with his.

They sat that way for a long time, until he finally stood up, wiped his cheeks, sighed deeply and said, "It's time to go."

"When will this *baka na senso* be over? It forces everyone to do such strange things," Aileen was telling Myrna two hours later, having just awakened her from sleep. "Poor Hideki. He should be in America studying English Literature and preparing to teach Japanese boys and girls how to live in peace. Now he'll be taking off to his death in about twenty-four hours and for no purpose. And there I was. I would have been willing to make love to a man I didn't love. When will this war end and some sanity return?" For once her sister did not have a clever reply.

"You haven't worn that blue dress for years," said Myrna the next afternoon. "This is a big deal for you tonight, isn't it?"

"It is for Hideki, and I guess for me too," said Aileen as she noted how loosely the dress that she used to fill out, now fit her. It was her favorite of the dresses she'd brought from America five years before.

"You sure you're not in love with this boy?"

"No, not love, but I feel so bad for him. I wish there were a way he could avoid this, but at this point, there isn't. I don't know if I'll ever understand the Japanese way." She went over and picked up her *Senninbari* sash. She recounted the stitches but knew that it lacked nearly a hundred stitches from being complete. "What can I give him, Myrna? I can't give him an incomplete *Senninbari* sash."

"I think he was letting you know last night what you could have given him, " answered Myrna.

"Myrna! I'm serious. What can I give him?"

"Why not give him a *tenugui?* You know, like in those *samurai* movies?"

Aileen went to a drawer and removed a white cotton hand towel and studied it. "You mean like this."

"Yes," said Myrna, "He could wrap that around his flying cap. Maybe you could write him some words of encouragement on it."

Aileen fingered the towel, then moved to the writing desk and removed a bottle of charcoal ink and a brush from the desk drawer. She carefully placed some newspapers under the towel and then wrote two characters on the towel, horizontally and in bold strokes. As the ink dried, Myrna came up and studied the characters. "*Hissho*," she said, thoughtfully. "Yeah, I guess that would do it. Where'd you come up with that?"

"I saw it downtown over a stand where they were collecting messages on flags. I think it would translate as something like 'Guaranteed Victory'." Aileen turned the towel over and then wrote in English "Love, Aileen".

"That sounds more like you," said Myrna with an approving nod.

Hideki was waiting for her at the main gate when she arrived at the air base three hours later. He wrote her name and address in the visitors' book, explaining to the guard that she was his cousin from Tokyo. After pinning her pass on her dress, she accompanied Hideki to the assembly area. Hardly a word passed between them as they walked. Finally, Aileen said "Hideki, wait a minute." She stopped, reached into her bag and handed him the *tenugui*. He looked at the characters and straightened visibly.

"*Hissho!*" he said forcefully. "Yes!" He started to wrap it around his soft flight helmet and then noticed the English words on the other side. Immediately he lost the military stiffness that the Japanese characters had caused and again said "yes" but this time softly. Suddenly the bugle call came over the loudspeakers sounding "assembly". Hideki tied the towel around his helmet and asked Aileen to arrange it so the English words would not show.

"I must say goodbye," said Hideki, standing straight now, holding Aileen's hands and looking at her intently. "I wish it could have been different." His eyes were dry.

"I wish it could have been different too, Hideki," was all Aileen could say as tears ran down her cheeks.

Hideki walked briskly to the assembly area and stood in line with thirty-five other men in flight suits, all looking as young and as innocent and as sober as he. They faced two civilians and an air corps major who stood in front of a table. The table held a bottle of *sake* and a black lacquered tray with forty inverted cups. Aileen joined the group of solemn family members behind the officials. The major called the men to attention, then introduced the two civilians as the mayor and deputy mayor of the nearby town. The mayor, a short, stocky man, seemed not to have suffered much from the food shortages of the war. He stepped to the microphone and began to extol "the great accomplishments of the imperial military forces." It did not take long for Aileen's attention to wander from the mayor's platitudes. She noted that three of the other pilots had *tenugui* around their helmets. Two of them had the standard red sun on the white background, but the third intrigued her. There were two characters with a similar meaning to her "*Hissho*" on the front, but on the sides were two embroidered tigers. They had been chosen, she knew, for their special meaning. Tigers not only symbolize strength, but they are known to "return to their lair." She recalled that when her father had resigned from Domei to take the position in Saipan, his co-workers had given him a carved wooden tiger, implying, Jun said, that they wanted him to come back. Aileen studied the young man with the tigers on his *tenugui* and wondered if they had been embroidered by his mother or his wife, or possibly a girlfriend. Jun had come back to Domei, she pondered, but as for this boy....Her musing came to an abrupt end as she realized that the mayor's speech had ended and the major's adjutant was passing the cups out to the pilots and the official party. The major removed the stopper from the *sake* bottle and poured each cup full. When that had been done, he called "*Kampai*", and all cups were drained in unison. When the cups had been gathered up, the mayor asked the crowd to join him in the traditional three cheers.

"*Banzai!*" they all cheered, both arms raised. "*Banzai!*" Aileen was certain that the shouts from the official party were louder than those from the crowd. "*Banzai!*"

"Right face!" came the command. "Double time, march!" Thirty-six young Japanese pilots trotted to their waiting planes. Motors started, propellers turned, and soon they were all flying off to the south to a base on southern Kyushu. There the pilots would spend the night while their planes would be drained of fuel and refilled with just enough to get them to Okinawa one way, three hundred twenty-seven miles, the next morning.

On the airstrip, soldiers officiously gathered up the *sake* cups and table, while Aileen and the others silently and tearfully walked towards the gate.

CHAPTER 23

I THOUGHT MY WAR WAS OVER," KEN SAID. THE NAME plaque on the desk in front of which he sat said "Douglas I. Furuya." To the left of the name was a captain's insignia; to the right the crossed rifles of an infantryman; and below the name were the words "Company Commander, Headquarters Co." "In fact, you were the one," Ken continued, "who said that because of my hand the only place where I could stay on active duty was teaching here at MISLS."

"The request came in yesterday for a dozen men who spoke Okinawan. They'll be invading there soon. That's classified, but everyone knows it, and someone had the idea that by having some men there who spoke Okinawan, they could prevent Japanese soldiers from fading into the population."

"That sounds like a good idea, Doug, but you know I don't speak Okinawan."

"No, but we thought we should send them under command of a senior officer."

"Since when is a second looey a senior officer?"

Doug reached into his desk and picked up a card to which were pinned two silver bars. He slid it across the table to Ken. "First looey isn't either, but it'll have to do. I made a list of men who give their descent as Okinawan. You can pick twelve, including some from the faculty, but no more than one faculty from any one division. I'd suggest you include Joe Higa and Jim Arakaki, both of whom graduated from college in Japan. Higa's in Division B, and Arakaki's in G, out at the 'turkey farm'. I understand Arakaki's disgruntled at having to teach *hakujins,* all of whom get commissions when they leave here. Actually most of the instructors would rather be out on the front lines, so I know you won't have trouble getting them to volunteer. Getting their division chiefs to agree is a different story. That's why I don't want you to take more than one instructor out of a division. Of course you don't have to take the assignment. Your hand can still exempt you from combat duty, you know, and with that and your Silver Star, no one would ever say a word." Ken looked at his right hand, still unconsciously working the rubber band contraption. He noted chalk dust on his fingers, evidence that he had switched back to writing with his right hand. He chuckled.

"I'll go. Of course. When do we go?"

"You're scheduled to leave at 1800 hours Wednesday."

"Wednesday? That's just five days from now."

"So it is," said Doug as Ken hustled out of his office.

Later that afternoon, Ken settled into his seat on the trolley out to the "turkey farm", so designated because it was an accumulation of hastily constructed barracks at the end of the trolley line on the southern border of Fort Snelling. There was room for only six teaching divisions on Fort Snelling per se, requiring this makeshift arrangement for Division G. The remoteness of the area and the temporary quality of the buildings did not make it a popular place, but at least it gave Ken a chance to review the work he'd done in the six hours since Doug had given him his assignment. He had chosen four men who were instructors, and eight who were students. He'd contacted six of the eight "volunteer" students so far, and they had all been enthusiastic about a chance to return to their genealogical homeland, even though most of them had never been there. He had contacted three of the four faculty and was now on his way to see the fourth. He had been careful to talk first to their chairmen. They of course had been unenthusiastic because of a shortage of replacements. It was easy enough to assign the top students from the graduating classes to the faculty, but it was apparent now that the Japanese American community had already been scoured for the really talented ones. In the end, the chairmen had reacted as Ken knew they would. *Shikataganai*. It cannot be helped.

When Ken arrived at the "turkey farm", he could see why it had gotten its nickname. The small barracks they used for offices, classrooms and living areas did resemble turkey coops. He couldn't resist looking inside one of the living areas. It held four cots, two small tables with two chairs apiece, a small chest for each man, and in the middle a coal-burning pot-bellied stove. Only men who had come from the detention camps would have considered it homey. Ken noticed with a smile that the brown blankets with US stamped in the middle were stretched tightly enough on the cots that quarters would have bounced off them.

He approached one of the shacks and knocked on the door with the sign "Chairman" on it.

"Come in," came the friendly response. "Oh, Lieutenant Hayakawa, I was afraid it would be you." The tone of voice had become less cordial. The chairman of Division G was Mr. Shigeya Kihara. A graduate of the University of California, he was a civilian who had been around nearly from the beginning. "Excuse me for being less than welcoming, but I got a call earlier in the day that you were looking for men who spoke Okinawan as well as Japanese and might be raiding the faculty. I suppose you want my permission to talk with Jim Arakaki."

"Yessir. The mission is to take twelve men who..."

"Yes, I understand the mission, Lieutenant. I'm sure it's a laudable mission. It's just that there's a laudable mission every month or two, and we get raided. A couple months ago, they needed extra men for Iwo Jima. A few months before that, Stilwell needed a special group, and on and on. Every time I think we have Division G set for doing our job, something happens to upset the apple cart."

"Well, sir...," started Ken.

"That's O.K., Lieutenant, I'm sure I'm not the only one in this war whose plans have to be revised from time to time, am I?" He smiled a smile of resignation. "You may talk to Arakaki. I'm sure he'll jump at the chance to get into the war. Please take a seat while I get him."

Ken could see dawn beginning to break over the Pacific behind them. He had to strain to look out the windows since the seats were strap seats lined up along the sides of the fuselage–bucket seats they called them. Half his team were seated along each side of the C3 airplane, hidden from the other half by supplies stacked and secured along the middle of the plane. Under each seat was a parachute, which the men had been instructed how to use before they entered the airplane. However all had agreed they'd go down with the plane before strapping on a parachute and jumping out over the ocean. Despite the uncomfortable riding conditions, Ken had slept well since their midnight departure from Travis Army Airfield near San Francisco.

"Lieutenant," said the young man sitting next to him, "if eet's O.K. wit' you, I like invite da guys to one luau at my parents' place when we come Hawaii."

"A luau, Takeda?"

"Yessir. Well, not a real luau with a *kalua* pig and all, but what we call one 'Japanese luau'. We roast some pig and make some poi, but den most of da rest is Japanese and haole food."

"We get to Hawaii in about an hour. Will that be enough warning for your parents?"

"Yessir. Dey nevah take long for one luau."

"I'll have to check and see when they can get us out, but if we have time, I'm sure the men would like that, Takeda."

An hour later, they were approaching Hickam Field near Pearl Harbor. They could see the outline of the sunken *USS Arizona* with its stacks above water. But from the air Ken could see no other evidence of the one hour of devastation that had occurred a little more than three years before. He thought of how much that one hour had changed his life as well as the lives of so many millions around the world. When on the ground, he was told his group was manifested for a flight leaving the next morning. Takeda talked to his parents, and they enthusiastically seconded his invitation. They agreed on the logistics of getting the men out to Haleiwa, where the luau would be, and they all hastily left the airfield for a day in Hawaii.

Ken found a telephone book and turned it to the S's. "I think Tyrus said he came from Kapahulu," he said mostly to himself. Seven Shimabukuros were listed but none on Kapahulu Avenue. The third Shimabukuro he called, however, knew Tyrus and gave him his parents' number.

"I'm Ken Hayakawa. I was a friend of Tyrus' in Italy and France," Ken said to the lady who answered the phone.

After a prolonged silence, the answer came back in a now tearful voice, "Yes, I remembuh Tyrus mentioning you een da lettuhs, you and Horace Yamashita and Kazuo Ishii from da mainland, and den da boys from Hawaii..."

"I'd like to come and talk to you and your husband today, if that would be O.K," said Ken. "We're on our way west and will be leaving tomorrow."

"Oh, yes. Dat would be nice eef no trouble to you, Mr. Hayakawa."

"No trouble at all, Mrs. Shimabukuro. How do I get to your place?"

It was almost noon when Ken approached the Shimabukuro home. It was a small individual house on a side street just off Kapahulu Avenue. Some of the wooden slats in the wall needed replacing, and a new paint job would have improved its appearance, but the hibiscus hedge and the large mango tree in the yard gave it a comfortable look. Inside, the furniture showed the rapid deterioration caused by a tropical climate, but everything was neat, and no dust was visible anywhere.

A fiftyish man dressed in blue work clothes with a name tag sewn over his left pocket declaring him to be "Fuji" greeted Ken. "Welcome, Mr. Hayakawa. My wife called me at da school—I'm da maintenance man dere—and said one of Tyrus' friends was coming by. Tank you foah spend some time wit us, eh?"

Ken noted a small table in one corner of the room. On the table was a large picture of Tyrus looking uncomfortable in a coat and tie, evidently his high school graduation picture. In front of the picture, still in their plastic boxes, were two medals, one a cross with a red, white and blue ribbon, which Ken recognized as the Distinguished Service Cross, and the other unmistakably a Purple Heart. Another picture showed a tall blond Army lieutenant colonel soberly presenting the medals to the Shimabukuros. To the right of Tyrus' picture, framed certificates that had accompanied the medals described the heroic actions that led to them. Behind the picture was a large cross with a solid base against which the pictures rested. On the front of the table was a squat candle which, judging by the amount of surrounding wax, had been lit frequently.

"Did you know that he had just saved a man's life when he was killed?" asked Ken.

"Yes. Da offisuh dat gave us da medal said so, but he deedn't know da details," said Mr. Shimabukuro. Ken related the details of Ty carrying the wounded Horace back to safety just before he was hit. He also told them of his swimming across the Arno River with the rope that ultimately allowed the whole battalion to cross. Quiet tears flowed from the Shimabukuros' eyes.

"There's something else I think you should know," Ken continued after a period of silence. He had been unsure whether to tell them this. "Tyrus had a...a... religious experience, a conversion, before he died."

Mrs. Shimabukuro looked up from her tears. "When we visited St. Peter's Cathedral in Rome, he was convicted of his, uh, sin, and he confessed to a priest right there in the cathedral. After that he really, uh, changed his ways. He lived about three months more, and his life was definitely changed."

"You doan need to hesitate tell us sin," said Mr. Shimabukuro. "We knew da boy. He was one problem raising up. Fighting, expelled from school, come veeseet da preenceepal, all dakine. We kept teenking dat down deep was one good boy. So dees ees one good news for us, eh?"

"See, Fuji, I tol' you prayers work," said Mrs. Shimabukuro, a huge smile now pervading her tears.

"In fact," Ken continued, glad he had decided to share this information, which might have offended some Issei parents, "he had decided to become a priest when he got back. He wanted to help other boys who had started out life like he had." Both parents continued to weep, now tears of joy.

Presently, Mrs. Shimabukuro stood up suddenly, wiped her tears, grabbed Ken's elbow, and said, "Boy. Come, come." She led him into the kitchen where the table was loaded with mangoes, pineapples and coconuts split in half, the juice in glasses. On the stove was rice cooking, and in the oven fish.

"Oh, Mrs. Shimabukuro. I don't want to impose on you," said Ken.

"No impose, Mr. Hayakawa, for one friend of Tyrus, and special dees kind good news."

Two hours later, Ken left the Shimabukuro house thinking he would not need to eat again for a week. Friends and relatives had gradually accumulated through the afternoon, initially quiet and respectful. Gradually they warmed up, particularly when, at Mrs. Shimabukuro's insistence, Ken reiterated the story of Ty's spiritual journey. Many reacted to the story with skepticism, but Tyrus's parents nodded vigorously each time Ken told it. Before he left, each parent individually assured him that the report of Tyrus's conversion and decision to become a priest was even more encouraging than the tales of his heroism.

Haleiwa was a beach side community at the opposite side of the island from the Kapahulu district. It took Ken three bus rides, one military and two civilian, to get there. When he arrived, he was easily able to find the Takeda luau on the beach. Three groups were arranged around a large bonfire. One group included a middle-aged couple–the Takedas–with their son and a couple of the men. Each of the other two groups had as its nucleus a pretty young girl, surrounded by three or four admiring young men. More careful inspection revealed to Ken that the men in the group around the senior Takedas were the married men in the detachment, while the bachelors were surrounding the girls.

After introductions, Ken told the Takedas how much he appreciated their hospitality. Their response was much as the Shimabukuros'. Though he thought that after that lunch, he'd skip dinner, he soon found he was eating the roast pork and poi and washing it down with beer. As the sun was setting over Haleiwa Bay, he asked Mr. Takeda about his family.

"We have five keeds. Da olduh boy, Harry, he graduated from da University Hawaii. He was one ROTC and went wit da 100th Battalion to Italy. He was keeled at one place, Monte Cassino."

"I joined the unit after Monte Cassino, Mr. Takeda. I didn't know him, but I know that was one terrible battle."

"Yeah. Den we have da two girls, Ella and Mary." He nodded towards the two groups, where the girls were still holding court. "Ella ees nurse, and Mary ees one school teachuh. Den numbah foah keed is Albert. He's weet da 442nd. I teenk dey're back in Italy now. And den Hubert,"–nodding to his son–"he's da brain in da family. He feeneesh numbah one in hees high school class, but he want join up befoah college."

"Do you live here in Haleiwa?" asked Ken.

"Yes. We leeve in one house neah da sugah fields until da keeds go school. Den we figuah we need move to town."

"You've done very well raising your family, I'd say," said Ken.

"Eet's been rough, but my wife work da company stoah, and I'm now one foreman. All da keeds ah good keeds. Dey get scholarships an stuff, and work. Eh, we make it. Eh, I teenk you guys from da mainland have it rough when dey move you from your homes to da camps. Eh, I doan teenk I could take dat, you know."

Ken opened another beer and thought about the Shimabukuro family and the Takeda family, different journeys but families that were close and supportive, a concept not foreign to Ken's experience.

CHAPTER 24

THE SUN MOMENTARILY GLINTED OFF THE ZEKE as it turned west over Okinawa. The pilot lifted his goggles and saw a profusion of targets - destroyers, ammunition ships, supply transports, and in the middle of them all, a small aircraft carrier. The scene was one of chaos. A burning oil slick with hundreds of men bouncing in the water marked a spot where an LST had just sunk. To the right of that, a minesweeper was nearly broken in half and sinking, its crew tumbling overboard. Several of the ships were burning. Small rescue craft were in amongst the bobbing survivors, pulling them aboard. The plane sputtered as it turned, a problem that had plagued it for the last hour, causing it to arrive a quarter-hour after the main flight. The fuel gauge had been on zero for the last ten minutes. The plane turned, leveled off and aimed for the carrier. For a few seconds, it flew unnoticed until suddenly it became the target of every gun in the fleet still firing. Holes appeared in the fuselage, and the right wingtip blasted off. The pilot found it harder and harder to hold the plane straight. The motor caught fire, and flames flared back over the cockpit. The pilot could still see the carrier and aimed his plane for the carrier's superstructure. Six hundred yards out a bullet smashed the cockpit and tore into the pilot's left ear. Blood spattered into the pilot's eyes, and he wiped them clear. Four hundred yards and the pilot could feel the blood spurting from the side of his head, sopping his jacket and the white towel tied around his flying helmet. Two hundred yards and he began to lose consciousness. "Must see! Must see!" he muttered and took a deep breath, focusing again upon the carrier's island. One hundred yards, and an explosion occurred under his left wing causing the plane to change course slightly to the right. The plane skidded on the flight deck looking much like a plane on a routine landing, but too close to the island.

The left wing struck the island, and the plane broke apart, catapulting into the ocean. The pilot was thrown out of the cockpit, landing a hundred yards from the carrier. He gained consciousness momentarily, turned to look at the carrier. "The bomb! It didn't explode!" But then he saw a huge fire where his wingtip had hit the carrier's island and smiled. "I did it." And then his eyes closed, and he went limp.

***

"Slow down, Schwartz, here's a Jap. I think he's the pilot that just hit the *San Jacinto*." Schwartz slowed the boat, and the sailor in front leaned over and pulled the pilot aboard.

"Is the sonofabitch still alive?" asked Schwartz.

"Naw. Sonofabitch's dead. Look at this scarf! I think I'll get me a souvenir." The sailor started to unwrap the white towel from the pilot's cap. but suddenly said "Aw, hell!" and he pulled his hand away. It was all bloody. "It ain't worth it!" He put his hand overboard and swished it to clean the pilot's blood off it. Eddie Dipalma from Brooklyn probably noted momentarily the Japanese characters on the towel but would not have known they meant "Guaranteed Victory". Had he persisted despite the blood and turned the tail of the towel over, however, he would have recognized "Love, Aileen" written with penmanship taught in a Seattle grammar school.

***

"C'mere a minute, Lieutenant. What do you make of this?" Ken walked over to the young man from Graves Registration, who was holding up the tail of the white towel tied around the pilot's flying helmet. "Why would this be written in English?" When Ken and his group stepped off the plane at the recently-captured Kadena Airfield in Okinawa, he was asked to help with identification of some Japanese pilots who had just been pulled out of the bay. He took two men with him and sent the rest to the temporary lodging assigned to them before deciding where they were to be used. Most of the dead Japanese were badly mangled, but Ken noted that the pilot he was being asked about had apparently only been hit in the left side of the head. His ear was gone and he had obviously bled to death.

"He has no identification in his pockets, Lieutenant. I guess his bomb never went off. Maybe it was a dud. These other guys are a mess." Ken looked at the inscription on the towel–"Love, Aileen"–and then turned the towel over.

"These two characters are *Hissho*, which means something like, uh, 'Guaranteed Victory'. I imagine that would be sort of a standard good wish when sending someone off to war."

"But how could committing suicide by smashing a plane into a ship be considered a victory?"

"I think the Japanese mind would consider it a personal victory if a man's death led to victory for his people. We do the same thing. We go on missions for flag and country that don't have much more chance of success than the *kamikazes*." Ken wondered if this young soldier had heard of the "Lost Battalion." "But I don't have any idea what this 'Love, Aileen' means." The two men knelt looking at the inscription for a few more moments, and then the soldier continued on his gruesome task. Ken dropped the towel and started to walk away. Then he suddenly turned back, untied the towel from the helmet, folded it carefully so that the blood, now dried, was on the inside and put it into his pocket.

"So, tell me again what your group is supposed to be doing here, Lieutenant." The speaker was a harried major whose job it was to assign all the smaller, supporting units to the large units on the rapidly moving front. The Army and Marine divisions had landed on the west coast of Okinawa against very little resistance, creating confusion as the follow up units were hurried ashore earlier than their planned dates. The major had been interrupted three times by calls on the field telephone in the five minutes since Ken had reported to him. "Your guys speak Okinawan. Is that different from Japanese?"

"Yessir."

"Well, how the hell should I know what to do with you guys, all these off-the-wall units coming across the beach." The phone rang again.

"I have a suggestion, sir," Ken said quickly when the major ended his conversation. "The front-line units already have their assigned translators for interrogating POW's. You're going to need these Okinawan-speakers mostly to deal with civilians whom we overrun and to separate out any Japanese who want to melt in with them. I'd suggest you keep this group attached to Army to be used as needed."

"That's a good idea, Lieutenant Hakawaka. I want you to go over to G-2 and tell them you're under their direction for all those reasons you just said." He returned Ken's salute brusquely and again picked up the ringing telephone.

Later that morning, Ken was talking to the G-2, the intelligence officer. Colonel Damechek had a little better idea how Ken's group of translators should be used and agreed with Ken's suggestion. "One more thing, though, Hayakawa, we need more contact with the translators with the front line units. At Saipan and also on Guam, they got a lot of information that we could have used. There wasn't a direct connection between them and us. One time we got intelligence we could have used only after it had been sent to Hawaii, processed and then sent back three days later. In addition to being in charge of these guys that speak the Okinawan dialect, I want you to be our contact with anything the front line translators pick up. That means you'll have to do a lot of traveling. I'll get you a Jeep and driver. Ever worked in G-2 before?"

"I had a little exposure to it in Italy, and then at the language school at Snelling, we were always dealing with intelligence about weapons, order of battle and so forth."

"You were with that Jap unit, I mean Japanese American unit, over there, the 4-something?"

"Yessir. The 442nd."

"I hear you guys were fantastic fighters. Last time I was in Hawaii, I talked to a friend who'd been with the 36th. He told me about you guys rescuing the 'Lost Battalion', when their other battalions couldn't do it."

"Well, we were all working together on it, but there sure were a lot of casualties."

"Is that where your hand got hit?"

"No, sir. That was a little later, but a couple of my friends got hit there."

"It's a hell of a war, Lieutenant. Anyway, I want you to spend a little time with Major Allen, and he'll tell you the kinds of things we're interested in."

Two days later, Ken was in a Jeep heading south to make contact with the translators in the 7th Division. The advance had now ground to a bloody halt. The Japanese had planned a strong defensive line across the southern part of the island at a place where the land rose suddenly into a series of defensible ridges. When Ken reported to division headquarters, he was directed to a nearby tent. "Your translators," he was told, "are working on a document that was found on a dead Jap officer."

"*Sensei!*" said the young Japanese American as he looked up from the document and recognized Ken. "I didn't know you were out here."

"Hamada, right?" Ken guessed as he thought back over his parade of students.

"Yessir, and this is Shigeo Ono. He went through Snelling before you got there, I think," Hamada said, nodding towards his partner. "Boy, you came at the right time. This paper we got off the dead Jap colonel tells all about their defense plans. We've been thinking they were just surprised and that's why we moved in so fast. But according to this, they expected us to land where we landed, cut the island in two and then turn south and north. Their plan is to let us get in and move far enough inland that we can't be covered by the guns from the ships, and then they'll defend the high ground. That's why everything's ground to a halt these last two days. You see those ridges there? There must be a million guns on them. But there are a couple things in this document we can't understand. Can you help us out with them? I mean, sir."

The three men bent over the document and wrestled with the few remaining confusing parts. Finally, they figured them out and then wrote out the translation in long hand, making three copies.

"Were there any more documents on the officer?" asked Ken. "This gives us the big picture, but from what you say, you need the details of individual gun emplacements."

"Naw. That's all," said Hamada.

"You take one copy and show it to your people, and I'll take the other two up to Army," said Ken. He talked to them a little more about their duties. They assured him that the function and usefulness of the translators was now well understood and appreciated by the commanders but that they still worried about being mistaken for the enemy by a well-meaning but trigger-happy GI.

"When we walk around after dark, we sing continuously–'The Star-Spangled Banner', 'America, the Beautiful', 'Stars and Stripes Forever', you name it. We'll be able to go on the road with patriotic songs when this war is over." Ken chuckled and headed back to Army headquarters, the two valuable copies of the translation and the original in his hand.

⚬

The next few days confirmed the accuracy of the captured document. Every attempt that the Army divisions in the south made to dislodge the Japanese from their ridges was beaten back. The Marine divisions were ordered north, and they had an easier time–until they came to the Motobu Peninsula. Mountainous and lined with deep gorges and few roads, it provided excellent natural defenses for General Mitsuru Ushijima's men. Ken, in his frequent trips to visit the translators in the front lines, sensed the growing frustration as attack after attack was repulsed, and the list of casualties grew.

He had a special mission when he visited his men on April 13 and 14. The death of President Roosevelt had been announced on the 13th, and many of the staff officers were sent to the front on those days. Ken wasn't sure how much grief the Nisei would be experiencing, for the president had signed Executive Order 9066, which had sent many of them and their families to the detention camps. He need not have worried, for the Japanese Americans were shedding as many tears as the others over the death of this man with the jauntily-angled cigarette holder and the spirit to match.

"Yeah, I know that he signed that order, Lieutenant, but what I mostly remember is what he said when they called for volunteers for the 442nd. I memorized it. 'The principle on which this country was founded and by which it has always been governed is that Americanism is a matter of the mind and heart; Americanism is not, and never was, a matter of race or ancestry,'" one man responded. The others agreed, even though they had not memorized the quotation verbatim.

⚔

If the front line translators were not kept busy with the static front and the lack of prisoners, the same could not be said for Ken's Okinawan translators in the rear. The plan was originally for them to separate Okinawan civilians from Japanese soldiers trying to avoid capture. It soon became clear that the rear-area translators' job was much larger and more important. Every day, the rear lines became more and more full of men, women and children displaced from their farms and villages, now becoming one of the most intense battlegrounds of the war. Shelter, food, water and medical care were needed immediately. Although the Military Government section of Army headquarters was tasked with this function, the numbers of refugees were soon overwhelming. One precept of dealing with such problems is identifying the leaders and governing hierarchy of the displaced people and using that framework as much as possible. Having been told that the invading forces were barbarians, none of the natural leaders stepped forward initially. The task of Ken's twelve, therefore, was to move among the people, develop their trust and find the men who could best help with organizing and controlling the refugees. Ken marveled at the fearlessness of these twelve as they mixed with the refugees. Weaponless, it would take only one Japanese soldier hidden among the people deciding to make one last heroic gesture for his emperor and they would be dead. Or perhaps an Okinawan with more loyalty to Japan than most of the people and who would consider the Nisei to be traitors. But none of Ken's fears were realized.

"No problem, Lieutenant," said one of his men, "the Japanese treated the Okinawans so badly that there're ten who'd give up a Jap soldier for every one who'd turn on me. And even those are more interested in where their next meal is coming from than in politics."

One day as Ken moved among the refugees, he saw one of his young men sitting on a shell-damaged wall talking with two bedraggled looking men his age. They wore threadbare Japanese uniforms. As he approached, he heard them chatting quietly in what he recognized as Okinawan, although not the regular dialect. It was more of a schoolboy slang, which Ken could not understand. "Sugiwara?" Ken said as he approached the men.

"Yessir?" Sugiwara jumped up startled. "Oh, Lieutenant. These are guys I went to school with. Remember I told you my parents sent me back here when I was ten to live with my aunt and uncle and to go to school? Well, these two guys were my best friends. We used to cut class and go fishing in the bay, and ... well, anyway, I saw these two in uniform and started to separate them out when I recognized them. They didn't know who I was at first. We haven't seen each other for five years. They just told me my uncle was killed." Sugiwara's voice trembled.

"Sorry to hear that, Sugiwara. How did that happen?"

"The Japanese took all the men in our little village and drafted them into the army about a month ago. They gave them a little training and some old weapons and then used them as front line troops. My friends say that on one of our pushes about four days ago, their unit was put in the front lines where they were like targets. Most of the men were killed or wounded, and that's where my uncle was killed. They don't have any loyalty to the Japanese, so they thought they'd take their chances as refugees, even though they would have been shot if the Japs caught them deserting."

"What about your aunt?"

"Our village is near Shuri Castle, and that's still behind their lines. As far as my buddies know, my aunt and cousins are O.K."

"Have you asked them about gun emplacements or troop dispositions?"

Sugiwara hesitated a bit. "I was just about to, Lieutenant." The two young men could speak Japanese passably, so Ken got out his map, and the four pored over it gleaning what information they could. It wasn't much, since they were told only where to go and nothing about the big picture or artillery support, but they were able to identify where their unit had been.

———

"Hayakawa, the general wants you present at the awards ceremony," said Major Allen to Ken a week later.

"You mean General Buckner?"

"Simon Bolivar himself."

"Why does he want me there? Because Takeda's getting a Silver Star?"   "I guess so. I think he wants to find out more about you guys and what you do."

"I've never talked with a three-star before."

"Just say a lot of 'yessir's and don't ask him why the battle's taking so damn long."

———

The next day, Ken was instructed to stand in formation with representatives of the division staff at the awards ceremony. Since they were still in a war zone and close to the fighting, the ceremony was more informal than the ceremony with General Clark in Italy. They wore battle dress and helmets. The sound of artillery could be heard in the distance. The citation for Hubert Takeda's medal described how he had, at great danger to himself, entered a cave and talked for an hour convincing Okinawan civilians to come out to be rescued. Eventually, more than two hundred came out. As Hubert had escorted the last ones out the mouth of the cave, an explosion came from out of the cave, killing the few holdouts. Hubert had been knocked to the ground but except for some ringing in his ears was none the worse for wear. The citation ended with the stock phrase about bringing great credit on himself and the United States Army. Ken silently added, "...and the Takeda family."

"Where is that Private Takeda from, Lieutenant?" General Buckner asked after the ceremony.

"He's from Hawaii, sir. He has two older brothers. One was killed at Monte Cassino, and another is still serving with the 442nd."

"Yes. I've heard about that unit. So Takeda's family is not in one of those detention camps?"

"No, sir, because he's from Hawaii. Only Japanese American families from the west coast were sent to the camps."

"What about your family, Lieutenant?" asked the lieutenant general.

"They're in a place called Manzanar in the California desert, sir."

"You have brothers and sisters?"

"I have a sister who is working in New York City, and a brother who has just joined the 442nd. I think he's in Germany now." Ken hesitated a moment and then added, "And also, sir, I have another brother. He refused the draft, and they sent him to federal prison."

"You mean they had the balls to draft you guys and then put you in prison if you refused? I thought you were all volunteers."

"We were all volunteers until early '44, when they said we could be drafted."

"Well, if you want my opinion, Lieutenant, that's a bunch of crap, drafting you guys. There may be some truth to the claim that they didn't know how loyal you were when the war began. History will tell us that answer, but to turn around and start drafting you a couple years later...that's just too much. I don't blame your brother. If I were in his shoes, I'd have done the same thing. Anyway, Lieutenant, I asked Colonel Damechek to have you here, because I wanted to find out what your men are capable of doing. I know they can talk people out of caves. They did that on Saipan and Peleliu and other places. I know they can interrogate POW's. Now Colonel Damechek tells me they're invaluable with organizing the Okinawan refugees and helping set up the military government. Do your men read Japanese?"

"Most of them do, sir."

"Do you have men who know the language well enough to write and translate surrender documents?" General Buckner asked. Ken told him about Higa and Arakaki, the two who had graduated from Japanese universities.

"Not that that damn Ushijima's ever going to surrender. He'll probably commit that whaddyacallit, harry-carry?"

"*Hara-kiri,* sir."

⚜

A week later, Major Allen picked Ken up and drove him to a cave where a large unit of Japanese had committed suicide by setting off explosives.

"One of your men was shot trying to talk them out of the cave—I'm not sure how serious the wound is. They're bringing the bodies out now and we need your help to identify the unit they're from," the major said.

Heavy late April rains had made most of Okinawa a quagmire, and Major Allen's jeep slipped and slid over the roads. The driver had learned his bad-road driving skills driving a taxi in Minneapolis before the war. Finally they skidded to a stop just below the entrance to a cave. Men were bringing bodies out on stretchers, many mangled beyond recognition. Ken saw a young Nisei sitting on a rock next to the cave mouth, smoking a cigarette and looking the other way. His left arm was in a blood-stained sling.

"What happened here, Hirakawa? It looks like you were hit," asked Ken as he approached the young man from behind. Hirakawa didn't move but continued to puff on his cigarette. "Hirakawa! What happened?" asked Ken again, raising his voice. Still no answer. Ken walked in front of him, and the young man jumped up, grimacing as he did because of his left shoulder. "What happened to you, Hirakawa?"

The young Nisei shook his head, pointed to his ears with his right hand and shrugged.

"The blast from the cave damaged his hearing, Lieutenant," said a medic as he approached the two. He went into the cave to try to talk the stupid Japs out and he got shot for his trouble. Fortunately, he was almost out of the cave when the ammunition went off or he'd be as dead as these guys they're taking out now. I mean to tell ya', Lieutenant, these American Japs got guts. You wouldn't catch me goin' into no cave. I'd shoot a flamethrower into it and say 'To hell with it' and go on."

"Is his hearing loss permanent?" asked Ken, though he knew the medic could not answer definitively.

"I don't know, sir. We'll have to see what happens in the next few days."

Ken walked over to the mouth of the cave where Major Allen had three of the more intact corpses laid. Ken fingered their colored collar tabs. "They're probably from the 23rd Regiment.. Are there any documents?"

"Not yet, but there are still a lot of men to bring out. They tell me there were more than a hundred in there." Ken and Major Allen watched the grisly procession without comment.

"You know, Major," Ken finally said, "our families back home are not going to believe...or understand what's going on out here. I mean, what drives us to the point where a bunch of men either blow themselves up, or other men burn them up by shooting hundreds of gallons of burning gas onto them? How are we ever going to tell this to our families back home?" Major Allen looked at Ken for a few seconds and then back at the parade of exploded flesh.

"Maybe we shouldn't tell them about it. Maybe we ought to just wave the flag, tell them a few general war stories, get back to work and forget the whole damn thing." A few minutes passed. "What family do you have back home, Ken?" It was the first time Major Allen had called him by his first name.

"I have a mother and father. I'm sure not going to tell them. I have an older sister. I'm not going to tell her. I have two younger brothers, but one of them thinks war is all glory. He's in the artillery and that's probably the best place for him. I pray he never sees the death and destruction his rounds cause."

⟡

If Ken had known what Peter was doing half way around the world, he would have known that his ebullient young brother had lost his innocence. Peter joined the army the day of his graduation and at his request been assigned to artillery when he reported in to Camp Shelby. His enthusiasm and athleticism–he had lost all his baby fat–had made him a model soldier through basic training as well as advanced artillery training. He had been shipped over to join the 522nd Artillery Battalion in France. By the time he arrived, the battalion had been detached from the 442nd and had just crossed over the Saar River into Germany. They moved fairly rapidly to the east, assigned to different divisions as they went. A move involved hooking their 105mm howitzers to trucks, moving a few miles, emplacing their guns, covering them with camouflage netting and awaiting a firing mission. Some days they'd move three times; other days not at all, allowing them to go on foraging trips for eggs and chickens in the countryside of southern Germany.

At first, Peter loved the work. But then sometimes when they moved they moved through their recent target area, and his brother's prayer would go unanswered. Soon, Peter's exuberance gave way to professionalism. He was merely a technician doing his job. But one particular episode he could not ignore. They had moved up to assess the results of their destruction of a large barn. The barn had been a small citadel of firepower that had held up the advance of an entire infantry battalion for half a day. "Good shooting, 5-2-2," had come the report from the forward observer. When Peter walked through the rubble of the barn, he counted no fewer than eighteen corpses draped over machine guns and antitank weapons. Good shooting.

On the day Ken was trying to identify the unit of the Japanese soldiers killed in the cave in southern Okinawa, his little brother was moving into the town of Dachau, just to the north of Munich. He should have been prepared for what he would encounter. Their unit had liberated several smaller concentration camps on their way to Dachau. Peter thought he was hardened to the sight of men and women, literally skin and bones, who stumbled out of the camps, embraced them and mumbled something in one of a multitude of languages.

"Hayakawa. You and Nakauchi, open the gate. We'll cover you, but be careful. I think all the Krauts are gone, but you never know," said the sergeant. Peter and Nakauchi walked through the foot-deep snow to the gate. It was padlocked. Peter raised his M-1 and shot the lock off. They opened the gate, and a mass of humanity came towards them. At least Peter assumed it was humanity. They appeared to be walking cadavers, eyes sunken and dark, the skin on their faces so taut they could show no emotion. All were dressed in black and white cotton uniforms with small round caps. Only a few were wrapped in ragged blankets. Most stumbled through the snow shoeless. Many fell and were helped to their feet by their comrades. Some could not be helped to their feet and stayed on the snow. One man stopped in front of Peter and with as much alarm as his distorted face could show said, "Japonisch?"

"No, we're Americans. You're safe." An English-speaking inmate volunteered to show them the camp. Half an hour later, he opened a door to a large building. Peter stepped inside, gagged at the stench but stayed long enough for his eyes to adjust to the dark. He saw corpses, looking not much worse than the live men and women he'd just seen, stacked one on top of the other. He estimated fifty of them before he stepped back outside and gulped some fresh cold air.

"The guards left two days ago. These are the people who've died since then," their guide said without emotion. The tears froze on Peter's cheeks as he began to dismiss the guilt he'd felt since seeing the eighteen dead soldiers in the barn.

In Okinawa, the bloody battle continued. The Japanese resistance was such that each small ridge required a concentrated full-bore attack before it was relinquished. Every yard of territory gained demanded nearly superhuman effort. April became May and May, June. Gradually the enemy-held area diminished. From Ken's vantage point back in the Army area, the stream of casualties, dead, wounded, sick and mentally exhausted, was unending. This included many of his translators, a few of them shot by mistake by their own comrades. They assumed the shootings were a mistake, although more than one of the translators had been assaulted by men who had become mentally deranged.

General Buckner had asked Ken to report to him several times since their first meeting. As the battle struggled on, he wanted to understand the Japanese mentality that would choose annihilation over surrender. Ken tried to explain from the paucity of his understanding the concepts of *on*, and *bushido*, the spirit of the *samurai*, and *gyokusai*: it's better to die for one's country than to live the rest of one's life in shame. The general began to get the picture and to give up the idea that he could appeal to General Ushijima for surrender on compassionate grounds. He realized that *hara kiri* was inevitable for his enemy. There would be no battlefield meeting between the two generals with a sword handed over to the victor and expressions of mutual respect.

"Maybe that's how a warrior should die, on the field of his greatest battle, whether he's the winner or the defeated," he mused to Ken one day.

By mid-June, the Japanese had been pushed into a small enclave on the southern tip of the island. Victory was near. General Buckner took a few of his staff, including Ken, now a captain, to observe the beginning of the last push. They stood behind a large rock on a hillside and watched. In the distance a salvo of five rounds, probably fired at random, was launched. "Hit the ground," someone yelled as the rounds approached. There was a roar as the rounds hit. One of them struck the large rock. When the dust settled, all stood up, unhurt–except General Buckner. A shard of rock had been driven through his chest. He died shortly. Four days later, General Ushijima committed *hara kiri*, and the battle for Okinawa was over.

CHAPTER **25**

T HE WAR NEWS FROM OKINAWA SEEMED unusually truthful. According to Jun, a minimum of propagandistic spin accompanied it. Aileen, not in contact with Hideki's family, had no confirmation of his death. She knew, however, there could be no other result. She noted that her despair was matched by the people who sewed stitches on her sashes. Months before, there was a certain amount of enthusiasm and optimism, but now, even though as many people stopped to add their words, the attitude was one of discouragement, messages of consolation almost, sent to men fighting a desperate last stand. If there was one point in time when Aileen thought the majority gave up hope, it was when, early in the battle for Okinawa, the huge battleship *Yamato* was sunk. It had been armed, they were told, to the level of impregnability. So there was no surprise when word came that the spirit of General Mitsuru Ushijima had joined those of all other men and women killed in wartime, at the Yasukuni Shrine.

Life in Tokyo, which could not have gotten any worse after the firebombing in March, got worse. Millions were evacuated to the countryside, but there was still not enough food. Even the availability of fish was rare. Mieko continued to make her visits to the countryside. Aileen noted the gradual disappearance of objects her parents valued–vases, silk-screen paintings, clothing–but she did not complain as she had when Mieko had traded her kimono. The incendiary bombings continued.

The official response to this suffering was still the conviction that Japan would ultimately be victorious. *Tonarigumi* leaders, with straight faces, still instructed their groups in self-defense with their sharpened poles. People practiced with chants of how the enemy would turn back because of the unbeatable spirit of Nippon. When the news of the German surrender came, Aileen thought that might have been the catalyst for the Japanese to seek an end to the war. Instead, a call was issued to fight on with the purity of a holy battle, unsullied by alliances with the unworthy white race. The Nakamuras shared their pessimism only in the privacy of their own home. Jun occasionally came home with a rumor of a peace party reaching out to the Allies, but that was never confirmed.

In July, Myrna started her third year of medical school and was assigned for the first quarter to the hospital in Hiroshima. Aileen hoped that might get her to an area less affected by the war, but Myrna's letters confirmed that very little of Japan had escaped the American air bombardment. Although her hospital was in the center of Hiroshima, because of the bomb damage, housing was at a premium near the hospital. She found a basement apartment in the suburbs. The advantage was that there were parks and walks where she could enjoy her rare free time. The drawback was that it took a 45-minute trolley ride and two transfers to get to the hospital. Nevertheless, she described great satisfaction at finally being able to see and treat patients after the years of basic sciences.

One evening in late July, a knock came at the Nakamuras' door. Aileen answered it and recognized Mr. Ueyama, her old boss at NHK.

"Please come in. Can I get you a cup of tea?" Aileen asked.

"Thank you very much, Aiko." Mr. Ueyama sat down and made small talk with Jun and Mieko while Aileen prepared tea. "We need you at the radio station, Aiko," he said when Aileen was seated.

"Oh, Mr. Ueyama, I..."

"Before you say anything, you would not be doing the same job as before. I know that bothered you, making up text for your, uh... for men from the country of your birth. But this would be translating English text that came in. The government has recently received a surrender demand from the Allies, and we are on the alert for communication back and forth. If any comes, we need to be immediately able to evaluate it. We decided to have an English translator on duty around the clock, but we don't have enough people."

"I have a different job now, though it's a volunteer job. *Senninbari*, and it's a full-time job, and one I think is very important," Aileen protested.

"Then we could put you on the midnight shift," said Mr. Ueyama,

"Midnight till 8 AM. We're close to where they distribute the cloths, so you could just leave the studio and have your cloth and stitches in about ten minutes. Not much work would be required, only if a message in English were received, or one sent out by the government in English. Many nights you'd sleep through the whole night. We wouldn't require you to broadcast yourself, so you wouldn't have to start smoking again." He added the last sentence with a sly grin.

"Well, I...." Aileen looked for help to her parents, but before they could give their opinions, Mr. Ueyama continued.

"I have a sense that you want this war over as soon as possible and with as little confusion and misunderstanding as possible. We know that our broadcasts are being picked up by the American Navy, which probably lies just over the horizon. It might be that your ability to clear up any problems in translation in something we broadcast will save lives." Aileen looked at Jun and Mieko, who were resolutely impassive.

"All right, Mr. Ueyama. I guess I can do it," Aileen finally said.

For the first week, Mr. Ueyama's prediction was accurate. Aileen had nothing of great importance to translate, but she did learn that steps were being taken towards peace. Though the steps were halting, perhaps this terrible war, a war that pitted her two countries against each other, causing millions of deaths and indescribable destruction, would soon end! The Allies had sent a message in late July from Potsdam, a small town near Berlin where they were meeting, describing their surrender demands. The Japanese were split on whether to reject it summarily, or to use it as an opening to barter for surrender terms that would save their pride of never having been defeated in war. The Big Six, the six government ministers with the responsibility for such decisions, were split 3:3. Kantaro Suzuki, an elderly admiral had been called back from retirement in April and made prime minister with the implied mission of getting the best surrender he could. Arrayed against him and other politicians was the military. Many of the older officers were willing to seek some sort of accommodation, but the younger officers were adamant against surrender. They felt even surrender with terms would bring great shame to them. Rumors of rebellion, should that happen, abounded. Complicating this was lack of clarity in the Potsdam Declaration on the position of the Emperor in post-war plans. In the end, the Japanese reply was ambiguous, neither rejecting the demands absolutely nor accepting them.

In later years when Aileen thought back to that morning of August 6, 1945, she remembered a feeling of distress, a free-floating sense of disaster, something for which any description missed the mark. She had not seen a flash in the sky, nor had she heard or felt a boom. But she had left the NHK building with a sure sense that something catastrophic had happened. By mid-morning, she began to hear fragmentary reports of a huge explosion in Hiroshima. Nobody had the whole story, but as more and more information came in, two things were present in every report: an explosion never before experienced in history had occurred, and it had occurred in Hiroshima. She bought an evening paper on her way home, and she and her parents studied it for clues of what might have happened to Myrna. The *pika-don*, or "flash-boom", as it was being called, had occurred at 8:15 that morning. There were reports of some *Bee-nijuukus* flying overhead, so it was assumed it was a bomb dropped from an airplane. Descriptions of the destruction were unbelievable, so unbelievable that reporters repeated that these were "unconfirmed reports". Nothing in the stories gave the Nakamuras hope that Myrna could still be alive. That night as the news reports came in to NHK, they all described the wasteland of several square miles created by the bomb. Only a few brick buildings remaining standing. People by the thousands had disappeared, "vaporized" was the term one reporter used. A news writer from Hiroshima told Aileen that the general hospital was right in the center of town, apparently at the point of maximal damage. The next day, Aileen studied casualty reports that came to the studio from the Interior Ministry. Myrna's name was not on any list, but that was no consolation, since 90% of the casualties were listed by the body part found, no identification possible. Aileen remembered the description of vaporization and began to realize they might never know for certain what had happened to her sister.

The first picture of the devastation was published in the evening paper, and Aileen and her parents stared at it wordlessly. "I've got to go to Hiroshima tomorrow and find Myrna," Aileen said.

"They won't let you go," said Jun. "They're only letting in emergency and medical teams. They have to evacuate the survivors, and they specifically said no one could come without permission."

"How will we ever know what happened to Myrna?" screamed Aileen, tears streaming down her cheeks.

"Maybe we never will, but our going there won't help," answered her father. Sobbing, Aileen ran to her bed and buried her face in her pillow.

Later that evening as they sat around a meager dinner, Jun broke the long silence. "The foreign reports are calling this an 'atomic bomb', something about breaking an atom in two. I don't know how that would create an explosion." His wife and daughter looked at him uncomprehendingly.

The next day, Aileen went straight home from NHK. She waited anxiously for Jun to return from Domei, although she knew he'd have no good news. He had more description of the bomb's characteristics, which was of no interest to Aileen, but he knew nothing more about casualties than she'd found at NHK the day before. She was getting ready to go to work after another nearly silent evening when there was a knock at the door. Jun answered it and after a few seconds called out excitedly, "Mieko! Aiko! Come quickly!" When Aileen arrived at the door, she saw a man with his head wrapped in a bandage and his arm in a sling. "He has a message from Myrna."

The man bowed to the two women and said, "Doctor Nakamura said to tell you she's all right. She has been busy taking care of the wounded and says she'll be home when they're all cared for, but that may be a long time."

"She wasn't...how come she wasn't hurt in the explosion? Wasn't she at the hospital? Are you sure? Myrna Nakamura?" Aileen sputtered.

"Yes I'm sure it is Doctor Myrna Nakamura. I don't know how she missed the explosion," said the man patiently.

"Please come in for a cup of tea," said Mieko.

"Thank you very much," said the man, bowing again, "But I must refuse your kind offer. I have to go to my home. They also don't know I have survived." After profuse thanks, the man left, and the Nakamuras stood embracing in the hallway for a long time, silent again but now with sobs of joy.

The next day, Aileen was again at her corner. Not many would pick up a needle and thread, though some did and then left in tears without sewing a stitch. Aileen was a study in mixed emotions, empathizing with the people but inwardly rejoicing that Myrna was safe and would be home before long.

That time came before Aileen expected. She arrived home that evening with a newspaper under her arm describing the second *pika-don*, dropped on Nagasaki that day. She heard retching in the back room.

"Myrna's home, but she's sick," said a worried Mieko. Aileen hurried back to see her sister prostrate, intermittently groaning and vomiting.

"It's some sort of GI upset due to the bomb," said Myrna between groans. "It has something to do with excess radiation, like I'd had too many X-rays all at once. The first day we were treating people for traumatic injuries, but by the second day, thousands began coming down with this. They die if we can't get enough fluids in them."

"Then you should be in a hospital!" said Aileen.

"No. There are too many already. In Hiroshima, we ran out of fluids. All we could say to a person was, "Go home and see if you can get enough fluid in orally." The hospitals in Tokyo are also full. When I started to come down with the symptoms, I came home as soon as I could. I was lucky to get a train right away, but I spent the entire time between cars throwing up outside. I wasn't the only one, and we had to share time at the window. You can tell from my smock, we didn't always make it to the window. I need to get as much tea and water down as possible in between heaves. You need to help me, Aileen." With that, she vomited again into a reeking pot she was holding. Aileen went outside, took several deep breaths and then went back into the kitchen. She found the largest kettle they had and started brewing some tea, the only thing they had plenty of.

The rest of the night, Aileen held her sister in her arms. Whenever Myrna was not throwing up, she would help her sip tea. Mieko and even Jun tried to spell Aileen from time to time, but she abruptly, even sharply turned down their offers. Through most of the night, Aileen felt sure her sister was losing everything she forced down. As dawn began to lighten the room, Myrna started to have diarrhea. Although that worsened the stench in the room, Aileen noted that her vomiting was lessened, and she was able to hold down more tea. By mid-morning, she was also handling some thin, but salty soup that Mieko had procured. Myrna's eyes were sunken. When Aileen pinched her skin, it retained its pinched shape rather than spring back to normal, a sure sign of dehydration. But for the first time, Aileen sensed a little progress, and she let Mieko attend her sister for a few minutes while she ducked outside to breathe some non-putrid air.

Later that next night, it was apparent that Myrna had turned the corner. Her fluid intake was clearly greater than her losses. She was still unable to eat solids–and just as well since not much solid food was available. Only a little rice and one yam remained, but no fish.

"You never told me how you avoided the *pika-don*," said Aileen once Myrna was resting comfortably.

"Ironically, I was sick that morning. I didn't want to infect my patients, so I stayed home. I was in bed, when I heard a terrible roar, and the house above me collapsed. It all came down into my basement apartment. My bed was against the wall so I wasn't hit. When I dug myself out and realized what had happened, I found a clinic and started to work. I had to walk away from the center of town because everything from my apartment into town was totally destroyed. You can't imagine how horrible the damage was! You could look towards downtown Hiroshima and see nothing but a few brick buildings still standing. Nobody was walking around. There must have been a hundred thousand people killed." Myrna started to sob, although in her dehydrated condition her tears were dry. "Anyway," she eventually continued, "I finally found a clinic that had survived enough that we could handle the wounded. I worked all day Monday and all night, got a couple hours sleep, and then I worked all day Tuesday and Wednesday. On Wednesday, we started seeing people with GI upsets. At first we assumed they were intestinal infections from contaminated food and water. But they all got worse rather than better. Eventually someone from the Ministry of Health told us what we were dealing with. Not that the information helped us treat anyone. But when I started getting nauseated, I realized I ought to get out of the area. I don't know when it's safe to go back."

"Not for a long time, girl," said Aileen with authority. "You're my patient, now, and you'll go back when I release you and not a minute before." Myrna smiled weakly.

Aileen returned to NHK that night, confident that Myrna was on the mend. In her two-day absence, the Japanese had sent out their acceptance of the Potsdam Declaration with the statement that they understood the declaration to not include "any demand which prejudices the prerogatives of His Majesty as a Sovereign Ruler." Within a day, the United States sent back its acceptance. Clearly, Aileen thought, the role of the Emperor still had to be clarified, but finally the war was nearly over, and without an invasion of the Home Islands. She sat down, and the tension, heartbreak and fury of the last four years began to ebb as the tears flowed. And she could not stop the tears all night though she had many more documents than usual to translate. Pouring out came the events of those four years: their inability to get passports to return to America before the war started; the lack of food that had almost become starvation; the desolation she felt when she thought her mother and sister's ship to Saipan had been sunk; the despair felt when she thought Myrna had been killed at Hiroshima; the helplessness she felt when she feared she and Jun would be lost at sea; and the despair when gentle Hideki flew off to sure death. And what would the future bring? Would the Japanese accept surrender, or would resistance groups interfere with the peace? Japan was still short of food. How soon would they have a diet that would end the starvation? And personally, would she ever get back to Seattle? Could she prove she was an American? Would her work at NHK raise suspicions that she was really Japanese at heart? *Was* she Japanese at heart?

On Okinawa, Ken greeted the news of the bombs with celebration, then awe, then horror as the pictures of the devastation began to filter back. The bleakness of the landscapes could only hint at what had happened to the thousands of people caught in the two cities. Fortunately he had plenty to concentrate on other than the bombs. For the first several weeks after the Japanese capitulation on Okinawa, pockets of soldiers, unable or unwilling to believe that the battle was over, still roamed about. The lot fell to Ken's men to convince them. That frequently meant squatting behind a wall, talking over loud speakers and awaiting the inevitable hail of bullets. At the same time, the problem faced with refugees now had mushroomed. A quarter of a million homeless people needed to be fed daily. Fear and distrust of Americans remained. Often it was necessary to convince the people that the plans for their care were to their benefit. More men of Okinawan heritage arrived from Fort Snelling, and Ken soon had them immersed in solving the civilian problem.

By late July, Ken had been given the added responsibility of helping with the plans for the invasion of the Home Islands. The Tenth Army— Ken was now officially assigned to the Intelligence section of Army—

would play a major part in the invasion, tentatively scheduled for several months later. He dreaded the thought of a few hundred Nisei translators acting as buffers between an angry invasion force and a frightened people desperately defending their homeland to the death. According to all their intelligence, the Japanese people were being so trained.

So hope mixed with horror as he began to pray that the bombs would bring an end to the war. Five days after the Nagasaki bomb, Ken was awakened from sleep at 2AM by a soldier saying that the translator listening to radio reports coming out of Japan needed him immediately. He dressed quickly and ran over to the tent. There he saw the translator pacing back and forth in front of his radio, earphones on, head bowed intently to catch every syllable. Ken had to touch his shoulder to get his attention.

"What's up, Ohashi?"

"Oh, Captain." Ohashi jumped. "It's the Emperor, I mean, it's over. This is from Tokyo, and it's all over, Captain!" Tears streamed down Ohashi's face.

"Calm down, Ohashi. Is the Emperor speaking?"

"No, sir." Ohashi took a deep breath. "This is an announcement that the Emperor is going to speak at noon tomorrow, Tokyo time, and announce the surrender."

"Let me listen." Ken put on the earphones. The announcement, as Ohashi had said, was to alert Japanese units to tomorrow's announcement, which would call an end to the war. Ken sat down and listened as the announcement was repeated. "Write it down, Ohashi. Let me get this message out."

Ken awakened Colonel Damechek and Major Allen. They insisted that Ken accompany them to tell the general. The general grilled Ken in depth on each word and every nuance of the report. Ken was glad he'd listened three times. The general told Ken to be present in the tent the next day when the Emperor's announcement was picked up. If it was as expected, he would get the word out to the troops immediately. Ken's next visit was with Higa and Arakaki.

"The Emperor doesn't speak regular Japanese, does he?" asked Ken.

"No, sir," answered Arakaki. "He speaks court Japanese. It's a little hard to understand, but between Joe and me, we can probably figure it out. They teach it a little in university, to guys that are going to be diplomats and stuff like that."

For Ken, the Emperor's announcement would be the equivalent of Doctor Kawamura's announcement three and a half years before: "The Japanese have bombed Pearl Harbor."

As he assembled his best translating team for the upcoming announcement, a curious event was happening in the NHK studios in Tokyo. Aileen was nearing the end of her shift, but the excitement of the night had put her in no mood to leave. All night long, messages had passed in every direction in anticipation of the Emperor's announcement. The NHK staff was told that the Emperor would not personally come to the studio, but that he had made a tape that would be delivered the next morning and played at noon.

The announcer for the 2AM to 8AM shift, Yoshio Oki, was taking a rare break. After a steady stream of reports, he was playing some music and resting at his microphone. Aileen, at her makeshift desk near the room's only door, reviewed the messages she'd translated that night. Suddenly there was a sharp rap at the door. Aileen arose and opened it. When she did, an Army major brushed past her. He drew a pistol and thrust it straight up in the air. "I demand to use the microphone to announce the revolution!"

Yoshio looked startled. "The revolution? What revolution?"

"The revolution that will restore the *Yamato damashii* spirit to Japan which those gutless politicians talking surrender are trying to take from it. We will defeat the white-skinned enemy on the soil of our beloved country, which has never been and never will be defeated on the battlefield."

Aileen had sunk back into her chair shaking, but Yoshio had regained his composure. "But Major, that would be impossible."

"Why?" asked the major, some of his bluster gone.

"We are under an air raid alert, and when that happens, no announcements can be made without the approval of the Eastern Army Headquarters."

"I will make the announcement without their permission," demanded the major, gathering courage and now pointing the gun at Yoshio.

The standoff continued with the major demanding he be allowed to call the rebellion into being, and the announcer refusing on the basis of standing operational procedures. Aileen wondered what she would do if the major shot Yoshio and then demanded she show him how to switch from music to microphone. She was sure she would show him. She was saved from this dilemma when the two men agreed to call the Eastern Army Headquarters.

"General Tanaka, please. I have a major here who wants permission to announce a rebellion," said Yoshio. The tone of his voice was as if he were getting permission from the sergeant of the guard to allow a man with an expired pass to enter the gate. After half a minute, Yoshio said, "Here he is, General," and handed the telephone to the major.

"Yes, General, this is Major...." He listened for a full minute with an occasional "Yes, sir." "But, General, we have ...." More listening, the pistol in his other hand now pointing towards the floor. "Yes, sir. But...." and finally, "I understand, General Tanaka." The major hung up the phone, put his pistol back into its holster, came to attention, did an about-face and marched out of the room.

Aileen and Yoshio looked at each other and let out a collective sigh of relief.

"What would have happened if you had given him the mike, Yoshio? Is there a revolution out there ready to happen?"

"Evidently General Tanaka didn't think so."

"You just saved hundreds or thousands of lives, Yoshio," said Aileen.

<hr/>

At noon that day, Aileen stood with head bowed on her usual street corner and listened with millions of other Japanese as the Emperor, in his stilted Japanese and high-pitched voice, announced their "acceptance of the provisions of the Joint Declaration of the Powers."

Five hundred miles south of Tokyo, in a tent on Okinawa, Ken listened, also with head bowed, and silently gave thanks to God.

CHAPTER 26

F OR MOST OF THE VICTORS ON OKINAWA, THE NEXT
several days were days of unalloyed joy. The war was over! It was
announced that most of the units scheduled to occupy Japan would
come from the Philippines. That announcement disappointed none of
the men on Okinawa, and all attention turned to learning how overseas
time credits qualified in determining priority of transfer home.

Ken could not determine why he felt no inclination to join in the
celebration. Due to combat service in Italy and his wound, he was near
the top of the list for going home. Still, that was not enough to relieve
his free-floating discontent. Though he still experienced some prejudice against himself as a Japanese American, he knew that the goal of
the Nisei to prove themselves as Americans had been overwhelmingly
met. He was sure that with time they would take their place beside the
English and Dutch and Germans and Irish and Italians and undoubtedly myriads more in the future as *Americans*. Yet his distress continued. He thought of medical school in his future–surely they could not
keep him out now–and worked the fingers on his right hand. With
continuing practice, he had again mastered the one-handed knot Doctor Kawamura had taught him at Manzanar. But the prospect of medical school had lost most of its attraction. Occasionally a vague sense of
guilt over the carnage filtered up from some deep area inside him, but
he quickly rationalized that feeling away. "They bombed Pearl Harbor." "They brutally invaded China." "They forced us to kill them,
almost to the last man." But was it "they"?

Three days after the surrender announcement, Colonel Damechek
gave Ken an unusual duty. "Tomorrow," he said, "the Japs are sending a
team to the Philippines to meet with MacArthur's boys to arrange the

details of the occupation. They'll land here and switch to one of our planes to fly on to the Philippines. They'll probably bring their own interpreters, but I want you to be around to make sure the transfer goes smoothly."

The next morning, Ken stood with hundreds of others at the airfield looking to the northeast for the approaching planes. Most of the men had come, curious to see this enemy they had fought for so long. Some were there for security reasons, and a few, like Ken, had come for the official transfer.

"There they are!" yelled a GI as he shaded his eyes with his hand. Ken could see more than a dozen airplanes approaching. Within minutes two Japanese bombers, painted entirely white, were distinguishable in the middle of the group. Two B-24's led, and several P-38 fighters flitted in and around them. The white bombers—now Ken could see the large green crosses painted on their wings and tails—landed and taxied to the waiting group. A staircase was hastily adjusted and wheeled up to the door of the first plane.

"What do I say to these SOBs?" Colonel Damechek asked of Ken as they mounted the steps.

"Welcome to Okinawa?" suggested Ken.

The door opened, and a small man with the insignia of a lieutenant general stepped out hesitatingly, blinking in the sunlight. Slowly, he descended the stairway.

Colonel Damechek stepped forward. He towered over the small man by eight inches. "Welcome to Okinawa. I'm Colonel Damechek," he said. Instead of a handshake or a salute, he pointed to a nearby C-54. "You and your men are to transfer to that plane for the continuation of your journey." Ken translated the colonel's remarks, and for the first time, the general looked away from Colonel Damechek. He shielded his eyes from the sun and looked at Ken, a confused look coming over his face.

Finally he said, "I am General Kawabe."

"He says he's General Kawabe, Colonel." Ken added, "He's General Umezu's deputy," referring to the Chief of Staff of the Japanese Army.

"O.K. Lead them over to the C-54."

Ken led them across the hundred yards to the waiting plane. He suddenly became aware that there was danger that some soldier might

decide to take his own vengeance on some of these high-ranking officers. Quickly he scanned the crowd. He only saw cameras snapping this
moment for posterity. He stopped at the stairs of the C-54 and motioned General Kawabe to climb up them. He waited as the rest of the
sixteen-man group from both planes moved up the steps. Each in turn
studied Ken, but the only to speak was one of the representatives from
the Foreign Office.

"And who are you, young man?" asked the elderly gentleman.

"Captain Ken Hayakawa, U.S.Army," answered Ken.

"Where is your family from?"

"California," Ken said aggressively. The man stopped and continued to look Ken in the eye. All the Japanese except this gentleman were
now inside the airplane. Colonel Damechek stood nearby, shifting his
feet and clearing his throat. Finally Ken, feeling uncomfortable, added,
"Okayama prefecture originally." The Foreign Office representative continued to study Ken, his uniform, and his captain's bars. He patted him
on the shoulder.

"It must have been a hard war for you, son," he said, then shuffled
slowly up the steps.

"What did he say?" asked Colonel Damechek, as the plane disappeared to the south.

"He asked where my parents came from, Colonel." He paused. "And
then he said it must have been a hard war for me."

Now it was the colonel's time to pause. "I guess it has been, hasn't
it? What's the name of that concentration camp where your parents
are?"

"Manzanar."

"Yeah. Manzanar."

⊷⊶

Over the next four days, Ken could not get the comment of the
elderly Japanese diplomat out of his mind. The war had been no harder
for him than for others in combat. He thought of Sergeant Honda and
Ben Watanabe and Tyrus and Kaz and the many others who had died.
He thought of Horace and others with more debilitating wounds than
his–their wars were harder. His time on the front line was only 102
days–he didn't count his Okinawa time since he was rarely in danger of
being shot, even though those days were included in the formula that
decided who went home first. He knew many soldiers who had been

exposed to immediate danger more than that. And sailors were always at risk from submarines. If the elderly Japanese and Colonel Damechek were right, it must have something to do with his roots and Manzanar. But at that point, conscious thinking disappeared into the haze of the unidentified stress he had begun to feel after the surrender announcement. He had learned to suppress those stressful feelings only by applying himself more diligently to his work. Much remained to do, settling the refugees and separation of Japanese soldiers and the occasional officer who might have been guilty of war crimes, from the Okinawans.

Two days after the Kawabe Mission had retraced its steps from the Philippines through Okinawa and back to Japan, Ken's world was suddenly rattled.

"You've been designated for the advance party," announced Colonel Damechek. "A group will go to Japan two or three days before MacArthur to make sure everything's ready for him."

"You mean to test the sincerity of the Japanese? If they're faking about the surrender, the advance party gets wiped out instead of MacArthur."

"Could be. All indications are that they're sincere, but I guess there's always the possibility of some guy deciding to take matters into his own hands for the pride of Japan. Anyway, you'll be in the translator section, under a Major Hanusa, who's on MacArthur's staff in the Philippines. The whole group will be under the command of a Colonel Magruder."

"Hanusa? I've never heard of him. I thought I knew all the Nisei in the translating business over here. Did he go through Camp Savage or Fort Snelling?"

"No idea, Ken, but you've gotta be ready by 0800 tomorrow."

In reality, it was three days later, 28 August, when Ken stood on the airstrip in the predawn darkness waiting to load onto one of the C-47's for the trip to Japan. There were about 150 men milling around waiting to load onto the forty-five planes forming the armada.

"Captain Hayakawa, I presume?" The words, spoken in unaccented Japanese, came from behind Ken. This was not the Japanese of a Nisei who had taken a brush-up course at the MISLS. He turned to identify the speaker but could not determine who had spoken. The only person within speaking range was a tall, blond major. He started to turn back when the blond major spoke again. "Captain Hayakawa?" Ken looked carefully at the major for the first time and noted his name tag.

"Major Hanusa?"

"That's right. We're going to be working together, Captain."

"Where'd you get the name Hanusa, sir, and how come you speak such good Japanese?"

"From my parents, and because I was raised in Japan." Major Hanusa laughed. "The name is Finnish. My folks were Japan Inland Mission missionaries for many years, and I was born there. I was in seminary when the war broke out, and you can guess the rest. Come on, this is our plane." Once on the plane, he introduced Ken to Colonel Magruder. The colonel showed the tension of leading the advance party. Although most of the men wore pistols, all knew that if there was a concerted attack by the Japanese once they were on the ground, the party would not be able to defend itself. And how cooperative would they be? Would they be hard negotiators even though they had surrendered unconditionally? After a few words with Ken, he settled back in his bucket-seat to get some sleep.

Colonel Magruder's tenseness was not shared by Major Hanusa. He spoke at great length about his idyllic boyhood in Japan. He liked the people, and he seemed to have enjoyed the uniqueness of being almost the only westerner most of his friends had ever known. He spoke of school outings and of having been accepted as one of them, even when in his teenage years, he grew to over six feet. He had literally shed tears when he got on the ship to return to the United States for college. He knew he wanted to return to Japan in some capacity, but he also knew that the call as a missionary should not be on the basis of simply a desire to live in that country. Finally in his last year of college, he felt that the call back to Japan was from God, not merely his own desire. With contentment he entered seminary, majoring in overseas missions. As graduation approached, he became aware that the politics of his beloved Japan had changed. Even his parents who had always assiduously remained apolitical wrote him that the militarists were getting the upper hand. He could no longer ignore the invasion of Manchuria, the Rape of Nanking and the Japanese expansion into Southeast Asia. When he heard of the attack on Pearl Harbor, he was devastated. When he finished seminary in 1942, he volunteered but not as a chaplain. He rightly estimated that his ability with the language could be put to good use. After intelligence training, he joined MacArthur in Australia and soon became his chief translator. Now, after three years, while the other men on the planes were entering an unknown and frightening world, Major John Hanusa was going home.

"There's Fujiyama!" he said excitedly, pointing out the windows to the left, just as the sun was rising to their right. "That's a great place to go hiking and camping, sailing on Lake Hakone. Beautiful! It's even more beautiful in the winter when it's covered with snow. We used to go there as a family and stay in an old hotel with hot natural spring baths in the basement. It took my folks several years to convince themselves that coed bathing was a part of the culture that we could participate in without violating our Christian principles." Major Hanusa's enthusiastic travelogue helped allay Ken's apprehensions. Even more so, they were allayed when he looked down to see the Third Fleet filling the bay, as the plane descended towards Atsugi Air Base.

"There're Halsey's boys!" said one of the men, also encouraged by the presence of the Navy.

As the plane descended, Ken was surprised by the countryside, the rice fields and country roads and streams. He wasn't sure what he expected, but after nearly four years of war, he didn't think things would look so peaceful. The plane circled the airfield once, and the men could see the large waiting contingent watching them. The landing was very bumpy due to the condition of the field, but soon they pulled to a stop. The door was opened, and a staircase was pushed to the door. Colonel Magruder took a deep breath and descended the steps, followed by Major Hanusa. As they set foot on Japanese soil, a Japanese lieutenant general came running up, his saber jangling. He came to a halt and stood up to his full five feet two inches. In English, he announced, " I am Lieutenant General Arisue, commanding the reception committee."

"I am Colonel Magruder, in charge of the advance occupation party for the Supreme Commander for the Allied Powers, General of the Army Douglas MacArthur." No one knew quite what to do after that. Ken, who had followed Major Hanusa down the steps, was being jostled by Signal Corps photographers maneuvering to get pictures of the historic moment.

Finally, General Arisue said in surprisingly good English, "Please follow me," and led the group across the field to some large tents. Ken did not notice any Japanese soldiers who appeared to be armed and aggressive. They appeared to be the administrative types who would be present at such a time. "Your trip must have made you thirsty. Please have a glass of juice." He offered Colonel Magruder a glass. The colonel reached out for the glass, then retracted his hand.

"No thank you." The general noted the action. He then deliberately drank the juice himself. Major Hanusa then stepped up, took a glass from the tray and drank it.

"I believe I will have one after all," said the colonel and took a glass.

The airfield was filling up with C-47's and their deplaning soldiers. After drinking the juice, the two staffs arranged for meetings between members of the staffs to coordinate the arrival of MacArthur and the first American combat troops scheduled for two days later. Ken and Major Hanusa, with the other translators hurried from group to group as needed. By the end of the day, Ken flopped exhausted onto his cot. He had just dropped off to sleep when he heard a rustling of his tent door. He jumped up, fumbling for his pistol.

"Hanusa-san?" said a face peeking through the tent flap.

"What do you want?" asked a frightened Ken in Japanese.

"I was told Mr. Hanusa was in this tent." The face now became a body, that of a captain in the Japanese Army Air Corps."

Ken put his pistol back into its holster and took a deep breath. "Major Hanusa is in that tent over there. Maybe I'd better show you, so you don't scare someone else who might have a quicker trigger finger than I." He put on his shoes and led him to the next tent. He called out in English before he entered the tent. "Major Hanusa. This is Hayakawa, may I come in?"

"Yes," came the sleepy answer.

"There's someone outside who seems to know you, Major," said Ken once inside the tent. Major Hanusa quickly put on his shoes and went outside.

"Isao!" he exclaimed and threw his long arms around the captain. They talked rapidly, and eventually Major Hanusa introduced Ken to Isao, his friend and classmate from childhood. Ken went back to his tent, wondering about the definition of "enemy".

The next morning, Ken awakened later than intended and realized he had slept soundly. The anxiety of the last several days that they would be walking into a trap had not materialized. The Japanese he had talked with told him there were men who would happily ruin the surrender process. However, the ones they knew of, they said, had tried the night before the Emperor's speech and failed. Most had then committed suicide. Security was tight, they assured him, but it was all at the perimeter of the base and did not intrude on the activities of those arranging for MacArthur's arrival. That second day, meetings of the various sections continued. By the end of the day, Ken thought it was about as dangerous as a home buyer and home seller arranging for the moving vans to arrive for the move out and the move in. It was also encouraging that planes continued to arrive, mostly Navy planes, and Atsugi was becoming well populated with Americans.

"I had us an invitation to dinner tonight, Ken," said Major Hanusa as they sat down to their dinner of warmed up field rations. "Isao invited us to the Japanese officers' mess, but Colonel Magruder didn't think it would be a good idea due to the non-fraternization rule."

"I'm sure it would have been more interesting food than what we're having now," said Ken.

"I'm not so sure. According to Isao, the food has been pretty sparse even for the army for the last year or so, but it would have been a good experience."

"So you and Isao have been friends a long time?" asked Ken.

"I guess I've known him all my life. His parents were two of the first converts at my parents' mission, and his father was one of the head elders."

"They tell me that being a missionary in Japan is a tough job, that the Japanese don't accept Christianity very readily," said Ken.

"That's right. There's a lot of family pressure against it. Even those who believe the message have an awfully hard time becoming Christians. It's almost as if they have to divorce their family and all their ancestors. I know Isao and his family had a very difficult time. Are you a Christian, Ken?"

"Yes. It's easier for Japanese Americans. We kids started attending church, almost because it was the American thing to do. When I got to college, I had to decide if I really believed it, and I decided that I did, you know, that I really was a sinner and that Jesus really had died for me. My parents weren't thrilled that we went to Christian churches, but they eventually pretty much accepted it.

You know what's been hard, though?" Ken continued. "Trying to figure where God comes into this stupid war. Germany at least is a

Christian nation, so how come we're all at war, killing each other by the millions? What happens when God gets prayers from both sides asking for success in battle? And Tyrus. I had a friend named Tyrus who had been a bad kid but then got converted in Italy and felt called to be a priest. I'm sure he would have followed through and been a real effective one. But he was killed saving another guy's life. Why couldn't God have gotten him over that barrier one second earlier and then let him become a priest? And then there are other things...." Ken stopped and tried to dig deeper into that part of himself just below consciousness that had been bothering him the last couple of weeks. He felt he'd been able to open it a bit, but then it closed down on him again. He let his sentence trail off.

"Well, Ken, you bring up problems that have bothered men for years, and there're no neat little answers," said John Hanusa after a few minutes' pause. "But one thing you might want to think about is that God gives us free will to do whatever we choose to. He gave us an example of a perfect life, and a guidebook so to speak, and the Holy Spirit, but it's up to us to choose. If we make bad choices, we face the consequences, either as individuals or as a nation."

"Did you have to argue with your conscience as to whether it was right for a Christian to join the Army and fight?" asked Ken.

"Yeah, I did. You can quote scriptures to support both positions, either of being a pacifist or of going to war for your country. We used to stay up long hours in seminary arguing about those things. The best argument for pacifism, I think, is the idea of turning the other cheek when someone strikes you. But I think that's directed at individuals and not necessarily at entire countries. I eventually came down on the side of 'obeying the authorities', which is a biblical principle. The tough thing there is whether or not it's a 'just war'. That puts the individual in the position of judging the authorities he's supposed to be obeying. It would have been hard being a German, because I think their war was a war of conquering territory and people and not a just war. From our perspective, I think it was easier to be convinced we were fighting a just war, since it started out as a defensive war. My main problem was fighting the Japanese. I've told you that my main memory was that of a gentle, peaceful people. They were very competitive in many ways and clearly thought that they had a superior culture, but in my experience they weren't warlike. I eventually had to face the fact that some were, and that group had gotten the upper hand. I had been just as guilty of stereotyping them as most Americans, but in the opposite direction. Anyway, I felt it was right for us to try to stop the militarists, whose goal seemed to be colonizing southeast Asia. In answer to your question, yes. It was very difficult, particularly when I realized that the guys we were killing in the front lines were average Japanese who'd rather be home working and raising a family, just like the average GI in the front lines."

Ken fell asleep that night thinking about his conversation with John Hanusa.

Early the next day, planes carrying the Eleventh Airborne Division began to land. Paratroopers ran down the staircases, rifles at the ready, hand grenades hanging from their battle jackets and formed up in squads ready for combat. Soldiers on the airfield, both Japanese and American, were somewhat taken aback by the military posture of the arriving paratroopers. Their mission had been to direct the incoming soldiers to assembly areas off the airstrip in preparation for movement into Tokyo, but at first it appeared there would be a battle. Finally the paratroopers began to relax and, a little crestfallen, allowed themselves to be led to their areas.

The most relieved man on the field that day was Colonel Magruder, who turned over the command of American troops to the division commander. He had arrived on one of the first planes, armed like his troops. Magruder's advance party had everything in preparation for the arrival of The General that afternoon, and there had been no bloodshed.

At two o'clock that afternoon, Ken stood on the airstrip at Atsugi Air base with hundreds of others straining for the first view of the plane that would bring General MacArthur to Japan. This was the culmination of the long, bloody road back, begun three years before in the steamy jungles of New Guinea, proceeding through bodies of water and on tiny islands with names previously unknown to almost all Americans.

"There he is!" came the cry, and in fifteen minutes, the silver C-54 with *Bataan* emblazoned on its nose came to a stop. The staircase was pushed to the plane, the door opened, and a 65-year-old man in khaki uniform with a disreputable hat, dark glasses and a corncob pipe in his hand stepped out. He paused at the top of the staircase as flashbulbs by the hundreds popped. A cheer arose from the surrounding soldiers, and

Ken tried to fight back tears. As he turned his head to the side to dry his cheeks inconspicuously, he noted Isao on the other side of John Hanusa. He was not cheering, but he was bowing from the waist. Ken thought of the Emperor, and now the Conqueror. The peace agreement allowed for the Emperor to remain in place but with decreased influence. How will this work out? he wondered.

Later, after the general's entourage left for Yokohama, John Hanusa told Ken, "I've gotten us orders to be at the surrender Sunday."

"You mean the one on the *Missouri*?" asked Ken.

"Yes. This is quite an opportunity, to be present at one of the most important historical events of our lifetimes. If I hadn't been able to wangle orders, I think I would have taken a quick frogman course and swum out there anyway. I convinced them there might be some last minute questions about the surrender document, even though both sides have gone over it with a fine-tooth comb."

Two days later, Ken and John had their spots on the quarterdeck of the great battleship pointed out to them. They were assigned to the far end of the ranks of representatives from all the Allied Powers. They were in direct view of the document signing table so if a problem arose, they could be beckoned for quickly. As Ken looked at the upper decks, he saw white-bloused sailors filling every available space. Scaffolding had been built to accommodate the cameras of the world's press.

Promptly at 9 AM, Foreign Minister Shigemitsu, struggling because of his wooden leg, led the eleven men from the Japanese delegation aboard. When the Japanese were in position, a chaplain gave the invocation, then "The Star-Spangled Banner" was played over the ship's public-address system. General MacArthur, flanked by Admirals Nimitz and Halsey, then appeared for the first time. He stepped to the microphone. "We are gathered here, representative of the major warring powers, to conclude a solemn agreement whereby peace may be restored." His message was short, and in Ken's opinion conciliatory, emphasizing the importance of such qualities as "higher dignity" and "sacred purposes" that would be required for a lasting peace. The signing then began, first with Mr. Shigemitsu and Army Chief of Staff General Umezu, followed by the representatives of the nine Allied nations. As Ken contemplated the scope of the war and the unnumbered casualties and the lives changed forever, he began to study the men in the Japanese delegation. He wondered how their lives had been and would be affected. Suddenly his eyes stopped on a small stooped figure in the rear rank. The man returned his gaze and nodded almost imperceptibly. Ken nodded back at Mr. Shimizu, the man who had made the disturbing observation to him on the Okinawa airstrip two weeks before.

General MacArthur signed the surrender documents—the last to do so. "Let us pray that peace be now restored to the world and that God will preserve it always. These proceedings are closed," were his concluding words.

Part V
Final Choices

保勝の利詁

CHAPTER 27

COME ON, AILEEN. YOU'RE APPLYING FOR A JOB with the Occupation, not answering a casting call for *Kabuki*," said Myrna. Aileen had searched the house for cosmetics long since used up and had found two empty jars. After adding a few drops of water to get the dried remnants out of the bottom corners, she was applying it to her cheeks, pale and drawn after the years of near starvation.

"I don't want to look like I'm going to die tomorrow. Does it look better if I tie my belt tightly or just let it hang loose?" The two sisters looked at the dress, the one she had saved like an icon from her days as an American girl. She had worn this dress on her last evening with Hideki. It was threadbare but ironed.

"Don't tighten it too much. You'll accentuate your thinness." Two weeks after the signing of the surrender, a notice had gone out that the Occupation was hiring bilingual men and women for secretarial duties. Interviews would be at the Dai Ichi building, the former insurance building across from the Imperial Palace which MacArthur used for his headquarters. Myrna, now recovered from her radiation sickness, was scheduled to return to a hospital for her ongoing studies the next week. She had agreed to accompany her younger sister down for her interview. Aileen put the last pin in her hair, carefully piled on top of her head and cascading over her forehead in controlled waves. The girls walked the two miles to catch one of the few remaining trolleys. It would take them all the way to the Dai Ichi building.

"Remember when the war broke out and that old man knocked that English book out of your hands?" asked Myrna.

"Yes, and I remember how much I wanted to slug him." The sisters laughed until tears came to their eyes, as they had nearly four years before. This time they had no fear of the other passengers regarding the scene with questioning glances.

$$\ast\mathord{-}\mathord{\leftarrow}\mathord{\bullet}\mathord{\diamond}\mathord{\bullet}\mathord{\rightarrow}\mathord{-}\ast$$

"You're American-born?" asked Private First Class Shimaoka in English, studying Aileen's application.

"I'm American," answered Aileen.

"What are you doing here?"

"I spent the war here. We were here when war broke out and couldn't get home." Shimaoka studied the slender girl standing in front of him.

"What did you do during the war?"

"I continued in college for a while, and then I worked."

"Where'd you work?"

"Uh, for NHK."

"The radio station?"

"Yes."

"You wait over there, miss. I'd better get the captain for this one."

In the inner office, Shimaoka told Ken his problem. "This girl says she's American, and she speaks English perfectly, but I don't understand why she spent the war here."

"There were a lot of Nisei caught here when they bombed Pearl Harbor. For some of them, their loyalty was with Japan, but for most I think, they remained loyal to the U.S., even though they had to keep quiet about it. What did she do, or say she did, during the war?"

"She worked for NHK," replied Shimaoka.

"Really? This isn't Tokyo Rose, is it?" Shimaoka laughed. "I'm serious," Ken continued. "They really want to find this Tokyo Rose. No one knows who she is, but they think she must be a Nisei."

"Well, I didn't ask her, captain. You want me to go back and ask her?"

"No. That's O.K. I'll talk to her." Ken took the application form from Shimaoka and walked out to the front office. "Aileen Nakamura?"

"I'm Aileen Nakamura," she said, standing up. Ken looked at the slight girl with the loose-fitting dress that had been in style six years before. He noted the black hair billowing over her forehead and the unsuccessful attempt to add color to her sunken cheeks.

"Come with me, please." Myrna waited in the outer room while Aileen followed Ken.

After reviewing her application, Ken asked, "Where's your pass-port?" Aileen described their inability to get passports but showed him her dog-eared certificate of identification. Ken looked at it, not com-pletely clear what it was. "Is your name on the family registry?"

"Yes, but not by choice."

"Tell me about your work at NHK?"

"I translated news reports and other things into English for the English broadcasts."

"What other things?"

"Introductions to songs."

"Propaganda?"

Aileen hesitated. "Some of it probably approached propaganda. Par-ticularly later in the war, I was sure they reported only the news that sounded good to them."

"To them? To whom?" asked Ken.

"To them. To the Japanese. They reported the news to their own people as well as over the English broadcasts in a way that sounded good; in other words avoiding the bad news."

"Do you consider yourself Japanese?"

"No. Well, yes... in a way. I'm an American of Japanese ancestry...like you. I've lived here with them for five years. There are a lot of good things you can say about the Japanese, but starting the *baka na senso* isn't one of them."

Ken hesitated at the vehemence with which Aileen described the war, then asked, "Are you Tokyo Rose?"

Aileen looked perplexed. "Tokyo Rose?"

"Yes. Tokyo Rose."

"Who's Tokyo Rose?" asked Aileen. Ken studied her. If she was putting on an act, it was an awfully good act.

Finally he said. "You know. The woman who tried to seduce the front line men to surrender... all the talk about their girlfriends at home and all that."

"I never wrote anything like that, and I don't know of anyone else who did. If any of the girls who read the script ad-libbed anything simi-lar, I never heard about it. What did the voice sound like?"

"Well I never heard her myself," said Ken, "but they say she had a real sexy voice."

Aileen thought of the girls she knew who did the announcing. "She was Nisei? Spoke without an accent?"

"That's my understanding," said Ken,

"Well I never announced myself," Aileen said and decided not to relate the incident of the voice trial and the pepper.

"I'll have to study your file some more, Miss Nakamura. Can you come back Thursday? On the way out, ask PFC Shimaoka to send to Seattle for a copy of your birth certificate."

Aileen passed on the information to Shimaoka. As they walked out, Aileen asked Myrna, "You ever hear of a radio announcer called Tokyo Rose?" Ken overheard the question and noted Myrna's look of non-comprehension.

***

"I met an interesting Nisei girl this morning," said Ken to John Hanusa, as he reported the day's activities to him. "At least she says she's Nisei."

"You don't believe her?"

"She has no accent, but she says she worked at NHK. I wonder if she's Tokyo Rose?"

"You think they'd get Tokyo Rose to infiltrate our headquarters as a spy and admit she worked for NHK?"

"Doesn't sound likely, does it, John? She denies doing any announcing, only the translation of the script, and of course nothing like Tokyo Rose was supposed to have said. But she did admit that some of what she wrote approached propaganda."

"Sounds to me like she's being pretty truthful."

"Yeah, maybe, but her voice was sort of sexy... I mean... you know what I mean."

John raised an eyebrow. "Yeah, I know what you mean."

"But she was pretty skinny. I imagine Tokyo Rose would have eaten pretty well."

"You're awfully observant, Captain Hayakawa," said John.

"Well, you know. According to her application, she lives here in Japan with her family. Maybe I'd better pay them a visit."

"I think you'd better. Luckily, MacArthur hasn't come out with a non-fraternization rule."

"Come on, John. This is business."

***

On Thursday, Aileen was in Ken's office. She was wearing the same dress but was without makeup–partly because Myrna had finally convinced her of the garishness of it, but also because she had used every last drop on her previous visit.

"I think I should visit your home, Miss Nakamura," said Ken.

Aileen looked surprised. "I guess we could arrange that. When would you like to come?"

"Right now." Still thinking in conspiratorial terms, he did not want to allow her to set up a false "family".

"Right now? Well, it's after 2 o'clock. My father should be home. My sister is at the hospital, but you saw her the other day, anyway."

"She's in the hospital?"

"*At* the hospital. She's a medical student."

"Was she a medical student in the States?"

"No. She was premed, but we've been here for over five years. She's a third-year student now." Ken thought that through and decided the dates added up.

"The Jeep's waiting for us outside, Miss Nakamura. Let's go."

Aileen sat in the back seat and pressed hard on her hairdo because of the wind. She luxuriated in the twenty-minute ride to her house, compared to the hour-and-a-half walk and trolley ride it took to get from home to the Dai Ichi Building. At first, she worried what it looked like, her riding in a Jeep. She soon realized that pedestrians didn't seem to notice, either out of courtesy or because the Occupation, starting its second month was now routine.

⋯⋯⋯⋯

After introductions, Mieko said "Please sit down, Captain Hayakawa, I will get tea." At Ken's protest, she said, "No, young man. It's no difficulty. We don't have many opportunities to offer hospitality these days. The tea is not the best, you understand." And she disappeared into the kitchen.

"And tell me, young man," Jun said as they sat down, "where is your family from?"

"Okayama."

"No. I mean in the United States," Jun clarified.

"We lived in Los Angeles, on Terminal Island, before the war. Our family was evacuated to one of the detention camps."

"Which one?"

"Manzanar. In California."

Mieko appeared with the tea in time to hear Ken's last answer. "I think most of our friends were evacuated to the camp in Wyoming or the the one in Idaho. If we had stayed in the United States, you two young people would probably never have met." It suddenly dawned on Ken that he was being treated as a potential suitor. He looked at Aileen. Her face was more crimson than it had been two days before with the cosmetics.

"Daddy," Aileen said, intending to correct his impression, but just then Myrna entered the house.

"Oh, you're the captain from the employment division. I'm Myrna, Aileen's sister." She looked around and then back at Ken. "What are you doing here, if I may ask?"

"Well, I...I'm doing what we call a background check," stammered Ken.

"For someone applying for any old job that needs both languages? You must stay busy doing background checks, Captain." She entered the bedroom to take off her white smock. Jun and Mieko looked confused.

"I was about to say," said Aileen to her parents, "that Captain Hayakawa is here for the purpose of... of... a background check." Jun and Mieko still didn't understand.

"Captain Hayakawa thinks Aileen might be 'Tokyo...what's-her-name'," said Myrna reentering the room.

"Rose. Tokyo Rose," said Aileen.

"Who's Tokyo Rose?" asked Jun. All eyes looked towards Ken.

"Well, she's the woman who was the announcer for the English broadcasts that were beamed to our troops in the Pacific. She supposedly tried in a sexy voice to make the boys homesick and want to surrender," said Ken.

"Is that right, Aileen?" asked Jun. "I thought it was just music and news."

"That's what I wrote. I don't know if any of the girls added anything on their own."

"And I don't necessarily think your daughter is Tokyo Rose. We just have to check everything out." There was silence as everyone tried to look as if they were concentrating on sipping their tea. Finally Ken said to Myrna, "You're a medical student? I was in premed when the war broke out."

"Yes. I did one year of premed at Washington, and I finished premed here and am now in my third year."

"Do you plan to continue med school in the States?" asked Ken.

"I don't see how I can do it. I doubt they'd give me much credit for medical school work done here. And I'm sure even if they accept more Nisei into med school now—you know they used to take only one a year at Washington—there are probably a lot of war heroes like you coming back who'll get first crack at it. I might just have to stay here, which is all right. I mean I like the Japanese. And they certainly will have a lot of medical needs in the next few years." Ken and Myrna talked some more about the medical training in the two countries. Suddenly she changed the subject.

"You know Captain —Ken, is that your name?—there's no way my younger sister could be this Tokyo Rose. First of all, I've never heard her say anything sexy to any young man. She's about as sexy as this teaspoon. But let me tell you about the 'Great Pepper Episode'." She proceeded to tell about the time Aileen peppered her throat so she'd flunk the voice test. Myrna embellished the story with great drama, and even Aileen was rocking with laughter when she finished.

"O.K. I'm beginning to get the point," Ken finally said when he stopped laughing. Shortly thereafter he took his leave.

"I'm sorry about my family," Aileen said as she walked him to the Jeep. "If I'd had a little more notice, I could have oriented them better to the purpose of your visit, and they would have behaved better. Except for Myrna. She'll say anything."

"It's not your fault, Miss Nakamura." Ken chuckled softly at the ineptness of his first intelligence investigation. "Anyway, come in on Monday, and we'll give you a position."

***

"So, did you root out old Tokyo Rose?" asked John Hanusa when Ken got back to the office. As Ken described his visit, John laughed as heartily as the Nakamuras had an hour before. "So Papa thought you were there courting his daughter, and you were really there trying to prove she's a spy. I'm glad you're going into medicine, Ken, and not into intelligence."

***

Monday morning found Aileen sitting in Ken's office as he explained, in perhaps too much detail, what her job would consist of. Suddenly

PFC Shimaoka burst into the room. "Captain! They just announced they've arrested Tokyo Rose. It's a girl from L.A. named Iva Toguri. She confessed."

"Iva Toguri?" repeated Aileen. "I know her. She didn't do those things you told me about. At least I'd be very surprised if she did. She was one of the announcers, but I never heard her say anything we hadn't written. And if you think I'm not sexy…well, anyway. Does that for sure let me off the hook?"

"You've been off the hook since that day at your house, Miss Nakamura." Ken finished describing the requirements of her new job. "Maybe I should come out some evening and apologize to your parents."

Aileen looked at him and said a little hesitantly, "I could tell them you send your apologies."

"Oh, I think I should probably tell them myself. It would be more courteous. And Miss Nakamura, it was your sister who said you weren't sexy, not me." Aileen blushed and left his office.

The "Apology Evening" at the Nakamuras went well for Ken. Aileen had instructed her parents the appropriate way to consider Ken, so there were none of the embarrassments of the first evening. Mieko insisted on serving dinner, meager as it was. That gave Ken the chance to reciprocate by bringing some food out from the Army commissary a few nights later. When Ken transferred Aileen from under his supervision to a different section the next week, Mieko questioned why. Aileen blushed and mumbled something about getting wider experience. But Myrna, never one to let something go unsaid, clarified the matter. "That girl has young Ken under her spell. He has plans for her, and it would look improper if he was her boss."

"No. Is that right, Aileen?"

"Would you keep your fat mouth shut, Myrna!" was all Aileen could answer.

A couple of days later, Ken moved from one room to another. As he packed his gear, he came across the white towel, now washed of its blood, he had taken from the dead *kamikaze* pilot six months before. He stopped suddenly as he read "Love, Aileen" and then *Hissho* on the reverse.

That evening Ken unloaded some commissary food on the Nakamuras' table. After the parents left the room, he took the towel out of his pocket and said, "Aileen..." Aileen took the towel, unfolded it and burst into tears.

"I'm sorry. I just wanted to know if you knew anything about this," Ken stammered. After a couple of minutes, Aileen controlled her sobbing long enough to ask where he had gotten the towel. Ken explained, leaving out the part about its being blood-soaked and the extensive damage to the pilot's face.

"Had he suffered?" asked Aileen.

"No. I don't think so," Ken lied. Holding the towel to her face, Aileen continued sobbing.

"You were in love with him?" Ken finally asked.

"No. I felt sorry for him. He should have been studying English literature in America, not flying his plane into some American ship. It was the *baka na senso!*" She suddenly looked up into Ken's face. "You believe me, don't you? I mean that I didn't love him. I want you to believe me." Ken took her wet face, brought it up to his and kissed her.

CHAPTER 28

S ERGEANT MURAKAMI? ARE YOU SERGEANT SHIG
Murakami?" Sergeant First Class Shig Murakami looked up at
his questioner, a tall husky private first class holding a large American
flag on a pole. Around his neck was a leather strap that joined in a cup
over his lower abdomen.

"Yes. Murakami. Dat's me."

"You used to be in the same unit with my brother, Ken Hayakawa.
I'm Peter Hayakawa," said the tall Nisei, a smile broadening his handsome face.

"Naw. You da little bruddah? Kenny said you goan come go join
up. What unit you een?"

"I'm with the 522nd. They asked me to carry the flag, probably
because of my height. I'm a little embarrassed, though, what with all
you guys who have seen so much combat."

"Aw, no mattah, bruddah. Most da guys who come ovah, you know,
dey're gone."

"Weren't you ever hit, Sergeant Murakami?"

"Naw. Well, yeah. On Mt. Folgorito, I got heet, but it was just one
flesh wound. I was back in two weeks, just een time foah da wah's end.
What's Kenny doing now?" The two combat veterans, one from a year
of the hardest fighting of the war and the other from a few months of
mostly mopping up operations, shared information on the men who
had come over with the third squad, third platoon, E company. Peter
rested the flag on the ground but held it straight upright with both
hands in an almost worshipful fashion, while Shig propped himself up
by leaning with both arms on his M-1. They were waiting on a side
street in Leghorn, Italy for the victory parade to start. It was the day the
surrender documents were being signed on the *Missouri* half a world

away. The 100th/442nd had been designated to be the first unit in the parade.

"Do you hear anything of Horace Yamashita?" asked Peter after he had told him his latest news of Ken.

"Yeah. You remembah Mike Matsunaga? Well he was telling me da uddah day dat Yamashita ees studying for lawyuh. You know he lost hees whole leg, but I guess he got one wooden one now. He was always talking about helping da Negroes, you know. Well he decided he could do da job bettah as one lawyuh. He's got guts, you know. He'll need 'em foah what he plans to do. What happened to yoah bruddah who said no and went to jail foah not joining up?"

"Howard? They let him out after about a year, and he went back to help our parents settle back in Los Angeles."

"Well, I doan blame him foah saying no aftuh what dey did to you guys from da mainland, but I bet he's goan have one tough time when all da guys who went, get back. And you have one seestah in New York?"

"Yes. I guess the big deal there from what Ken writes is that she's fallen in love with his old roommate, who's a Caucasian."

"She's goan marry one *haole*? Dat's goan make yoah parents mad, eh?"

Before Peter could answer, the parade director came by in his jeep and yelled for Peter's color guard and Shig's platoon to get ready to move. "As soon as the band goes by," he yelled, "You guys get going." The color guard lined up, moved forward on command and did a left turn.

"Platoon, tensh-hut! Sling arms! Fohward mahch! Column left, mahch!" called Sergeant First Class Shig Murakami in quick succession, and the parade began with the Nisei leading the way. The cheers of the Italians and the non-combatant American soldiers lining the street soon drowned out the band.

***

"Dor, I'm worried about how your father's going to accept this," Dave Larson said as the taxi pulled up in front of the ramshackle house on Terminal Island a few weeks after the victory parade in Leghorn. "What if he says no?"

"We'll just have to take one step at a time," said Dorothy, squeezing his hand as he helped her out of the cab. The two walked up the creaking steps. Dorothy opened the door. "Mom! Dad! We're home!" she called out.

Shoji and Toshiko entered from the back room. "Dorothy!" was all Toshiko could say before she started to weep. Dorothy wrapped her arms around her embarrassed mother.

"It's O.K., Mom. I'm home." Shoji stood quietly in the doorway, impassive. Dave shifted his weight and looked at the floor.

"Mom. Dad. You remember Dave from Ken's UCLA days," Dorothy finally said, releasing her mother.

"Yes. I remember him. How are you, David?" said Toshiko formally. "Kenichi tells me you also were in the war in Europe and that you also were wounded." Without waiting for a response, she added, "Please. Sit. Sit. I will get some tea." She left for the kitchen. Before sitting, Dave walked firmly over to Shoji and extended his hand.

"It's good to see you again, Mr. Hayakawa." At first, Shoji looked Dave in the eye and did not move his hand. Finally, he slowly raised it and shook Dave's hand.

"Yes," he said in a somewhat imperial tone. "Please, sit down. So, Fumiko, how was your trip? Your mother says you came by airplane?"

"Yes, Daddy. It was quite an experience. They have women who serve drinks and meals on the airplane. And it was so fast! Can you imagine that only twenty-four hours ago we were getting on the plane in New York City? The plane only made three stops." Shoji just shook his head. Toshiko brought the tea, and she and Dorothy talked more about the wonders of modern air travel. Dave and Shoji drank their tea and pretended to listen to the women's conversation, avoiding eye contact with each other.

"So, how are things going, Daddy, now that you're back?"

"Better. Better."

"Mom says Howie was able to get your boat back. Where is Howie?" Dorothy said after a pause.

"Yes. He got the boat back," said Shoji. "He should be home soon."

Dorothy had many questions about Manzanar, particularly how the last few months there went as the people returned to their homes, and how their acceptance had been when they got home. Her mother described the empty shelves they encountered in the home, the shelves on which she and Dorothy had so carefully packed the family's excess clothing before going to Manzanar. She then brightened, went to a back room and returned, happily unwrapping the kimono and obi she had retrieved from the church. Although Toshiko did most of the talking,

Dorothy noted that her father had more self-confidence than she remembered hearing from her mother's letters. He seemed more the father of old who sat regally by while the rest of the family prattled on about inconsequentials, then gave the final word that ended all discussion. She noted that Toshiko usually deferred to her husband's opinion, as she had before. What had happened to this man who had become emasculated in the camp and dependent on smuggled whiskey?

Suddenly Dave interrupted the conversation. Sitting on the edge of his chair, he blurted out, "Mr. Hayakawa, I would like permission to marry your daughter, Dorothy. During the last nine months we have fallen very much in love. I have known many girls, probably too many, but she is the only one I have ever wanted to spend the rest of my life with." He sighed a sigh of relief. Shoji sat upright in his chair, his face taking on a severe look.

"No! My daughter will not marry a *Gaijin*! I did not send her to New York to forget she is Japanese! Fumiko, you will stay home now and find a Japanese boy and marry him. I will not have grandchildren who are not *Nihonjin*!"

"Daddy. I did not forget I'm Japanese while I was in New York. If anything, I became more aware of it when there were no other Japanese around. And, Daddy, what I found was that the Japanese qualities that you and Mom taught us go very well in an American culture–hard work, courtesy, self-control. We can compete and do very well. We don't have to stay as a separate community. We can integrate into American society and be respected for ourselves. I didn't fall in love with Dave because he's a *Gaijin*. I fell in love with him because he's a good man. He's kind and considerate."

"Poppycock!" said Shoji, his face reddening as he stood up. "We did not teach you to speak to your elders in such a fashion!" With that, he stormed into the back room. Dave slumped back into his chair, and Dorothy started to sob.

"Never mind," said Toshiko, "I will talk to him. You must understand, David, that old Japanese belief is that Japanese is number one and other races are inferior. Even though Shoji has lived in this country many years, it's hard to erase old belief."

"I understand, Mrs. Hayakawa," said Dave. "My father feels the same way–for Caucasians. I'm sure he'll have a similar response when we tell him." Toshiko looked questioningly at Dave.

"He will?" she said, obviously not needing an answer. "Hmm."

At that point, Howie came through the door. "Dor!" he yelled and embraced his sister. "Oh. I haven't washed the fish smell off yet." But Dorothy would not let him go until she had held him a long time, then introduced him to Dave.

When he came back after washing and changing his shirt, Dorothy asked him to tell them how he got Shoji's boat back.

"Well, you remember Dad had left the boat with Mr. Brandt, who was going to sell it and send Dad the proceeds? And we never heard from him? Well, I finally found him. He owns another boat shop in Long Beach now. I just went in and asked him what had happened. When he remembered who I was, he sort of turned white and muttered something. Finally he said he'd sold the boat but was sure he'd sent the money. I let him fumble around in his papers as if I believed he could come up with some proof. Finally he told me who he'd sold it to and how much he'd gotten for it. I went and found the guy and the old boat. He'd used it mostly for pleasure and had kept it up pretty well, certainly improved the living quarters. Anyway, I told him Mr. Brandt would buy the boat back at twice the price he'd sold it for, and..."

"Had Mr. Brandt said that?" interrupted Dorothy.

"No. But I went back and told Mr. Brandt what I'd told the new owner and that I expected him to do that and give the boat back to Dad."

"And he agreed to that?"

"With a little persuasion. I told him we had a cousin who was a lawyer and who was anxious to get into the area of restitution of Japanese property."

"We don't have a cousin who's a lawyer, Howie," said Dorothy.

"I know that, but Mr. Brandt didn't. Anyway the thing that finally convinced him, I think, was when I told him I was an ex-convict. He didn't want to challenge a lawsuit and an ex-convict. He did very well financially during the war, so buying the boat back at double the price wasn't hard for him to do. I've been able to get similar concessions for about five other guys from Terminal Island whom he treated in the same way. Now when I walk into his office, he just groans and says, 'What now?'"

"So you and Dad are back in the fishing business?"

"Yeah. Just like old times."

"That's what's made the difference in your father," said Toshiko. "When we got back, he was just as depressed as he'd been at Manzanar. All he'd do was lie around and drink. When Howie came home and got the boat back, that's what gave him life again, although it wasn't easy to get him out to sea again."

"No," said Howie. "I had to almost drag him out the first time. He didn't want to do anything. I finally convinced him that we needed two to run the boat. I gotta admit, I did a couple of dumb things on purpose to prove that I needed him to keep me out of trouble. Anyway he gradually started to get interested again. And I don't think he drinks much any more, sometimes a beer after we've had a successful catch."

"And that's why he reacted so strongly to your request about marriage. Three months ago, he wouldn't have cared. Now he feels he's in charge again as the father and husband and he's doing what he sees is his duty. Maybe he's calmed down enough so I can talk to him." Toshiko left for the back room.

"You were talking a minute ago about being an ex-convict," said Dorothy. "How do you feel about that?"

"Not very good. I know I brought dishonor onto our family. But I still think I was doing what was right. Somebody had to protest what they were doing to us. Ken and Pete protested by joining the Army and putting themselves in danger. I protested by refusing to be drafted and going to prison for it. I'll have to deal with that for many years, maybe all my life. Most of the guys coming back from Italy now don't understand or approve of what I did. A couple do, but most just think I was a coward. I think Ken understands. He and I had a pretty good talk when he visited me in prison before he went to Okinawa."

"Well, it was a tough choice, Howie. I'm glad I'm a girl and didn't have to make that choice."

"You've made another choice that may be hard to resolve," said Howie, nodding to the back room, where they had heard occasional outbursts from Shoji. "I wonder how Mom's getting along with her project."

When they sat down to eat, Shoji sat at the head of the table but added nothing to the conversation, which in any event was superficial. It was as if all were waiting for the imperial opinion. Finally it came.

"So, David," said Shoji, "my wife says your father does not believe my daughter is good enough for you."

"Well, sir, that's not exactly it. He doesn't believe in inter-racial marriages."

"Hmmm," mused Shoji. "Does he think that if an American married a Japanese, the American race would be weakened?"

"I don't think he's thought it through, sir. I think it's just a prejudice on his part."

"Prejudice. Prejudice." Shoji mused some more. "We must rid ourselves of prejudice. I must speak with your father." The Hayakawa emperor had spoken.

⚬

The November sun, still warm in Saipan, shone through the small home's living room windows, glassless since the apocalyptic three weeks of war seventeen months before. Inside was a solemn assembly. Presiding in front of a table with a cross and an old photograph draped in black bunting was a tall, broad-chested Saipanese, his hair now completely white. He was dressed in an ill-fitting dark suit. In a quiet voice he prayed.

"Heavenly Father, you know what it is to lose a son, and so you know my broken-heartedness, and that of his mother and brother and sisters and friends. So we ask for your comfort as we mourn for our beloved Martin. Thank you for letting us know how he died and the fact he died serving others. When we think of our suffering in the recent years, it was so little compared to that of Martin's, and yet his was so little compared to that of Jesus. Mostly we thank you for sending Jesus that we might be forgiven our sins, that we will one day have a great reunion with Martin before your throne, and that in the meantime we might live life abundantly. Thank you for the end of the terrible war, and we pray for the continued healing of your people on Saipan." Pastor Villagomez wiped his cheeks and turned with a smile. "Let us rejoice for Martin, who is now in the presence of God. His travails are over."

The small group rose slowly and filed outside where a table was laden with fresh fruits and raw reef fish. In the group were Mrs. Villagomez and their daughters, Sumi and Asako. Also present was Juergen, taller but more slender than his father and bearing the same handsome face. Next to him was his wife, in kimono for this occasion, and their son, now five years old. They had recently returned from Japan, and Juergen was in the process of setting up a medical clinic in Garapan. The Tenorio family was present also, and holding Masayo's hand was a young man dressed in the uniform of a Marine corporal. They were passing around a tear-stained letter, the one from a survivor of the concentration camp where Martin had been, which described his work as a pastor in the camp and his eventual death.

"Thank you for coming, Jose," Pastor Villagomez said to Mr. Tenorio. He gave similar greetings to the rest of the family, and when he came to Masayo and her Marine, "I was happy to hear of your engagement. You know, though, that there's a lot of red tape involved in marrying a local girl, don't you?"

"Yessir. I've already started the application process. Masayo says you have agreed to give us premarital counseling," said the young man.

"Yes. I'll be happy to. And as long as the approval process takes, you'll both be qualified to be pastors and marriage counselors in your own right by the time we're through. How has your family received the news?"

"They're not too happy. But when they meet Masayo, I give them about two days to be won over by her."

"That may be a little optimistic," said Pastor Villagomez. "But at least she speaks English well. Did she tell you the story of how she learned English?"

"The story of Aileen and the classroom on the mountaintop? I've heard it a hundred times."

CHAPTER 29

KEN HAD PROGRESSED FROM HAVING TO THINK up an excuse to visit Aileen. Now they met daily for lunch in the Post Exchange snack bar, and he drove her home after work. Mieko would insist he stay for dinner, most of which he had supplied from the commissary. One evening as they drove home, he said, "We got a response from King County Hall of Records in Seattle today. They said they have no record of an Aileen Nakamura born in their county."

"What!" exclaimed Aileen, "They must have made a mistake. I'm sure it was that county. We lived just four blocks from the King County Courthouse all our lives. I'll check with my parents, but I'm sure that was the right county. If they can't find my birth certificate, I won't be able to get a passport."

"Absolutely!" affirmed Mieko a few minutes later, "August 15, 1922, and March 24, 1921 for Myrna. Northwest Memorial Hospital. I'm certain that's in King County."

"The letter was very short," Ken mused, "almost as if they had not looked into it much. I think I have a way to check it out."

That night as he drove home, he admitted to himself that he was in love. With the few girls he'd dated at UCLA, love had never come to mind. Infatuation for a few weeks with one of them, perhaps, but nothing more. His commitment to his pursuit of medicine had always been a good excuse. I need to apply myself to my studies, he'd say. No time for romance. But with Aileen, the thought of one day saying goodbye and parting ways left him with an empty feeling down in that area of him which he'd been trying to unroof over the last few months. Through his friendship with John Hanusa, he had begun to identify the distress that he could not get into words. It had to do with the war he, an American, had fought against his people, the Japanese. This dichotomy was his same old problem, but now it had to do with hundreds of thousands of people killed and lands destroyed from Honolulu to New Guinea to Burma to Tokyo, and not whether he preferred hamburgers or seaweed. John's distinction between the Japanese militarists and the average Japanese person had helped a lot. As he got to know more Japanese, he appreciated that distinction more and more.

Three weeks later, a short Nisei with a pronounced limp walked into the Hall of Records of the King County Courthouse in Seattle. "I'd like to talk to the chief of the department," he said to the young woman who met him at the counter.

"Miss Petragini," the young woman called to the back, "there's a little man out here that wants to talk to you." Miss Petragini, her gray hair in a bun on the top of her head, and only a few inches taller than Horace Yamashita, came to the counter and looked Horace over.

"May I help you?" she asked in a suspicious tone of voice, one that did not signal a desire to help.

"Yes," answered Horace in a business-like tone, "I'd like a copy of a birth certificate. I have an official request from the Army." He handed her a sheet of paper.

Miss Petragini took the paper and in a more co-operative tone said, "Yes. I'm sure we can help." She started to walk to the back and suddenly stopped. "Oh! Aileen Nakamura. No. I mean, her birth certificate is not available. I mean, you need to talk to the county clerk. It's uh...." Flustered, she handed the paper back to Horace. "Mr. Ericsson. His office is two doors down the hall."

"We have no birth certificate for any Aileen Nakamury or whatever her name is," said Mr. Ericsson, talking to Horace in his outer office. "We looked and couldn't find it."

"Perhaps it's because you have her name wrong," said Horace courteously. "If I could look for it with Miss Petragini, perhaps I could...."

"No. No. Quite out of the question. You'll have to take our word for it."

"Mr. Ericsson, Miss Nakamura is an American citizen. Issuance of her passport depends upon supplying her birth certificate. I'm aware that constitutional rights of American citizens of Japanese ancestry have been abridged over the last few years, but the legislatures and the courts are beginning to correct those wrongs. Large financial penalties are being assessed on those people who *continue* to abridge the rights of American citizens." Horace took a deep breath. He hoped Mr. Ericsson was not sufficiently informed to know that Horace's statement reflected his hopes for the future rather than an accurate description of the present.

"You a lawyer?" asked Mr. Ericsson.

"Law student." Mr. Ericsson looked at Horace's lapel, where a small metal replica of a Silver Star ribbon was pinned. He did not know exactly what medal it was, but he had seen his limp when he had entered the office. He studied Horace a few moments more.

"Sharon," he finally said to his secretary. "Go tell Miss Petragini to find the woman's birth certificate for this man."

"You want me to help you find it?" asked Horace when he had returned to the record room.

"No, young man. I want you to know we do not lose records in this record room. Do you want her sister's also?" She was back in twenty seconds with both birth certificates. "Now, young man, we cannot give you the birth certificates themselves, but we will make true copies and have them notarized. I am a notary public. There will be a fifty cent charge for each."

"You're a doll, Miss Petragini. I mean thank you very much," said Horace, finally smiling, as he took a dollar bill from his wallet.

Ken was told in early November that he would be changing jobs. He would be the Army Liaison Officer to the Allied-Japanese Economic Consultation. That meant he'd represent the Army in the discussions and implementation of changing the Japanese war economy back to peacetime manufacturing.

"But, Colonel, I have no background in business or engineering," said Ken in protest.

"The State Department is supplying the experts in that, Captain. Your main job will be to oversee what they're doing and keep me apprised of what's happening. Furthermore you were requested by name. I don't know by whom. Your ability to speak Japanese will come in handy, because the guys from State don't speak it real well."

"So you speak some Japanese, do you?" asked Ken of Doctor Keith Carmody, the young State Department man in charge of the consultation.

"Not a bit. I can say *sayonara*. That means 'hello', doesn't it? Or 'goodbye'?"

"Goodbye," said Ken.

"No. My qualification for this job is a Ph.D. in Industrial Management. I volunteered for the Navy but then found out I had diabetes, so I went back to school. When I got my degree, I volunteered again, thinking they'd use me in Europe. I took three years of French in college. So here I am. I know nothing about Japan except what I've seen in the newsreels."

"Well, I guess we'll be learning together. Now who is this man we'll be meeting tomorrow?"

"A guy named Shumitsu." Doctor Carmody made it rhyme with jujitsu.

"Shumitsu?" repeated Ken.

"Yeah. Something like that."

The next morning as Ken and Doctor Carmody approached the somewhat stooped elderly gentleman in his 10-year-old suit, Ken smiled.

"Mr. Shimizu, we meet again."

"Yes, Captain Hayakawa. It was my hope that you could be assigned to this joint endeavor."

"So you were the one who requested me?"

"I am not in the position to make requests of the Occupation, young man, but I am finding that a courteously placed suggestion is very effective with the Americans."

"May I ask, sir, why me?"

"A perceptive question, Captain," answered the diminutive official. "I thought it best to have somebody who was both Japanese and American to be involved in this rebuilding. America will hate us for many years because of this war, and they will hate Japanese Americans too. But there will come a time when the hate will wear out, and our two countries will become partners and eventually friends. We Japanese are industrious people, as the Americans are. We have allowed ourselves to become detoured in the last fifteen years with dreams of territorial power. Those dreams have now been dashed as many of us predicted, but in the future our power will be economic power practiced in a peaceful world. Japanese Americans will have central positions in the new relationships, and I thought it important that you be present at the beginning of this next era."

"You seem to be old friends," said Doctor Carmody, a little suspiciously.

"Well, you could say that," said Ken. "I'll tell you later." The three sat down to talk. The plan was to approach manufacturing plants and factories, determine what they had been producing, suggest what they might produce in the future, assess the damage and how much it would cost to repair the equipment, and then to arrange for a loan. Just what part each of them would play in this program was a mystery to Ken.

When they finished planning and agreed to approach the first factory that afternoon, Mr. Shimizu asked Ken, "Have your parents returned from their detention camp?"

"Yes sir, they're back in Los Angeles," he answered. Mr. Shimizu waited. "They, uh... my father got his boat back and is back to fishing, uh..." Mr. Shimizu continued to wait. Ken shifted in his chair. Why am I telling this man everything, Ken asked himself. "My sister's getting married. Uh. My brother's back from, uh, detention and helping my father. Uh."

"And when are you planning to return?" Mr. Shimizu finally asked.

"I'm not sure, sir." Because of Aileen, Ken had asked that his rotation date be put on hold. More uncomfortable silence. "I, uh, was planning on going to medical school when I got home."

"No!" interrupted Mr. Shimizu, "you must stay."

"Stay? Why must I stay?"

"To help your people into the future."

On the way home, as Ken described his last conversation with Mr. Shimizu to Carmody, he became more and more upset. "How can he tell me I must stay? It's not my job to help them into the future. They'd be doing just fine if they hadn't gone crazy with this war, and that wasn't my fault. What makes him think he can tell me what I must do?"

❦

In the next three weeks, fortunately for Ken, Mr. Shimizu made no more claims on his future. The three men worked from before dawn till after dusk at their project. They found that most factories had already made the transition to a peacetime product. Even many of the most damaged factories had resumed work, in many cases with very tenuous repairs, which frequently broke down. The owners and managers were surprised, some were incredulous, that the Occupation was willing to help them with their repairs. Carmody often found himself in the position of trying to persuade owners to accept the help he offered.

"They're an easy people to work with, aren't they, Ken?" said Keith

Carmody as the two sat at Happy Hour at the end of the third week, "They're very self-reliant."

"They have a lot of pride. Even those who accept help struggle with their consciences," replied Ken.

"And old Shimizu (he pronounced the name properly now) sure knows how to get his way. When he and I have a different opinion on what a factory should switch to, we talk around about it until I'm thinking I made his suggestion in the first place. Have you noticed that?"

"Yeah, I have, Keith. He's a persuasive guy in his own gentle way."

"Does that mean you're thinking you'll stay here and help 'your people' into the future."

"Naw. I don't think so. But like you say, they're a good people to work with," replied Ken. Keith Carmody studied Ken as he finished his beer.

⌦

"Are you a Christian?" Ken asked Aileen one chilly December evening as they strolled her neighborhood.

"I don't think so," she answered. "In Seattle, Mom and Dad let us choose our religion for ourselves. We'd sometimes go to Christian churches and sometimes to the Buddhist temple, so we ended up making no choice. Religion didn't seem important to them, and so it wasn't to us. It wasn't until I got to Saipan and met the Villagomezes and their congregation that I began to feel that what you believed about God made a difference. From the beginning, I felt comfortable with them. They're really a loving people. But I was just beginning to get the message when the invasion came. I told you how Pastor Villagomez risked his life to get Daddy and me out, didn't I? Well, since I got back, I haven't had much time, or taken the time, to think more about it." They walked on in silence for a few more minutes.

"How would you like to come visit John Hanusa's old church over Christmas?" Ken asked. "It's in western Honshu, and the trains go there now. We'd go Saturday and stay through Christmas Day, then come home the next day–Wednesday. You'd have to take one day off work. John says you could stay with one of the families in the church."

"I'd like that, Ken."

⌦

The next Saturday, Ken, John and Aileen climbed aboard the train to Kobe, where they would change to the small rural train for Toriyama.

With some difficulty, they found three seats together. The car for Allied personnel, designated by a large yellow ball painted on the side of the car, would have been less crowded. But John had insisted they travel on the regular car. "I've never seen you two out of uniform," said Aileen.

"First time we've been on leave," explained John. He was settling back in his seat, obviously enjoying the trip. Of the three, he was clearly most at home despite his height and the color of his skin. He served as tour director, pointing out interesting points of geography, embellishing them with the history involved. He always started in English but soon reverted to Japanese when he came to a part of the story that could only be explained in Japanese. Nearby passengers were soon leaning in to hear their conversation, obviously confused by this unusual trio: *The Japanese young woman looks and dresses Japanese, but her accent is a little unusual. The Japanese young man dresses American, and his accent really is funny. The American young man speaks the best Japanese of all and obviously is very familiar with our country!* They were soon the center of attention for the whole car. Ken and Aileen felt embarrassed at the attention, but John barely noticed. He'd experienced this before.

It was late afternoon when the small train pulled in to Toriyama. John was first off the train. Before Ken and Aileen could descend, thirty men and women, bowing and talking excitedly, surrounded him. Introductions were made, and the entourage started down the street. Willing hands, of young men who'd been hearing of Hanusa-san for several years, picked up their luggage including four large bags of commissary food Ken and John had brought.

The group stopped before a modest home three blocks from the train station. "Aileen, you'll stay here with Mrs. Onuma," said John. "They've planned a dinner in the church tonight, and she'll bring you there." Four blocks later, they came to a small square building with a freshly painted sign in front indicating that this was a Christian church. When they entered the building, Ken noted a cross on a rectangular table set on a simple raised altar. The altar also supported a pulpit, more like a lectern. Folding chairs filled the room, and many more were stacked against the wall. That was it–nothing more was in the room. John stopped and surveyed the room quietly for several minutes while the chattering young porters carried the luggage through the back door. Finally John continued through the back door followed by Ken. There in the fenced back yard stood a large meeting hall even now full of women preparing the evening meal. There was also a small house where the luggage had been taken.

"Come on in," said John, entering the small house. "This is the home where I spent most of my growing up years." Though it was small, the furnishings and kitchen were Western. "None the worse for wear," said John.

"No, John-san," said the elderly man who had led the greeting party. "We have cleaned it every week, waiting for you and your father and mother to return."

"How has it been, Mr. Hishikari? Has it been more difficult here because you're Christians?" asked John.

"Oh, yes. The *kempeitai* and the *tonarigumi* leaders were always trying to frighten us into closing the church. But we continued, with the elders taking turns preaching, and they never did anything to us. In fact, the congregation grew during the war. Unbelievable. But we tried not to be too obvious. The sign on the front of the church fell down early in the war, and we didn't get around to getting a new one up until about a month ago. I hope God will not doubt our faith because of that."

"I think God will think you were being 'wise as serpents and harmless as doves'," said John.

⚬─◆─⚬

Since the war had ended only four months ago and the Japanese still suffered major food shortages, Ken was amazed at the sumptuous dinner that night. Fresh vegetables and fish, mixed with the commissary food, were served in abundance. The program, delayed by the length of the dinner, primarily focused on John and his parents. Testimonials of the thirty-year ministry John's family had had went on and on. Some praised the gentle personality attributes of the Reverend Mr. and Mrs. Hanusa. But most told of life-changing decisions they had made as a result of the Hanusas' ministry. Those changes put them in a tiny minority in Japan and sometimes separated them from families. As the evening wore on, Ken became weary. He leaned over towards Aileen, seated next to him at the head table, and started to comment on the length of the testimonials. But he saw that she was paying rapt attention to every word. Refocused, he sat up straighter in his chair and tried to pick up the speaker's train of thought.

After the program was over, Aileen commented, "This reminded me a lot of the congregation in Saipan." People clustered around John, leaving Ken and Aileen to themselves. "They certainly love the Hanusas. And they seem to be sincere in their Christianity. The general feeling I picked up in my last several years in Japan is that Christianity is fine for westerners, but we Japanese have our own religion. This group wouldn't agree. Their faith seems to have pulled them through these last terrible years."

"At home, there was always a struggle from both directions," replied Ken. "Some felt that out of loyalty to our race, we should be Buddhists. But an equal number joined a Christian church as part of their accepting the American way of life. Both of those approaches miss the point of what becoming a Christian is all about. It's the content that's important, not the externals. So, Japanese and a person of any race can become Christians. We can develop our own externals and traditions as long as the central content remains the same."

"What do you mean by the central content?" asked Aileen.

"That God created the world and everything in it, and when people sinned by going their own way, he came to earth as Jesus and died to pay for the sins of all people. Our only responsibility is to accept that death for ourselves and with his help, honor him with our lives." Aileen silently studied Ken's face.

The next two days the group visited various church members in their modest but clean homes. Many homes displayed small shrines with a picture of a young man in uniform, not unlike the shrine in the Shimabukuros' home in Hawaii. John felt sad since most of these men had been boyhood friends. In the homes that contained no pictures, the childhood friend was there, laughing with John at memories of their childhood. Some memories included boyhood pranks which Ken knew the Reverend Mr. and Mrs. Hanusa, would not have been proud of. Nor could he imagine this Army major, one of General MacArthur's chief translators, being involved in such activities.

Christmas was celebrated solemnly both Christmas Eve and Christmas Day, the church full, all the folding chairs in use. On Christmas Day, John gave the sermon. Ken noted with delight that Aileen dwelled on every word.

On the train back to Tokyo, Aileen shared her thoughts. "You know one of the things that struck me the last few days. Normally Japanese look on New Year's Day as the most special day of the year–a day when they should patch up quarrels and, in general, start out the year on the right foot. But here, these folks consider Christmas as the most important day."

"My parents also made use of the tradition that says what happens on New Year's is prophetic for the year to come. My father always visited people on New Year's Day, particularly those loosely connected to the church, or those slack in attendance."

"That goes along with what Ken and I were talking about the other day," replied Aileen. "Christianity can be for Japanese even though some traditions might be changed, because the central part of Christianity is for everybody."

"If it weren't for that," said John, "my parents' lives would have been wasted." He settled back in his seat and soon was dozing, making up for lost sleep over the last several nights. Talking with his friends–often into the early hours of morning–had taken precedence over sleep. Aileen was deep in thought as her gaze skipped across the countryside.

"John," said Aileen several hours later, just before they separated at the Tokyo train station, "I need to talk to you. Will you be in your office tomorrow?"

"Yes," he answered, with a questioning look on his face.

That night when Ken went through his mail, he found one with a return address of Doctor Broderick Wilson, admissions dean at the University of California medical school.

UNIVERSITY of CALIFORNIA, School of Medicine
Office of Admissions December 12, 1945
> *Dear Mr. Hayakawa,*
>
> > *As regards your application for admission to the University of California School of Medicine, which has been pending since 1941, we are happy to offer you a position in the class beginning September 1946. If you accept this offer, please inform me in writing at your first opportunity, and we will send you the packet of materials you will need in preparation for matriculation in our school.*
> >
> > *I have recently been in contact with Doctor Tosh Kawamura, and he informed me that you had not at-*

tended Creighton University but had volunteered to serve our country in the Army. It was through him that I received your present address. It is my sincere hope, Mr. Hayakawa, that you will be able to accept our offer. Sincerely, B.L. Wilson

Broderick L. Wilson, M.D., Dean of Admissions

CHAPTER 30

T HE NEXT DAY AT LUNCH, AILEEN SAID, "KENNY, I have to tell you what happened today!" She spoke softly–almost in a whisper–the kind one uses when conveying something of great importance.

"What happened?"

"Remember I told John I wanted to meet with him? Well, I told him how impressed I was by the people in his church, how they really seem to believe that God is involved in their lives. It must have been hard for them over all those years living as such a minority and with a faith that most Japanese would think was western, particularly during the war. But they obviously have a deep inner conviction that they have something worth risking their lives for. It reminds me so much of the church in Saipan. They all have something–or someone–they can trust in. I told John I wanted the same thing. I never had anyone I could bring my worries and fears to. Mom and Dad would listen politely, then tell me what I *should* be feeling, and Myrna would make a joke out of it. Anyway that's what I told John. You know what he said?"

"No."

"He said that what they had and what I wanted was–Jesus. Then he said I could ask Jesus into my heart–that was the term he used–right there and then. So I did. It was as simple as that. Well, not quite as simple. When I started to pray, I was overwhelmed by how self-centered I am, and I felt I first had to tell that to God. John called it confession. When I finished, everything seemed–lighter–and clearer. Did that ever happen to you?"

"Not quite as definitely. When I joined the church as a teenager, I had to make a public declaration of faith, but it wasn't until I was in college that I realized how important that declaration was. One weekend after my roommate had gone home, I spent time praying and reading the Bible. By the end of the weekend, I decided that the Christian gospel was the only thing that made any sense to me. I felt I'd already made the decision and I was just confirming it then."

"Isn't it a great feeling? I mean, my anger at the stupid war (this time she said it in English and without the vituperation that always accompanied *baka na senso*), and Hideki's unnecessary death, and my worry over getting my citizenship back became sort of secondary." Aileen held her fork in her hand, ignoring her lunch. "Being a Christian is a personal decision, not something you are because you come from a certain culture."

"Well, I can't tell you how happy I am that you made that decision, Aileen," said Ken, also leaving his lunch untouched. "Because if two people are going to spend the rest of their lives together, they should hold the same beliefs."

"Yes," said Aileen looking vacantly at her lunch, her fork still poised in her hand. Several seconds passed, and she began to slowly raise her head. "What'd you say? Spend the rest of our lives together? Are you proposing marriage to me, Kenny Hayakawa?"

"Yes. I guess I am," answered Ken, looking intently at the blushing Aileen. "I mean, I know I'll have to ask your father, but I think *we* should talk about it first, don't you?"

Aileen started to weep.

"Does that mean yes?" asked Ken.

"Don't ask silly questions," said Aileen through her tears.

"And if that's not enough," said Ken. "Read this." He handed her the letter from Doctor Wilson.

"Oh, Kenny!" Aileen said as she read the letter, "Just what you've been waiting for all these years. Can you get out in time to start in September?"

"I think I can," Ken said. With the excitement of the morning, Aileen did not note the lack of enthusiasm in Ken's last statement.

Later that evening as Ken and Aileen walked in her neighborhood, bundled against the cold, he said "I didn't think your father was going to agree so quickly to our getting married. I knew he liked me, but I thought he'd at least go through the motions of asking me about my future plans, whether I could support his little girl and all that."

"With Myrna and me both being so 'American' and outspoken, I think he was just thankful that you asked at all. I told them about your acceptance to med school, so I guess he figures you can support me."

"You know, Aileen, I'm not sure I want to go to medical school."

"What?" Aileen stopped and looked at him. "I thought that was your dream all these years," she said softly. "I know you turned down the acceptance to Creighton, but that was to help prove our loyalty as Japanese Americans. You've done that." She held up his wounded hand and kissed it gently. "Why aren't you sure now?"

"Well," Ken answered hesitantly, "there may be something more important for me to do. I mean medicine is very important, obviously, helping people, curing their diseases, relieving their pain, and all. But in the last few months, the thing that really excites me is helping the Japanese get back on their feet. They...we...are a good people, with a lot of drive and ambition. My desire in the next few years is to see the Japanese and American people become friends. That's going to be a huge job, and I don't have a real good idea how to do it, but I think we, as Japanese Americans, can be at least a part of the answer." Aileen was silent. They continued to walk, hand-in-hand, which they had not done previously, aware of the Japanese tradition against public shows of affection.

"Ever since the surrender and even before, I've been trying to deal with something down deep that I couldn't get clearly in mind. It was all involved with the fact that as a Christian I was trying to kill all these people and particularly the Japanese, who to some extent were 'my people'. I kept thinking I should be trying to resolve the old problem of being Japanese or American, and here I was trying to kill them. I prayed and prayed that I'd get a clearer picture of this unrest, but it was too deep. The answer didn't come as quickly as the night I had to get an answer on whether to go to Creighton or the 442nd. But now I think I'm coming closer. Maybe God wants to use me...us...as reconcilers. Being both Japanese and American, not either-or, puts us in a position to help heal the wounds. I'm not sure how that works out in practice, in the Army or as a civilian, in the government or in business, here or in the U.S., but I think that's the way to go." Ken stopped and turned to Aileen, now holding both hands. "What do think?"

Without hesitation, tears running down her cheeks, Aileen answered, "Let's go."

Their discussion turned to other topics, but before Ken left, he said, "There's one more man we need to talk to. Will you come with me to see him tomorrow?"

✦

Mr. Shimizu bowed to Aileen the next evening as they sat down at one of the newly-opened coffee shops, a far cry from the place where Aileen and Hideki had shared their tea less than a year before. "Captain Hayakawa has spoken glowingly of you, Miss Nakamura, and I understand congratulations are now in order."

"Thank you, Mr. Shimizu. And he has spoken to me of you with great respect," Aileen answered bowing primly.

After the three were seated and had been served coffee, Ken began to tell Mr. Shimizu what he had told Aileen the evening before. The elderly diplomat listened impassively, occasionally sipping his coffee. Ken would hesitate periodically, hoping for a word of agreement, or even a nod indicating he was being heard. Receiving none, he continued until he realized he was repeating himself. He took a deep breath, sighed, and stopped. A full two minutes passed before Mr. Shimizu spoke. "Japan has just lost a war of unparalleled destruction. As a nation, we have dishonored and shamed ourselves. We have never experienced that before and we don't know how to absorb that, Captain Hayakawa, Miss Nakamura, but we will learn. The world is new. It will not be long before it will be routine to pick up a telephone and speak to someone halfway around the earth, or to get on an airplane in one of our countries and get off in the other country. International trade will soon become the normal way of business, and as damaged as Japan is today, we will soon be a leader in manufacturing and trade. Attitudes will have to change, and it will not be easy to do. No longer will we be able to isolate ourselves emotionally, but we will need to open up and learn how men and even women of other countries think and feel. This has never been the Japanese way. I and my generation will not understand it, much less be able to participate in it. You two young people and your generation will have to show us the way, even if we don't approve or don't listen. When I first met you, Captain Hayakawa, I told you that it must have been a difficult war for you, but now I also think of the great opportunities you have." Mr. Shimizu smiled for the first time since Ken had started speaking, took a sip from his coffee cup and settled back in his chair.

Epilogue

あとがき

W AVES LAPPED GENTLY AT THE BOW OF THE *President Wilson* as it entered Tokyo Bay. Ken and Aileen leaned on the rail, transfixed by the developing shoreline. More than a year had passed since they left Japan, and already from this distance they could appreciate the renovation from the war damage. Occasionally one would point out some change from their last remembrance, but mostly they stood quietly watching.

Much had occurred since their visit with Mr. Shimizu in the Tokyo coffee shop. First had been the necessity of obtaining permission to marry from the consulate. When it was established that Aileen was an American citizen and the possessor of a fresh new passport, permission came quickly. John Hanusa married them in the chapel of the *Dai Ichi* building. They honeymooned in an old hotel on the shore of Lake Yamanaka with a clear view of Mount Fuji. Snowed in by a late spring snow, they stayed an extra three days, enjoying the natural hot spring baths in the hotel basement. When they returned to Tokyo, Ken's demobilization orders had arrived. After a tearful goodbye with Jun, Mieko and Myrna, they boarded a troopship bound for Oakland. One of just three married couples on board, they were assigned their own stateroom and to the ship's officers' dining table. They rarely ate with them, as they were frequently in their cabin suffering seasickness. Hardly a honeymoon cruise, they decided.

They spent several days in the San Francisco Bay area, awaiting Ken's discharge. While there, he followed up on contacts with the State Department started in Japan. He decided that at least at first, his mode of bridge-making would be through aid programs administered by the State Department. He was awarded the Legion of Merit, to join his Silver Star, Bronze Star and Purple Heart, at his discharge ceremony at the Presidio of San Francisco. The awarding officer summarized his service in such glowing terms that Aileen joked to Ken that she wasn't certain they were referring to her humble husband. Ken noted that his day of discharge was exactly three years after the day he had arrived at Camp Shelby. He reminisced with Aileen about the changes that had taken place during those three years.

Their visit to Terminal Island, which Aileen had long dreaded, turned out to be a thoroughly enjoyable time. The Hayakawas quickly fell in love with Aileen and were soon confiding in her more than they were in Ken. The relationship of Howie and Shoji, working together again on the boat had continued to be good for both, and long forgotten was Shoji's dependence on whiskey. Howie's activities during the war were still not well-received by much of the Terminal Island community, but that did not seem to bother him much. He had the appearance of a man at peace with himself. Peter was still on occupation duty in Italy, but Toshiko was proudly announcing that he would be following Ken to UCLA when he returned home.

One night when Howie and Shoji were out at sea, Toshiko related the story of Dorothy and Dave's wedding. Once Shoji had learned that Mr. Larson had questions about an interracial marriage, he suddenly became leader of his own anti-prejudice league forgetting, Toshiko said with a chuckle, his own racial prejudice. When it was reported that the Larsons would not be attending the wedding, Shoji decided it was time to take matters into his own hands. Against everybody's advice, he took the train up to San Luis Obispo to talk to Mr. Larson. He flatly turned down Dave's offer to go with him. When he returned two days later, he announced that the Larsons would be attending the wedding. No amount of wheedling by anyone in either family would extract from the two men what they had talked about, but when the wedding time came, the Larsons were there and as far as anyone could determine were in favor of the whole proceedings. Dave and Dorothy left soon after the wedding to return to New York City, and to Toshiko's surprise Shoji and Mr. Larson talked by phone about once a month, sharing information on the newlyweds.

Ken's orientation to the State Department required nine months in Washington, D.C. On their way back, they returned to Seattle to visit the Nakamuras. Jun, though now in his mid-sixties, had been asked to be the American representative of a Japanese firm, and he had quickly accepted. The week in Seattle had been very nostalgic for Aileen. A few of her friends had returned to Seattle from the camps - most had gone elsewhere - and several evenings were spent sharing experiences.

The *President Wilson*, which would take them back to Japan, left from Los Angeles, and that gave them the unexpected opportunity to visit Masayo -she now went by the name Margaret - and her husband in

Camp Pendleton. They sat in a circle and laughed as their infant daughter began to try her first steps, and Margaret giggled when she whispered to Aileen that she thought she might be pregnant again.

The sea was much calmer on the return trip to Japan. This time, only Aileen was nauseated, and inexplicably only in the morning.

"You know what I was thinking about last night, Kenny," Aileen asked as the ship approached the Tokyo dock.

"No," answered Ken.

"Our baby will be a symbol for us. Conceived in America, born in Japan."

THE END

Bibliography

A Time to Choose is fiction, however, I have attempted to accurately portray the historical, geographical and cultural background of the action in the story. In so doing, I have obtained information from the following books, only a few of the books that could have been used for this subject.

World War II - Time-Life Books, various volumes and authors, Alexandria, VA, various dates. A comprehensive history of World War II

The Setting Sun of Japan. Carl Randau & Leane Zugsmith, Random House Books, New York, 1942. Two reporters travel extensively in Japan and Southeast Asia just before the start of World War II.

A Farewell to Manzanar. Jeanne Wakatsuki Houston & James D. Houston, Houghton Mifflin Company, Boston, 1973. The touching detention camp memoirs of a seven-year old, told thirty years later.

Americans: The Story of the 442nd Combat Team. Orville C. Shirey, Infantry Journal Press, Washington, 1946. The comprehensive history of the storied Nisei unit in Europe.

Lost Battalions: Going for Broke in the Vosges Autumn 1944. Franz Steidl, Presidio Press, Novato, CA. 1997. The true story of the rescue of the "Lost Battalion" by the 442nd Regimental Combat Team.

Yankee Samurai: the secret role of Nisei in America's Pacific Victory. Joseph D. Harrington, Pettigrew Enterprises, Detroit, 1979. The story, through first-person interviews, of the graduates of the Military Intelligence Service Language School as translators and interpreters in the Pacific.

Honor by Fire: Japanese Americans at War in Europe and the Pacific. Lyn Crost, Presidio Press, Novato, CA. 1994. A wartime correspondent interviews veterans of both fronts fifty years later, weaving her personal accounts into their memories.

Tokyo Rose, orphan of the Pacific. Masayo Duus, translated by Peter Duus, Kodansha International, Tokyo, distributed in the US through Harper & Row, New York, 1979. The story of Tokyo Rose, told from one woman's viewpoint.

The Sacred Warriors: Japan's Suicide Legions. Denis Warner & Peggy Warner with Commander Sadao Seno, JMSDF (Ret), Avon Books, New York, 1982. Complete history of the feared *Kamikaze* squadrons.

The Fall of Japan. William Craig, Dial Press, 1967. Thoroughgoing account of the last year of World War II for the Japanese Empire.

Photograph by Carolyn Blight

About the Author

This is the first novel for Edward Blight. Born in Santa Barbara, California and educated at The Citadel and the University of California, San Francisco School of Medicine, he served as a physician in the US Army for twenty years. Following eighteen more years in academic medicine, he retired in the summer of 2000. A chance encounter with a Japanese American patient led to the research that brought forth this novel. Blight currently lives with his wife in Pacific Grove, California.